IT'S A LOVELY DAY TOMORROW

IT'S A LOVELY DAY TOMORROW

Margaret Thornton

HEADLINE

First published in 1992
by HEADLINE BOOK PUBLISHING PLC

10 9 8 7 6 5 4 3 2 1

British Library Cataloguing in Publication Data

Thornton, Margaret
It's a Lovely Day Tomorrow
I. Title
823 [F]

ISBN 0–7472–0626–0

Typeset by Keyboard Services, Luton

Printed and bound in Great Britain by
Clays Ltd, St Ives PLC

HEADLINE BOOK PUBLISHING PLC
Headline House
79 Great Titchfield Street
London W1P 7FN

In memory of my mother and father and Grandma,
and the Blackpool boarding house.

Chapter 1

There had never been a season like it. They swarmed from the excursion platform at Central Station in their thousands. Harassed-looking women with pale pinched faces, their tightly permed hair confined in almost invisible hairnets. Jolly-looking men, pallid too, like their wives, sporting Fair Isle pullovers and white pumps, joking and talking loudly. This might prove to be their last taste of freedom for some considerable time, so they'd laugh and be happy, and be damned to that Hitler and Chamberlain and the lot of them. Plump, perspiring grandmas in navy spotted dresses, grandads with handkerchiefs knotted over their bald heads.

And the children . . . They dug furiously with their wooden spades – or the coveted metal ones for those of a more advanced age – scattering the sand far and wide, often over the protesting adults, in their attempts to construct the biggest and best sand-castle ever seen. The boys wore knee-length serge trousers and the girls were often arrayed in frilly party frocks. A trip to Blackpool was quite an occasion for which you dressed up in your best clothes, never mind the unsuitability of the attire. 'Now, try to keep it clean, our Doris. Cost a lot of money, that frock did . . .' You could hear the cries of anxious mothers echoing across the beach. Many of the children gathered round the red and white striped booth of the Punch and Judy man, laughing uproariously at the antics of the funny hook-nosed character whirling his baton. 'That's the way to do it . . .' Mr Punch bellowed in his nasal tones while dog Toby, with a frill round his neck, sat meekly watching it all. And what would a visit to Blackpool be without a ride on a donkey? Bells jingled and hooves thudded rhythmically as the youthful jockeys urged their patient steeds to greater endeavour across the stretch of smooth golden sand.

The grown-ups sprawled in deck chairs, beetroot-red faces lifted towards the sun. They paddled in the sea, the men with their trousers turned up and pullovers discarded to reveal collarless shirts and braces, the women lifting their skirts to their knees, forsaking modesty for that blissful feeling of sand between the toes and cold water lapping round their ankles. Then, clanking metal spades along the pavements, carrying tin buckets filled with sand and shells and seaweed, they trooped to their boarding houses for high tea at half past five. You could see it through the lace-curtained windows of hundreds of houses – boiled ham with salad, triangular-cut bread and butter, and a plate of 'fancies'.

'Hey, look at t'Tower . . .' many an astonished holidaymaker would cry as they stared upwards, craning their necks, at the gigantic ironwork structure pointing into the blue sky, a staggering 518 feet.

'Looks as though it's movin', don't it? Hey, you don't suppose it is, do you?'

'Go on, Albert, you daft 'aporth! 'Course it's not moving. It's been there well nigh fifty year. I reckon it'll stand up a bit longer . . .'

The Tower did look as if it were swaying when you stared at it for long enough, an optical illusion often noticed by the awe-struck visitors.

It had been a record-breaking season. The number of railway passengers arriving at Easter and Whit was up one fifth on the previous record, but for Blackpool, in this summer of 1939, the outbreak of war came two months too early. The season staggered to an abrupt end instead of finishing in the blaze of glory which would have been a fitting climax to twenty years of growth in the holiday trade in this, the king of all holiday resorts.

Blackpool had lived up to its motto, 'Progress', throughout the Thirties. The culmination came in 1939 with the opening of the Odeon Cinema, the new Opera House, the casino at the Pleasure Beach, and the new bus station in Talbot Road. In 1940 the Central Station was to be rebuilt at a cost of two million pounds . . . But Adolf Hitler put a stop to that.

'Gosh! I don't think I've ever felt so tired,' said Jenny Bradshaw. She collapsed gratefully into the depths of a shabby armchair in the kitchen of her mother's boarding house and wiped her hand across her perspiring forehead. 'Phew! It's a scorcher today an' all. Trust

Mother to insist on having the bedrooms bottomed on a day like this. She's a slave driver all right!'

'She is that,' replied Violet Carter with feeling.

Violet was Jenny's sister, her junior by eight years, but unlike her both in looks and temperament. Jenny was small and pert with dark curly hair and a prettiness that inclined towards plumpness, whereas Violet was tall and thin – 'like a yard of pump water', her mother often said, with scant regard for her younger daughter's feelings – with straight blonde hair that fell limply to her shoulders.

'You've got to admit, though, that she pulls her weight,' Violet went on. 'She works just as hard as we do. I sometimes wonder where she gets all her energy from. She's not getting any younger and she's as strong as a carthorse.'

Jenny nodded in agreement, smiling at her sister. Trust Violet to see both sides of the question. She was a kindly lass, always ready to see the best in folks. 'Yes, you're right. Mother can do more than her share when she's a mind – when she's not too busy telling us what to do. And we've all been rushed off our feet this summer. I can't ever remember a season like it.'

The season had started way back in the spring, at the Easter weekend. There had been a few visitors then, but at the end of May, in Whit week, it really got going. They had been full up ever since, until this last week or two. The visitors were mostly regulars, from the inland towns of Lancashire – from Rochdale and Oldham, from Burnley, Blackburn, Accrington and Chorley and, above all, from Wigan. There was a sign by the front door which read '"Pleasant View", Landlady, Mrs Carter from Wigan'. It had been the custom at the time the house was built, at the end of the last century, for landladies to advertise in this way. It made visitors from the landlady's home town feel welcome, and went a long way towards ensuring their return the following year. It was an old-fashioned custom, but then Annie Carter was old-fashioned in many ways.

With regard to other aspects of her boarding house, though, she'd had to move with the times. There were now washbasins in all twelve bedrooms and a WC on each landing. Even so, there was quite a bit of queuing and peeping round bedroom doors to see when it was free. They provided full board – cooked breakfast, midday dinner, and high tea – and all their visitors agreed that they

3

got good value for money, many of them returning year after year.

'It must have been dreadful in the olden days,' said Violet, leaning back in the armchair opposite her sister. She folded her hands behind her head and sprawled her long legs across the clipped rag hearthrug. If her mother saw her she would accuse her of slouching. But Annie Carter was still upstairs, sorting out the sheets and pillowcases in the big cupboard on the landing, and the sisters knew that they could safely snatch five minutes' peace. 'Mother's always telling us gruesome tales about what it used to be like. Just imagine – visitors bringing their own food and expecting it to be cooked just the way they wanted it! It doesn't bear thinking of. It's hard enough now.'

Jenny laughed. 'I don't know about it being the olden days. I don't think it's all that long ago. I remember something of the sort when I started working for Mother. And she's told me many a time how some landladies used to charge a shilling a week for the use of the cruet. Mother never did that, though.'

'No, you can say what you like about Mother, she's not stingy.' Violet stretched languidly and gave a loud yawn – something else her mother wouldn't approve of – then rose to her feet. 'Tell you what, Jen. I'll go and make a nice pot of tea. Mother'll no doubt be wanting one in a minute, and your Tom'll be calling round soon, won't he? I'll go and put the kettle on.'

Jenny closed her eyes as her sister disappeared into the back kitchen. What she had said to Violet was true. She couldn't remember ever feeling so tired. She was weary, both physically and mentally. A glance in the mirror that morning had shown her that she didn't merely feel tired, she looked it as well. Her greenish-hazel eyes that normally shone with merriment – Jenny could, as a rule, always find something to smile at – appeared dull and lacklustre, ringed with dark shadows. She glanced down now at the cotton dress she was wearing, green with a pattern of large white daisies. It had been so clean and crisp-looking when she had first run it up on her sewing machine last year. Now she was aware how shabby and dishevelled it was, like Jenny herself felt. The hem was coming undone and hung down limply and there was a button missing from the bodice, but it was good enough for working in. At one time Jenny had made a strict rule for herself, that she would always change out of her working clothes into something pretty and presentable before her husband Tom came home from work.

4

Now, more and more often, Tom was coming home to a Jenny who hadn't bothered to change, who hadn't combed her hair and washed her face. Not that he ever seemed to notice . . .

It was hardly surprising that she was tired, though, with all the work that had to be done in the boarding house. Mountains of crockery to be washed up, beds to be made or changed, washbasins and lavatories to clean, the fire to light in the lounge – there were very few days, even in the middle of the summer, when it wasn't necessary – fresh food to be bought every day, and meals to be cooked for more than twenty people, as well as serving at the tables. A young girl came from across the road to help with the serving when they were extra busy, and Cousin Ada came once a week to 'do' the bedrooms, but most of the work fell to Jenny and Violet and their mother.

Jenny had been glad when the visitors had dropped off about two weeks ago, but she still felt just as exhausted. It was all this talk of war, she supposed. It was enough to make anyone feel weary. And now the Germans had invaded Poland . . .

'I knew it! I knew this would happen,' said Tom, later that afternoon. He leaned forward, his grey eyes gleaming with fanaticism. 'I could have told you we hadn't heard the last of it when Chamberlain came back from Munich, waving his scrap of paper. Peace for our time, indeed . . .'

Jenny suspected that Tom had wanted it to happen. He just couldn't wait to don a khaki uniform and go off to defend his country. And for what? All for some quarrel in a faraway land which was none of their business anyway.

'At least Mr Chamberlain tried, Tom,' said Jenny. 'And I don't care what you say now, at the time most people were glad to believe him. I feel right sorry for him. He seems a nice little man, and he was only trying to avoid a war. Only complete idiots would want to go to war again so soon.'

'The trouble is, we know too much now,' remarked Annie Carter. She glared belligerently through her thick-lensed spectacles. 'It doesn't do to know too much about what's going on. In the last war, we had no idea what was happening over there. And a good job too – we just had to get on with our lives as best we could. We found out soon enough when something serious had happened.' She sighed as she settled her considerable bulk more comfortably in the sagging easy chair.

5

Jenny thought her mother was looking tired. She could do with a good rest – couldn't they all? – but it didn't look as though there would be much respite for any of them. If rumours were to be believed, they might soon have to accommodate a houseful of evacuees.

'They tell us far too much,' Annie repeated, nodding aggressively. 'There's far too much news in those bloomin' papers.'

'That's why they're called newspapers, Ma,' said Tom with an uncharacteristic touch of humour. 'Because they tell us the news.' He smiled and winked at Jenny.

Annie went on as though she hadn't heard him. 'I don't hold with all this reading. Sheer waste of time, I call it. Our Violet's always got her head stuck in a book. And you're not much better, our Jenny. Always reading those silly magazines when you should be working.' Annie sniffed and glared at her daughter.

Jenny had to bite her tongue, as she frequently did at her mother's remarks. She did like magazines and nice romantic books; nothing too heavy though, none of the books that Violet read – great thick volumes with small print. Jenny felt that she would go mad if she couldn't escape now and again into her make-believe world. She had the sense to know it was only make-believe; Jenny had her feet firmly on the ground. But her mother's comments were unfair. She only read her magazines when she had finished her work. It was no use arguing with Annie, though. She would always have the last word.

Jenny was only too glad that she could escape, when her day's work at the boarding house was over, to her own little home round the corner with Tom and their little daughter Patsy. Poor Violet had to put up with Mother all the time, and her younger sister was even less inclined than Jenny to stick up for herself. Violet had been such a clever girl at school, always top of the class. She read all sorts of serious books – Dickens and Trollope and Thomas Hardy and goodness knows what else – like Mother said, she was always reading. She had wanted to be a teacher, but Mother had soon put paid to that idea.

'Where's the sense in educating a girl?' she had said. 'You'll only go and get married, and what use will all that book-learning be then? No, my lass, you'll leave school, same as I did, and come and work here with me.'

6

So Violet had left school at fourteen – that was in 1934, the year that Patsy was born – and had worked in the boarding house ever since. Jenny didn't know how she stuck it, day in and day out, putting up with other's caustic comments. No doubt Violet would get married some day, but she was nineteen already and there never seemed to be any sign of a boyfriend. Jenny had been married when she was nineteen.

She glanced across the room to where Violet was holding an animated conversation with Tom. She thought, as she often did, that her sister could do so much more with herself if she tried. Her faded blue and white gingham frock with the Peter Pan collar, and the shapeless cardigan that she wore over it, did nothing to enhance her appearance. But then, who am I to talk? thought Jenny, realising full well that just recently she hadn't been bothering much what she looked like either. Violet's hair was a pretty pale-blonde colour, almost flaxen, and might wave slightly if allowed to, but she always fastened it back tightly with a pair of childish slides. It made her features look even more angular, her nose even sharper. Her eyes were her best feature, hazel like Jenny's, but much greener, with long dark lashes.

Jenny, too, as a girl had cherished wild ideas of finding employment in the wide world outside. She knew that she wasn't as brainy as Violet, but she'd always been lively and interested in what was going on. It would have been lovely to work in a shop, a ladies' dress shop maybe, or in Boots at the lending library. But Mother had put a stop to her fancy ideas too. Jenny also had worked for her mother since she was fourteen; that had been in 1926.

At least she had met Tom and escaped, even if it was only to the next street. If Annie had had her way, they would have had two rooms in the attic. But Tom had insisted on their own home. He could stick up for himself, and for Jenny, when he wanted to, and Annie seemed to admire him for it. No one ever seemed to stand up to Annie, except Tom occasionally, and Cousin Ada, of course . . .

Jenny hadn't really been listening to the conversation going on between Tom and Violet. She had heard it all so many times before. All about Hitler marching into the Rhineland way back in 1936, and about the Spanish Civil War. Jenny couldn't understand what that had to do with the present situation, but according to Tom it was a victory for the Fascists and another step nearer to the inevitability of war between Britain and Germany.

Violet knew such a lot about it. She and Tom often had these involved discussions. Jenny thought at times that Tom would have been better married to Violet; but she, Jenny, was the one he had fallen in love with, and she knew that he loved her still. There was no mistaking the ardour, at certain times, in his pale-grey eyes – an ardour that she couldn't always answer.

'So you agreed with Mr Churchill then, did you, Tom?' Violet was asking now.

'Yes – I agreed with him. I think he was right to call for rearmament, but the Cabinet wouldn't listen to him. And most people wouldn't have wanted it at that time. A lot of people called him a warmonger, but he was right, you see, after all.'

'Mr Chamberlain began to wake up to reality, though, didn't he, when Hitler invaded Czechoslovakia?' Violet's green eyes glowed intensely as she looked at her brother-in-law.

'He had no choice, Vi.' Tom spread out his hands in a dismissive gesture. 'Chamberlain brought pressure on the Czechs to hand over a large part of their country to Germany. There were three million Germans living in Czechoslovakia, you know, so I suppose they did have some cause for complaint. But even that wasn't enough to satisfy Hitler.'

Czechoslovakia, and now Poland. But to Jenny, and to most other people too, she suspected, these countries were so far away. And what business was it of Britain's anyway?

'It's got nothing to do with us,' she protested now, finally joining in the conversation. 'Why can't they sort it out amongst themselves? It's ridiculous dragging us into it.'

'We can't give way to aggression, Jenny,' Tom replied patiently. 'The British and French have both threatened war, unless the Germans withdraw from Poland.'

'And do you think they will?'

'No – I don't,' said Tom flatly.

Annie sighed. 'Well, we'll all know soon enough. That Mr Chamberlain's talking to us all on the wireless tomorrow, isn't he, Tom?'

'That's right, Ma. At eleven o'clock.'

'You're coming round here then, are you? It'll happen be best if we're all together when they tell us what's going to happen.'

'Yes – we'll all be here, Mother,' Jenny replied wearily. She couldn't wait to get away today, back to the security of her own home with Patsy and Tom. Perhaps when she got Tom on his own she might be able to convince him of his foolhardiness in wanting to enlist. It was a forlorn hope, though, she feared. 'We'd best be off now. Our Patsy's gone out with Cousin Ada this afternoon. She's taken her down to Pablo's ice-cream parlour for a treat, but she'll be bringing her back soon for tea.'

'Huh!' Annie grunted, as she always did when Cousin Ada's name was mentioned.

There was little love lost between Annie and her niece. Jenny knew that it was because, in Ada, Annie had met her match. Ada, just like her aunt, had a caustic tongue and a fiery temper, but they concealed a surprisingly tender heart. Ada thought the world of Patsy. Jenny and Tom's little daughter had proved to be a very great blessing to them all. Patsy was the only one who could find the chink in the armour that both Annie and Ada wore to protect themselves. Against what? Jenny often wondered. Could it be against loving, or feeling things too deeply? Tough northern folk such as they often found it difficult to show their emotions. It took the innocence of a child to break down the barriers.

Ada came back with Patsy soon after Jenny and Tom arrived home.

Patsy was jumping up and down with excitement. 'It was lovely, Mummy. I had a great big ice cream with nuts on it, and red stuff squeezed all over it out of a vinegar bottle. And Auntie Ada had a milk shake in a big glass. She had a right long spoon to scrape out the last little bit, didn't you, Auntie Ada?' She pulled at her aunt's hand, her eyes, hazel-brown like Jenny's, gleaming with the remembered wonder of it all.

'Yes . . . We've had a grand time, haven't we, lovey?' Ada stooped and gave the child a quick hug, then fondly stroked her fine ginger hair. 'Eh dear, I don't know I'm sure,' she said quietly, turning to Jenny and Tom. 'It makes you wonder what it's all about. One minute we're sitting eating ice cream at Pablo's, as right as ninepence, and the next minute we could be at war with those bloomin' Germans. Whatever is the world coming to? I think they've all gone mad.'

9

'I'm sure they have,' said Jenny. She looked pointedly at her husband. 'That's what I keep telling Tom. I'm sure it's not worth fighting about, whatever it is, but I can't get him to see sense.'

Tom shook his head sadly. 'It's not me that needs to see sense, love. It's all them bigwigs, the top brass. Small fry like us, we just have to do as we're told . . . Anyroad, we'll all know the worst tomorrow.'

'How's your ma?' asked Ada, somewhat ungraciously. 'I daresay she'll have a lot to say about it all. She's always got an axe to grind about summat.'

'She'll be glad when we know for certain,' said Jenny. 'Same as the rest of us. It's this waiting that gets you down . . . We're all going round for our dinner tomorrow. I wouldn't want Mother and our Violet to be on their own.'

'No, I suppose you're right,' replied Ada grudgingly. 'Families have to stick together at a time like this. I shall have me work cut out tomorrow seeing to my ladies. They're getting all hot and bothered about it already, I can tell you, and it hasn't even started yet. That reminds me, I'd best be getting back to 'em. It's supposed to be my half-day, but they're not much good at fending for themselves.'

Ada departed with a curt nod at Jenny and Tom and another hug for Patsy. Her cousin was a good sort, thought Jenny as she watched Ada's stocky figure walking purposefully down the street. Ada was employed as housekeeper-cum-companion to two maiden ladies who lived near the centre of Blackpool. It was a pity she'd never married, but there didn't seem to be much likelihood of that happening now. She was too set in her ways. She looked years older than she really was, with her iron-grey hair scraped into a roll and skewered with lethal-looking hairpins, and her face red as though with enthusiastic scrubbing and devoid of any trace of make-up. Yes . . . it might have made a world of difference to Ada if she'd got married.

Jenny said as much to Tom as she turned from the window and started laying the table. 'Our Ada'd have made somebody a good wife. She's such a hard worker and a wonderful cook. It seems a waste for her to be looking after them two old biddies.'

Tom laughed. 'A fellow wants a bit of something else from a wife besides hard work and nice meals. I like my food as much as the next man, but I like a bit of the other now and again as well.' He looked slyly at Jenny from beneath lowered eyelids. 'I can't see Ada providing any of that there, can you, Jen?'

Jenny flicked the cloth over the table in a deft movement as though she hadn't heard his last remark. Silently she turned to the sideboard drawer and started taking out the knives and spoons.

'Anyway, I reckon she's left it a bit late for getting wed now, hasn't she?' Tom continued. He knew jolly well that Jenny wouldn't answer him when he started making provocative remarks. She was a bit strait-laced at times, was Jenny. She responded to his lovemaking – usually – in the depths of the double bed, but it certainly wasn't something to be talked about in the middle of the afternoon. 'Your Ada must be pushing forty now, isn't she?' he asked.

'Yes – thereabouts,' said Jenny. 'There was a milkman that seemed keen on her a year or two back, a widower he was – d'you remember? – but she sent him packing. He lived in a tiny little house in South Shore and Ada said she'd be a fool to leave a comfortable home to go and live in a one-bedroomed cottage.'

Tom shrugged. 'I suppose she was right if she was only thinking of marrying him for the comforts he could provide. I must admit she seems happy enough living with the Frobisher ladies.' He chuckled. 'It tickles me the way she always calls them "my ladies".'

'Yes . . . I don't suppose she'll change now,' Jenny agreed. 'She's always laughing about it and saying she's on the shelf. But she says she knows when she's well off. If she's happy living in somebody else's home, then it's got nothing to do with us.'

Jenny never ceased to be thankful for her own little home, humble though it might be. Home, to Jenny and Tom and five-year-old Patsy, was a two-bedroomed terraced house, identical to hundreds of others, in the area of Blackpool known as North Shore. Solidly built of Accrington brick, these houses had sprung up all over the town soon after the turn of the century.

There was no garden, the door opening straight off the street into a tiny hallway, the floor of which was covered with orange and brown linoleum in a pattern of squares and rectangles. A strip of rather worn red carpet covered the stairs which led up immediately behind the front door. The room at the front of the house, which Jenny usually referred to as the best room or the front room, was rarely used except at Christmas or on very special occasions. The rest of the time it smelt musty and slightly damp. They couldn't afford to have a fire in both rooms, and it was nice to have a room to keep for best, in the way that you always wore your best clothes on a Sunday. A cumbersome three-piece suite in maroon moquette, and a bow-fronted display cabinet were the only items of furniture, and even so the small room seemed overcrowded.

Jenny kept her best china tea service, patterned with pink roses, in the cabinet, together with an accumulation of treasures acquired over the years. A china lighthouse emblazoned with 'A Present from Scarborough' was a reminder of their honeymoon. There was a Coronation mug of Edward VIII – commemorating the non-event – and one of his brother, King George VI; a box covered with varnished seashells; a paperweight with a pattern of tiny flowers; a silver-plated butter dish and a set of small glasses with gold rims. Treasures very rarely used or noticed, and dusted once a year at spring-cleaning time.

The back room was the heart of the house. Jenny loved this room, which they always called the kitchen. It wasn't a kitchen at all really. The cooking was done in a minuscule scullery, the back kitchen, opening off the main room. The furniture in the back room was second-hand, all that they could afford, bought at a saleroom. A dining table and four chairs, a bit shabby, but serviceable; two comfortable fireside chairs, and a Victorian oak sideboard with a pattern of fruit and flowers carved on the doors.

In this room were Jenny's real treasures, her most precious possessions, bought one by one after a great deal of scrimping and saving. There was a wind-up mahogany gramophone – a modern one without a horn, with the speaker cleverly concealed in the cabinet – a wireless with a sunray design cut into the front, and a mirror shaped like a flower with petals of pink and green glass, which hung over the fireplace.

On the sideboard stood Jenny's pride and joy, a figure lamp that Tom had given her on her last birthday. It was in the shape of a lady; gilded and completely naked, she stood on her toes holding in her upraised arms an enormous beach ball through which the light filtered, shedding an orange glow in a dark corner of the room.

'Disgusting!' had been Annie's comment when she saw the figure. 'You should be ashamed of yourself, our Jenny, having a thing like that in the house. Whatever will people think?'

But Jenny didn't care about what people thought, or about what her mother said. She would do as she pleased in her own home. To

Jenny the female figure represented beauty and joy, and the freedom that she herself so fervently desired.

And now, what was to become of them all? Was the freedom so painfully fought for and won only twenty years ago to be thrown away at the whim of a power-mad dictator?

'That Hitler's crazy,' Jenny persisted, later that night after Patsy was tucked up in bed. 'They're all crazy. I reckon that if the leaders of all these nations want a war, then they should get together and fight it out amongst themselves, like children do in the school yard. They're just like children anyway, wanting something that doesn't belong to them. That's all that wars are ever about, isn't it? Wanting land that someone else has got.'

Tom didn't answer. He stared into the fire, preoccupied with his thoughts.

'If the ordinary people refused to fight, they couldn't have a war, could they?' Jenny went on. 'Then they'd be forced to sort it out. It's only complete fools who want to fight.'

Tom sighed. 'Look, Jenny love. We've been over all this before. I've told you – we can't give way to aggression. We must defend our rights, and protect the nations that are being persecuted.'

'But why enlist, Tom? It isn't as if you were a very young man.'

'I'm only thirty-one, Jenny. I haven't exactly got one foot in the grave yet.' Tom could be very pedantic at times.

'Thirty-one is quite old – for a soldier. And if you persist you may well end up with two feet in the grave. There are lots of men who are younger than you. They'll be called up first. Just wait until they send for you – please, Tom.'

'I can't, love.' Tom shook his head. 'My father died defending his country, and what's it all been for? I couldn't live with myself if I didn't go and carry on where he left off.'

'That's not strictly true, Tom. Your father died from Spanish 'flu, the same as mine did, well after the war.'

'But it was as a result of the war, wasn't it? His chest was weakened, and his heart, and he had no resistance left.'

'Perhaps if he had died on the battlefield you might feel differently. It's not just a game of toy soldiers, you know. I heard my dad talk often enough about the trenches. The mud and the noise of the shells and the stench of decay . . . He couldn't seem to get it out of his mind. Mother wouldn't listen to him. She used to

13

tell him to shut up. She didn't want to hear such horrible tales. But I heard him talking to Uncle Bert many a time. I was only a little girl. I wasn't supposed to be listening, but it's something I've never forgotten.'

Jenny hadn't forgotten either that it was drink, not the war, that had finally killed her beloved father. He had been a frequent visitor to the pub round the corner, driven there, no doubt, in an effort to subdue his gruesome memories and to escape from his wife's nagging tongue. When the Spanish 'flu epidemic hit the town, his weakened body and mind could put up no resistance. Jenny supposed that her mother must have wept at her husband's death, although she didn't remember seeing her do so. What she recalled most vividly was Annie's determination to start afresh. She had scraped together what little capital she had, and the insurance money, and put a deposit on the Blackpool boarding house. They had moved there from Wigan in 1921, Annie and nine-year-old Jenny, and Violet who was then a baby of ten months.

'There'll be no trenches this time,' said Tom. 'We're much more up to date now. A lot of the fighting will be done in the air. Not that I fancy joining the RAF. Glamour boys, that's what folk call them, with their curly moustaches and swanky voices. No, the Army's good enough for me. Anyway, it may be all over by Christmas, and I'd never forgive myself if I went and missed it all.'

Tom didn't really think that the war would be over by Christmas, but there was no point in alarming Jenny. He couldn't make her understand that it was a question of honour, something that he knew he must do. Of course he realised it wasn't like a game of toy soldiers. Jenny was inclined to be scathing about his soldiers, as though he was a little boy who'd never grown up, playing endless games. She didn't understand that, to him, they were real, fighting imaginary battles helped him to sort out problems in his mind, and they also evoked vivid memories of his father.

He remembered the set of Britain's cavalry figures that Dad had bought him for his eleventh birthday, just after the war ended. Tom had loved the Life Guards on their black horses, with their red uniforms and swords upraised, and the bandsmen with cymbals and trumpets and drums. Other sets had followed: infantrymen; the kilted Scottish regiments; gunners – some lying down and some

14

standing up, with guns ready to fire; and native warriors – Zulus, Egyptians and North American Indians.

Tom and his dad had played for hours, planning battle campaigns, arranging their men in strategic positions, retreating and advancing. And after his father died Tom saved his pocket money to add to his collection. He had carried on collecting even after he was married. His latest acquisitions were tanks and ambulances and armoured cars – new models that were just coming on to the market. He couldn't make Jenny understand that this was far more than just a game. To Tom, it was at times as real as life itself.

Jenny understood so little about him these days and Tom feared at times that they were growing apart. She looked tired lately, and she had lost some of the vital sparkle which had attracted him when he first set eyes on her. That had been nine years ago on his first visit as a holidaymaker to Pleasant View. How bonny she had looked then, her dark curly hair framing her elfin face, and her hazel eyes – sometimes green, sometimes brown – twinkling merrily as she smiled at him and Bob.

He had discovered that this pretty girl in the frilly apron, serving at the tables, was the landlady's daughter. He'd had to put up with a few black looks from Annie, although she had agreed, somewhat grudgingly, that Tom could take Jenny out.

'Make sure she's in by half past ten, mind,' she had warned him. 'I'll have no girl of mine gallivanting about till all hours. She's only seventeen.'

Annie could be a battle-axe all right, but Tom got on with her well enough now. You just had to show her that she couldn't always have her own way. She worked those girls far too hard, though. It was no wonder that Jenny looked so weary, and that she had developed recently, to Tom's dismay, a sharp edge to her tongue. Like her mother . . . No – Tom brushed the thought away hurriedly. His beloved Jenny could never turn out like her mother. God forbid! Never in a thousand years.

She didn't really mind the toy soldiers. To Jenny, that was just what they were – toys – another instance of how some men never grew up. She just knew that she had to dust them. There was a selection of them arranged on the chest of drawers in the bedroom. The others – boxes and boxes of them, neatly catalogued – were stacked away in the drawers. Across the top of the chest were red-coated guardsmen, marching as to war, together with Tom's father's war medals, a peace mug celebrating the Armistice, with the flags of the Allies surrounding a globe of the world, and a Toby jug depicting General Kitchener.

Jenny didn't mind this memorabilia of war cluttering up their bedroom. After all, a bedroom was only a place where you went to sleep. There was never any time for lounging in bed. It was a habit that Annie had never encouraged.

'You die in bed,' had been a favourite expression of her mother, when Jenny, as a young girl, had wanted a lie-in.

Perhaps – one day – Jenny thought longingly, she night have a posh bedroom, with a dressing table and wardrobe in bird's-eye maple, and a quilted satin eiderdown. Perhaps – one day – they might be able to afford a semi-detached house in Marton or Layton, or even Bispham . . .

But Jenny knew that Tom had set his heart on returning – one day – to Yorkshire.

Chapter 2

They had travelled by train to Blackpool from Castleburn, for a week's holiday at the seaside. It would have been easier to go to Scarborough, or Whitby or Bridlington, and Tom would have preferred it. He didn't care much for crowds and noise but his mate Bob had been insistent. Bob wanted to see the Tower and the new promenade, and the Golden Mile. And Stanley Park, he had heard, was just like being in the country. Bob was twenty-two years old and he'd never been to Blackpool, something he meant to put right without further delay. So Tom had tagged along somewhat reluctantly, but he had never regretted it.

There had been a slight reduction in the number of visitors to Blackpool in this summer season of 1930. The depression was hitting the Lancashire mill towns and the Yorkshire woollen trade too, but, so far, Tom had always managed to find employment as a builder and he could well afford a holiday.

They found the boarding house in a side street near the promenade. It seemed to be just what they were looking for and there was a sign in the window saying 'Vacancies'. Pleasant View attracted many visitors who came on spec, with its bright yellow paintwork, polished brass door knocker and letter box, and scrubbed stone steps edged in white with a donkey stone. 'Pleasant View' was a misnomer, though, if ever there was one. The only view was of a row of identical houses across the street, red-brick and three-storeyed with attic windows, each set in its own paved front garden behind a low wall topped with iron railings. If you climbed to the attic bedroom at the front of the house and stood on tiptoe on a chair you could see the sea – just – a triangle of water, sometimes greeny-blue, but usually grey, shimmering between the slated rooftops.

There was no doubt, however, about the north-country welcome that awaited you at Pleasant View. Annie Carter prided

17

herself that her boarding house was a home from home. Her Lancashire hotpots and steak and kidney pies were out of this world, as were her home-made Eccles cakes and almond tarts that graced the table at tea time. The feather mattresses were comfortable, the sun shone all week, and the company was congenial.

Bob had found himself a girl right at the beginning of their stay, when they went dancing at the Tower. She was a mill girl from Oldham, and Bob knew that it was unlikely that he would ever see her again. Tom, however, returned to Yorkshire with happy memories of Jenny, the lively girl who had gone out with him a few times that week. He loved her gaiety and the wholehearted delight that she took in all that went on around her. 'Ooh, look, Tom. Look at that . . . Aren't they lovely?' or 'Isn't it exciting?' she would cry joyfully at the sight of the donkeys on the sands, or the milling crowds on the ballroom floor, or the brightly coloured marigolds blooming in the rock gardens on the promenade. He remembered how her greenish-brown eyes lit up and sparkled with happiness, how she would almost skip and dance for joy, like a child. In some ways Jenny was childlike; she had an appealing innocence and naïvety which had made her irresistible to Tom. He guessed that treats, even such simple ones as riding on a tram or dancing at the Tower Ballroom, were rare occurrences for Jenny, tied as she was to the drudgery of her life in the boarding house.

Annie Carter could be rather a tyrant and Jenny appeared at times to be almost frightened of her mother. But Tom, astutely, had perceived a softness in the older woman's glance, behind the thick-lensed spectacles and behind the shrewd look that she had given him when he had asked if he could take her daughter out. He suspected that her bark was a great deal worse than her bite and that her grudging manner concealed a real affection for her daughter. It was only natural, after all, that she should be anxious about someone who wished to start courting Jenny and, already, Tom's thoughts were heading in that direction. He felt sure that when and if the time came he would be able to surmount Annie Carter's objections.

And so he wrote to Jenny, a chatty, friendly letter, telling her how much he had enjoyed her company, and that he hoped he would see her again. Much to his delight she wrote back, and later that year, when the Illuminations were on, he managed to snatch a long weekend from work. The following summer he visited

Blackpool again, this time without Bob, and spent a week at Pleasant View. And no one was more amazed than Tom, unless it was Jenny herself, when, that autumn, Annie allowed her daughter to visit his home in Yorkshire for a whole week.

Annie had been surprisingly agreeable about the visit.

'Yes, you can go, lass, if you've a mind,' she said, graciously for once. 'It's about time you had a holiday, and we've not got many folks booked in for that week.'

Jenny's proposed visit was to be at the end of September. By then the Illuminations season would be in full swing, but it was mostly weekend trade.

'Mrs Hanson and I can manage,' said Annie, referring to a neighbour who sometimes came in to help out, 'and happen Cousin Ada can come in more often if we're pushed. Her ladies, as she calls 'em, don't seem to mind her helping here a bit . . . That Tom seems a nice lad, quiet and steady like. Of course, he's not from Lancashire. I must admit I'd like it better if he were, but I reckon Yorkshire's not all that far away. It's not like getting friendly with a Londoner. I'd better drop a line to his mother first, though, before you go. It would only be proper.'

So Annie wrote and Tom's mother replied, saying how much she was looking forward to meeting Jenny.

She had never been so far from home before and Jenny was bubbling over with excitement as she said goodbye to her mother and sister at Central Station and climbed on to the Preston-bound train. That was where she would change for the train that would take her across the Pennines – the backbone of England, that separated Lancashire from Yorkshire, she remembered being taught at school – towards Tom's home town. She was apprehensive about the change at Preston. Supposing she couldn't find the right platform? Supposing the train went without her? A kindly porter, however, pointed her in the right direction and she boarded the train and leaned back against the prickly upholstery feeling a real sense of achievement. She was a traveller now. The sepia photographs on the carriage wall opposite her showed seaside views of the distant resorts of Scarborough, Bridlington and Filey, all places in Yorkshire, Jenny thought. The only seaside resort that she knew, apart from Blackpool, was Southport, where she had been once on a day trip. Perhaps, someday, she might travel even further afield than Yorkshire. She hugged the thought delightedly to herself as the train chugged away with a hiss of steam and a screech of wheels in a cloud of dense grey smoke.

After Preston, the flat landscape of the Fylde gave way to gently rolling hills, and the hedges dividing the fields were replaced by dry-stone walls. Then the hills became steeper, sweeping stretches of moorland coloured purple with heather, their vastness broken by outcrops of rock and grazing sheep. Jenny had never seen so many sheep. She leaned forward in her seat and eagerly watched it all. It wasn't just a different county; it was like a different world. She ate the potted-meat sandwiches, carefully wrapped in grease-proof paper, that her mother had prepared for her, then sat with her hands tightly folded in her lap, trying to still the fluttering sensation in her tummy and the thudding of her heart against her ribs. Because, as the train clattered along, gobbling up the miles, nearing her destination, Jenny's apprehension was growing.

She felt shy and nervous, almost sick with anxiety. It was three months since she had seen Tom, time enough to forget quite a lot about him. And when all was said and done, she didn't know him very well at all. The whole of their time together, when added up, amounted to less than a month. They had corresponded regularly, though. Not a week went by without a letter from Tom, and Jenny had written almost as frequently. When he had begged her to come and stay at his home in Castleburn, Jenny hadn't needed much persuading. It would be wonderful to have a week away from the drudgery of the boarding house – and from Mother too, Jenny admitted to herself – but now that she was here she was beginning to have second thoughts. Suppose Tom's family didn't like her? Suppose she didn't care as much for Tom when she saw him on his home ground?

The train slowed down and squealed to a stop and Jenny read the signboard – Castleburn. She had arrived. She tugged her battered leather suitcase off the rack and struggled to open the carriage door. Then she stood on the empty platform and looked round uncertainly. Where was Tom? He was supposed to be here to meet her. She stood in the unfamiliar station and watched the train disappearing into the distance, a tiny puzzled frown wrinkling her brow. Then she saw him, and she wondered why ever she had been so worried. He was dashing along the platform, his sandy hair

20

flopping over his brow, his grey eyes shining with delight at seeing her again. He looked so comforting and familiar that Jenny felt as though she were coming home.

'Jenny, love!' His arms went round her in a bear-like hug. 'It's real grand to see you. I'm sorry I'm late – Mr Jenks from down the road brought me in his car and I had to wait while he filled her up with petrol. Come on, let's be having you.' He picked up her heavy case in one hand and put his other arm protectively round her waist.

Mr Jenks's old Hillman car felt like a Rolls Royce to Jenny. She leaned back in the worn leather seat and watched the grey-stone houses flash past. They looked strange after the red-brick houses of Lancashire, but very welcoming.

Tom's home stood on the outskirts of the town in a short cul-de-sac. It was solid and square, like the houses that children draw. The other houses in the street were terraced, but the Bradshaw home, standing on its own at the end of the street, was detached. It was perfectly symmetrical. The green front door was flanked by two large square windows, each with four panes of glass, and there were two identical windows directly above. The roof was of grey slate and two chimney pots sat squarely in the middle, one of them puffing out clouds of smoke, in spite of the warmth of the September day.

Martha Bradshaw came bustling out of the kitchen at the back of the house when she heard the door open. She was a tiny woman, only about five feet in height, grey and prematurely wrinkled. Her brown skin was crisscrossed with a network of deep lines and she was dressed entirely in black. Her long skirt almost reached the ground and the only touch of colour on her dress was the pink cameo brooch which she wore at her throat.

'So you're Jenny,' she said, her beady brown eyes looking appraisingly at the girl. 'Come on, lass. Let's have a look at you.' She put her head on one side, like a bird, and nodded once or twice, then a huge grin lit up her tiny features. 'Aye – I reckon you'll do. Our Tom said as how you were a bonny lass, and you are that – right bonny.'

Jenny smiled uncertainly. 'I'm very pleased to meet you, Mrs Bradshaw.'

'Well, come on in, lass, and make yourself at home. And you, Tom – don't stand there gawping like one of Lewis's dummies.' His

21

mother gave him a not too gentle poke in the ribs. 'Take Jenny's case up to her bedroom.'

Jenny knew right from the start that she would love Martha Bradshaw. The Bradshaws were 'not without a bit of brass', as Tom's mother was fond of saying. Mr Bradshaw had been a foreman builder, and Martha had worked long hours in the woollen mill up to and after her marriage, enabling them to 'put a bit on one side'. Tom had followed in his father's footsteps and was employed as a bricklayer by the same firm. Now there was just Martha and her unmarried daughter Lilian living at home, and Tom, of course, who was two years younger than Lilian.

There were five children in the Bradshaw family. Jack, the eldest, still lived in Castleburn with his wife and family, but the next two, Hilda and Joe, had moved away when they married. Both of them, however, had chosen partners from Yorkshire, and their homes, in Bingley and Bradford respectively, were not too far distant.

'Yorkshire folk don't often get wed to strangers from foreign parts,' Martha Bradshaw remarked, as the three of them sat drinking tea by the black range in the kitchen. There was a small parlour and a dining room, too, at the front of the house, but the family usually gravitated to the kitchen.

Jenny cast a startled look in Martha's direction. Was that what they thought of her, because she came from the other side of the Pennines? A stranger . . . Her own mother, she recalled, had made a similar remark about Tom. But it wasn't as if she was going to marry him. There had been no talk of that, not yet. Jenny experienced a moment of panic. Oh dear! She did hope that she hadn't got off on the wrong foot.

Martha noticed her discomfiture. 'Eh, dear . . . You didn't think I was meaning you, did you, lass? Nowt of the sort. I was just going to tell you about our Jack.' She leaned forward and grasped hold of the hissing kettle with a red knitted pan holder and poured the contents into the brown earthenware teapot which stood on the hob. 'I think this'll stand a drop more water . . . Now, what was I saying? Oh aye, our Jack. He got friendly with a foreigner after the war. He served in Palestine during the war, did our Jack. Anyroad, he met this 'ere foreigner, a lass from London she were . . .' Jenny smiled to herself. Londoners, to her own mother, were always classed as foreigners and seemingly they were to Martha Bradshaw as well. 'She was the sister of one of his mates in the Army, but nowt came of it. He got wed to a girl from round t'corner.' She gave a chuckle and leaned across and placed her lined brown hand over Jenny's. 'Tek no notice of me, lass. I allus says what I think. Our Tom'll tell you that. I believe in calling a spade a spade, like most Yorkshire folk do!'

'I'll say you do, Mam,' said Tom, smiling at her fondly.

He always referred to his mother as Mam and he obviously thought the world of her. Jenny couldn't help comparing his feeling for his mother with her own for Annie. Did she love her mother? She supposed she did, although she had never thought much about it before. Annie certainly wasn't the sort of person to enkindle spontaneous affection, not like Tom's mother was. This undoubtedly was a happy household; she could feel the warmth encompassing her already. She sipped her tea, feeling very much at home.

It was when Lilian, the daughter next in age to Tom, came in from work that Jenny became aware of a faint feeling of tension, of unrest . . . Nothing that she could put her finger on, but the cordial atmosphere that had pervaded the house had been disturbed. Not that Jenny could say that Lilian had been anything but pleasant to her. She called out a cheery 'Hello, you must be Jenny' as she quickly swilled her hands under the kitchen tap. Her handshake was firm, but cold and rather damp – she hadn't bothered to dry her hands properly – and Jenny noticed a coolness in her eyes as she told Jenny, 'We've heard a lot about you.'

Jenny was struck by the startling resemblance between Lilian and her mother; the same build and stance, the same rapid movements of the head and hands and the same beady brown eyes, but in Lilian's the vital spark of warmth was missing.

Lilian worked in the local Woolworth's store in the High Street and had done so ever since it opened, about ten years before. She threw her working overall over the back of a chair and sat down at the well-scrubbed pine table. Jenny had noticed that the chair at the head of the table, a wooden Windsor armchair, was left unoccupied. It had been so when she and Tom and Martha had eaten their tea earlier, and Jenny had felt puzzled; it looked by far the most comfortable chair. Why didn't someone sit on it? Now Lilian, also, sat on one of the smaller chairs at the side of the table.

After a studied glance round the room, Jenny guessed at the

reason. She felt that it was an unspoken tribute to the memory of Albert Bradshaw, Tom's father, who had died, she had been told, a couple of years after the end of the Great War, as her own father had done. Photographs of Albert Bradshaw, along with other family groups, abounded in every room. An individual study of him in a stiffly starched collar, sporting a prolific growth of beard and moustache – not unlike the king, George V, when he was younger – stared down from the mantelpiece over the place at the head of the table where Jenny was sure he had once sat.

Martha fussed round her daughter. 'Here you are, lovey. We've saved you some nice ham and pickles. We had our tea earlier. We knew you wouldn't mind. Jenny was fair famished after all that travelling . . . This tea's not long been mashed. I reckon we can squeeze out another cup or two . . .'

As she ate her meal, Lilian chatted about her work at Woolworth's store, where she was in charge of the sweet counter. They had had a busy day.

'I should think that's every little girl's dream,' Jenny remarked. 'When I was a child I used to think how lovely it would be to work in a sweetshop – you know, like all little boys want to be an engine driver. Did you, Lilian?'

'Yes, I suppose I did.' Lilian gave a curt nod, her eyes on a dish of custard tart which had followed the plenteous helping of ham. She didn't look at Jenny as she answered. 'I'd always fancied working in a shop of some sort. Good job I did too, because I wasn't clever enough to do owt else. Our Hilda was the brainy one. Went on to the Grammar School, she did . . .' Jenny was aware of a note of envy creeping into the young woman's voice. 'Miss La-di-da she was an' all, I can tell you, going to a posh school. Me and the lads had to make do with the Senior School up the road.'

'Same here,' said Jenny with feeling. 'I wasn't brainy either. It's my sister as is the clever one.' She gave a self-conscious laugh. Lilian was making her feel slightly uncomfortable. She glanced concernedly in the young woman's direction, but Lilian was tucking into her custard tart as though she hadn't had a meal for a month.

Jealousy . . . could that be what was plaguing Lilian? thought Jenny. She found it strange; she had never been envious of her own sister's ability. She had always accepted the fact that they were just different, as sisters often were. Poor Lilian . . . it must be dreadful to have a feeling like that gnawing away at you. She made up her mind to try to get to know Lilian this week and to make an effort – hard though it might be – to like Tom's sister.

Martha Bradshaw threw a little more light on the subject the next morning as she and Jenny were washing the breakfast pots. 'Now, don't you be taking too much notice of our Lilian, She's allus been like that, ever since our Tom came on the scene. She was only a little lass, nearly two years old, and I reckon she felt as how she'd got her nose pushed out. That's why I fuss round her, happen a bit more than I should, to make up for it. Eh, lass . . .' Martha gave a sigh, '. . . it's not easy being a mother. You can't allus show your feelings, not the way you'd like to.'

Jenny looked at her enquiringly, but without having any idea of what to say. She wasn't accustomed to heart-to-heart talks – Annie certainly didn't indulge in them – but Martha didn't need an answer.

'You're not supposed to have favourites.' She shook her head. 'Any mother knows that, but it's hard. Aye, it's hard, lass.' She emptied the bowl of soapsuds down the drain and wiped her hands on the towel. Then, still talking, she started to stack the breakfast pots away on the dresser. Ordinary actions, and the words were delivered in matter-of-fact tones, but the feelings expressed came from the heart. 'He's been my sun, moon and stars ever since he came along, has that lad. And when Albert died, it was Tom as I turned to for consolation, young as he was. He was a comfort to me. He was that . . . Mind you,' Martha looked at Jenny and lowered her voice confidingly, 'it were a bit of a shock, I can tell you, when I first knew I was expecting him. I thought I was going through the change and then, would you credit it, the doctor told me there was another bairn on the way.'

Jenny felt faintly embarrassed. Her own mother, so forthright about most things, was strangely reticent when it came to talking about 'women's problems'. Jenny remembered the humming and haaing there had been when Annie had tried to explain to her about periods. 'Being unwell', she always called it. Jenny had already known about it, but had refrained from saying so. She had just listened to her mother going on about not washing your hair or eating ice cream, and on no account should you ever have a bath when you were 'like that'.

'Aye, he's always been a good lad, has our Tom,' Martha went

25

on, 'and I've prayed that he'd meet a nice lass.' She beamed at Jenny. 'And I reckon he couldn't have done any better.'

Jenny felt again that the older woman was jumping to conclusions, but, at the same time, she was happy that she was being made to feel so welcome. So all she said was, 'Yes – we get on very well, Tom and me. And . . . thank you for inviting me, Mrs Bradshaw.'

'Like I was saying, I've tried not to make it obvious,' Martha continued. 'Not that the others would have cared much. They've all made a fuss of our Tom, with him being the youngest. I've had a grand family, thanks be to God, and they're all different, Jenny. Aye, as different as chalk and cheese. That's one of the best things about being a mother, watching how they all turn out. Our Lilian though, she's a deep 'un. Always has been. I'm blessed if I know what makes her tick at times.'

Poor Lilian, Jenny thought again. It certainly seemed as though envy was at the root of the girl's difficulties. This feeling was increased when she met the eldest brother Jack and his family, and noticed the easy camaraderie that existed between the two brothers, despite their difference in age. Again, Lilian seemed to be on the outside, looking in. But Jenny's persistent attempts at friendship won through. Lilian began to chat to her more animatedly, although Jenny noticed that the older girl hardly ever let their eyes meet in a direct glance. However, she did go so far as to offer to lend Jenny her bicycle, so that she and Tom could go for rides in the surrounding countryside.

Tom had taken a week's holiday from work so that he could be with Jenny all the time.

'You can ride a bike, can't you, love?' he asked her when he heard Lilian's offer.

'Of course I can,' she replied eagerly. 'I do errands for Mother on my bike. And sometimes I go for rides in the summer, with my friend Eileen. We go to the sandhills at Squire's Gate, or up to Nobreck. It's so flat in Blackpool, it's lovely for cycling.'

Tom laughed. 'Well, it's not so flat here. You'll find you have to push a lot harder. But you might as well make use of our Lilian's bike, then we can see something of the countryside.'

As the week went by, Jenny found herself more and more delighted with all that she saw on this her first visit to Yorkshire.

26

Castleburn was a bustling market town and roads converged from all directions into the cobbled market square where the farmers from outlying villages brought their produce every Wednesday morning.

Jenny wandered happily round the stalls, a basket over her arm. They were shopping for Tom's mother, but Jenny was doing more stall-gazing than shopping. Tom took it all for granted – he had seen it all before and he didn't care much for shopping anyway; he said it was women's work – but Jenny was enchanted by the sights and the sounds and the smells. She gazed in awe at the stalls piled high with apples, pears and oranges, and the biggest cabbages and cauliflowers she had ever seen; eggs with deep brown shells; enormous round cheeses; jars of home-made lemon curd and honey. Jenny breathed in deeply. She could almost taste the aromas which emanated from all the different kinds of produce. A decaying, cabbagey smell from the greengrocers' stalls, the pungent scent of overripe cheeses, a sugary, minty smell from the sweet stall.

'Ooh – look, Tom. Let's buy some of that Yorkshire mixture,' she cried in delight, feeling like a child again.

Tom indulgently produced sixpence and they bought a huge bag of boiled sweets – red and yellow pear drops, stripy mints, fruit cushions and butter drops.

Jenny bought three yards of material, a blue cotton print with a pattern of white daisies, from an apple-cheeked old woman. 'It's for our Violet,' she told Tom happily. 'It's about time she had a new frock for best, and Mum and I can run it up for her as easy as not.'

Then she chose a cup and saucer in fine china with a gold rim, emblazoned with a design of pansies, as a present for her mother. 'Mum likes a nice cup of tea. She's got nothing as posh as this, though. It'll look a treat on her dresser.'

Tom smiled at her fondly. 'You're always thinking about other people, Jenny. Come on, let's buy something for you. What would you like?'

Eventually she chose a bowl of china flowers, brightly coloured anemones in red, blue and purple. 'Aren't they pretty, Tom?' she said. 'I'll put it on my chest of drawers and then I'll think of you every time I look at it. Oh, Tom – I'm so happy!'

27

Jenny's cheeks were flushed with excitement and her eyes danced delightedly as she tried to take in every detail of the scene around her and imprint it for ever on her memory. They walked up to the far end of the market to the animal pens. Here were squealing piglets, squawking hens, geese, ducks, and fluffy week-old chicks.

'Oh, Tom – look. Aren't they sweet?' Jenny reached out a finger and tentatively touched the pale-yellow feathers of a tiny chick.

Tom laughed good-humouredly. 'Come on, Jenny. They don't stay like that, you know. Little chicks grow up soon enough into bad-tempered hens, like that lot over there. Anybody would think you'd never seen real live chicks before.'

'I haven't.' Jenny stared at him, wide-eyed with the wonder of it all. 'Don't you realise? I'm a town girl, not an old country bumpkin like you.'

She was fascinated by the countryside around Castleburn. The grey-stone houses, nestling beneath clumps of sycamore trees whose leaves were already tinged with the first yellow and orange of autumn; grazing sheep; cascading waterfalls; gently flowing rivers. Surrounding it all were the limestone hills, grey and forbidding, but here and there carpeted by a sweep of purple heather, then unexpectedly giving way to rich pasture land, shining emerald-green when lit by a sudden burst of sun peeping from behind the clouds. And Castleburn itself was so picturesque, with its fourteenth-century castle, which gave the town its name, at one end of the main street, and at the other end the parish church with its square Norman tower.

The last day of Jenny's visit they picnicked by the river. Nearby were the ruins of the twelfth-century Cistercian abbey, standing like a sentinel in the well-tended meadowland. Jenny pulled her cardigan more tightly round her shoulders. There was a distinct nip in the air today, although the sun was shining. Autumn was fast approaching, as was Jenny's return to her native Lancashire. It was only just across the Pennines, but to her it felt as though it were a million miles.

She sighed. 'It's so peaceful here, Tom. You don't know how lucky you are, living in a place like this.'

'So what's wrong with Blackpool, then?' he replied, grinning at her. 'I thought you liked living there, Jenny?'

She shrugged. 'Oh, I like it well enough, I suppose. I didn't know any different till I came here. I don't remember much about Wigan. I was only nine when we moved, so Blackpool's the only place I've known well. I'm not sand-grown though. Neither is our Violet, but she nearly is. She's lived there since she was about ten months old.'

'Sand-grown? What's that?'

'It's what they call you if you're born in Blackpool. They're very proud of it, are Blackpool folk. "I'm a sand-grown 'un", you'll hear them say. My friend Eileen's sand-grown . . . Everybody seems so much more friendly here, though.'

'Aye – there's nowt much wrong wi' Yorkshire folk, lass,' said Tom, laughing and exaggerating his native accent. 'Come on, though, Jenny. You can't tell me that Blackpool folk are much different. They seemed all right to me, the ones that I've met.'

'Yes, I suppose so. The trouble is, we're so busy we don't get round to making many friends. We're too busy making money, though to hear Mother talk, you'd think we hadn't two ha'pennies to rub together.'

'What about the winter, when the visitors have gone? What do you do then?'

'Oh, there's always plenty of jobs. Painting, decorating, sewing curtains, mending sheets . . . We never seem to have a spare minute.'

'Your mother certainly gets her money's worth out of you, love. I don't think she appreciates you.'

'She's all right,' said Jenny grudgingly. 'I try not to take too much notice of her, or else I'd get upset. She's had a hard life, Tom. Working in the cotton mill, then in the boarding house, and she finds it hard to show her feelings. I suppose she must love Violet and me, but she doesn't show it very much. Still, she's let me come here, hasn't she?'

Tom put his arm round Jenny and she leant against his shoulder. His tweed jacket felt rough against her cheek, and she could smell the characteristic maleness of him that she was beginning to know so well. A mixture of brilliantine and a faint trace of tobacco smoke. Tom smoked when he was outside, but never in the house. His mother didn't approve, and he would never do anything to upset her.

'It's been lovely having you here, Jenny,' he said, squeezing her

29

more tightly towards him. 'And they all like you so much. My mother can be a bit of a terror till you get to know her, but she's taken to you right enough, love.'

'I think she's lovely, Tom,' said Jenny simply. 'I felt scared at first. I thought she might be – you know – sanctimonious, but she doesn't keep going on about her religion, does she?'

Jenny had been overawed at first by the illuminated text hanging in the Bradshaws' parlour, 'Christ is the head of this household, the unseen listener to every conversation, the unseen guest at every meal'. She had wondered what was in store for her, glancing uncomfortably over her shoulder, fearful that the unseen presence could read her innermost thoughts.

Jenny wasn't much of a churchgoer. Annie had made sure they went to Sunday school – Violet still went, of course – and Jenny had been confirmed when she was thirteen, but now there never seemed to be time for regular worship.

She had gone to church with the Bradshaws on Sunday morning, not to the Norman parish church, but to the Wesleyan Methodist chapel round the corner in a side street. Mrs Bradshaw led the way, dressed in black as always. Black coat, and a black velour hat pulled well over her brow, and a huge black Bible under her arm. They sat upstairs in the gallery and Jenny joined in with them as they sang lustily:

'What a friend we have in Jesus,
All our sins and griefs to bear.
What a privilege to carry
Everything to God in prayer.'

Jenny knew that to Martha Bradshaw, as to all these Wesleyan Methodists, Jesus was like a real friend.

'No, Mam doesn't talk about her faith much,' Tom said now, 'but it's very real to her.'

'Not like my mother,' said Jenny feelingly. 'She's always on about what God thinks about this, and what He should do about that. I don't know why she claims to be such an authority on the subject. She never even goes to church now . . . No, that's not fair of me. There's never time to go.'

'You can always find time to go if you want to,' Tom answered, somewhat self-righteously, Jenny thought. 'Mam always insisted that we went and it's a good habit to get into. It stands you in good stead, and you never forget what you've learned as a child.'

'Surely it should be more than a habit, Tom? Shouldn't it be something that you do because you want to?'

'It's that as well, Jenny, but there's nothing wrong with forming good habits.'

Jenny was beginning to realise that Tom was a creature of habit. Work six days a week, church on Sunday, meals on the table at the appointed time. 'A place for everything, and everything in its place', she'd heard him say, and was to hear him say again, many times.

'I signed the pledge when I was twelve,' Tom went on. 'That was something that Mam insisted on.'

'Signed the pledge? What's that?'

'Pledging never to let strong liquor pass your lips. I did it in memory of my father. He was a firm believer in temperance. He was a good man, Jenny. You'd have liked him.'

'I'm sure I would, if he was anything like your mother. There's nothing wrong with having a drink though, surely?' Jenny was puzzled by this 'holier-than-thou' attitude. Her own mother wasn't averse to a drink of sherry or Guinness especially at Christmas time, and there was always a half-bottle of brandy in the sideboard cupboard, ready for emergencies. 'Do you mean to say that you never have a drink at all?'

'Well, I do now – occasionally. I go and have a pint now and again with the fellows I work with. But not a word to Mam, mind.' Tom laughed. 'She won't have alcohol in the house, so I abide by what she says. No – you're quite right, Jenny – there's nothing wrong with having a drink. It's knowing when to stop, and some folks don't.'

Jenny nodded thoughtfully. Her own father had been a case in point. Maybe if he'd had a more sympathetic wife there would have been no need for his frequent visits to the pub. She felt a little confused. She liked the Bradshaws very much and her feeling for Tom was gradually growing into something far greater than liking, but she wondered if the example set by Martha Bradshaw might be too hard to live up to. They were such kind people though, and to Jenny, accustomed to her mother's carping criticisms, kindness could cover a multitude of other faults.

'Your mother's a lovely person, Tom,' Jenny said again. 'I shall miss her – and I shall miss you too. Oh, Tom . . .' She buried her head against his shoulder, 'I don't want to go back.'

Tom suddenly realised that he would miss Jenny more than he could bear. He had known that he was very fond of her before she came to Yorkshire and throughout the week that fondness had grown. Now Tom knew, without any doubt, that he loved her and that he didn't want to part from her, not ever. He put both his arms round her and held her close, then he put a finger beneath her chin, lifting her face so that her greeny-brown eyes, now brimming with tears, looked into his grey ones. 'Then don't go back, love,' he said softly. 'Stay here with me. Oh, Jenny – I love you so much. Will you marry me? Please say that you will.'

Jenny nodded. 'Yes . . .' Her voice was the merest whisper. 'Oh, Tom – I love you too.'

As Jenny declared her love, Tom's lips closed over hers in a possessive kiss. He had kissed her before, many times, but this time it was different. It was as though he were laying claim to her as his own. I've said that I love him, thought Jenny to herself. I'm sure I do . . . And if love meant feeling safe and secure and wanted, then indeed she did love Tom.

Happily, they made their plans. The first thing that they must do, of course, was to break the news to Martha, and to Lilian . . . Martha was delighted and threw her arms first round Tom and then round Jenny, kissing her on both cheeks. Jenny smiled, flushed and happy, but at a loss for words.

She stole a glance at Lilian. The young woman had an unfathomable expression on her face, her mouth set in a grim line and her eyes staring unfocused at nothing. Jenny had tried hard all week, but had to admit to herself that she couldn't really take to Lilian. But now she felt sorry for her. Could it be that the girl was jealous that Jenny had a young man whom she was going to marry, while for her there was not a sign of one? Or could it be that she was fonder of her brother than she realised and didn't like the idea of another girl taking him away? As her mother had said, Lilian was a deep 'un. There was no doubt about that.

Lilian turned to her now and gave a brief smile which didn't reach her eyes. 'Congratulations, Jenny,' she said politely, if a trifle coldly, holding out her hand. 'I hope you'll be very happy. And you too, our kid,' she added, nodding at Tom.

Jenny knew that at the end of the week she must go home, but Tom would come over to Blackpool next weekend, they decided, by which time she would have broached the subject with her mother. He could get a train after work on Saturday, and go home again on Sunday. He would ask Mrs Carter, formally, if he could marry her daughter. Then they would go and buy a ring, and they would get married next summer. They would have a little grey-stone house in Castleburn, and they would live happily ever after . . .

'Go and live in Yorkshire?' said Annie Carter, her voice shrill with annoyance. 'Have you taken leave of your senses, girl? Of course you can't go and live in Yorkshire. You're staying right here.' She tapped her finger aggressively on the table top. 'You're needed in the boarding house. How do you think I'm going to manage if you go gallivanting across to the other side of the Pennines?'

'But . . . but Tom's asked me to marry him, Mother. He's coming to see you next weekend, to talk about it.' Jenny felt like crying; in fact she could feel the pricking of tears behind her eyelids already at her mother's harsh words.

'He can talk till he's blue in the face. You're not leaving here. You're under age, my girl, and don't you forget it. You're only eighteen and you'll do as I say. I don't mind you marrying him,' she added condescendingly. 'He's a nice enough lad. But if he wants you, he'll have to come and live here.'

'But how can he, Mother? His job's in Castleburn.'

'Then he'll have to find another one, won't he?'

And that was just what Tom did. He loved Jenny far too much to think of losing her, and there were all his brothers and sisters in Yorkshire to look after his mother. And Martha, he knew, though she loved her youngest son so much, would only wish them well.

There was no shortage of building work in Blackpool and Tom was soon able to find employment. Annie had her plans all worked out for the young couple.

'You can have two rooms on the top floor,' she told them. 'One for a bedroom and one for a sitting room. And you can have your meals down here with us, the same as you've always done.'

Tom, however, was adamant in his refusal and Jenny loved him for the way he stood up to her mother. They were having their own home, he declared, no matter how small it was. They were going to start their married life under their own roof. And so they did, at number sixteen Green Street – another misnomer – just round the corner from Pleasant View. It was the tiniest little house, two up and two down, but it was their own.

Tom and Jenny were married at the end of September 1932 – just a few weeks before Jenny's twentieth birthday – at the parish church round the corner. Jenny wore a dress of pale lavender georgette, and Violet and Jenny's best friend, Eileen, who were her bridesmaids, wore lemon crêpe de Chine. It was a very small wedding. Mrs Bradshaw said that it was too far for her to travel, but the family was represented by Tom's eldest brother, Jack, who was his best man. Lilian, somewhat to Jenny's relief, didn't attend either. After a meal at the Co-op café the happy couple set off for their honeymoon in Scarborough.

Jenny was apprehensive. To say that she was scared would be putting it too strongly – she couldn't be scared of dear Tom – but her experience of men was limited. There had been one or two boyfriends before she met Tom, amounting to little more than a quick kiss and a fumble by the back gate. And Annie had told her nothing at all.

Eileen's elder sister Jean had got married when Jenny and Eileen were twelve. The two girls had whispered together and giggled and guessed, and in the end Eileen had asked Jean outright what it was that you had to do. Jenny had been incredulous when Eileen passed on the information. It all sounded so ridiculous. Why on earth should anybody want to do that? Now, seven years later, she thought she understood. She could feel a faint stirring of desire, coupled with a churned-up feeling in her stomach, as she anticipated her wedding night.

She need not have feared. Tom was a gentle and considerate lover, and Jenny guessed that for him, too, it was the first time. After the initial shock she found it a pleasant enough experience. Nothing to make a song and dance about, to be sure, but Tom seemed happy enough, and if Tom was happy, well then so was Jenny.

Tom was filled with a quiet happiness, secure in his love for Jenny and her love for him. Sometimes he found it hard to believe that this lovely girl was his, that they were now man and wife. He had known that she was apprehensive about their wedding night, but no more so than he had been. He found it hard to express his feelings, to show her how much he loved her, but he was determined that he was going to be a good husband. He would work his fingers to the bone, if need be, to provide a comfortable home for his beloved Jenny. And he would learn to love her with his body as he already loved her with his mind.

Jenny loved Scarborough, finding it, though a seaside town, a complete contrast to Blackpool. They climbed up from the harbour to the ruins of the twelfth-century castle, then through the graveyard of St Mary's church where Anne Brontë was buried, to the maze of tiny streets and fishermen's cottages surrounding the market hall.

'It all seems so old compared with Blackpool,' Jenny remarked, gazing around happily. 'There's nothing old in Blackpool. Even the cliffs aren't real – they've been made by man. It's like another world here. There's only one thing wrong though – the sun sets in the wrong place.'

Tom burst out laughing. 'Oh, Jenny – you are a funny girl. Whatever do you mean?'

'In Blackpool the sun sets behind the sea. I've watched it sometimes. It's lovely, Tom. The sea's all dancey and sparkly, like diamonds, and the sky goes a pinky-red colour. Here the sun just disappears behind the houses, and it seems all wrong somehow.'

'Ah, but here the sun rises over the sea. You didn't think of that, did you? We could get up early and catch it one morning.'

But they never did. It was a luxury for Jenny to have a lie-in and then to tuck into a hearty breakfast of bacon and eggs that she hadn't cooked herself. The boarding house was very much like Pleasant View, but here Jenny was a guest, and that made all the difference.

They stayed for a week in Scarborough, and when they returned home they spent two whole days sampling the attractions of Blackpool. Jenny was seeing it all for the first time from a visitor's point of view. There were so many things that she hadn't done; residents very rarely sample the pleasures of their native town. They danced at the Tower ballroom, they rode on a clanging tram to Fleetwood, and they stared open-mouthed at the dubious delights of the Golden Mile. Jolly Alice, the fattest woman in the world; the bearded lady; the giant rat; and the star attraction of 1932, the Rector of Stiffkey, starving himself for fourteen days inside a large barrel.

'It's all a fraud,' Jenny heard a passer-by remark. 'If you go round the corner at twelve o'clock, you'll see him supping in the pub.'

Number sixteen Green Street was like paradise to Jenny. She still worked just as hard in the boarding house – after giving Tom his breakfast, she dashed round the corner to her mother's and started again – but at night she could go back to her own little home.

It was there, in June 1934, that Patsy was born. June the twenty-first is the longest day of the year, and it certainly felt like it to Jenny. But when, at five minutes before midnight, the tiny red-faced, red-haired baby was put into her arms, she knew that it had all been worth it. But the birth had been a difficult one and the doctor warned Jenny and Tom that it was unlikely that there would be any more children.

Chapter 3

Patsy sat on the front doorstep of her grandmother's house, her black doll in her arms. She nursed it lovingly, rocking backwards and forwards in rhythm with the tune that was going round and round in her head:

> 'There's a friend for little children,
> Above the bright blue sky.'

They sang that song at Sunday school and it was one of her favourites. Patsy knew that the friend in the song was Jesus. She had often gazed up into the bright-blue sky, hoping that one day she might see Him looking down at her from way above the clouds, but so far she hadn't been lucky.

The sky was bright blue this morning and the sun was warm even though it was only ten o'clock, holding the promise of a real scorcher of a day. Patsy fiddled with the ribbons of her sun bonnet. It felt itchy and uncomfortable, but Mummy insisted that she should wear it to keep the sun off her head. She got a headache if she stayed in the sun too long, her fair skin soon became red and sore and the freckles on her face even more pronounced.

Patsy hated her freckles. Every morning she peered into the mirror, hoping against hope that they might have gone away. Mummy laughed and called her a vain little miss, saying that freckles and auburn hair always went together. At least Mummy called her hair auburn and not red.

The boys at school called her redhead, or ginger, or – even worse – carrots, and it was so hard not to take any notice of them. She could feel the dreaded tears pricking her eyes, then they would laugh and dance round her, taunting her and shouting, 'Cry baby!'

The only thing that Patsy didn't like about school was the big boys who would link arms in the playground or on the way home so that she couldn't get past. Patsy knew only too well that she was timid and she hated herself for it, but it was hard when you were so tiny. She was the smallest girl in her class. Her teacher, Miss Banks, was lovely. She often gave Patsy a hug, saying that it didn't matter about being small, and that the best things came in little parcels.

It mattered to Patsy though. How she wished that she could be tall. Maybe when she was a grown-up lady she would be. Her hair would still be ginger, but perhaps it would get darker, then she could wear a pink dress. Mummy never let her wear pink. She said that it clashed with her hair. She always dressed her in blue or pale green or lemon.

I shall have red shoes too, thought Patsy, holding her legs out stiffly in front of her and surveying her sensible brown Clark's sandals. She would have a wardrobe full of red shoes, some with high heels, some with bows, some with buckles. It was a long time to wait, though, when you were only five.

Patsy sighed. She laid Topsy, her black doll, carefully on the step and ran to the iron gate. She leaned over and looked anxiously down the street. There was no sign of them yet. She couldn't even hear the sound of the drum in the distance as she sometimes could. Oh, please God, don't let them not come today, she prayed in a muddled manner, the words all mixed up in her head; but God would understand what she meant.

She dashed through the house, along the hallway, through the kitchen where Daddy was sitting reading the newspaper, and into the back kitchen. There was a delicious smell of apples and roasting meat. Grandma was standing at the big scrubbed white table in the middle of the room, her hands covered in flour, making an apple pie. Mummy was peeling potatoes at the sink and Auntie Violet was drying the pots.

'They've not come yet, Mummy,' Patsy cried. 'D'you suppose they're not coming today?'

'What's that, lovey?' said Annie, putting down her rolling pin and looking fondly at the little girl through her thick-lensed glasses. 'Who's not coming?'

'She's waiting for the band, Mother – the Salvation Army band,' Jenny explained. 'She likes to listen to them on a Sunday morning.'

'Oh aye – the Sally Army.' Annie grunted. 'Let's hope all their singing and Bible-bashing does a bit of good today. I reckon it's a bit late for a miracle to happen, though. Here, lovey – have a nibble at this.' She held out a piece of apple dipped in sugar to Patsy. 'Off you go now – shoo. You'll be in the way if you stay here.'

Patsy lingered, lolling against the table, looking longingly at the cut-out bits of pastry and the apples and the spice. Sometimes Grandma let her help. She would give her a lump of dough and a small rolling pin, and a dear little pastry wheel that made a crinkly pattern when you ran it up and down, and Patsy would make her own little apple tart. Grandma was flustered today, though. Her face was red and she kept wiping it with a big handkerchief. Grandma never got cross with Patsy, but the little girl thought it best not to outstay her welcome. Anyway, she wanted to go outside again and wait for the band.

'Listen, Patsy – I can hear them now,' said Jenny, her head on one side. 'Come on, love. Let's go and see them.'

Jenny took hold of Patsy's hand and they dashed out into the front garden. The band was just turning the corner. Patsy stared, wide-eyed, as they came nearer. The black-uniformed men and ladies were marching smartly, like the soldiers that marched across her daddy's chest of drawers. She loved the clashing cymbals, the jingling tambourines, the trumpets and horns and the booming drum, and, above all, the lady with the glockenspiel. She held it high in the air, the sunshine glinting on the metal keys, which made a tinkling sound as she tapped them. It was like fairies dancing, Patsy thought. It made her feel all shivery inside.

The band stopped just outside Pleasant View and Jenny and Patsy stood hand in hand and listened as they sang their hymn.

'Tell me the old, old story,
Of unseen things above,
Of Jesus and His glory,
Of Jesus and His love.'

Patsy joined in the chorus with them. Her voice was sweet and clear, and although she sang slightly out of tune with the Salvation Army songsters, they didn't seem to mind. Several of them smiled at the little ginger-haired girl who was usually one of their audience on a Sunday morning. When they had finished singing, Jenny gave her daughter three pennies out of her apron pocket, and Patsy ran into the street and popped them into the wooden collecting-box that a lady was holding out.

'Thank you, my dear. God bless you,' the lady said.

She was pretty, her black bonnet with the big bow at the side framing curly brown hair and a cheerful face. Patsy felt happy and warm all over. Perhaps, when she was a grown-up lady, she would join the band. They might not approve of red shoes, though. Patsy looked down at the feet of the songsters, men and women alike all clad in sensible black lace-ups. Black stockings too . . . No, they would definitely not approve of red shoes, she thought sadly. Perhaps it wouldn't be such a good idea, after all, to join the band. Oh dear, life was very puzzling sometimes.

The band disappeared down the street and Jenny turned to go back into the house. 'Are you coming, Patsy?' she asked.

'In a bit, Mummy. I won't be long,' said the little girl seriously, nodding at her mother. 'I'll just teach Topsy that song.'

Jenny would have liked to have stayed outside too, but her mother would accuse her of neglecting her duties if she didn't get back. Even though they had been invited to Sunday dinner Jenny was still expected to do her share. It was too nice to be indoors on such a day. They should be taking a picnic, as they did occasionally, and lunching on the sands near North Pier or at Stanley Park. It was certainly not the weather for a big Sunday dinner – roast beef today, with Yorkshire pudding, roast potatoes, carrots and garden peas, and apple pie and custard to follow – but, whatever the weather, this was the ritual on a Sunday. Jenny usually cooked her own Sunday dinner. Sunday was a day that she tried to keep apart, to spend with Tom and Patsy, but her mother had insisted that they should all be together today. She looked up at the cloudless blue sky and felt the warmth of the sun burning her arms through her thin blouse. She sighed as she stepped inside again. You could scarcely believe, on such a glorious day, that there could be news of imminent war and bloodshed.

The back kitchen looked dark and felt hot and oppressive after the brilliant sunshine outside.

'She's happy now, is she?' asked Annie. 'She's heard the band then?'

'Yes, she's satisfied now. That'll keep her happy for a while. She's teaching the song to her doll.'

40

'Poor little mite,' said Annie, shaking her head. 'She's lonely. She should have had a little brother or sister.'

Jenny felt herself bristling with indignation at her mother's tactless remark. Why did she do it? Annie knew as well as anyone that Patsy's birth had been a difficult one and that, though Tom and Jenny had wanted them, no more children had come along. But her mother could never leave things alone. She always had to rub salt into the wound.

Jenny forced herself to speak calmly, but there was a sharp edge to her voice. 'That's hardly my fault, is it, Mother? We would have loved another child, but it just wasn't to be. I know Tom would have liked a son – men usually do – but he doesn't complain. He thinks the world of our Patsy.'

'Aye. A lad would have been able to play with him, with those bloomin' toy soldiers.' Annie banged her rolling pin on the table with more force than was necessary. 'I don't see him playing with Patsy so much. He hardly takes any notice of her, does he?'

'It's just his way, Mother. It doesn't mean that he loves her any less. And Patsy's contented enough. She plays with her dolls, and she loves books. She's always drawing and colouring, and she'll be reading as well before long. Her teacher says she's doing ever so well at school.'

'She's a solitary little soul, though. You've got to admit it, our Jenny. She could do with a few more friends. She spends too much time with grown-ups.'

'She's all right,' said Jenny resignedly. 'She has plenty of friends at school from all accounts, but I'm always too busy to have any of them round to play with her. And I don't like her running wild in the street. You wouldn't either, Mother. You've had enough to say about Eileen's lads charging up and down, making a nuisance of themselves. Anyway, they're mostly boys round here, and I know our Patsy doesn't care much for boys.'

'Aye, happen you're right.' Annie nodded. 'Well, the way things are shaping, she'll perhaps have a houseful of evacuees to play with soon. I reckon we'll have to do our bit if the worst comes to the worst. Aye, you're right, our Jenny. Patsy seems happy enough on her own. You've brought her up nicely and I'm not denying it.'

That from her mother was praise indeed. Jenny didn't tell her that at times Patsy was far from happy on her own. The child desperately wanted a little brother or sister. Jenny had tried to explain to her that God sent babies and that somehow she didn't think he would send any more to their house.

Patsy, however, was not so easily dissuaded. Jenny had overheard her bedtime prayers occasionally, when the little girl hadn't known she was listening. After the usual list of requests asking God to bless all and sundry – Mummy and Daddy, Grandma, Auntie Vi, Auntie Ada, Granny Bradshaw and all the aunts and uncles in Yorkshire – there followed an impassioned plea: '. . . And please God, could I have a little brother or sister? I'd like a sister best of all, but if you can't manage that, then I'd like a really best friend. Thank you, God. Amen.'

When her mother had gone inside Patsy picked up her beloved black doll again and sang to her.

> 'Tell me the story simply,
> As to a little child,
> For I am weak and weary,
> And helpless and defiled . . .'

Patsy loved music. They sometimes had a percussion band at school, but she was always allocated a triangle, much to her annoyance. Probably, because she was so small, the teacher thought she wasn't capable of holding anything else. How she would love to clash the cymbals together, with her head proudly upraised and her arms outstretched, but it was always the tall girls who had that honour. And it was always the boys who were chosen to play the drums. Life – and teachers – was so unfair at times.

The sun disappeared momentarily behind a cloud and Patsy shivered. Still holding Topsy, she ran into the house. All the family were in the kitchen, gathered round the wireless set, their faces stern and unsmiling.

'Come on, my little love,' said Annie, holding out her arms.

Patsy climbed on to her grandmother's lap and snuggled against her flowered apron. Grandma always wore one of these voluminous aprons when she was working. The one she had on today had a pattern of blue and orange flowers and was edged with orange bias binding. Patsy leaned her head against Grandma's broad chest. It felt all soft and comfy, like an enormous feather pillow. Oh, she did love her gran. Patsy couldn't understand why Grandma often looked so cross and spoke so impatiently to Mum and Auntie Vi. And when Auntie Ada came, that was even worse. She and Grandma were forever shouting at one another. Grandma didn't shout at Daddy, though, and she never, never shouted at Patsy.

Jenny looked at her daughter cuddling up on Annie's lap and marvelled again at their close relationship. There must be a soft core to her mother, hidden deep beneath the tough exterior, but it was only Patsy who seemed able to reach it. Jenny imagined that when she and Violet were children their mother must have cuddled them like that, but her recollections of that were very faint. And yet at times of crisis, as now, her mother relied so much on the closeness of the family bond.

As eleven o'clock drew nearer they were all quiet, each lost in their own thoughts. Then the flat, sombre tones of the Prime Minister came over the air.

'I am speaking to you from the Cabinet Room at Ten Downing Street. This morning the British Ambassador in Berlin handed the German Government a final note stating that, unless we heard from them by eleven o'clock that they were prepared at once to withdraw their troops from Poland, a state of war would exist between us. I have to tell you now that no such undertaking has been received, and that consequently this country is at war with Germany.'

'Oh, dear God in heaven!' gasped Annie, putting her hand to her bosom, which was rapidly rising and falling. 'Whatever is going to become of us all?'

Jenny noticed that her mother had turned pale. Patsy, disturbed by her grandmother's outcry, quickly slid off her knee and went to stand near Jenny. She put her arm round the little girl and fondled her silky auburn hair, wondering, as her mother had done, just what was going to be the outcome of it all.

'Sshh, Ma,' Tom admonished, but not unkindly. 'Let's just listen and hear what he has to tell us.'

They listened in silence as Neville Chamberlain told them how his long struggle to win peace had failed. Hitler had been determined to attack Poland, come what may, and the only way of stopping him now was by force.

Jenny resisted a desire to say to Tom, 'Well, I hope you're satisfied now. This is what you've been waiting for.' One glance at her husband showed her that the fanatical gleam that had been in his eyes for the last few weeks, whenever the possibility of war was mentioned, had disappeared. Now Tom looked worried, his grey eyes clouded with a quiet desperation. She looked at him and smiled, and he smiled sadly back at her.

'. . . Now may God bless you all,' said the Prime Minister in tones of unbelievable sadness. 'May He defend the right. It is the evil things that we shall be fighting against – brute force, bad faith, injustice, oppression and persecution – and against them I am certain that the right will prevail.'

As the broadcast ended Jenny reached across and turned the knob of the wireless set. They had all heard enough and there was nothing more to be said. They sat in silence for a few seconds, each preoccupied by their own thoughts, then the stillness was broken by a strangled cry from Annie. A wordless shout, as though she were choking, that sounded something like 'Help!' Then Jenny noticed, with mounting horror, that her mother had slumped forward in her chair, her spectacles askew, her arms limp, her face deathly pale.

'Quick – she's fainted!' Jenny rushed to her mother's side. She took hold of her hand and stroked her forehead which was beaded with sweat. 'Come on, Mother. It'll be all right,' she said soothingly, as though to a child. 'We'll all be here together, whatever happens. It'll be all right, you'll see.' There was no response. 'Get the smelling salts, Violet,' she ordered. 'They're in the sideboard drawer, I think, somewhere. For heaven's sake be quick, Vi!'

Violet scrabbled about in the drawer and produced a small bottle of yellowish crystals. Jenny took off the top and waved the bottle under her mother's nose. Annie's eyelids began to flicker, then she blinked dazedly and stared round the room as though it were all strange to her.

'Come on, Ma. Have a drop of this.' Tom had found the half-bottle of brandy which was kept, mainly for medicinal purposes, in the sideboard cupboard. He poured a good half-inch into a glass tumbler. 'Come on, Ma. Never say die.' He put his arm around Annie's shoulders and held the glass to her lips.

Annie moaned again, but she sipped at the liquid, then, falteringly, took hold of the glass herself. They all watched her in silence, waiting for her to gradually come to her senses.

'What's the matter with Grandma?' said Patsy, in a frightened whisper. 'Is she poorly?'

'Just a bit,' said Jenny. 'She'll be all right in a minute, dear. It's so hot in here, and she' been working hard all morning, hasn't she, making us a nice dinner?' She turned to her sister. 'Perhaps you could take our Patsy out for a little while, could you, Vi? Just a walk round the block?'

Violet nodded. 'Come on, Patsy love. Have you brought your doll's pram? Right then – let's give Topsy some fresh air, shall we?'

Annie was coming round now. 'This is a right carry-on and no mistake,' she said, muttering feebly to herself. 'I could strangle that Hitler with me bare hands, causing all this fuss and bother.'

Tom chuckled. 'Don't worry, Ma. I'll do it for you if I get half a chance.'

'And making me faint an' all,' Annie went on, her voice a little stronger now. 'I've never fainted in me life.' She drew a large handkerchief from her apron pocket and wiped the beads of sweat from her upper lip and forehead. 'I'll be all right now. I'm not going to let a pint-sized crackpot like that Hitler get the better of me, and that's for sure.'

'That's the spirit, Mother.' Jenny smiled at her and patted her shoulder. 'Now, you just take it nice and easy and I'll go and get on with the dinner.'

'Thanks, lass.' Annie nodded at her. 'I'll come and join you in a little while. Just let me get me breath back. He's not going to stop us from having our Sunday dinner, and that's a fact.' She shook her head sadly at her daughter's retreating back, then turned to her son-in-law. 'Eeh, Tom – it's a bad do. It is that. Whatever is going to become of us all?' she asked for the second time. 'They told us twenty years ago that it were the war to end all wars. A fat lot they knew, I must say. Well, lad, you'd best get your uniform on and give that Hitler what for. He's got no business turning people's lives upside-down like this.'

'You're right there, Ma.' Tom forced a small, sad smile that didn't reach his eyes. 'I shall be at the recruiting office first thing in the morning. You can be sure of that.'

'You're a good lad, Tom. Our Jenny picked a winner when she married you.' Annie grinned at him. 'But . . . I don't know, lad . . . whatever happens, I've got a funny feeling that things are never going to be the same again, not for any of us.'

Chapter 4

Jenny and Tom stared uncertainly at one another. Now that the time had come for him to leave they both seemed at a loss for words. He humped his heavy suitcase on to the train then turned to smile encouragingly at her. She felt a surge of affection rush through her as she looked at him; a slight figure – Tom was not much taller than she was – in his belted trench coat and soft felt hat, a stray lock of sandy hair flopping over his brow, unable to disguise even now, at the moment of departure, the look of eagerness in his grey eyes. The next time she saw him he would be in khaki, leather suitcase replaced by a kitbag.

'Take care of yourself, Jenny love,' he said, as he put both his arms around her and held her close to him. 'And Patsy an' all.'

'And you as well, Tom. You take care . . .' she whispered, knowing as she said it what a senseless thing it was to say to someone who was going to war. And yet it was what people always said. Take care . . . She almost laughed at the absurdity of it, then she realised that her laugh had turned to a sob and that her eyelashes were wet with tears.

'I'd best get on, love, else they'll go without me and that'd never do.' Tom gave an embarrassed little laugh, then he looked steadily at Jenny, a last lingering look, before his lips came down upon hers in a kiss that said far more than his stumbling words could utter.

All the way down the platform, the length of the train, couples were doing the same, then, at a shrill blast from the guard's whistle, all the men clambered aboard. They leaned from the carriage windows, waving, blowing kisses, shouting last anxious messages at the women who ran alongside.

'Keep yer pecker up, love . . .'

'Don't forget to write . . .'

'I'll be back by Christmas, you'll see . . .'

47

Then the train gathered speed and, one by one, the heads vanished back inside.

Jenny stood on the platform and watched the train disappear in a cloud of grey smoke. The acrid smell hung heavily in the air. She could taste it at the back of her throat. She took out her handkerchief and wiped a stray tear from her cheek and a black smut from her nose, then she resolutely turned and made her way towards the barrier.

As she had known in her heart all along, there had been no point in arguing with Tom. His mind was made up. On the second day of the war he had enlisted at the local recruiting office, and now he was on his way to a training camp. Now that he had finally gone, Jenny couldn't sort out her confused feelings. Of course she was sad to see him go. He was, when all was said and done, her husband, the father of her child, and war was a dreadful thing. She had prayed – to an unsympathetic God, it seemed – that he would not go, that he would at least wait until men of his age group were called up. Now she prayed that he would be safe.

Please God, she muttered silently, take care of him. Don't let anything dreadful happen to him. She knew it was a childish prayer, and yet how else could she pray? No doubt thousands of other women were at that very moment praying the same prayer. Wives, sweethearts . . . mothers and sisters too. She spared a thought for Martha Bradshaw and for Tom's sisters Hilda and Lilian, who would be saddened at the thought of him going to war. The wives and mothers of German soldiers would doubtless be praying too. How could God be expected to sort it all out? It was so very confusing.

Yet Jenny had to admit to herself that she was relieved at Tom's departure. She had known that it was inevitable, therefore it was better to get the parting over quickly, with the minimum of fuss, so that they could all get on with what they had to do. Just recently, relations between the two of them had been strained. Jenny knew only too well that she had been irritable lately, liable to nag at Tom – and at Patsy too – for the least little thing. Her only excuse was that she was tired. She would insist to her mother that she must spend a little more time in her own home, giving Patsy attention.

Tom had been remarkably patient with her. His greatest fault was his obstinacy. Even now, he was seeing his recruitment as a glorious challenge. With a bit of luck, though, it might not be for very long. There was talk of it all being over by Christmas. Perhaps a separation would do them both a world of good. Last night, as she lay in Tom's arms, they had managed to recapture some of the happiness and contentment of their early love. Jenny had never known bliss or ecstasy or magic – words frequently bandied about in the romantic stories that she read – but she and Tom had been happy enough together once. Maybe they would be so again, when all this was over.

Central Station was as crowded as Jenny had ever seen it. There were already a few recruits in khaki and airforce blue, and a lot of men in civilian clothes, going off to join their regiments, with headscarved or turbanned women saying goodbye. And on the excursion platform, another trainload of evacuees was arriving.

Pleasant View now had its quota. Annie had opted for children under school age with their mothers, and seven women with, between them, twelve children had been billeted on her. They were from the Liverpool area, a happy-go-lucky crowd, determined to make the best of things. Some of the children were unruly – Annie had removed all knick-knacks from the mantelpiece and the top of the bookcase in the lounge as a precautionary measure – but they responded to a 'good clout round the ear'ole', as one mother put it, or to a raucous shout of 'For God's sake, give over, you little perisher!'

To Annie's relief the mothers looked after their own offspring. After all, there was little else for them to do. Their days were spent on the sands or the promenade making the most of the still sunny weather. When the children were in bed at night the women gathered in the lounge, knitting, playing cards, smoking and, above all, chatting.

'It's a chance to have a bloody good holiday,' one young woman had remarked to another in Jenny's hearing. 'We love Blackpool, our Fred and me, so he says to me, "Off you go, love, you and the youngsters, and have a good time while you've got the chance."'

'Aye, you're right, Sal,' her friend replied. 'We'd best make the most of it while we're here. Seems funny, doesn't it? You'd never think there was a war on, if it wasn't for this bloomin' blackout.'

Jenny agreed. The thing that had brought home to them all that they were really at war was the extinguishing of the lights.

49

'The lights are going out all over Europe. We shall not see them lit again in our lifetime.' That was what an English statesman had said at the start of the war in 1914. And so it was again, only twenty-five years later. The lights were out all over Britain.

Streetlighting had been officially extinguished on September the first, blackout regulations were enforced and the use of car headlights was banned. All houses, factories and shops had blackout curtains at the doors and windows. Jenny had stocked up with material, cheap black cotton at a shilling a yard, from the local market, enough for all twelve bedrooms and the downstairs rooms. She and Annie and Violet had been busy making it up on the old Singer sewing machine and now the house was dark enough to satisfy any prying ARP warden.

Apart from the blackout, it was all rather boring. They had been prepared for a supreme test of their courage and endurance. Now all they could do was wait.

Jenny glanced across to the excursion platform where yet another train was arriving. She saw nurses standing at the barrier, in case any of the children needed medical treatment, together with the officials waiting to welcome the evacuees.

As she stood at the bus stop, the long crocodile of children made its way through the barrier on to the station forecourt. Some had kitbags over their shoulders, some carried battered suitcases. They all had a gas mask in a cardboard case slung round them, from which fluttered paper labels bearing their names and addresses. In spite of the warmth of the September day they were all smothered in an abundance of clothing. Belted gaberdine raincoats, prickly serge trousers, grey socks concertinaed round thin ankles, knitted woollen pixie hoods. Many of the boys sported school caps atop their short back and sides. They held hands, walking two by two like the animals entering the Ark. They too were entering a safety zone, but many, obviously finding it all very bewildering, were in tears. Some looked scared stiff, no doubt homesick already after an agonised parting from Mum, and some were chattering excitedly, looking upon it all as a great adventure.

Jenny had volunteered as a helper at a North Shore reception centre, offering tea and sympathy. She would just have time to dash home and grab a quick midday snack before doing her afternoon stint. Her mother had given her the day off from her duties in the boarding house as a concession to Tom's departure. Annie had been more sympathetic recently, but it had taken a major war, Jenny reflected ruefully, to bring about a change of heart.

The local reception centre for the evacuees was in the Sunday school building attached to the Methodist church. It was the main hall, high-ceilinged and painted in a bilious shade of green. The walls were decorated with biblical scenes from both the Old and New Testaments – Daniel curbing with upraised hand three ferocious lions; Moses receiving a message from the burning bush; a rather stylised Jesus in a white robe blessing a crowd of children; and the same figure surrounded by swarthy fishermen with boats and nets – pictures obviously chosen for visual appeal rather than for any coherent message running through them. The room was hot and stuffy and Jenny felt sorry for the children, most of whom, as she had noticed before, seemed to be unsuitably clad, muffled up to their ears in warm clothing. It was doing nothing to stifle their exuberance, however; the noise in the room was deafening, as a couple of hundred children chattered excitedly, all at the tops of their voices. Apart from a few, here and there, who were still crying, sobbing and sniffing audibly, unable to restrain their streaming eyes and running noses.

Jenny joined the ranks of ladies in flowered aprons whose job it was to take round the food and drink. In the centre of the room was a long trestle table covered with green and white checked oilcloth. The children were sitting down now, being marshalled into position by a horsey-looking woman wearing a hat with a feather in the side, like Robin Hood. She was in charge of the proceedings and Jenny knew her as Mrs Davenport, a local bigwig, who was the wife of a solicitor. In front of each child was a thick white plate and cup, but no saucer. Jenny, armed with an enormous enamel teapot, went round pouring dark-brown liquid into each child's cup. The tea, with milk and sugar already added, looked strong and certainly not to a child's taste. Many of them, most likely, would have preferred lemonade but, as everyone was constantly being reminded, there was a war on and you had to count the cost. There didn't seem to be any complaints, however.

A second battalion of ladies followed with plates piled high with fish-paste sandwiches and rock buns. The buns made a heavy clonking sound as they dropped on to the plates, but most of the children were eating as though they were ravenous. It had been a long time since breakfast, and now they were fortifying themselves, no doubt, for whatever hazards lay ahead.

When tea was over, the children went to sit on long benches round the sides of the room, while the ladies retired to the kitchen to face the gargantuan task of washing up. Mrs Davenport and her minions, two other velour-hatted ladies, seated themselves importantly at a table at the end of the room. They consulted long lists of names attached to clipboards. Jenny noticed that Mrs Davenport was sitting with her knees wide apart, revealing a vast expanse of blue *Directoire* knickers. Several of the boys giggled and pointed, to Jenny's amusement. She was waiting to have a word with this important personage; she had decided, only that day, to have an evacuee herself. She would have a little girl, she thought, about Patsy's age, who would be company for her daughter. She hadn't told Patsy yet. She wondered if all these children were spoken for, or if there might be one to spare.

Mrs Davenport was starting to speak now, in deep, booming tones, more like a man's voice. The group of giggling boys was once more reduced to hysterics, pushing one another, going red in the face and shoving grubby handkerchiefs into their mouths to stifle their laughter.

'Charles Anderson,' read out Mrs Davenport, 'James Baker, Richard Bates, Peter and Paul Carson – ah, twins, I see, jolly good – Simon Davis.'

Six boys trooped out and stood in a line in front of the table.

'Now, would you young gentlemen like to go with this lady? Righty-ho, off we go then. Jolly good!'

The boys hitched up their rucksacks and followed a pleasant-looking woman through the doorway. Jenny went back into the kitchen. She was nervous of interrupting Mrs Davenport now, when she was so busy. That august lady tended to look down her nose at lesser mortals like tea ladies. It might be better to wait until there was a lull in the proceedings, and if she stopped out there much longer her fellow workers would be accusing her of neglecting her duties.

A quarter of an hour later, when Jenny poked her head round the kitchen door, the lists of names were still going on and the number of children had visibly diminished. Several women were walking round the room now scrutinising the evacuees, for all the world as though it were a cattle market. Jenny couldn't help noticing that it was the most attractive children who were being chosen and offered homes; pretty little girls who looked as though they would give very little trouble, or bigger boys who looked sturdy and able to help with household chores. Jenny felt a lump come into her throat. It was heaven help the less attractive children – the ones with spots perhaps, or buck teeth or steel-rimmed spectacles – poor little mites. Beauty was far more than skin deep, but how apt people were, Jenny mused, to judge by first appearances. They would all be found homes in the end, but how awful it must be to be left there, waiting and wondering.

Apart from these children who were being singled out, the others were still being dealt with alphabetically. As Jenny watched, she saw a little girl waving wildly, obviously trying to attract someone's attention.

Jenny went over to her. 'Did you want something, dear?' she asked.

'Oh, yes please, lady. I'm dying to go to the lavvy and I daren't go on my own. Can you show me where it is, please, lady?'

She was an appealing child with short black hair cut in a straight fringe and enormous blue eyes that were looking pleadingly at Jenny. She had noticed her at tea time – one of the few children who had said 'thank you' when the tea was poured out. She had been looking after a little boy then, making sure that he had enough to eat and drink and didn't stuff his mouth too full. Obviously the child had been well brought up, whoever she was. The little boy was still at her side, Jenny noticed.

'Of course I'll show you,' said Jenny. 'Come with me, lovey. What about your friend? Does he want to go as well?'

The little girl turned to him. 'Do you want to go, Ben?' she asked. 'To the lav,' she added in a loud whisper.

The small boy nodded, so Jenny took them each by the hand and led them out of the back door to the concrete yard.

'There you are,' she said, pointing to a green door. 'And that's the one for you, young man.' She pointed to another door.

'Wait for me, Ben,' said her young charge, with some urgency. 'I 'spect it'll take me longer than you. Girls always take longer than boys,' she added in a matter-of-fact voice.

Jenny suppressed a smile. She, too, had always thought, as a child, that it was one of the unexplained mysteries of life why boys could always be so quick about it.

'Don't worry,' she said. 'I'll wait here for both of you.'

She was certainly an engaging little girl. She would make an ideal companion for Patsy, and perhaps bring her own daughter out of her shell. Of course, that wasn't the main idea, Jenny thought guiltily. These poor little mites were in need of love and care, and if she could provide a home for one then she would do so. She would try and arrange it with Mrs Davenport.

Ben came and put his hand shyly in Jenny's again, and a minute later the little girl joined them.

'I'm all right now,' she said brightly. 'I was frightened I was going to wet my knickers, like the babies at school do sometimes. It makes a big pool on the floor, and the teacher gets ever so cross. But I haven't. Mum gets cross too if something like that happens. She bought me some new navy-blue knickers to come away.'

'You should have gone sooner, dear,' said Jenny. 'Why didn't you?' There had been a constant procession of children going outside all afternoon.

'I dunno.' The little girl gave a shrug. 'I don't know the other children very well. Only Ben.'

'Why is that, love?' enquired Jenny. 'I thought there would be a lot of you from the same school?'

'My school nearly all came last week,' the child explained. 'Y'see, me mum's only just made up her mind to let me come. And his mum an' all.' She jerked her thumb in Ben's direction. 'So we had to come with a lot of kids that we don't know.'

She obviously needed the support of a grown-up, thought Jenny. Her air of self-possession was probably just a veneer. She couldn't be much older than Patsy.

'What's your name, dear?' Jenny asked.

'Rosie White. Well, my proper name's Margaret Rose – I was called after the princess, y'see – but everybody calls me Rosie.'

'Well, that's lovely,' said Jenny. 'You look just like a rose with those pink cheeks.'

'What are you called?' asked Rosie. 'I can't go on calling you lady, can I?'

'I'm Mrs Bradshaw. Jenny Bradshaw.' Jenny hesitated. 'You can call me Auntie Jenny, if you like. I was wondering . . . would you like to come and live with me, at my house? I've got a little girl about your age. That's if we can arrange it,' she added quickly, hoping she hadn't spoken too soon. 'We'll have to go and see that lady, Mrs Davenport.'

'Ooh, yes please, lady . . . I mean Mrs . . . I mean Auntie Jenny. That would be lovely.'

Jenny noticed that Rosie's eyes had filled up with tears, and as she looked at her she felt a lump in her own throat and a prickle under her eyelids.

'Come on then,' she said cheerfully. 'Let's see what we can do.'

'Oh dear I nearly forgot,' said Rosie suddenly. 'What about Ben? This is my friend, Benjamin Williams, and I promised his mum I'd look after him. He lives down our street and he's only a little boy. Can he come too?'

'I think we can find a nice home for him.' Jenny nodded reassuringly. 'Not with us, though. There isn't room in my house, but my friend Eileen wants a little boy to go and live with them. She has three boys of her own. She lives a few doors further along our street, so you'll be able to keep your eye on him, Rosie. Is that all right?'

Rosie nodded happily. Jenny hoped that the billeting officer would approve. Women like Mrs Davenport made Jenny feel ill at ease and inadequate, but she felt that she would fight tooth and nail for these two children.

Fortunately, there was no problem.

'We haven't got to the Ws yet,' said Mrs Davenport, consulting her list. Watts . . . Weston . . . White . . . Yes, there it is. Margaret Rose White. But your mother has already got her quota, hasn't she, Mrs . . . it's Mrs Bradley, isn't it?'

'Bradshaw,' Jenny corrected her. 'But this is for me. It's me that wants this one,' she said, ungrammatically. Oh dear, this woman was getting her all in a fluster as usual. 'And I'll take Benjamin Willams, if I can, for my friend Mrs Sykes.'

'Righty-ho then. Jolly good,' boomed Mrs Davenport. 'Off you go.' She turned back to her papers in a gesture of dismissal. Then, as an afterthought, she flashed Jenny a toothy smile. 'Thank you so much, Mrs . . . er . . . Bradley. We do appreciate your help. We all have to do our little bit, haven't we?'

Rosie chattered excitedly all the way home, like a little bird chirping away at Jenny's elbow. Ben, on her other side, was very quiet at first.

55

They came from Liverpool, Jenny discovered, though she had already surmised as much from their accents. She didn't know the city, but from Rosie's description she gathered that they lived near the docks.

'Uncle Bill takes me to see the big ships sometimes,' Rosie said proudly. 'Well – he's not me real uncle, you know. He's a friend of me mum's.'

'She's got lots of uncles,' Ben joined in, suddenly coming to life. 'That's what my mum says. Haven't you, Rosie? Your mum's got lots of friends, hasn't she?'

'Yes.' Rosie nodded. 'She meets them at the pub. It's called the Jolly Roger and it's at the end of our street. Me mum works there sometimes, then I go to sleep at me Auntie Nellie's across the road. Well, she's not me real auntie . . .'

'Just a friend of Mummy's?' enquired Jenny. The child seemed to have led a very chequered existence.

'Yes, that's right,' said Rosie. 'Then me mum sometimes takes her friends home for a cup of tea.'

For a cup of tea? thought Jenny, raising her eyebrows. She felt her heart warming more than ever to the little girl at her side.

'Mum earns a lot of money, working at the pub.' Rosie nodded again vigorously. 'She buys me lots of nice clothes. She bought me this new coat to come away in. Do you like it, Auntie Jenny?'

'Yes, indeed I do, dear. It's very smart.'

Rosie was neatly dressed in a navy-blue belted gaberdine raincoat. It looked stiff with newness and came to well below her knees. Room to grow into Jenny guessed, but at least Rosie looked smarter than most of the children at the hall, in their shabby hand-me-downs. Her mother obviously believed in dressing her nicely, no matter how that lady came by her money, and she was a polite little thing too.

'My mum's ever so pretty,' Rosie went on. 'I think you're pretty too, Auntie Jenny . . . different, though.' Rosie screwed up her eyes and pursed her lips, looking appraisingly at Jenny. 'My mum's hair's longer'n yours, and it's blonde.'

'Bottle blonde,' added Ben briefly. 'That's what my mum says.'

'I'm sure she's lovely, dear,' said Jenny hurriedly. 'She must be nice to have a pretty little girl like you. Did she come to the station with you this morning?'

'Yes, but she had to go before the train left. She was meeting a

56

friend, you see. She looked nice, didn't she, Ben? She had her new red coat on, and her red shoes.'

'She looked all right,' said Ben grudgingly. 'My mum stayed with us till the train went, didn't she, Rosie? And she kissed us goodbye and waved to us. My dad's at work, you see, so he couldn't come.'

'His dad's a docker,' said Rosie, pointing at Ben. 'And my Uncle Bert – that's my Auntie Nellie's husband – he's a docker too.'

'And what about your daddy, dear?' Jenny asked tentatively. It would be as well to find out. If she didn't, Ben would no doubt tell her.

'I haven't got a daddy,' said Rosie briefly, her little mouth closing in a tight line. 'I've never had one.'

It was as Jenny thought. Moving on to safer ground, she discovered that Rosie was five years old.

'But I'm nearly six,' she added importantly. 'I'll be six this month. I'm older than him.' She pointed her thumb vaguely in Ben's direction. 'He's only just five. That's why his mum asked me to look after him, 'cos I like looking after little children. Oh, Ben, I nearly forgot!' Rosie clapped her hand over her mouth. 'I've got your stick of rock in my bag. I'll get it out for you when we get home.'

Jenny smiled to herself. The child was at home already, and she hadn't even seen her new abode.

'A lady gave it to me,' said Ben.

'Yes, that's right.' Rosie nodded. 'Do you know, Auntie Jenny, when we got on the bus at the station a lady gave us all a stick of rock. It's pink and it says "Blackpool" all through it and it tastes all minty. I had a little suck of it, then I put it away for later. Ben was getting his hands all mucky with his, so I said I'd look after it for him. Do you like Blackpool rock, Auntie Jenny?'

Jenny agreed that she did, but she hadn't had any for ages.

'Then I'll give you some of mine,' said Rosie. 'I think it's my very favourite, after pear drops. I love pear drops, and I like aniseed balls, too.'

'And sherbet dabs,' added Ben, 'and jelly babies.'

Listing all their favourite sweets kept the children happy until they arrived at Eileen's front door.

Chapter 5

Ben suddenly went quiet again when Jenny knocked at Eileen's front door. He put his thumb into his mouth and Jenny noticed with alarm that his big brown eyes were filled with tears, one of which was already trickling down his cheek. Poor little fellow. It had been a long day and a traumatic one too. Leaving behind his home and his parents, and travelling to an unknown town with largely unknown companions – except for Rose, to whom he seemed to cling like a lifeline. And then to encounter a host of strange ladies, bent on organising his existence. He had been remarkably brave so far, but this final ordeal seemed to be proving too much for him.

However, Eileen would make him feel at home if anybody could. Jenny wasn't too sure about Eileen's boys, though. Ronnie and Ray, the twins, aged six, and their three-year-old brother Larry, were a bunch of tearaways and no mistake. Patsy was often intimidated by the twins at school, but it wasn't worth falling out with Eileen about it. Patsy, she knew, would have to learn to stand on her own feet, and while parents were arguing about their offspring, the children were just as quickly making friends again.

Jenny smiled at Ben and squeezed the hot little hand still clinging tightly to hers. 'Cheer up, Ben,' she said. 'You'll like Auntie Eileen. I know you will – she's lovely.'

The door opened, and there was Eileen, smiling at them. 'Well, well, well! What a surprise!'

She looked at Jenny, who winked at her and said quietly, 'This is Ben Williams. He's come to stay with you.'

Eileen crouched down and put her arms round the little boy. 'And he's very welcome, I'm sure. Just wait till my three boys know they've got a new friend. They'll be tickled pink.'

Ben sniffed back his tears and wiped his nose hurriedly on his coat sleeve, then he grinned conspiratorially at Jenny. Yes, she knew that he would be as right as rain with Eileen. Her comfortable bulk was having a soothing effect on him already. Jenny sometimes envied her friend's happy-go-lucky attitude to life. Maybe, with three unruly boys and a husband who seemed to be work shy, it was the only way to cope with things. Nothing seemed to ruffle Eileen.

'And who are you, dear?' Eileen rose to her feet, taking Ben's hand, and smiled at Rosie. 'Are you Ben's sister?'

'No, I'm Rosie White. Margaret Rose really – after the princess, you know. I've been looking after Ben all day, but I 'spect he'll be all right now.' She nodded gravely. Eileen obviously met with her approval. 'I'm going to live with Auntie Jenny,' she added contentedly, grinning at her new friend.

'Well, that's lovely. You'll be just down the street, and you'll be able to see Ben whenever you like.' Eileen beamed at the little girl, her eyes opening wide. Eileen was round all over; round tortoise-shell-rimmed glasses, a button mouth constantly making a round O of surprise, and sausage curls atop a pleasantly plump body. 'Are you coming in, Jenny?' she asked. 'Charlie's taken the lads on to the sands for a while, so there's only me here. We can have a nice cuppa and a chat.'

'No, I'd best not, thanks, Eileen. I've left Patsy at me mother's. Not that she'll worry – she loves being at her gran's – but I'd best get back.'

'OK. Let's be having you then, young man.' Eileen picked up Ben's rucksack. 'Gosh – that's heavy. Whatever have you got in there, Ben? Yer dad's hobnailed boots? Or is it yer mum's mangle.'

Ben giggled, all trace of tears now gone. He waved a cheery goodbye to Jenny and Rosie and followed Eileen into the house.

'She's nice, isn't she, Auntie Jenny?' said Rosie as the door closed behind them.

'I think so,' Jenny agreed. 'I've known Eileen for years and years. Ever since I was a little girl, not much older than you. We were in the same class at school. She looked after me when we first came to live in Blackpool. It all felt strange at first, you see – like it does to you now, Rosie. Eileen helped me to settle down, and we've been the best of friends ever since. I expect my little girl Patsy will look after you when you go to school with her, just like

60

Eileen looked after me.' Jenny knew that it was far more likely to be the other way round, Rosie looking after Patsy.

'Oh, I shan't need looking after, Auntie Jenny,' Rosie said brightly, as if reading her thoughts. 'I always take care of the little 'uns, like Ben. There were some other little kids down our street an' all. They were too small to come away with us on their own as 'vacuees, but their mums used to leave 'em with me in the street, 'specially in the summer when we could play out late at night.'

Poor little lass, thought Jenny. I reckon she could do with mothering in spite of all her grown-up talk, and if I have anything to do with it, that's what she'll get. All kids needed affection and a cuddle now and then, no matter how self-assured they appeared to be.

'Did you say school, Auntie Jenny?' Rosie asked, wrinkling up her nose. 'Will I have to go to school, same as I did at home?' The faint disgust showed in her voice.

'Of course you will, dear,' said Jenny, laughing. 'I hope you'll be staying with us for . . . quite a while, and everybody has to go to school. Or else we'll have the school board fellow after us.'

'Yes – he was always coming down our street.' Rosie nodded. 'Some of the big girls used to stay off to look after their kid brothers and sisters. But I like school really. I'm on the third reading book now,' she added proudly. 'It's all about a farmer called Old Lob, and a cow called Mrs Cuddy.'

'Well, fancy that! Those sound like the books that our Patsy's on.'

'Are they?' Rosie's eyes lit up with interest. 'Does Patsy like going to school, Auntie Jenny?'

'She likes it well enough, but you'll be able to ask her yourself in a minute, Rosie.' Jenny paused with her hand on the gate of Pleasant View. 'This is my mother's boarding house, where I work sometimes. We'll just go in and pick up Patsy – she's been staying with her gran – then we'll all go back home.'

Rosie stopped dead outside the gate, her big blue eyes suddenly apprehensive. 'Auntie Jenny,' she began hesitantly, 'd'you think she'll like me – Patsy, I mean? You're her mum, aren't you, and she may not want me to . . . I mean . . .' Her voice petered out and she gave a worried little sigh. 'Oh, you know what I mean, don't you, Auntie Jenny?'

What a perceptive child she was. Jenny gave her a hug. 'I know exactly what you mean, Rosie, but don't worry. I've got love enough for both of you, and I know that you and Patsy are going to be very good friends.'

Back home at 16 Green Street, the two little girls stood and stared, brown eyes and blue eyes warily studying each other.

Patsy turned to her mother. 'D'you mean she's going to stay here for ever, Mummy?'

'Well, I shouldn't imagine it will be for ever, dear, but for . . . quite a while.'

'D'you mean to sleep and everything?'

'Well, of course.'

'But – where will she sleep?'

'There's a spare bed in your room, isn't there, Patsy? Another little bed just like yours. Auntie Vi came to sleep there once, don't you remember, when Daddy and I went to a party?'

Patsy bit her lip and nodded. 'Will she have her dinner with us too? And her breakfast and her tea?'

'Well, of course she will, you silly sausage. She's come to live here.'

Jenny began to feel uneasy as she saw her daughter's forehead wrinkle in a frown. Then, just as suddenly, Patsy grinned, a heartwarming beam that lit up her whole face.

'Ooh, that's lovely, Mummy,' she cried. 'I've always wanted a special friend, and now I've got one.' She dashed across the room and grabbed hold of Rosie's arm. 'Come on. Come upstairs with me, an' I'll show you my best doll an' everything.'

Rosie went with her, turning to grin slyly at Jenny as they went through the door. Rosie, too, had seemed worried for a few moments, her head turning anxiously to look first at Patsy, then at Jenny as they talked about her. It was going to be all right, though. Jenny flopped wearily into an armchair. Gosh, she was tired. All told, it had been an exacting day. She would make herself a nice cup of tea, then start getting some supper for herself and the two girls.

'This is Topsy – she's my best doll. I've got some more dolls as well. They're all sitting over there on the other bed. That's going to be yours, isn't it, Rosie, so I 'spect we'd better move them. And that's Teddy – I've had him since I was a baby – and that's Golly. D'you like his coat? Mummy made it for him, but he's gone and lost a button . . .' Patsy prattled away happily to her new friend. 'D'you like dolls, Rosie? Have you got a best doll?'

Rosie looked down at the black doll that Patsy had placed so lovingly on her lap. Had she only known it, she was greatly privileged. Topsy was entrusted to very few people. 'No,' she said, shrugging her shoulders. 'I never cared much for dolls. I think dolls is a bit soppy. She's nice, though,' she added hastily, hearing Patsy's little gasp of horror. 'It's just that – well – I s'pose I've never really had a proper doll of my own, except for an old pot one of me mum's. She's black, your Topsy, isn't she?' Rosie gently stroked Topsy's head with its tufts of woolly hair, and laid the doll down to see if it closed its eyes. 'See, she goes to sleep an' all. Why d'you have a black doll, Patsy?'

'We learned all about little black children at Sunday school. There's people that goes over the sea to teach 'em all about Jesus. Mish – mish – mishonries they're called,' said Patsy seriously. 'So I asked Mummy if I could have a black doll, and she bought me Topsy when I was four. The lady at Sunday school said they're just like us really – black boys and girls, I mean – but their skins is a different colour. Their houses is different, though. We put our pennies in a little box at Sunday school – it's like a little house with a grass roof, same as the black boys and girls live in. D'you go to Sunday school, Rosie?'

'Naw . . .' Rosie shook her head vehemently. 'We go down to the docks on a Sunday to see the big ships, me and Uncle Bill, and sometimes me mum comes with us if she's not busy.'

'What about your daddy? Does he go with you as well?'

'I haven't got a dad.'

'D'you mean he's in the Army, like my daddy? I haven't got a daddy just now, 'cos he's gone away to fight the Germans. Is that what you mean, Rosie?'

'No. I've never had one.'

'Why? Is he dead, your dad?'

'Dunno.' Rosie shrugged. 'Never mind about dads an' all that . . . How old are you, Patsy? You're not as big as me, are you? Come on – stand up. Let's have a look.'

Patsy unwillingly stood next to her new friend. As she had feared, Rosie was nearly a head taller. 'I'm growing, though,' she said indignantly. 'Mummy says I'm growing all the time. She says I've fairly shot up since I was five.'

'When was you five then?'

'Last June.'

'Well I'm nearly six. I'll be six this month. September the twenty-third.'

'Then that's why you're bigger'n me. I 'spect when I'm six I'll be as big as you . . . Rosie – d'you think Mummy'll let us have a party for your birthday? I do sometimes.'

'Don't suppose so – with there being a war on an' all.'

'Well, she'll buy you a nice present then. I know she will. Would you like a black doll, Rosie? Just like my Topsy?'

Rosie's eyes lit up with delight. 'I think I would,' she said slowly. 'I think that would be real lovely.'

'We'll ask Mummy then. Come on, let's go and ask her now.' Patsy tugged at Rosie's hand and the two little girls smiled happily at one another as they went downstairs.

'We'll see . . .' said Jenny, at Patsy's plaintive request on Rosie's behalf. She smiled at the two little faces looking up at her so beseechingly, Patsy's more so than Rosie's, however. The little evacuee, she thought, must already have taken a few knocks and disappointments in her short life and Jenny would love, if possible, to buy her the doll. But it was the expense . . . Sometimes there was little enough money left for necessities such as clothes, let alone dolls. 'I'm not promising, mind,' Jenny told them, 'but . . . we'll see.'

'Yer mum didn't say yes, did she?' Jenny heard Rosie say later, when she thought she was out of earshot.

'No . . . she said "We'll see",' replied Patsy thoughtfully. 'That's what she always says. It usually means yes.' Least she didn't say what she sometimes says to me,' she added brightly. 'Money doesn't grow on trees you know, Patsy . . .' It was an excellent impression of her mother's voice, and Jenny had to suppress her laughter.

Annie offered to help with the expense of the doll. 'I'll chip in with a bob or two,' she said. 'She's a nice little lass, that Rosie. A bit forward, mind you, but she's none the worse for that, and she'll be good for our Patsy. She'll help to bring her out of herself.'

Violet, too, had contributed a shilling, and the new black doll, which had cost 7s. 6d., was now hidden in Jenny's wardrobe away from the curious eyes of the little girls.

Rosie had settled down very well in her new home. The morning after her arrival when, very early, Jenny had tiptoed into the girls' bedroom, she had found them both asleep in Patsy's bed, dark head and ginger head lying close together on the pillow.

'Stay in your own bed, Rosie dear,' Jenny told her kindly. 'There's more room, you see, and you'll sleep better on your own.'

'It was my fault, Mummy,' said Patsy. 'I heard Rosie crying, and she said she felt lonely, so I asked her to come in with me.'

'I never was crying!' Rosie's pointed little chin stuck out aggressively. 'It's only babies what cry.'

'You were then. I heard you.'

'I might have been sniffing – I had a bit of a cold – but I weren't crying.'

'You said you were lonely, though.'

'So what?'

Jenny came to the rescue. She put her arms round Rosie. 'There's nothing wrong with crying, my love. We all do it sometimes and it makes us feel better.'

Rosie snuggled closer to Jenny. 'I might have been crying . . . just a bit,' she admitted. 'I was thinking about me mum, and I wondered if she was missing me.'

'She's sure to be missing you, dear, but she knows that you're all right, and that's the main thing, isn't it? She knows you'll be safe here, and we sent her that postcard, didn't we?'

An official franked postcard had been issued to all the evacuees, to be sent home to parents, bearing details of their new addresses. Rosie had printed painstakingly, under Jenny's guidance, 'Dear Mum, I like it here. Auntie Jenny is lovely. (That had been Rosie's own idea.) There is a little girl called Patsy. I hope you are well. Love from Rosie.'

After that, there had been no more tears, and the two little girls were getting on so well together it was as if they had known one another all their lives. The only cloud in the brilliant blue sky of life for Patsy – apart from her daddy being away, of course – was the small matter of school. She had assumed that Rosie would be in her class and, unwittingly, Jenny had also given her that impression. Mrs Davenport had called round, however, the next day, to ensure that Rosie reported for school the following Monday, in the afternoon.

'Local children in the mornings, evacuees in the afternoons,' she boomed in her officious voice. 'Thank you, Mrs Bradley. I'm pleased to see that Margaret Rose is settling down.'

'But why, Mummy?' pleaded Patsy. 'I wanted Rosie to come with me. Why can't she?'

'I suppose the school would be too crowded with all the extra children,' Jenny explained wearily, 'and rules are rules. We all have to do as we're told.'

It was a nuisance, though. It would have been far more convenient to have both children going out and returning at the same time each day. As it was, Jenny had one little girl with her all the time and, with her duties at the boarding house, it was inconvenient to say the least.

Rosie, too, was disappointed with the arrangement. She found herself in a class full of strangers. Mrs White had been somewhat dilatory in making up her mind about her daughter's evacuation, and consequently Rosie's schoolfriends from home had been allocated to a different part of Blackpool the week before Rosie arrived.

Jenny put up with a day or two of grumbling, then she decided to do something about it. The thought of officialdom, in the shape of an awesome headmistress, had her trembling at the knees, but for the sake of the children she would face a lion in its den if necessary. This headmistress, however, was very understanding.

'Rules are made to be broken,' she declared, 'and we must do all we can to make sure our little visitors are happy. Certainly, Mrs Bradshaw. We'll make room for Margaret Rose in Miss Banks's class with Patricia.'

Patsy was overjoyed, especially as Miss Banks let them sit together at a big double desk at the back of the room, a place only allotted to the most reliable children. At last she had an ally who would defend her against all foes.

'Hiya, titch,' yelled Ronnie, one of Eileen's twins, when he encountered Patsy in the playground on the first morning of the new arrangement.

'Ginger nut! Carrots!' taunted Ray, the other insufferable twin, tweaking Patsy's hair and running away.

'Leave my friend alone. Don't you dare touch her!' cried Rosie.

'Aw, shurrup you! You're only a 'vacuee,' retorted Ray, 'same as that soppy kid we've got staying with us. Wet the bed last night, he did. He's a baby. Even our Larry doesn't wet the bed.'

'And don't you say a word about my friend Ben either.' Rosie clenched her fists, her blue eyes glistening with rage, then, quick as a flash, she darted forward and gave the astounded Ray a hefty punch on the jaw.

'Punch her back,' yelled Ronnie. 'Cheeky little kid. She's not gonner get the better of us.'

Rosie turned on him. 'D'you want to fight an' all?' She danced up and down, shaking her clenched fists menacingly in his face.

'Leave her, Ronnie. She's only a girl,' said Ray disdainfully. 'She's not worth bothering about.'

Arms slung round one another's shoulders, the twins skulked away, to Rosie's glee and to Patsy's heartfelt relief.

She was never troubled by either of them again. Eileen remarked to Jenny, later that week, that her boys were quite taken with Rosie.

'She's a real good sort – for a girl, I mean,' Ronnie had told his mother.

Ben, also, noticed a change in the twins' attitude from that day on, but he never knew the real reason. Ronnie and Raymond Sykes, the terrors of the neighbourhood, had more than met their match in Rosie White.

'What would you like to do for Rosie's birthday?' asked Jenny. 'I thought we might take a picnic and go somewhere for the day. Where would you like to go?'

The birthday fell on a Saturday and Annie had magnanimously given Jenny the day off from her chores so that she could spend it with the children.

'The Pleasure Beach!' cried Patsy, her eyes gleaming with delight. 'Or Fairyland – or the Boating Pool. Or p'raps we could ride up to Fleetwood on a tram.'

'We can't do all those things,' laughed Jenny. 'There wouldn't be time. As it's Rosie's birthday, perhaps we should let her have some say in the matter.'

'I don't mind, Auntie Jenny.' Rosie smiled happily. 'I don't know where any of those places is, but there is one thing I'd like to do.' Her big blue eyes looked appealingly at Jenny.

'And what's that, dear?'

'I'd like to have a ride on a donkey.'

They rode on a clanging tram along the promenade to the Boating Pool at North Shore. Rosie was enthralled, as Patsy always was, no matter how many times she visited the place, by the gaily painted paddle boats and the automated ride with its jolly wooden animals. Rosie chose a giraffe and Patsy an elephant, and they climbed on to the high backs where they clung tightly, trembling with trepidation and excitement. After they'd had a drink of fizzy red pop from the stall with the striped awning, they walked along the beach towards North Pier. Or, to be more correct, Jenny walked and the two little girls ran and skipped barefoot across the sand, their sandals in their hands, for a blissful paddle in the sea. The ridges left by the tide hurt their feet, and the sea seemed a very long way off, but it would be such a pity to put their shoes on. Then they dug with their little wooden spades and made a fine castle decorated with shells and seaweed.

Jenny had brought a picnic and they ate ravenously. What did it matter if there were grains of sand in the meat-paste sandwiches and sausage rolls? This was a banquet fit for a king, fittingly rounded off with cornets bought from a nearby ice-cream stall. The ice cream was yellow and creamy, melting quickly to run in rivulets down their sandy fingers. But that was no problem as there was a rock pool handy for a quick wash.

Rosie had her coveted donkey ride. How she had loved the funny creatures, with their long ears and their heads too big for their bodies, when she had seen them from the bus window on her first day in Blackpool. Now her wish was coming true. Rosie's donkey trotted along briskly, the bells on its harness jingling. The child's hair streamed backwards in the sea breeze and her cheeks were flushed more rosy than ever with excitement.

Patsy's donkey followed behind more sedately. It wasn't Patsy's idea of fun – she had only agreed to have a ride to keep her friend company – and she was relieved when she could clamber safely to the ground again.

'That was lovely, Auntie Jenny,' Rosie cried. 'Ooh, I'm having such a nice birthday. It's the best one I've ever had.'

There had been two cards in the post this morning, one from Mum with a half-crown postal order, and one from Uncle Bill. And all her new friends had given her cards too – Auntie Jenny and

Patsy, and Patsy's grandma and Auntie Vi as well. But the best thing of all was that beautiful black doll – almost like Patsy's – lying in the box with its eyes closed, in a dear little red and white spotted dress. Rosie hadn't been able to speak for two minutes, she was so thrilled.

Now they were off again for a walk along North Pier. Through the turnstile they went, along the wooden planks, their footsteps making a hollow plonking sound. Through the chinks in the floorboards they could see the rough sea far below, for now the tide was coming in. Patsy was always frightened that she would fall through one of those ominous cracks. It was impossible, she knew – she was far too big – but the heart-stopping fear was always there.

It was incredible to think there was a war on, thought Jenny, as they made their way back along the pier. They had been blessed with perfect weather in these early war days, as though God was trying to compensate in some way. Blackpool had never looked more magnificent. Never, by any stretch of the imagination, could you call it a beautiful place, but it had a grandeur that was all its own; the gulls screaming overhead, the bracing breeze – as always – tangling the hair and stinging the cheeks, and the vast panorama of mile upon mile of sea and sand.

To the left, as far as the eye could see, stretched boarding houses and hotels, topping the man-made cliffs and the three-tier promenade. To the right, there were more hotels and shops, the dubious delights of the Golden Mile and, looming above it all, the massive ironwork structure of the tower, like a sentinel keeping guard. The only sign that they were at war was the huge, concrete invasion blocks which had been erected by the sea wall.

To round off the day they visited Patsy's favourite place, Fairyland, at the end of the Golden Mile. Here they were transported in little carriages through dark tunnels, suddenly coming upon a glade where fairies were dancing, goblins were hammering, and elves were dozing upon scarlet toadstools. It was a wonderland that never failed to enchant Patsy, and now Rosie was equally thrilled.

'It's been a lovely birthday,' she said again when they arrived home. 'Ooh – Auntie Jenny – I am glad I came to live here. I hope I can stay for ever.'

'Ooh, so do I!' echoed Patsy. 'D'you think she can, Mummy? Stay for ever I mean?'

Jenny shrugged off the embarrassing question with a remark about the children's bedtime. It was late and they were both very tired . . .

'Come on now. That's enough excitement for one day. Supper . . . and then off to bed. You can hardly keep your eyes open, Patsy. Ooh, that was a big yawn, Rosie! Come on now, the pair of you. Up the wooden hill . . .'

Jenny's heart had missed a beat at the child's outspoken remark about staying for ever. She was glad, of course, that Rosie had settled down and was happy, but how upset the little girl's mother would be if she could hear her. Children were completely self-centred at times, wrapped up in their own little world. So long as they were well cared for and contented, that was all that mattered to them. Jenny thought that quite possibly they were right. One had to be tough and develop to the full the art of self-preservation in order to be able to exist in such a crazy world.

Chapter 6

'. . . A new year is at hand. We cannot tell what it will bring. If it brings peace, how thankful we shall all be. If it brings us continued struggle we shall remain undaunted.

'In the mean time I feel that we may all find a message of encouragement in the lines which, in my closing words, I would like to say to you – "I said to the man who stood at the Gate of the Year, 'Give me a light that I may tread safely into the unknown.' And he replied, 'Go out into the darkness, and put your hand into the Hand of God. That shall be to you better than light, and safer than a known way.'"

'May that Almighty hand guide and uphold us all.'

'And God bless him, too,' remarked Annie Carter, as the King's broadcast ended. 'I reckon he's made a grand king, in spite of that stammer of his. If anybody'll keep our spirits up, it'll be him. He's a darned sight better than that there brother of his, with his fancy woman.' Annie sniffed. 'A fine old mess we'd be in if he was king, I can tell you. I reckon we had a lucky escape when he abdicated.'

Jenny and Tom looked at one another and grinned. She was still the same old Annie, but she hadn't the power to dampen their spirits today. After all, it was Christmas Day, the season of goodwill, traditionally a family time, and for this Christmas at least the family was all together.

Tom had been granted a forty-eight-hour leave, to Patsy and Jenny's delight, and he had arrived home late on Christmas Eve. He would have to go back on the afternoon train on Boxing Day, but there would be time enough to think about that when tomorrow came. They were all determined to enjoy what was left of the day.

'Yes, I agree with you, Ma' said Tom diplomatically. He tried to agree with his mother-in-law whenever he could – to keep on the right side of her – although it was difficult at times. But this time, what she said was true. The king, in his quiet way, was giving his subjects hope and encouragement. 'Yes, we're getting along very nicely with George the Sixth, and that was a fine speech he made.'

'Do you think he's right, Tom?' asked Jenny. 'About the new year bringing peace, I mean? He seemed to imply that it could soon be over, didn't he?'

'Who can tell, love? Personally, I don't think so.' Tom shook his head. 'There have been some bad losses at sea, but apart from that it's hardly got started yet. And when it does, well, I think we may be in for a long, hard struggle.'

'I read in the paper that Chamberlain wonders if we're fighting the right enemy,' said Violet, leaning across the table and looking earnestly at Tom. 'He hates the Communists, doesn't he? And now that the Russians have invaded Finland – well, it makes you wonder, doesn't it, Tom?'

'Leave it alone, can't you, our Violet?' snapped Annie. 'I'm sure Tom's had enough of war talk, and it's Christmas Day, for goodness' sake. Why can't you talk about summat more cheerful?'

'It's all right, Ma,' said Tom. 'I don't mind. Funnily enough, there's not much talk in the barracks about the war. There might be when it hots up a bit, but all that the fellows want to talk about when they get together is football or their families or girlfriends.' Or their conquests with the ATS girls, he thought. And not just the single men either, he added to himself, but he wasn't going to tell Annie or Jenny about that.

'What do you do all day, Tom?' asked Jenny, as if she'd been reading his mind. 'I mean, you're not fighting or anything yet, so what is there to do?'

'It's all highly secret, Jenny,' said Tom. He put a finger over his lips. 'You know what the posters say, "Careless talk costs lives".'

'I can't see that it would make any difference,' retorted Jenny. 'There's only us here, and we're not likely to go blabbing to anyone, are we?'

'You can't be too careful, love. That's one of the things we're taught. We do a lot of square-bashing and cleaning our kit. They're very keen on spit and polish, I can tell you. But we seem to spend an awful lot of the time sitting around on our arses waiting for something to happen.'

'Tom! Watch your language!' said Annie, sounding very

72

shocked. 'You never used to talk like that. Whatever's got into you?'

'Sorry, Ma.' Tom grinned. 'That's barrack-room talk. I was forgetting meself. Still, no harm done, eh? They're not listening.' He nodded towards Patsy and Rosie who were engrossed in a game of snap at the other end of the room.

'You can't be too sure,' said Annie. 'Little pigs have big ears. You never know what they overhear, and that Rosie doesn't need much encouraging, I can tell you,' she added in a whisper.

'She's a grand little lass, though, isn't she?' said Tom. 'That was a good move you made, Jenny, taking an evacuee. She's done our Patsy a world of good already. I've seen such a change in her, and it's giving the poor little kid a home as well. It's funny her mother didn't want her at home for Christmas though, isn't it?' he added quietly.

'She happen thought it would unsettle her,' said Jenny, 'and Rosie seemed happy enough to stay here. Our Patsy would have been heartbroken if she'd gone, 'specially at Christmas.'

Mrs White, Rosie's mother, had been over to Blackpool in November on a special 'Visit to Evacuee' cheap day-return ticket. Jenny had found her to be a happy, friendly person and she had taken quite a liking to her, in spite of her peroxide-blonde hair, vermilion lips and nails, and tight skirt. Mrs White had been very grateful for what Jenny and her family were doing for Rosie, and seemed content to leave her daughter in Blackpool for an unspecified period.

Many of the evacuees who had been billeted in Blackpool had returned home now. There were no air raids, they were homesick, and what was the point of staying in Blackpool in the winter? As far as the unaccompanied evacuees were concerned, the Government's demand for a small parental contribution towards the children's support may have had something to do with the drift homewards.

Daisy White explained that she had taken a job at the munitions factory since Rosie's departure and that she did a lot of night work.

'Huh! It's easy to see what her night work is!' Annie had observed derisively.

Jenny, however, was willing to reserve her judgement, in spite of all her mother's comments about Daisy White being a 'fancy

73

piece and no better than she ought to be'. The woman seemed fond of little Rosie and had made a fuss of Patsy, too, when she came over for the day. Jenny felt that Daisy had made the right decision in leaving the child where she was. After all, one never knew when things were going to 'hot up', to use Tom's phrase, and the safety of the children, the future generation, should be of primary import-ance. Jenny did have a sneaking feeling, however, which she wouldn't for the world admit to her mother, that Daisy White was considering her own best interests as well In leaving the child in Blackpool A letter had come from her about a week ago, explaining that she would be very busy over the holiday period and couldn't see her way to having Rosie at home, but she hoped they would all have a lovely, happy Christmas. She had sent a book of Enid Blyton stories for Rosie, and one for Patsy as well, so the children were well pleased. Rosie hadn't minded at all that she wouldn't be with her own mother at Christmas.

The day had been a happy one so far. Food was still fairly plentiful, and Annie had managed to buy a small chicken which she had eked out with her own home-made stuffing and huge helpings of roast potatoes and vegetables. The pudding had been made several months ago with dried fruit bought before the war started – Annie still had a stock of this in her cupboard for emergencies – and the children were excited to find tiny silver charms and threepenny bits wrapped in greaseproof paper hidden in the pudding.

'Hey – what's this?' Rosie exclaimed. 'There's summat hard in me mouth.' She grimaced and spat it out onto her plate. It was a tiny silver pixie which Jenny told her was a lucky charm. 'It wouldn't have been so bloomin' lucky if I'd swallowed it,' Rosie retorted, to gales of laughter from the grown-ups.

She was highly delighted all the same – obviously the custom was new to her – and she hid the charm away in her handkerchief which she stuffed up her knicker leg. Patsy found a threepenny bit which she was allowed to keep, but the adults gave their findings back to Annie to be used again another year, God willing. They pulled crackers and wore paper hats and exchanged gifts, making believe for this one day that they were living in a perfectly normal world. The war had encroached insidiously, though, even into the Christmas preparations.

'Well, I think it's a poor do,' Annie had complained, 'that

there's no midnight Carol Service at the church this year. It's coming to something when that has to be stopped. I don't see the sense in it at all.'

'It's because of the blackout,' Jenny explained. 'They can't cover up those big stained-glass windows. Besides, I don't know what you're worrying about, Mother. You haven't been to the Carol Service for years.'

'That's not the point,' retorted Annie. 'I might have gone this year. I'd just like to have been given the chance, that's all.'

'Well, how about us going in the afternoon then?' Jenny had suggested. 'They're having the service earlier in the day so it'll be over before it gets dark.'

'It wouldn't be the same at all,' Annie moaned.' No, if they can't have it at the proper time, then they can have it without me.'

And of course there were no carol singers coming to the door either. All whistles, hooters, horns, gongs or other musical instruments were prohibited out of doors 'in accordance with official instructions'.

Patsy and Rosie had each received as a gift a smart gas-mask case made of shiny blue leatherette. Jenny had noticed in the local toy-shop that there were toy barrage balloons on sale, and one of the Christmas cards they had received showed Santa Claus being shot down – but fortunately unharmed! – by anti-aircraft guns.

There was not much money to spare for presents, but the children received snap cards, games of Ludo and Snakes and Ladders, and Jenny had made a new dress out of odds and ends of material for each of the beloved black dolls. There were, of course, the customary sugar mice, chocolate coins covered in gold foil, and apples and oranges in the stockings, so all told it was proving to be a very pleasant day.

'Snap!' shouted Rosie loudly. 'There, I've won, Patsy. Let's have another game now, shall we? What about Snakes and Ladders? That looks good. I know, let's ask your dad to play with us.'

'All right,' agreed Patsy. 'Daddy, will you come and have a game with us – Snakes and Ladders?'

'Why not?' said Tom amiably. 'I don't think I'm needed here, am I?' He grinned at the three women who were beginning to clear away the debris left behind by a satisfying meal.

'No, lad. You'll only be in the road in the kitchen,' said Annie.

'Me and the lasses'll soon side this lot away. Go on with you. Make yerself scarce.'

Tom joined in the children's game somewhat restrainedly. He had always found it difficult to communicate with his little daughter, though he loved her more than he could say. He was unable to put his feelings into words, and having no idea how to talk to the child on her on level, he had preferred to leave her upbringing mainly in Jenny's capable hands. Consequently, father and daughter seldom conversed, and he couldn't remember her ever asking him before to join in a game.

He found himself, to his amazement, getting more and more engrossed as the two little girls shook the dice and climbed their coloured counters up long ladders and slid them down slithery snakes to land at the bottom of the board again.

'Now it's your turn,' said Rosie excitedly, giving Tom a nudge. 'Go on – let's see if you can get a six. If you do, you'll be at the bottom of that ladder, and then you'll nearly have won.'

What an astute little thing she was, thought Tom, working out her own and everybody else's moves in advance. In games, as well as in life, so much depended on how the die was cast. To his surprise he threw a six, and in two more moves he had won the game.

'Hurrah! Daddy's won,' shouted Patsy.

'That was a good game, wasn't it?' said Rosie. 'Shall we play again . . . er . . . I don't know what to call you,' she added, a tiny frown wrinkling her brow as she looked at Tom.

'What about Uncle Tom? Won't that do?' asked Tom, feeling suddenly very pleased with himself.

'It might,' said Rosie seriously. 'I was wondering though . . . You see – I've never had a proper dad, like Patsy has you, and I was wondering if I could call you . . .'

'Call him Daddy, like I do,' chimed in Patsy. 'He won't mind, will you, Daddy?'

Rosie shook her head, her blue eyes clouded with concentration. 'When I was a very little girl,' she said, 'we used to go and see me mum's dad – he was me grandad – and he lived on the other side of the river. Me mum used to call him Pop. He was ever so nice and kind, but then he died. He looked a bit like you do.' Rosie put her head on one side and pursed her lips as she looked at Tom appraisingly. 'He wasn't very big, and he had floppy hair like yours, and the same colour eyes. Of course he was a lot older'n you – but you look like him. D'you think I could call you Pop, like me mum called me grandad?'

'I think that would be a lovely name,' said Tom, feeling an unfamiliar warmth spread all through him. The little lass was a charmer and no mistake, and if she was the means of him getting closer to his own daughter, then that was all to the good. He put an arm round Rosie and drew her towards him, then he put his other arm round Patsy. 'All right then, that's settled. I'll be your pop – and your dad,' he said, hugging them both. 'And now I've got two little girls instead of one. Isn't that nice? Now, shall we have another game of Snakes and Ladders, and see if you can beat me this time?'

Jenny stared into the pitch blackness of the room which was unrelieved by even the tiniest chink of light. There was a street lamp outside the window which, before the days of blackout restrictions, had cast a glow into the bedroom through the thin cotton curtains. Now the streetlamps were extinguished and the blackout material at the windows was more than a match for any encroaching moonlight or starlight. Jenny was unable to sort out the jumble of thoughts in her mind. Tom's leave had been such a very short one; now, just when she was beginning to get used to him being home, it was nearly time for him to go back again. It had seemed odd at first, having him there, almost as though he were a stranger. She was glad, though, that he and Rosie seemed to have taken to one another, and that Patsy, encouraged by her new friend, had drawn closer to her father. But it was their own relationship – hers and Tom's – that concerned Jenny. There was a constraint between them, not spoken of or acknowledged openly but there nevertheless.

Earlier, when they had come to bed, Tom had opened the curtains and they had made love by the faint light of the moon. Tom had always been a gentle and considerate lover, but tonight his embraces had been more demanding. It was as though some of the savagery of war had entered into him. Once or twice Jenny had to bite her lip to stop herself from crying out against the rough onslaught of his body.

She knew, however, that it was partly her own fault because she was resisting him. If only she could give of herself, fully and unrestrainedly, maybe there would be an end to this warring and tension hidden deep inside her. Jenny was only too well aware that she was withholding some vital part of herself, but she couldn't have explained why. It was almost as though she were making love to a stranger. She tried to shrug away the absurd thought, but it persisted. Tom seemed . . . different. At times Jenny felt she didn't know her husband any more. She had, however, kissed him fondly and told him how she would miss him. She loved him – of course she did, didn't she? – and prayed every night when she went to bed for his safety, but his lovemaking left her strangely unmoved.

She also felt that Tom was holding something back, in spite of the ardour of his embraces. He seemed distracted, his mind elsewhere, no doubt on some far-flung battle line. He had always been a man of action rather than of words, finding it difficult to give voice to his feelings of love for her. He was as taciturn in lovemaking as he was in other aspects of his life and Jenny knew, without being able to put it into words, that his approach to her was unimaginative. She had never known another lover and therefore was unable to make comparisons, but she knew instinctively that some vital spark was missing.

She lay and listened to Tom's rhythmic breathing. His physical needs satisfied, his body and mind were now at rest. But Jenny was wide awake. She felt tears of frustration spring unbidden to her eyes and course hotly down her cheeks. Whatever was the matter with her? What was it that she desired so much? Jenny couldn't answer her unspoken questions, but she knew that she would recognise it, when – and if – she ever found it.

Chapter 7

Violet Carter leaned forward and looked at herself searchingly in the flyblown mirror. Irritably she pulled out the childish slides that constrained her hair and shook her head wildly from side to side. Unfettered, her pale-blonde hair fell forward, waving gently on either side of her angular face. She seized a comb and tugged it through the fine silky locks. Her friend Joyce was right. It was time she had a new hairstyle and tried to smarten herself up.

A stray tress flopped over one eye and Violet stopped, comb poised in her hand, as she leaned forward to examine herself more critically. That was just like Veronica Lake's hairstyle in her latest picture. Perhaps it would suit her, Violet, if she were to encourage her hair to fall that way. Why not? An unfamiliar excitement gripped her as she combed and patted and preened.

She should put on her dress first, though, before doing her hair, or else it would all want doing again. She opened the massive oak wardrobe and took out her one good dress. It hung limply on its padded hanger. But, as Jenny had told her, it looked better on than off, and her sister had helped her to liven it up with a black velvet bow at the waist. Jenny was so clever with her fingers, and knew just what to do with a bit of stitching here and a bit of ribbon there to make old clothes look fashionable. Violet undid the long zipper at the back and stepped into the dress. The dark-red marocain suited her fair complexion. Jenny had assured her that she looked nice in it when they had chosen it together at the Co-op Emporium on Violet's eighteenth birthday. The padded shoulders gave her that extra width that her slim figure needed and the sweetheart neckline was just right to frame her necklace of imitation pearls. Violet opened the dressing-table drawer, took out the creamy-white beads and fastened them round her neck. Then she patted her nose and cheeks with a swan's-down powder puff and daringly applied a touch of Tangee lipstick, bought yesterday in Woolworth's.

Now she was ready. She folded her arms tightly across her thin chest as if to stop the rapid beating of her heart. She wondered if it was worth it – all the dressing up and prinking and preening, to say nothing of the fluttery, frightened feeling deep in her tummy – just for a visit to the Tower Ballroom. Tonight Violet was going dancing for the first time in her life.

There was a knock at the bedroom door and Jenny poked her head round. 'Can I come in?' she asked. She did so without waiting for an answer; the sisters had always been good friends in spite of the eight years' difference in age and the dissimilarity of their temperaments. 'Mother said you were still up here getting ready. "Tarting herself up" was what she really said, but you know what Mother is.'

The two young women looked at each other and giggled.

'You do look nice, Vi,' said Jenny warmly, affection shining in her eyes as she looked at her sister, 'and you've done something different with your hair as well. Come here, though – let's comb it back. It's flopping over your face.'

'It's meant to . . . I thought it looked like that film star – you know,' said Violet hesitantly. Oh dear! If Jenny thought it looked silly it would perhaps be better to fasten it back.

'Oh, you mean Veronica Lake.' Jenny nodded. 'Yes – you're right, Violet. You look the image of her. Just wait till Mother sees you, though. She'll say you're a fancy piece.' The sisters giggled again. 'Where are you meeting your friends, Vi? Outside the Tower, or are they coming here?'

'No – I said I'd meet them at the bus stop at seven o'clock. The dance halls close at ten o'clock, you know, so we have to go early to get our money's worth. Sheila lives near the bus stop and Joyce lives near you, Jenny, at the other end of Green Street.'

'Yes – I've seen her going past. She looks a nice girl. I'm glad you've made some friends at the factory, Vi. It's done you a world of good, you know, going out to work.' Jenny smiled at her sister. 'It's a good job you stood up to Mother, or you'd still have been slaving away in the boarding house.'

'Well, it's partly thanks to you and Cousin Ada. I don't know what I'd have done without you.' Violet's voice trembled a little. 'She's still a bit funny with me – Mother, I mean – now that the RAF lads are here and she's all that extra work. And I'm scared of what she'll say when she sees me wearing lipstick. I've never worn it before. Does it look all right, Jenny? Oh gosh! I almost wish I wasn't going. I feel so worked up.'

'Go on with yer bother.' Jenny gave her sister a quick hug. 'I've told you – you look lovely. Now, you'd best be off. You've only five minutes to get to the bus stop. Put your coat on and nip downstairs. Just shout to Mother as you go out, then you'll not have to put up with a lecture. And for heaven's sake, enjoy yourself, Vi, and forget about Mother for once in a while.'

'OK – I'll try.' Violet didn't sound very confident, but she smiled at her sister. 'Thanks, Jenny.'

'Off you go then. I'll tidy up here for you.'

Jenny knew that to forget about her mother was easier said than done, but there had already been a big change in Violet since she had gone to work at the aircraft factory in March of that year – 1940. Vickers Armstrong had opened an aircraft assembly plant for the manufacture of Wellington bombers at Squire's Gate, on the airport site. Sub-factories had been established in other parts of the town to minimise the effect of possible air raids, and it was at one of these that Violet was employed. The upper floors of Talbot Road bus station had been camouflaged with black paint and now provided jobs for hundreds of men and women at the north end of the town.

Jenny had been hardly able to believe her ears when her sister had declared her intention, a couple of months ago, of going to work at the factory.

'It isn't as if I'm needed at home, Jenny,' she had said. 'All the evacuees have gone now, and half a dozen civil servants don't need much looking after, do they?'

The staff from the Ministry of Pensions had moved to Blackpool, and after the exodus of the evacuees a few of these Government officials had been billeted on Annie. The allowance of one guinea a week per person was a welcome bonus to the landladies, but the civil servants, on the whole, didn't take as kindly to the move as the evacuees had done.

Blackpool had shivered that winter under the heaviest snowfall ever recorded in the town. Annie grew sick of the complaints and the requests for warmer blankets from 'them southerners', as she called them, accustomed to warmer climes.

'Bloomin' Londoners,' she grumbled. 'Proper nesh, they are.

Can't stand a bit of God's fresh air, and they want waiting on hand and foot. Thank goodness there's only six of 'em.'

Nevertheless, she had been outraged to hear that her younger daughter intended to volunteer for war work.

'Have you taken leave of your senses, girl?' she cried, going red in the face. 'Of course you can't go and work in the factory. How the heck do you think I'm going to manage here, with all these bloomin' civil servants?'

'There's only six of them, Mother. You said so yourself,' replied Violet with an unusual show of spirit. 'I'm sure you and Jenny can manage half a dozen young women, especially with Cousin Ada coming in on a Saturday. Anyway, we've all got to do our bit, and if I don't volunteer for war work I'll be called up before long, as likely as not. Then I might end up in the ATS or the Land Army.'

'She's right, Mother,' Jenny agreed, willingly supporting her sister. She was glad that Violet was learning to stick up for herself at last. 'I'll do a bit extra if it's necessary, although these civil servants don't seem to be much trouble as far as I can see. We've all got to make a few sacrifices.'

'There's a war on you know, Mother,' Violet added pertly. 'Hadn't you realised?'

Jenny suppressed a giggle. Good for you, our Violet, she thought.

Annie was not amused. She went redder than ever as she yelled at her daughters. 'We'll have less of your lip, my girl. And you can shut up too, our Jenny. It's got nowt to do wi' you. And you, young woman, you don't come of age for another year or more,' she went on, wagging her finger at Violet, 'and until then you'll do as I say, and after that an' all if I've got owt to do with it.'

Annie's northern accent became even more pronounced. It always did when she was under stress as she was at this moment. The thought that Violet was eligible for war work, that she might, in fact, be called up into one of the women's services had given Annie quite a turn. It was something she hadn't even considered. Violet was her little girl – in spite of her daughter being nineteen that was how she still thought of her – and she couldn't bear the idea of parting with her, not just yet. She was well aware that she was often brusque and short-tempered with the lass, but her gruff manner disguised a deep love which tore at her heartstrings sometimes. Violet had come along eight years after Jenny, at a time when Annie had thought there would be no more children. Violet was her own little 'Lammas lamb' as countryfolk sometimes called a baby born late in life – Annie's own mother had often used the term – and was all the more welcome for her late arrival. Not that Annie had ever told her so . . . Dear me, no. That wouldn't do at all. Daughters had to be kept firmly in their place.

Annie was in a quandary now, though, right enough. She carefully wiped down the draining board, all the while wondering how she could get herself out of this little lot. It had been second nature to Annie to protest when Violet had suggested working at the factory. Now she was beginning to see that it might be the lesser of two evils, that it might, in fact, be not such a bad idea at all. She certainly didn't want the lass going into the ATS or even the Land Army, but how on earth was she going to retract now without losing face?

She slowly squeezed out the dishcloth, playing for time. Violet was quite right of course. It didn't take three of them to look after half a dozen young women, but Annie had something else up her sleeve that her daughters didn't know about yet. She still might be able to keep Violet at home if she played her cards right. She turned to face them. 'And you two don't know it all either,' she said, nodding meaningfully. 'Them stuck-up civil servants from London may well be leaving here soon. They'll be moving round the corner on to t'prom. A posher place'll suit 'em better, I don't doubt.' Annie sniffed. ''Cos we're going to have some RAF lads comin', so there!' She folded her arms across her broad chest and smiled gloatingly at her daughters. 'So it'll be all hands on deck, I can tell you, when we get a house full of troops. You can forget all yer fancy ideas about working at t'factory.'

'It's the first we've heard of it, Mother,' replied Jenny indignantly. 'Why didn't you tell us?'

'I don't tell you everything, madam. Only what I want you to know. But I suppose you'd better know now. The billeting officer came to see me yesterday while you two were out gallivanting in town. He looked at the bedrooms and went snooping into the back kitchen – he were a polite enough young fellow, though, I'll say that for him – then he said he thought I'd got room for about twenty of 'em. So that's that, young lady. You can put that in yer pipe and smoke it.' She nodded aggressively at Violet and marched out of the room.

Violet turned and looked helplessly at Jenny, tears of disappointment beginning to well up in her lovely green eyes. 'I'm afraid she may be right, Jenny. It seems as though I really will be needed here, if there's going to be twenty RAF lads to look after.'

'No!' said Jenny, banging her fist on the table. 'She's not going to get away with it this time. You've a right to go out to work if you want to, and I think it's very patriotic of you to volunteer for war work. Listen – I think I know of a way of getting round Mother. Cousin Ada was saying she'd like to do a bit more to help the war effort. She feels she's wasting her time looking after those two old ladies, but they employ her as a companion so she can't very well take another job. How would it be if we ask her to come here another couple of days a week? The Frobisher ladies don't seem to mind her coming here, so long as she's back in time to get their tea.'

'Ooh, Jenny, do you think she would? That would free me, wouldn't it, to go and work at the factory?' Violet's eyes began to shine with renewed hope, but clouded again just as quickly as she thought of Annie's reaction. 'I don't know, though. Mother might not take too kindly to having Ada here more often. You know what they're like when they get together. There'll be fur and feathers flying.'

'Oh, don't be such a defeatist, Violet. Mother can't have it all her own way. Like I told her, we've all got to make a few sacrifices. Anyway, we'll go and ask Ada first. Then, if she agrees, we'll tell Mother it's all settled.'

'A "fait accompli", you mean?'

'A what?' Jenny gave a puzzled frown.

'Fait accompli. It's French. It means what you just said. It'll be already decided, so she won't be able to do anything about it.'

Jenny laughed. 'Exactly. I don't know your fancy French words, Vi, but that's what I mean. She'll have no choice.'

Ada Wainwright had been employed as a housekeeper-cum-ladies' companion by the Misses Frobisher for about twenty-five years. The two maiden ladies were now in their seventies. They had been born in the middle years of Victoria's reign, when the practice of keeping servants was becoming more widespread among the middle classes. Their father was a prosperous doctor, his patients drawn from the residents of the Raike's estate, one of the more affluent areas of Blackpool. It was on this estate that the

Frobisher ladies – Miss Alice and Miss Maud – still lived, in a solidly built semi-detached house of shiny red Accrington brick.

Ada's mother was Annie Carter's eldest sister, but it wasn't to be near her aunt that Ada had moved to Blackpool. She had, in fact, moved to the seaside several years before Annie and her family. She had liked the idea of working in the clean fresh air of Blackpool, rather than in the grimy, smoke-filled atmosphere of her native Wigan. There was little love lost between aunt and niece, but as they resided in the same town it was only natural that Ada should spend her days off with the Carters. Family ties were strong in the north of England and, as Annie often said, blood was thicker than water.

When Ada first moved to Blackpool old Dr Frobisher had just died and the two maiden ladies had recently set up home together. They couldn't manage without a maid. Neither of them had ever worked for a living or been trained in anything other than the gentlest of domestic chores. Miss Maud occasionally lent a hand in the kitchen and could make a very nice fruit cake when she felt inclined. Miss Alice was an adequate seamstress, taking care of all the mending of the household linens. Apart from that, as Annie Carter succinctly expressed it, 'they were neither use nor ornament'.

Ada was forced to agree with her aunt, although she personally had nothing to complain about in her place of employment. The Misses Frobisher were kindly ladies who had made sure that the young Ada, leaving home for the first time, was happy and contented. At first she had been submissive, as befitted a servant, but gradually, over the years, her position in the household had changed. Now she walked a tightrope between servant-companion and equal. She cooked the meals and served the two ladies, then she sat at the same table with them, eating the same food, but keeping her apron on as a symbol of her subservience.

Ada was a veritable treasure. Neither of the ladies knew how they would manage without her. They had even allowed her to take a little extra job, helping out at her aunt's boarding house one day a week. In the evenings she sat with them in the dining-cum-living room, listening to the wireless. She had her own domain, though; a snug housekeeper's parlour at the back of the house where she entertained her own friends and relations. It was into this room that she ushered Jenny and Violet one afternoon in March 1940.

Jenny wrinkled her nose fastidiously, as she always did, on entering the house. The predominant smell was of lavender polish. Ada kept the house scrupulously clean, but underlying this perfume were several less pleasant aromas. Cooking smells emanated from Ada's kitchen into the hallway – they'd obviously had cabbage today – combined with the more sinister, subtle smell of old ladies. The Misses Frobisher would have been horrified at Jenny's thoughts. Didn't they have a bath once a week on a Friday? Ada always kept a good fire going, even in summer, to ensure that the water was nice and hot, and they changed their undergarments once a week too.

Jenny held out her hands to the comforting warmth of Ada's fire. This was such a welcoming room. The brass fender gleamed with recent polishing, as did the candlesticks which stood on the mantelpiece topping the black range, and the brass toasting fork at the side of the fireplace.

'It's still pretty chilly for the time of year,' Ada remarked, 'but we're nice and snug in here. Sit yerselves down and draw up to the fire.' She pointed to the two red moquette armchairs on either side of the fireplace; Ada herself sat on a cane-seated dining chair which she pulled away from the table.

'Now, to what do I owe this honour?' she asked. 'I don't usually have the pair of you visiting me together. Aunt Annie's let you off the leash this afternoon, has she?' Ada grunted with laughter, but Jenny and Violet didn't join in. 'What's up?' said their cousin, looking at their serious faces. 'There's nothing wrong, is there? Aunt Annie's not ill or anything, is she?' Ada's face crumpled with concern.

'No, it's nothing like that,' Jenny assured her. 'We've come to ask you a favour, Ada. Well, it's Violet really.' Jenny smiled encouragingly at her sister.

'You tell her, Jenny,' said Violet in a whisper. 'You'll know what to say better than I do.'

Ada listened as Jenny explained about her sister's decision to work at the aircraft factory, and about Annie's vehement objection to her doing any such thing.

'So we wondered, Ada, if you'd be willing to help us a bit more? Perhaps another couple of half-days a week? Then it would release Vi to go and work at the factory.'

Ada's gimlet-sharp eyes narrowed speculatively. She nodded

thoughtfully once or twice. 'Hmm, I see. Yes, I certainly do see . . . But Aunt Annie's reckoned without me. Just you wait till I've finished with her. She'll be singing a different tune then! She's no right to stand in your way, Violet.'

'You mean – you'll come then, Ada?' asked Violet eagerly.

'Of course I'll come, lass. I'll be only too pleased to help. I'll have to ask my ladies first, though, and see what they say. But I don't see how they can object, if I'm helping the war effort. I was saying to Miss Maud only the other day that it was time she got off her fat bottom and did a bit more, now there's a war on.'

Jenny smiled to herself. She doubted that Ada had used exactly those words, though she was never afraid of speaking her mind, even to her employers.

'And what did Miss Maud say to that?' asked Jenny.

'Oh, she agreed with me,' said Ada. 'She says they're going to stop taking sugar in their tea, now we're rationed, and she was looking through the cookery book to see if she could find a recipe for an economical fruit cake. Not that she's likely to find one in Mrs Beeton.' Ada raised her eyes to the ceiling. 'They all need about a dozen eggs. And Miss Alice has started knitting socks for the troops, same as they did in the Great War, she says. Well, it makes a change from sewing fancy lace on pillowslips. I reckon we'll all have to do without frills and flounces for a while yet, by the look of things. We'll have a nice cup of tea, though. Things aren't so bad that we can't enjoy a nice cuppa.'

Ada bustled into the kitchen which opened off her small parlour, from where she carried on a shouted conversation with her cousins. 'How's that evacuee of yours – that little Rosie? She's still here, I take it?'

'Yes, she's still here, Ada. Most of them have gone now, of course. They'd all gone from Mother's by the end of last year, as you know, but I don't know what our Patsy would do if Rosie's mother decided to have her home again.'

Jenny didn't know what she would do either. She found it difficult to remember a time when she had had only one little girl, and not two. Patsy was her own dear child, of course, and would always have a special place in her affections, but Jenny had found, to her joy, that what she had said to Rosie that first day was very true. She had love enough for both of them, and her fondness for the little girl from Liverpool grew stronger with every day. Parting

87

from her would leave an aching void in Jenny's heart, but it would be time enough to think about that when it actually happened.

'She's not been over to see her again then, that Daisy White?' called Ada.

'No, not since before Christmas.'

'Huh! I reckon she's better off without her, poor little mite. I can't see that dolled-up madam having much time for children. She thinks she's it and no mistake.'

'You've only met her once, Ada.' Violet joined in, sounding indignant. 'She is the child's mother, and she seemed very fond of her from what I could tell. Besides, it's difficult travelling in wartime. She might not be able to get a train just when she wants one.'

'I don't know so much about that,' Ada retorted. 'I've heard as how them top nobs in the Government are encouraging people to go on holiday as usual. They say it'll help to keep folks' spirits up. They reckon that Blackpool's going to be bursting at the seams this Easter what with the RAF being here, and them civil servants from London an' all.'

'Well, Mother won't have room for any visitors and that's for sure,' said Jenny. 'She's going to be full up with RAF blokes. And how can folks go on holiday when food's rationed? It doesn't make sense.'

'I've heard tell that Blackpool's quota of rationed food has been doubled for the holiday. A woman were telling me about it in the butcher's the other day.' Ada came back from the kitchen with a laden tray and placed it on the table. 'And visitors have been told that they needn't use their food coupons, so long as they stay for less than six days at a place that's registered for catering. So now you know.' She picked up the brown earthenware teapot and filled the three cups to the brim. 'So I reckon that Daisy White could get here easy enough if she'd a mind . . . But you're a kind lass, Violet.' She smiled warmly at her cousin as she passed her a cup of tea. 'Trust you to see both sides of it, and happen you're right. The trouble with me is me tongue's so sharp it's a wonder I don't cut meself at times!'

At least she knows it, thought Jenny, as she sipped the strong hot tea. She thought again, as she often did, what a grand person her cousin was, beneath all that bustle and bluster. She hoped the Frobisher ladies realised how lucky they were to have Ada.

'Call in and see my ladies before you go, won't you?' asked Ada now. 'You know they're always glad of a bit of company.'

'Yes, we'll do that,' Jenny agreed. 'Come on, Vi. Drink up your tea. We'd best be making a move or Mother'll have the police out looking for us.'

The Misses Frobisher were sitting one either side of the huge fire in the living room, which was overfilled with heavy Edwardian furniture. A massive mahogany sideboard with a built-in mirror, elaborately embellished with spindles and fretwork, towered almost to the ceiling. The dining table and chairs were of mahogany too, with padded leather seats and backs, each one weighing a ton, Ada avowed as she pulled them out each week for a ritual dusting.

The room was stuffy and claustrophobic, the stale smell even more prevalent in here, combined with the smell of camphor which drifted from the dark woollen clothing of Miss Alice and Miss Maud.

'Well, well, well! We've got company, Maud,' said Miss Alice in a gruff voice. 'Here's Jenny to see us, and young Violet too. Isn't that nice?'

Miss Maud nodded. 'Company,' she echoed, in gentle, twittering tones. 'Very nice.'

Jenny thought, as she always did, that they were like an act at the Palace of Varieties; Miss Alice tall and thin, Miss Maud short and fat, continually echoing her sister's words. They were kindly old souls, though, always taking an interest in Ada's relations. They had very few living relatives of their own and lived vicariously, relishing the joys and sorrows of the Carter and Bradshaw families. Patsy, surprisingly enough, loved visiting them. She never tired of playing with the numerous china ornaments that adorned the lounge. Jenny was always on pins in case the child should break one, but the old ladies were very indulgent.

'And how's your dear husband?' enquired Miss Alice. 'We're so pleased he's serving his King and Country.'

'Mm, King and Country,' agreed Miss Maud.

'He's very well,' replied Jenny, speaking loudly and enunciating each word clearly. Miss Maud, in particular, was rather deaf. 'He's in France now, but I don't know exactly where. It's all very secret, but I hear from him every week.'

'Dear boy,' said Miss Alice. 'We remember him in our prayers every night.'

'Every night,' echoed her sister.

'And how are you, Violet dear?' asked Miss Alice. 'No young man to show off to us yet?' She gave a throaty chuckle.

'No young man?' asked Miss Maud coyly.

'I'm very well,' replied Violet dutifully. 'No, there's no young man yet.' She gave a weak smile. The sisters asked her the same question every time they met.

'Bring Patsy to see us soon, won't you, Jenny?' said Miss Alice eagerly. 'And that nice little Rosie too. She's a dear little girl.'

'Dear little girl,' repeated Miss Maud pensively. 'They're both such dear little girls. You must be very proud of them, Jenny.'

Miss Alice glared at her sister as if she were a child who had spoken out of turn.

The two young women were glad to escape into the fresh air, even though it was bitterly cold.

'Well, that's that,' declared Jenny. 'I knew Ada would turn up trumps. You'll be working at the factory in no time, Vi.'

'Maybe,' said Violet, casting a worried glance at her sister. 'Mother's not going to like it, though.'

'Then she can jolly well lump it,' said Jenny emphatically.

Annie Carter didn't like it, but she knew when she was beaten, and she certainly wasn't going to have that bossy madam Ada Wainwright telling her what to do. No one would think, to hear her talking a week later, that she had once been opposed to the idea.

'My younger daughter's working at the factory, you know,' she said proudly to the RAF billeting officer when he called round the following week. 'She went and applied all by herself, bless her. She didn't wait to be called up. But we've all got to do our bit, haven't we, young man? My niece Ada is going to come and help us, so we'll be able to manage twenty RAF lads as easy as winking.'

Jenny listened in wry amusement. Mother was a caution and no mistake. She wouldn't admit that, for once, she had failed to get all her own way. Jenny knew that poor Violet was having to suffer the rough edge of Annie's tongue because of it all, but her sister had been stoical in her refusal to budge from her resolution. She had applied to work at the factory the next day.

Violet loved every minute of it. The din of the machinery, the excited chatter of her colleagues as they yelled at one another across the work benches and, above all, the feeling that at last she was doing something to help the war effort. Every morning she left the house at a quarter to eight, clad in the regulation boiler suit, her long blonde hair hidden under a turban.

She had to admit that the work – riveting endless pieces of metal together, in a long assembly line – was boring and mindless, unsuited to someone with her agile brain, but then she had never been able to achieve her full potential, so what did it matter? Mother had put paid to her wild ideas of becoming a teacher years ago, and Violet had obediently, if reluctantly, worked in the boarding house with no hope of escape. She had almost welcomed the outbreak of war, though she felt guilty at such selfish thoughts, glimpsing through the dark clouds of hostility and oppression a chance of an undreamed-of freedom for herself.

The factory was like another world to Violet. *Music While You Work* and *Workers' Playtime* blaring from the tinny radio; hastily snatched meals – spam and chips, or rabbit pie – and strong cups of tea from the staff canteen; and the friendship of jolly girls like Sheila and Joyce.

Violet had never had a close friend before. Of course there was always Jenny; she was a wonderful sister, but she was a lot older than Violet and she had her own husband and little girl. Violet had never minded that until recently. She had been content – or had convinced herself that she was content – to share Jenny's happy home life. She had enjoyed looking after little Patsy, chatting to Tom, going shopping with Jenny – playing the part, in fact, of the typical unmarried sister.

And there had always been her books; Violet had lived in a make-believe world, laughing and crying with the characters of Dickens and the Brontë sisters and her particular favourite, Thomas Hardy. Now, she was beginning to realise that there was another world apart from Jenny, apart from her books. She wondered what it would be like to have a home and family of her own, to have a boyfriend, first of all . . . Violet had never, in all her nineteen years, been alone with a young man, except for Tom, of course, and that didn't count.

She had two nice girlfriends, though, and that was a good start. They had such fun together, she and Joyce and Sheila. Violet hugged the thought to herself as she hurried along the street to the

91

bus stop. She was glad now that they had persuaded her to go dancing with them tonight.

Violet no longer felt afraid. Her high heels clattered confidently on the pavement and she lifted her head, smelling the tang of the sea drifting towards her on the gentle breeze, feeling all around her the gentle balm of a lovely May evening. She was going to enjoy herself. It was going to be a great adventure.

Chapter 8

The ballroom was like a scene from a Hollywood film, all gold and glitter and gaiety. Tiers of red plush seats behind gilded balconies, and flashing crystal chandeliers led the eye upwards to the painted frescoes on the ceiling. Here, flower-bedecked maidens and elegant youths cavorted together in a make-believe world.

To Violet, standing on the edge of the ballroom floor with Joyce and Sheila, the scene had a feeling of unreality. She felt as though, any moment, she would wake up and find herself in her narrow single bed in the small attic room. She blinked, dazzled by the lights, and dug her fingernails hard into her arm, wincing at the self-inflicted pain. She had read in stories of characters pinching themselves to make sure something was really happening, but never had she needed to convince herself that her life was not a dream.

She had visited the Tower before on many occasions. As a child she had been fascinated by the fish in the cool greenness of the aquarium downstairs; she had sympathised with the monkeys and the lions encaged in the pathetic apology for a zoo, housed on an upper floor of the Tower building; she had watched, enthralled, the ballet performed by local children, which took place on afternoons in the summer. She had felt envious of those precocious little misses, she recalled, teetering on their toes, frilly tutus sticking out at right angles, to reveal glimpses of pink satin knickers. She had looked at her own sensible Clark's sandals and her gingham dress, and had sighed. Mother didn't approve of dancing lessons for Violet and Jenny, even if she could have afforded them.

Violet pulled herself back from her reverie. Tonight it was her turn. She was going to dance on that same ballroom floor – if someone asked her. If not, she could always dance with Sheila or Joyce. It wouldn't be quite the same thing, of course, but girls often danced together. There was nothing odd about it.

'But I can't dance!' she had protested, when Joyce and Sheila first suggested that she should go with them to the Tower. 'It's no use. I've never been dancing in my life and I'd only make a fool of myself. Besides, Mother doesn't hold with dancing. She says it's cheap, letting a fellow put his arms round you like that when you don't even know him.'

Sheila gave a hoot of laughter. 'Honestly, Vi, you are the limit! You're not going to let that mother of yours dictate to you all your life, are you? Why don't you stick up for yourself? You've already shown you've got gumption by coming to work here, so don't give up now. Let her see you've got a mind of your own.'

'I'll bet your sister has been dancing, though, hasn't she?' said Joyce. 'I think your Jenny's ever so pretty. I've seen her going past our house. All that dark curly hair,' she added wistfully. 'I'd give anything to have hair like that.' Joyce dragged her turban off her head and ran her fingers through her own mousy mane. 'Look at mine! As straight as a yard of pump water.'

'At least you've got plenty of it,' moaned Sheila, pulling off her own turban to reveal wispy fair locks, the colour and texture of doll's hair. 'Look at this!' she wailed, peering at herself in the mirror of the factory cloakroom and pointing to her wide forehead. 'I've got no hair at all here. I'm practically bald.'

'Give us your comb,' said Joyce. 'It just wants pulling forward a bit, like this . . .' She combed Sheila's sparse hair over the broad expanse of forehead. 'There – that's better.'

'Not that it makes much difference,' Sheila went on, 'not during the day anyroad. We've always got our heads smothered in these bloomin' turbans. It's a wonder any hair grows at all. I'm telling you, girls, I'll be as bald as a coot before this flippin' war ends.'

Violet smiled quietly to herself. Oh, she did like Sheila and Joyce. They were forever fussing about their hair or their faces, but they had been so kind to her since she started work at the factory. She combed her own hair vigorously – her scalp felt itchy after being covered all morning by the turban – and fastened it back tightly at either side with tortoiseshell slides.

'You're the lucky one, Vi,' said Sheila enviously, 'having hair that colour. It's like pale-golden corn, ripening under the summer sun.' She clasped her hands together and gave an exaggerated sigh.

'Bloomin' heck! Listen to her,' laughed Joyce. 'Proper poetic she is, our Sheila. Sounds as though she's swallowed a dictionary.'

94

Sheila giggled, her glossy red lips parting to reveal small pearly teeth. Sheila was like a doll, with her blonde hair, a round baby face and eyes of a startling blue which she opened wide now as she stared at her friends. 'You don't think I made that up, do you? Oh, come off it – I haven't got a brain in me head. Violet's the brainy one. I read it in *Woman's Own*.' She giggled again. 'Honestly, though, Violet. You are lucky, having hair like that.'

'Why do you fasten it back, though?' protested Joyce. 'I've never seen you without those silly slides. Here – give 'em to me.' She held out her hand, and Violet obediently took out the slides and handed them to her friend. 'Now – let's have a look.'

Joyce combed Violet's hair forward. It fell gently to her shoulders, softening her angular face.

'There – you look real pretty, Vi. Now, promise me you'll start doing your hair like that. Don't forget – there's all those RAF lads at your house now. You'll knock 'em sideways.'

Violet laughed. 'I might – do my hair different, I mean – not the bit about the RAF. I'm not all that bothered about them.'

'Ooh, why on earth not?' Sheila's blue eyes opened wide with astonishment. 'I'd give anything to be in your shoes. All those ge-or-geous men!' Her mouth made a round O of delight. 'We've only got room for one bloomin' civil servant at our house – a right la-di-da piece she is an' all. Why aren't you bothered about them, Vi? I would be, I can tell you.'

Violet didn't doubt it at all. Much as she liked Sheila, Violet knew that the girl had quite a reputation for being 'one for the men', as Joyce put it, and not averse to pinching other girls' boyfriends too, if she got the chance. There were a couple of girls at the factory who wouldn't speak to Sheila and that, so Joyce had told Violet, was the reason.

Violet shrugged. 'Oh, I don't know. I've never been used to lads. There was only me and our Jenny at home, and Mother was that strict with us we never had much chance to get to know any boys. I never know what to say to them.'

'I'll bet your Jenny finds plenty to say to them,' said Joyce, nodding her head meaningfully. 'She looks a proper live wire. I can't see her being told what to do by your ma.'

'Oh, she's had to toe the line, same as me. But she's got her own home so it's easier for her now. Our Jenny's always had more go about her than me, though, and she's a lot prettier too.' Violet sighed. 'That always helps.'

'You'd look just as pretty as Jenny with your hair loose,' argued Joyce. 'Don't say I haven't told you, but no doubt you'll please yourself no matter what I say.'

Violet had once more fastened her hair back and was replacing her turban. 'I can't have it all flying about now, can I, not while I'm working? But I'll think about it. I might even think about coming dancing with you.' Violet looked wistfully at her two friends. 'But I don't know how to do it. Will you show me?'

'You don't know how to do what?' Sheila rolled her eyes and sniggered. 'Find yerself a feller and you'll know what to do all right, I'll tell you, Violet.'

'Oh, give over, Sheila. You're embarrassing her.' Joyce scowled at her friend. 'We're not all like you. You're man-mad.'

Violet had turned bright pink and was nibbling nervously at a piece of loose skin on her thumb. Joyce was right. Sheila did embarrass her at times. Violet knew that of the two girls she much preferred Joyce, who was generous and warm-hearted and full of good old Lancashire common sense. Sheila was flippant, what Mother would call a 'fast little cat'.

'We'll teach you how to dance, won't we, Sheila?' Joyce said now.

'Of course we will.' Sheila pushed playfully at Violet's shoulder. 'You'll be as good as Ginger Rogers before we've done with you.'

They practised in Joyce's bedroom to the tinny strains of a wind-up gramophone.

'South of the border, Down Mexico way . . .' crooned Joyce. 'Come on, Violet. Hold on to me. A foxtrot's dead easy. It's only like walking backwards to music.'

Violet twisted and turned and tottered, then they all collapsed on the bed, shrieking with laughter.

'Now, you go home and practise dancing with the sweeping brush in your back kitchen,' said Sheila.

'Don't be so daft!' Violet laughed. 'Mother'd think I'd taken leave of me senses. She'd be packing me off to a loony bin.'

All the same, Violet practised secretly with a chair in her small attic bedroom.

'One, two, three . . . One, two, three, Little Sir Echo, How do you do? . . .' she sang.

And after three or four sessions the girls felt that Violet was ready to make her début on the dance floor.

The main problem was finding someone to dance with. The whole room seemed to be spinning round, as Violet watched more and more couples take to the floor. She'd had one dance with a rather spotty RAF lad whose dancing prowess was on a par with her own. They had spent most of the time falling over one another's feet and saying sorry.

The ballroom floor was a sea of air-force blue, interspersed with bright splashes of colour from the girls' dresses. Although hundreds of girls were dancing, there were countless numbers of them standing on the edge of the floor as well. The male population of Blackpool had increased, due to the coming of the RAF, but so had the female population with the intake of civil servants from the ministries in London. Violet watched Sheila dance past to the rhythm of a foxtrot, her eyes closed, her head resting dreamily on the shoulder of a young RAF recruit.

'Bloomin' heck!' moaned Joyce, 'I'm sick of standing here like a wilting wallflower. We'll go on for the next one, Violet, you and me.'

'Let's hope it's a waltz then. I can do that best.'

But Reginald Dixon at the organ struck up with the strains of 'Little Angeline'.

'Come on,' shouted Joyce. 'It's the Palais Glide. We can all do that.'

Violet and Joyce – and Sheila, who had returned somewhat bemused – joined hands and ran on to the ballroom floor. This was a jolly dance that Violet enjoyed. She had learned it during her last year at school at the end-of-term – all-girl – party. They linked arms with two more girls and two lads joined on the end.

'She was sweet sixteen, Little Angeline, Always dancing on the village green . . .' they chanted in chorus as they cavorted round the ballroom. The magnificent floor of mahogany, oak and walnut reverberated with the din of a thousand feet.

As the organist played the last resounding chord – 'Poor – little – Angeline . . .' – Violet felt her feet, unsteady in the unfamiliar high-heeled shoes, slipping from under her.

'Help! Oh, gosh!' she yelled, grabbing at Joyce as she fell heavily to the floor, her red marocain skirt flying up over her thighs. In a panic she pulled it back over her knees. Whatever would Mother say? Showing all her underwear in the middle of the ballroom floor! She sat up, dazed and dizzy, feeling her face flush with embarrassment. She saw a sea of faces above her. Joyce was looking worried, but Sheila, typically, was having a fit of giggles.

'Come along, luv. See if you can stand up.' One of the RAF lads who had joined on the end of the line held out his hand to help her to her feet.

Violet looked up into a pair of grey eyes filled with concern, then she followed the line of his nose – it seemed to go on and on – leading to a wide, humorous mouth. Aware that she was staring, she grinned sheepishly, then grasped his hand and staggered painfully to her feet.

'That's the way to do it, Vi,' whispered Sheila. 'Fall at his feet. Clever girl! I'd never have thought of that.'

'Shut up!' hissed Violet, frowning at her friend. Really, Sheila was the limit at times.

The RAF lad held out his arm for her to cling to. 'Now – come and have a sit-down. Have you hurt your leg?'

'No,' replied Violet. 'It's not my leg. It's my . . . er . . . I mean – I sat down rather heavily.' She felt the blush spread right to the roots of her hair.

The lad grinned. 'OK then. Let's be having you.' He guided her to an upholstered bench in an alcove set back from the ballroom floor.

'I'm Tony,' he said as they sat down. He held out a brown hand, scrubbed clean, but Violet could see fine traces of ingrained dirt in the pores and under the fingernails. 'Tony Harris. Aircraftman Second Class – commonly known as A/C Plonk.' He grinned again, even more widely, and a lock of soft brown hair fell over his forehead.

Violet held out her hand, smiling at him. 'I'm Violet Carter. Vi, if you like.'

'No, I prefer Violet,' replied Tony. 'It suits you.'

Violet wondered fleetingly what he meant. She had always thought that her name didn't suit her at all, conjuring up as it did an image of a delicate little flower, whereas Violet felt herself to be big and clumsy.

'A modest violet,' Tony went on. 'I guess you're a bit shy, aren't you?' He raised an eyebrow questioningly.

'I suppose so.' She gave an embarrassed little laugh. 'You're billeted in Blackpool, are you, Tony?' she asked.

'Yes,' he replied. 'That's right. In North Street. I've been here about three weeks. It's not bad as billets go – good grub, pleasant landlady – what more could you want?'

'That's just round the corner from us,' Violet told him. 'My mother has a boarding house – we've got RAF lads too – twenty of them.'

Tony pulled a wry face. 'Seems as though I've been sent to the wrong billet then, doesn't it? Just my luck! Never mind – you're not so far away if you're only round the corner.'

Violet felt herself blushing again. She wasn't used to conversations with boys taking this sort of a turn. In fact, she wasn't used to talking to men at all, except for Tom. There was something in Tony's speech – the way he had of talking right at the back of his throat – that reminded her of Tom.

'You're from Yorkshire, aren't you?' she asked.

'I am that,' said Tony proudly. 'My accent gives me away, does it?'

Violet nodded. 'My brother-in-law comes from Yorkshire, and he talks just like you. He's from Castleburn, in the West Riding.'

'Oh yes – I know it well. We used to go there on charabanc trips. It's lovely there, by the river. I'm from Leeds, meself. There's nowt so lovely about that, not in the centre of the city anyroad. It's all muck and chimneys. Still, it's home, but God knows when I shall see it again . . .' Tony stopped abruptly. He was silent for a moment, staring straight ahead. 'I keep nagging me mother and dad to move out of Leeds, away from the danger. I've an uncle who's got a farm, Ilkley way, and they could go there, but me ma's that stubborn, there's no budging her.'

'There's not much happening yet, is there?' asked Violet. 'There's no bombing or anything over here?'

'No, not yet, but I reckon there will be soon enough, when old Hitler gets going. There's plenty of fighting on the other side of the Channel. I suppose we're bound to get our share here before long.'

'We were certainly prepared for it, weren't we?' said Violet earnestly. 'Gas masks and air-raid shelters and everything, and then nothing happened. It was an anticlimax all right.'

'A pretty girl like you shouldn't be worrying her head about things like that.' Tony winked at her. 'You take it all very seriously, don't you?'

'Yes, I suppose I do,' said Violet. 'I like to know what's going on, and why. I used to chat to my brother-in-law, Tom. He always knew what was happening in different parts of the world. He's in the Army, over in France. What about you, Tony? What are you training for?'

'Engine mechanic, same as I was in Civvy Street. I'd like to have seen some action though – dropped a few bombs on Jerry – but it looks as though I'll be non-operational. They train you for what they think you'll be best at, you see.'

'At least you'll be out of danger, won't you, working with the ground crew? And the aeroplanes have to be maintained.'

'That's one way of looking at it, I suppose,' replied Tony, 'but some blokes think it's a cushy number, staying on the ground. I'm inclined to agree with 'em.'

'You're an engineer in Civvy Street, are you?'

'Garage mechanic. I worked at a big garage near City Square. I spent most of the time flat on me back, tinkering with rich folks' cars. Can't you tell?' He grinned ruefully as he held out his calloused hands.

'A sign of good honest toil.' Violet smiled at him. 'My mother always says "Where there's muck, there's brass".'

'It depends which way you look at it.' Tony laughed. 'There's not so much brass come my way yet. And you don't catch yon fellows with their Rolls Royces getting their hands dirty. They pay me to do that. Still, I don't begrudge 'em their fancy cars. I'll have one like that meself one day with a bit of luck – if I get through this lot in one piece.'

'Have you got a car, Tony?'

'No – not me. A BMX motorbike. It's a smasher, Violet.' His eyes lit up with pleasure. 'It's shut up in me dad's shed at the moment. It wouldn't be patriotic to use it now. Anyroad, petrol's rationed, and she doesn't half gobble it up. That reminds me – do you fancy a drink? I've got a right thirst. Shall we go to the bar?'

Violet hesitated. 'I don't know . . . I've never . . .' She bit her lip. 'You'll think I'm stupid, I know you will, but I've never been in a pub in my life. Mother doesn't approve and . . .'

'Your mother isn't here, is she?' Tony grinned. 'Anyway, it's not like a real pub, and you don't need to have anything alcoholic if you don't want it. Have a lemonade – or you could try a shandy. That's a nice drink and they don't put much beer in it.'

Violet sipped daringly at the shandy. The taste was bitter – she ran her tongue round her mouth tentatively – but pleasant nonetheless.

Her mother would go hairless if she could see her, but, as Tony said, her mother wasn't there. She smiled to herself, feeling all warm inside. It was turning out to be a lovely evening.

'Do you feel like dancing again?' Tony asked. 'Your – er – leg's all right now, is it?' he added, grinning.

'Perfectly, thank you,' said Violet, a trifle huffily, but Tony didn't seem to notice.

He must be nearly six foot, she thought, which was fortunate because she was a tall girl. Their steps blended well together – Tony was no great shakes at dancing either – and Violet felt the firmness of his arm round her waist, the roughness of his chin brushing against her forehead.

'This is a lovely way to spend an evening . . .' the organ played, and Violet smiled to herself again. Yes . . . it was a lovely evening.

'Bid me discourse, I will enchant thine ear,' whispered Tony.

'What?' asked Violet, frowning.

Tony laughed. 'That's what it says up there – over the stage.' He pointed to the gilded lettering. 'Is it a quotation or something?'

'Oh, that – yes, it's Shakespeare,' replied Violet.

> 'Bid me discourse, I will enchant thine ear,
> Or, like a fairy, trip upon the green,
> Or, like nymph with long dishevelled hair
> Dance on the sands and yet no footing seen.

We learned it at school.'

'You're quite a lass, Violet Carter,' Tony whispered, holding her close. 'I can't pretend I know what it means, but I like the bit about the dishevelled hair.' She felt his hand caressing her own hair. 'And the dancing on the sands. Shall we go and have a dance on Blackpool Sands, Violet? Away from the crowds where nobody can see us?'

Violet giggled. 'Me mother'd kill me!'

'How about the Winter Gardens then? They've got a smashing dance floor there. Will you go with me one night, Violet?'

Violet nodded. 'Yes – thanks. I'd love to.'

'The Empress Ballroom's used as a gym during the day,' Tony went on. 'We do our PT there. The Winter Garden's fairly buzzing with us all. Kit inspections in the Floral Hall, training films in the Opera House, Morse code lessons in the Olympia . . .'

'And dancing, as usual, at night?'

'Yes, that's right. We work hard, so why shouldn't we play hard too?'

'Vi – don't go home without me, will you?' Joyce ran after them as they walked hand in hand off the ballroom floor. 'I don't like asking you really.' She looked pointedly at their clasped hands. 'But Mother'll be ever so mad if I walk home on my own, and Sheila's still mooning around over that fellow.'

'Of course I won't leave you, you daft thing,' Violet assured her. 'We came together and we'll go home together. Wait for me outside the cloakroom.'

'What about . . . ?' Joyce whispered, nodding her head in Tony's direction.

'I don't know,' Violet whispered back, 'but it doesn't matter anyway. See you later.'

Dusk was falling as they walked home through the quiet streets. Tony linked arms with Violet and Joyce, one on each side of him. Double British Summer Time meant that it was still light at ten o'clock at night.

'Daft time to be going home from a dance, isn't it?' remarked Tony. 'Still, I suppose the bigwigs know what they're doing, making sure we're all tucked up in our beds at a reasonable hour.'

'"Early to bed, early to rise" – I suppose that's what they're thinking,' added Violet, 'and we've all got to be fresh for the next day's work, haven't we?'

They left Joyce at the end of Green Street and walked the fifty or so yards to Pleasant View in a companionable silence. Violet hoped that her mother wasn't looking out of the window. She didn't feel like going into a long, involved explanation about Tony tonight. Soon, perhaps – for Violet felt sure that he would be around long enough for her to have to do some explaining – but tonight was all her own, to be shared with no one.

She found herself wondering what would happen if he kissed her. His nose was so very long, and hers, too, was anything but short. Surely they would get in the way? They paused by the gate.

'Thanks for a lovely evening, Violet,' Tony said softly, squeezing her hand. 'Don't forget about the Winter Gardens. I'll call round and see you soon, and meet your ma. OK?'

'Yes.' Violet nodded contentedly. 'OK. Thanks, Tony – for everything.'

He didn't kiss her. She didn't know whether to be glad or sorry.

Chapter 9

Pleasant View was a hive of activity. The RAF recruits stampeded up the stairs; they queued on the landing for the WC – you could hear their ribald comments – 'Come on, Sam. What the hell are you doing in there? Making your will? Too many baked beans, more like . . .'; they devoured the tasty meals that Annie and Jenny prepared, and at night they congregated in the lounge, playing cards, or reading, or writing letters, or they gathered round the old upright piano.

'Bless 'em all, bless 'em all, The long and the short and the tall . . .' they chorused, as Jack, an AC2 with a touch as gentle as an elephant, thumped out the tunes. There were only twenty of them, but it seemed more like a hundred. The place echoed with their clatter and clamour and cheerful chatter.

The house was more like a home than it had ever been. You couldn't help but be affected by their good-humoured gaiety and zest for living. Annie's maternal heart was touched, and she responded to them with a warmth that her own two daughters couldn't evoke. She had always wanted a son, but the good Lord hadn't seen fit to send her one. Daughters were all very well, but you couldn't be free and easy with a daughter. You had to keep them on a tight rein – let them know who was the boss – or goodness knows what tricks they might get up to. What wouldn't she have given to have a son like one of these lovely lads.

'Now, think on, our Jenny – we've got to make them feel at home,' she told her daughter, soon after the RAF recruits arrived. 'What does it matter if there's a bit of noise? We'll just have to put up with it. I'm having none of this lights-out-by-ten business and keeping quiet in the lounge as though they're in gaol. That Mrs Barber across the road, she's trying to rule hers with a rod of iron. Poor lads!' Annie sighed. 'They're somebody's sons – all of 'em –

and they'll have to face God knows what dangers when they start flying them aeroplanes.'

'They're not all going to be pilots, Mother,' Jenny tried to explain. 'They're training for all sorts of jobs – electricians, mechanics, wireless operators, and all that . . . They won't all be flying aeroplanes.'

'So you know it all, do you, madam?' said Annie, folding her arms and wagging her head at Jenny. 'It's called the Royal Air Force, isn't it? So I reckon they'll all be flying when it gets started. They've got the Army – soldiers like your Tom – to fight on the ground and do the ordinary jobs.'

Jenny turned back to her endless task of peeling potatoes. There was no point in arguing with her mother. To Annie the RAF meant only one thing – flying. To Tom it meant glamour. 'Posh voices and curly moustaches' was how he summed up the Royal Air Force. The 'Brylcreem boys', they were sometimes called, but the ones that were billeted at Pleasant View were ordinary enough. Friendly, likeable lads from modest backgrounds such as Jenny's own. There didn't seem to be anything glamorous about them. They were always ready for a laugh and a joke. Jenny was growing accustomed to the wolf whistles and the shouts of 'What are you doing tonight, darling?' and other such remarks when she went into the dining room in her frilly apron. She found herself looking forward to her encounters with them. There was nothing like male admiration to make a girl sparkle.

Even Violet was coming out of her shell and smiling shyly at their facetious remarks. Not that Violet was at home all that much nowadays. When she wasn't at the factory she was often out with Joyce and Sheila, or with the RAF lad she had met at the Tower, Tony Harris, but Annie made sure that she pulled her weight in the house at weekends.

Annie was a different person since the arrival of the airmen.

'Eeh – you're a rum 'un and no mistake! Get on with yer bother!' she chuckled in response to their teasing, her face going red and her short-sighted eyes filling up with tears of merriment, so much that she had to take off her glasses and wipe her eyes on her voluminous apron. They called her Ma, and sought her out to chat to her about their girlfriends or their families, and there was nothing she wouldn't do to make them feel at home.

The only person who seemed to be oblivious to the charms of the

Royal Air Force was Cousin Ada. She went about her duties stoically, her mouth set in a grim line, never a flicker of amusement showing in her sharp eyes.

'This is a right carry-on. It's like a bear garden,' she moaned, rubbing furiously with her duster at a ring-mark left by a wet glass on the piano. 'There'll be no decent furniture left, I'm telling you, Aunt Annie, by the time this lot's got themselves away.'

'It's no business of yours,' retorted Annie. 'It's my furniture – you're just paid to keep it clean – and it's all in a good cause. I don't begrudge the poor lads their pleasure, and if the furniture takes a bit of a hammering it's just too bad. Anyway, I reckon there'll be compensation if they do any damage, after it's all over – but it's still got nowt to do with you!'

She glared at Ada, who glared back. Relations between them hadn't improved since Ada had started coming three times a week, but Jenny suspected that her mother and her cousin enjoyed their verbal sparring.

Ada was a good worker, strong and willing, in spite of her grumbling. She could 'bottom' a room in next to no time, and the windows sparkled and the furniture gleamed at the onslaught of her yellow duster. She was a source of amusement to the male guests, though she was unaware of it.

'I know what she could do with,' Jenny overheard one fellow saying to his mate, with a nudge and a wink, and a nod at Ada's back, stiff as a ramrod, 'and it isn't a plate of fish and chips.'

Jenny grinned to herself. She was inclined to agree with him. Poor old Ada; somewhere along the line she had missed the boat. She joked quite freely about being an old maid, and on the shelf, but working in a household full of personable young men, Jenny thought, must make her even more aware of her spinsterhood. There was nothing to be ashamed of in being a spinster, to be sure, but, if Ada didn't mind, why did she go on about it so much? She might have been better off settling for that milkman who had designs on her, if the married state meant so much to her.

Tom was now serving on the other side of the Channel. His letters home were guarded – Tom was not one to divulge military secrets – but, even so, many of his phrases were blacked out by the censor's pencil, so Jenny had very little idea of where he was or what he was doing. He was more concerned about what was happening at home; how was Patsy, and was that dear little Rosie still with them? – than with his own news. Jenny missed him in an undemonstrative sort of way but his letters, instead of bringing him closer, seemed to make Jenny feel even more detached from him. He had never been a good letter-writer – neither was she – and the phrases he used were stilted and constrained. They told Jenny nothing at all. She thought of him fondly, but she didn't yearn for him. She was too busy cooking and looking after the RAF lads, and caring for Patsy and Rosie to worry unduly about Tom. He was doing what he had longed to do. He was serving his country in a time of mortal danger. Jenny prayed nightly for his safety, but she felt sure that he was content and that valour would bring its own reward.

At first, Jenny had waited on the RAF recruits in the dining room, carrying a heavy tray stacked high with plates of steaming food. It was back-breaking work, and time-consuming too. Pleasant View was badly designed for serving visitors. The back kitchen, where all the cooking was done, opened off the living-room – generally referred to as the kitchen – which meant that Jenny had to carry her laden tray through the kitchen, along the hall, and into the dining room scores of times before they were all served with their dinner, pudding, and a cup of tea to follow.

'There must be an easier way,' she grumbled to her mother. 'Whoever designed this house didn't give much thought to the poor waitress.'

'You never complained before,' retorted Annie, 'when we had visitors from Wigan and all over. You think you're too good, do you, madam, to wait on His Majesty's Forces? I reckon you should be proud, never mind being so toffee-nosed about it.'

Jenny seethed inwardly, but she managed to bite her tongue, as she usually did. There were times, though, when she could have hit her mother. She probably would, one of these days.

'It's not like that at all, Mother,' she replied sharply. 'Besides, I had our Violet to help me before, and young Mary from across the road.' Violet still helped at weekends, but Mary had found regular employment at Woolworth's and was no longer available. 'I've been thinking,' she went on cautiously. 'If we had that wall knocked through, we could have a serving hatch from here straight through into the dining room. It would save a lot of unnecessary work.'

106

'It'd cost unnecessary brass too,' Annie retaliated. 'You must think I'm made of money.'

All the same, the joiner from round the corner was there the next day, jotting down measurements in his well-thumbed notebook.

'Nothing too elaborate, mind,' said Annie, 'but it's a good idea of mine, don't you think so, Mr Gibson? It came to me as quick as a flash in bed last night. Now, why don't we knock a hole in the wall, I says to meself, straight through into the back kitchen. It'll save our Jenny such a lot of traipsing backwards and forwards. She's run off her feet, poor lass.'

Jenny smiled to herself wryly. 'It was a brilliant idea of yours, Mother,' she remarked after Mr Gibson had departed, scratching his head and grumbling about labour costs and the shortage of materials. 'However did you manage to think of it?'

'We'll have less of your lip, my girl,' was Annie's only comment, but Jenny noticed a faint smile hovering round her mother's lips, and a momentary flash of humour softening her eyes as she nodded curtly at her daughter.

The work was completed in about ten days. Now the airmen formed an orderly queue at the hatch, plates in hands, while Jenny and Annie spooned out dollops of mashed potato or steamed pudding, and generous helpings of bright yellow custard or thick brown gravy.

The two women became expert at stretching the meagre allowances, concocting tasty dishes out of corned beef and spam, dried egg and wholemeal flour, and eking out as well as they could the statutory rations of two ounces of butter, four ounces of cheese and four ounces of bacon for each person.

'I think we'll make a Woolton pie this morning, Mother,' Jenny declared, one bright sunny morning towards the end of May.

'And what might that be when it's at home?' asked Annie, sniffing.

'You know – Lord Woolton – the fellow in charge of the Ministry of Food. It's named after him,' Jenny explained. 'They mentioned it on *The Kitchen Front* the other morning.'

'Go on then – what do we need?' asked Annie. 'I must admit, you're a dab hand at stretching the rations, our Jenny. You're getting to be a fair cook an' all,' she added, somewhat grudgingly.

107

That from her mother was praise indeed. Jenny cheerfully gathered together the ingredients – equal quantities of diced potatoes, cauliflower, swedes and carrots, a few spring onions (quite a luxury), oatmeal and gravy browning. When she had cooked them for ten minutes on top of the stove, she transferred the mixture into enamel pie dishes, covering the top of each one with a pastry crust.

'There,' she said, as she pushed them into the oven, 'that's your Woolton pie. It can cook nice and steady all morning, then we'll serve it up with some rich brown gravy. It'll be a dish the King wouldn't turn his nose up at, I'll tell you, Mother.'

'You're full of the joys of spring this morning,' commented Annie. 'What's that in aid of? Have you had a letter from Tom?'

'No, Mother. I haven't heard from him this week. But it's as well to keep our spirits up if we can. There's no point in being downhearted. We've got Mr Churchill leading us now, and he's the right man for the job, according to our Violet.'

With the resignation of Neville Chamberlain at the beginning of May 1940, Winston Churchill had become Prime Minister and formed a National Government. He had inspired everyone with his rallying call to the nation: '. . . I have nothing to offer but blood, toil, tears and sweat.' Chilling words, but destined to bring a glow to the heart and a lift to the spirit of every true Briton. Jenny had been against the war and all that it stood for from the beginning, and she still remained uninterested in political manoeuvring, but she was moved by the leader's words.

'Aye, our Vi usually knows what she's talking about,' replied Annie. 'She's like a dog with two tails, isn't she, since she met the RAF bloke? He seems a nice lad. He was on the front row when noses were given out, sure enough, but apart from that he's all right. I reckon she could do a lot worse.'

'He can't help his nose, Mother. I think he's quite a nice-looking lad,' Jenny replied. 'But give our Violet a chance. She only met him about three weeks ago. It can't be all that serious yet.'

'Strange things happen in wartime.' Annie nodded knowingly. 'I remember what happened in the last war – it only seems like five minutes ago an' all. Young couples nipping down the aisle together when they'd only known one another five minutes. Anyroad, time will tell, and he's a nice lad.'

Annie had taken to Tony Harris the first time she'd met him. He had called round and courteously asked if he could take Violet dancing, and now they went out together a few nights a week. It was the RAF uniform that had done it, Jenny reflected. To Annie, the boys in blue could do no wrong and Violet had redeemed herself in her mother's eyes by bringing one of them home. Annie's attitude towards her daughters was – for some of the time – a good deal more tolerant these days. War was a great leveller of personalities.

Violet had a sparkle in her eyes and a spring in her step that her sister had never seen before. Jolly good luck to the girl, thought Jenny; it was high time she had a bit of pleasure. Jenny wished her well, but hoped that she wouldn't get hurt. Violet was still like a child in many ways, naïve and extremely vulnerable, and Tony Harris was her first boyfriend. She wasn't experienced in dealing with men . . . not that I'm all that knowledgeable either, thought Jenny wryly, married at nineteen to the first man that asked me . . .

The Woolton pie was a great success. The steaming platefuls of the tasty mixture, topped by a tempting golden-brown crust, gave off a mouthwatering aroma. Jenny could hear the comments of the lads.

'Jolly good grub!'

'Even better than my mother makes.'

'This lot'll stick to your ribs, all right.'

'You've scored a winner with this concoction,' Annie commented. 'It didn't cost much either. Well done, lass.'

Jenny smiled happily at her mother. Her spirits were high today. She smiled at Sergeant Robert Cunningham too, as he diffidently approached the serving hatch, his empty plate in his hand.

'Can I be like Oliver Twist and ask for more?' he said quietly, holding out his plate.

He was a well-spoken young man who had been the sergeant in charge of the billet for the last few weeks. He wasn't much older than the rest of the men – Jenny guessed that he would be in his middle twenties – but he seemed different from them in subtle ways. He sometimes sat apart, not joining in the boisterous revelry in the lounge at night. He didn't appear stuck-up, though, just quieter. He was usually reading or writing letters, but Jenny had seen him on occasions laughing and joking with the other lads, and he was very popular with them all.

'You may certainly have some more, Sergeant Cunningham,' Jenny replied, giving him the courtesy of his full title. Most of the lads were referred to by their Christian names – they liked it that way – but she hadn't had much conversation with the sergeant yet. She put a second substantial helping on to his plate. 'I'm glad you enjoyed it. It's Woolton pie.'

'Just like they're serving at the Savoy Hotel in London.' The sergeant's blue eyes twinkled. 'My compliments to your chef. No doubt she trained at the Savoy too?'

'Our Jenny's the chef,' Annie joined in eagerly. 'She's done us proud with this, hasn't she, Sergeant Cunningham?'

'She has indeed. They'll all be queuing up for second helpings. Look – here they come.'

Jenny found herself blushing as the young sergeant smiled at her. She felt a glow of happiness spread right through her, from the tips of her toes to the top of her head. It was inexplicable.

'Jenny, do you think you could manage to come in tonight and see to the suppers?' Annie asked, when the mountain of washing-up had been cleared. 'Mrs Barber's asked me to go with her to a whist drive at the church hall. It's in aid of the war effort, so I said I'd try and go. Besides, I like a good game of whist. You'll probably be on your own – our Violet'll be out with that Tony, as likely as not.'

Jenny popped in occasionally in the evening, but, as a rule, after they had served the tea and washed up, her time was her own.

'Yes, I'll try, Mother,' she replied. 'You go and enjoy yourself. You could do with a change.' She smiled at her mother, feeling unusually benevolent towards her. Annie, too, was surprisingly warm-hearted today. There must be something in the air. . . . 'I daresay Eileen will come in and look after the girls for a while, if I ask her. Charlie'll see to the boys for her.'

Eileen's husband Charlie wasn't in the forces, nor was it likely that he ever would be. He had flat feet, short sight and an asthmatic chest. Jenny suspected in the past that he was work shy too, but he was holding on pretty well to his present job on the maintenance staff of the Electricity Board. It wasn't exactly a reserved occupation, but Charlie was exaggerating its importance at the moment. Civilian fellows had to try to justify themselves some-how, surrounded as they were by a sea of air-force blue and with their mates joining up left, right and centre.

Charlie was always willing to look after the three boys and Ben, the evacuee, who was now happily settled with them. That left Eileen free to go round and have a chat with her old friend Jenny, or to look after Jenny's two little girls, as she readily agreed to do this evening.

Jenny brewed the tea in a large enamel pot, then opened the serving hatch into the lounge – which was really the far end of the long dining room – to count heads. Some of the lads would be out, dancing, or at the pictures, but there was usually a few of them in throughout the evening. There were eight of them tonight. Jenny noticed Robert Cunningham in a corner by the window, his dark curly head bent over a book. She put the cups and saucers on a tray with the milk and a small amount of sugar, and pushed it through the hatch, then she carried in the teapot and a plate which held a selection of Peak Frean's biscuits. She had wondered whether or not to take in the tin – the lads weren't bothered overmuch about niceties like doilies and traycloths – but, if she did, they'd probably eat the lot. They had already had three substantial meals – cooked breakfast, midday dinner and high tea – but, as her mother said, they all seemed to have hollow legs.

'Tea up, lads,' she called cheerily. 'I'll leave it here on this little table. Just come and help yourselves.'

Robert Cunningham looked up from his book and smiled at her. She smiled back. They looked at one another for a few seconds – it seemed much longer – their eyes appraising one another, until Jenny, flustered, looked away. She bent over the tea table and started arranging the spoons in the saucers, busily engaging her hands and her mind with the small task, anything to stop the pink flush that was staining her cheeks, and the slight trembling of her fingertips.

The lads congregated round the table, pouring out the strong brown liquid, helping themselves to milk and sugar and biscuits. Jenny turned to go.

'Aren't you having a cup of tea, Mrs Bradshaw? Do stay and have one with us.' The sergeant was at her side, looking down at her from his lofty height. He was tall, like their Violet's young man, about six foot, she guessed.

Jenny smiled at him. 'Why not?' she said. 'I think I will. I'll just go and get another cup.'

Her feet seemed to have wings as she sped along to the kitchen and back again. Whatever was the matter with her? Behaving like a silly schoolgirl, just because a young man had smiled at her and asked her to have a cup of tea.

'Come and sit here,' Robert Cunningham gestured quietly to the armchair opposite him.

Jenny was glad to sink into its comfortable depths. She had been on her feet most of the day and the rest was more than welcome. She closed her eyes for a second and put her hand to her mouth, stifling a yawn.

'Are you tired?' The sergeant looked at her in concern. 'I'm sure you must be, looking after a houseful of airmen. You don't get much rest, do you, Mrs Bradshaw?'

'I'm all right – really I am.' Jenny nodded. 'Just a bit weary, but a cup of tea will soon bring me round . . . and my name's Jenny,' she added, smiling at him.

'Yes – I know. It's a pretty name – it's just right for you. I'd like to call you Jenny, if I may? I'm Robert – or Rob, if you prefer it.'

'No . . .' Jenny looked at him steadily. 'I think I prefer Robert.'

He grinned at her. 'That's settled then. Now – Jenny – we can't have you run off your feet like this, working all the hours God sends. I've been talking it over with the lads, and we're going to make a rota of volunteers to help you with the chores – washing up, peeling the potatoes, that sort of thing. Do you think that's a good idea?'

'Oh yes – that would be wonderful – Robert.' Jenny leaned forward in her chair, her eyes lighting up at the prospect of more help in the kitchen. 'Mind you, I don't know what me . . . my mother will say. She thinks that you lads are already doing enough, serving your King and Country. I think she feels that it's a privilege for us to look after you; it's our contribution to the war effort.'

'And a jolly good show it is too,' said Robert, 'but that doesn't mean that you can't do with some help. Anyway, we're supposed to pull our weight, you know. The top brass are very keen on us sharing the workload and showing our appreciation. We had a lecture about it the other day . . . So we'll start tomorrow after breakfast. Two lads to do the washing-up, and two to peel the spuds. OK?'

'That's marvellous.' Jenny smiled her thanks at him, experiencing again the warm glow of contentment that she had felt earlier in the day.

She viewed him surreptitiously as she sipped her tea. Tall, dark and handsome was a phrase that sprang readily to mind, one often used in the romantic stories she read; it fitted Robert Cunningham to a T. Here was a young man to whom Tom's description of 'glamour boy' might very well apply. His black hair was thick and wavy and his eyes were grey-blue, like the Irish sea on a summer's day.

'Have you been writing home, Robert?' Jenny looked enquiringly at the notepad and the couple of addressed envelopes which were lying on the wide arm of the chair next to him.

'Yes – to my parents, and to my . . . to a young lady I know in Coventry.' Robert reached into his breast pocket for his wallet and produced a small snapshot. 'This is Marjorie,' he said, holding it out to Jenny.

'Your girlfriend?' she asked, raising her eyebrows.

'Sort of. I've known her for ages – we were at school together,' Robert explained. 'She's a nurse at a hospital in Coventry. I expect we'll get married when all this is over. That is if . . .' He hesitated. 'I can't ask her to marry me while everything is so unsettled. One day, perhaps.'

She's a lucky girl, thought Jenny ruefully, feeling a sudden wave of jealousy engulf her, to be replaced almost immediately by a realisation of her own stupidity. What on earth was she thinking about? She was a married woman – happily married, or reasonably so, she had always supposed – and Robert was just a lonely RAF lad seeking a bit of female company to while away the evening. But the thoughts about the girl in the snapshot continued. I wonder why he doesn't ask her to marry him now? Lots of young couples were getting married with very little thought for the future. Perhaps he wasn't very sure of his feelings, or perhaps she wasn't . . . ? Jenny looked at the photo of a round-faced smiling girl, with short hair waving gently above a wide forehead. She was wearing a simple cotton dress and leaning against a gate leading into a field. Just an ordinary girl and an ordinary English scene, the sort of photograph that thousands of young men must be carrying about with them at this moment.

'She looks nice,' said Jenny, handing it back to Robert.

'She is.' He smiled and tucked the photo back into his wallet.

'And do you come from Coventry as well, Robert?'

'Yes. I work – or should I say, I used to work with my father. He has a small business there.'

Jenny couldn't help but notice Robert's somewhat refined accent as he referred to 'my father'. I would probably have said 'me dad', she thought.

'The shop's on the outskirts of Coventry,' Robert went on. 'He sells radios and gramophones and small electrical appliances. That's why I'm training to be a wireless operator. I've always enjoyed tinkering around, trying to make things work. We'd just started selling gramophone records as well, in a separate part of the shop. That's the side of the business I'd like to build up eventually.' He hesitated, then added quietly, 'God willing.'

There was a split second's pause, in which they looked at one another in complete understanding. Jenny shuddered inwardly. These young men must all have to live with the knowledge that their plans and hopes and dreams might never reach fruition. Yet one had to go on planning and hoping and dreaming, holding fast to the faith that there would be a future.

'Do you like music, Robert?' Jenny asked quickly, to put an end to the emotive silence.

'Yes, I do,' he replied eagerly. 'Tuneful music, that is. Nothing too highbrow. I like Chopin, and Mozart – and a good brass band.'

Chopin and Mozart sounded very highbrow to Jenny. She couldn't remember ever having heard any of their music. Mozart was that boy-genius, wasn't he? Composing symphonies and suchlike when he was only five years old. But she knew something about brass bands, though her knowledge was second-hand.

'Tom – that's my husband, he's in the Army – he has some brass-band records,' she said enthusiastically. 'He likes regimental marches and that kind of thing.'

Just for a moment Jenny thought she saw a fleeting glimpse of regret on Robert's face – or could she have imagined it? – as she mentioned Tom. But he smiled and nodded and answered her eagerly. 'Good stirring stuff. I like them myself. And what about you, Jenny? What are you doing with yourself while Tom's away, apart from looking after us, of course? What do you do in the evenings?'

'I listen to the wireless quite a lot when the girls are in bed. And I knit – Patsy and Rosie keep me busy. Or I read – I love reading . ._. What's that book, Robert?' Jenny pointed to the blue leather volume which was pushed down the side of the chair. The gold lettering on the spine was practically worn away and the cover was shabby, showing signs of constant handling.

'Oh, this is an old favourite. You can tell by the state of it. It's by Thomas Hardy – *Far from the Madding Crowd*. I must have read it dozens of times.'

'My sister reads Thomas Hardy's books.' Jenny was glad that she had at least heard of the author. 'She was a clever girl, our Violet. She still is, of course. She got a few of Hardy's books as prizes at school.'

'And have you read them, Jenny?'

'No, not me.' Jenny laughed. 'I'm afraid Ethel M. Dell's about my limit. I like a nice romantic book – nothing too serious, though – and it has to be a good story.'

'Then you would like Thomas Hardy, and he's not difficult to read either. You couldn't find a much more romantic book than this.' Robert held out his shabby copy of *Far from the Madding Crowd*. 'It's about three men, all in love with the same woman.'

'What a very lucky lady,' said Jenny, laughing again. 'And does it end happily? I think the best stories are the ones with a happy ending.'

'It has a . . . satisfying ending.' Robert narrowed his eyes thoughtfully. 'Yes, it was the only possible ending really. The man who had loved her steadfastly throughout – Gabriel Oak – won her in the end.'

'He's certainly got the right name,' Jenny commented. 'There's nothing more steady than an oak tree.'

'He was the salt of the earth, was old Gabriel. Nothing could shake him, and Bathsheba treated him shockingly at times. Here, Jenny – would you like to read it? I promise you won't find it boring.' Robert held out the book again. 'Read it, and then tell me what you think about it. Do you think Gabriel deserved Bathsheba, or – which is more to the point – did she deserve him?'

Robert smiled, wrinkling the laughter lines around his eyes and mouth. His face lit up, and Jenny noticed that his eyes shone a deeper blue, as blue as the cornflowers that bloomed in the summertime in Martha Bradshaw's cottage garden. She had so enjoyed her little chat with him – she was sure he had enjoyed it too – and she hoped they would be able to repeat it before long. She was lonely . . . and so was Robert. And Tom was so very far away . . . but Robert was here . . .

Chapter 10

Jenny glanced curiously at the letter with the Yorkshire postmark as she picked it up off the mat. She didn't correspond regularly with Tom's relations; none of them were keen on letter writing, but now Jenny thought she recognised Martha Bradshaw's spidery handwriting. She hoped it wasn't bad news – a letter usually denoted a crisis of some sort – or maybe Martha was worried about her son's whereabouts. That was only natural, but Jenny knew she wouldn't be able to help her. She hadn't heard from Tom for a fortnight and the news from France was not good. Worrying reports were filtering through of the retreat of the Allied Forces and their evacuation from Dunkirk; where Tom was she had no idea.

She slit open the thin blue envelope and scanned the contents, smiling as the written words on the page so quickly evoked her fond remembrance of Tom's mother. Jenny could almost hear her speaking. She was, she wrote, '. . . pretty well, considering, apart from a twinge of rheumatics and that's only to be expected, isn't it, Jenny dear, because I'll be 78 next birthday . . .' Martha was incredible for her age. It was hard to believe that she was so much older than Jenny's own mother, who was not yet sixty. Martha went on to say that she was concerned about Tom, but prayed continually for his safety and felt sure that '. . . the good Lord will watch over him'.

Jenny caught her breath as she read the next words. '. . . Our Lilian has not been well and I worry about her. She's so pale and listless and shows no interest in anything except her work. This war seems to be getting to her though there's not much sign of it here apart from the blackout. A week in Blackpool would work wonders for her, all that lovely sea air, and I'd be so pleased, Jenny love, if you could put her up . . .'

Lilian arrived a few days later and Jenny went to Central Station to meet her. An uneasy friendship had existed, over the years, between the two young women. Jenny felt that Lilian was never entirely comfortable in her presence, envious perhaps of the intimacy of the bond between husband and wife, a closeness that it seemed unlikely Lilian herself would ever experience. She was thirty-three now and, as far as Jenny knew, had never had a boyfriend. Jenny had hoped that she would meet someone, but the years had passed and Lilian was still single. Poor Lilian . . . It was odd that that was how Jenny always thought of her.

Jenny's heart went out to her sister-in-law as she saw her coming along the platform, her thin frame pulled sideways with the weight of her heavy suitcase. The headscarf knotted tightly under her chin did nothing to add to her appearance, and the brown costume jacket which she wore over a limp summer dress had seen better days. Jenny was struck again by Lilian's resemblance to Martha Bradshaw, more apparent as the years went by. Jenny feared that Lilian was spending too much time in the confines of home with only her mother for company, and so she was growing like her. Not that it was Martha's doing; Jenny knew that Martha had often urged her daughter to go out more and to make friends, but to no avail. Lilian looked like an elderly woman already, well ahead of her time.

Her beady brown eyes lit up at the sight of Jenny and she seemed genuinely pleased to see her. Maybe there would be a chance this week for the two young women to draw closer together. Jenny hoped that it might be so. She was aware of a stiffening of Lilian's body as she embraced her, as though she was unused to physical contact, then she put her head on one side in a birdlike movement as she awaited Jenny's kiss on her cheek. Her face was unlined, unlike her mother's, but in every other way she might have been almost the same age.

And Jenny, to her chagrin, found her so incredibly boring. She braced herself mentally as Lilian launched herself into yet another tale about Woolworth's. Her place of employment was the young woman's only topic of conversation, which was hardly surprising, Jenny thought, when you considered that it was all she ever did. Her life revolved round the shop and its employees.

'. . . and we've heard tell as how sweets'll be the next thing to be rationed, Jenny. It might only be a rumour, mind, but we're not

118

getting the stocks in with sugar being rationed . . . I asked 'em to move me to the hardware counter. It didn't seem patriotic somehow to be serving sweets when there's a war on . . .' Jenny didn't see the reasoning behind this remark. '. . . so I'm selling hammers and nails and suchlike now. It seems a bit more meaningful, if you see what I mean.' Jenny didn't.

Patsy and Rosie, however, were excited at having a visitor, Rosie especially so at acquiring a new auntie that she hadn't met before.

'Can she sleep in our room?' Patsy had asked eagerly. 'Then Rosie and I can sleep together. There's plenty of room in my bed and we won't giggle and keep her awake, honest we won't.'

Jenny had readily agreed when Lilian said she didn't mind sharing a room with the two girls. The sleeping arrangements had worried Jenny. There was an empty space in the big double bed . . . but that had been Tom's. She was reluctant to share with Lilian, and she knew intuitively that Lilian wouldn't like it either, but, luckily, the girls had come up with the obvious solution.

They were delighted at having an auntie who actually worked in Woolworth's – a magical place, full of all manner of entrancing objects, where they were occasionally taken as a special treat – and Jenny was very relieved when Lilian offered to take them there on Saturday afternoon.

'It's much bigger than your titchy little Woolworth's,' Patsy assured her, remembering the somewhat inferior store from her visits to Castleburn.

'Yes, it's enormous,' Rosie joined in, 'and there's all sorts of things what you can buy for sixpence.'

Jenny breathed a sigh of relief as she watched them disappearing down the street. She was finding it a strain having Lilian there, especially as the young woman very rarely left her side. Martha's idea had been for her to benefit from the bracing sea breezes – she certainly looked washed-out and weary – but Jenny had managed to persuade her only once, so far, to walk on the promenade on her own. Jenny couldn't accompany her; she still had her duties at the boarding house – or billet, as it was now called – although Annie had been very accommodating about giving her a few hours off now and again.

When she had tidied round, Jenny plumped up the cushions on

the easy chair; she'd sit down in a minute and have a well-earned rest. She gave a tut of annoyance as she heard a noise at the front door. Lilian and the girls were back early. Damn! She had been looking forward to an odd half-hour or so on her own. It sounded like a key turning in the lock, but Lilian didn't have a key . . .

The next minute Tom walked into the kitchen; staggered would have been a more fitting description, for this was a very different Tom from the one who had gone off to war the September before with a light in his eyes at the thought of facing – and vanquishing – the enemy. Now he looked dead on his feet, completely dejected and disillusioned.

'Tom . . . I can hardly believe it.' Jenny rushed over to him and put her arms round him placing her cheek against his.

His kiss was just a perfunctory peck on the cheek. 'Hello, love. I'm whacked . . .' was all he said as he flung his kitbag on to the floor.

'But . . . why didn't you let me know? I'd no idea . . .'

'There wasn't time, love. I got a train as soon as I could after we landed at Harwich. Eh, Jenny . . . it were a bad do. I can't tell you all about it now. I'm fagged out.' He leaned his head back in the easy chair and closed his eyes. 'Make us a cup of tea, love . . .'

'Your Lilian's here,' she told him later, when he had divested himself of his army gear and seemed a little more relaxed.

'Lilian . . . where? What's she doing here then?' He glanced around him in bewilderment, seeming disorientated and confused.

'She's having a little holiday. Your mother thought a few days here would do her good. She's gone into town with the girls.' Tom hadn't asked about them yet.

'Oh aye, our Patsy . . . and young Rosie,' he said now, as though he were just bringing them to mind. 'It'll be nice to see 'em again.' But his grey eyes didn't shine with anticipation; Jenny could see that they were dulled with disappointment and a quiet anguish.

Tom was home for a couple of weeks, awaiting his call back to his camp in the south of England. Jenny's heart ached when she saw how changed he was. She silently watched him as, from time to time, he went into a trance, staring fixedly across the room. Even his beloved Patsy and dear little Rosie, to whom he had taken such a fancy at Christmas, failed to arouse more than a token response to their fun and laughter.

But Jenny, to her surprise, found that she had reason to be

grateful for Lilian's presence. The brother and sister had been quietly delighted to see one another. Jenny had seen an odd tear glinting in the corner of Tom's eye as he greeted his sister. He had hastily brushed it away as Lilian, seemingly without emotion, kissed his cheek. Lilian wasn't much of a one for kissing, but her joy at seeing him again so unexpectedly showed in her flushed cheeks and shining eyes. Jenny tried not to be resentful at Tom's tears; she hadn't evoked such a response at his first sight of her, she thought wryly, but Lilian, she knew, was a reminder of his home in Yorkshire, and his childhood. His links with his family had remained strong. Even though they very rarely corresponded his heart was there, amidst the dark limestone hills, and Jenny knew that, eventually, the hills of home would call him back.

Now with the unforeseen arrival of her brother, Lilian was persuaded to make the most of the fresh sea breezes and the delights that, even in wartime, Blackpool had to offer. The two of then went for long walks on the promenade or around Stanley Park, and Tom, for a time at least, seemed to forget his worries and preoccupation with the war. Jenny had no idea what they talked about when they were together. She wondered if Lilian was boring Tom, too, with her endless tales about Woolworth's, but she thought not. The memories of the pair of them stretched further back than Jenny could go, and Yorkshire folk were great on reminiscing . . .

Poor Lilian . . . She had so little in her life and if her brother could bring her some happiness, even for just a short time, then Jenny was glad. The young woman looked happier and much healthier now than when she had first arrived, and Jenny was pleased to be able to share her husband. The sharing, though, could never be anything but unequal. Jenny was Tom's first love. His feeling for her surpassed everything. Jenny had always known that and she knew also, to her regret, that her love for her husband did not nearly measure up to his love for her. She had been pleased to see him, though, there was no doubt about that, and there was no sign of the constraint between them of which Jenny had been so painfully aware at Christmas. But Tom was dreadfully weary; not a gallant hero, which, she was sure, was how he had pictured himself before this wretched war started, but a tired and a sadly disillusioned man. Her relief when he walked through the door, after so many weeks of worrying and wondering about his whereabouts, had been overwhelming. Still, though, there was this feeling of unreality, that Tom was just a visitor and that soon he would be gone again.

Lilian lay in bed, staring unseeingly into the darkness which was illuminated only by a tiny flicker from the nightlight next to Patsy and Rosie's bed. She was wide awake and she knew that sleep might elude her for hours. It had been like this ever since Tom had arrived home a few days ago. She could hear the regular breathing of one of the little girls, and a gentle 'put-put-put' noise coming from the partly open mouth of the other one. Comforting sounds from children wrapped in the deep slumber of innocence. It was the sounds from the next bedroom that Lilian was listening for, and yet dreading to hear. She bent her head towards the wall and waited. Then she heard them; murmuring voices, too low for her to hear the words – she wasn't sure that she wanted to hear them – then the rhythmic sound, faint yet unmistakable, of the creaking of the bedsprings. As it grew louder Lilian put her head beneath the bed covers, weeping hot bitter tears of frustration and loneliness . . . and jealousy.

Lilian couldn't fully understand her feelings, but she knew that her envy of Jenny at times amounted almost to hatred. Tom had always been special to Lilian; ever since he was a tiny baby she had thought of him as her own. No one knew of the depth of her feeling for her brother – not her mother, nor her other brothers and sisters, nor Tom himself – an affection so deep that sometimes even Lilian herself was frightened by the intensity of it. That was the reason she had never formed a lasting attachment, never married, because there was no one who could in any way measure up to her dear Tom.

She had been jealous at first of the tiny newcomer who was taking up so much of her mother's time and attention. She had been the baby of the family until then, made much of by her sister and two elder brothers, and she had resented sharing the limelight. Tom had been a good baby; she recalled how he had lain for hours at a time in his cot, not crying, his serious grey eyes just staring placidly around him. Their mother had bathed them together in the big zinc tub on the hearth – it was several years later that they had an upstairs bathroom – as there was less than two years separating the two children. The rest of the family – Jack, Hilda

122

and Joe – were several years older, so it was inevitable that the younger two should be drawn together.

The young Lilian had watched, fascinated, as Martha changed baby Tom's nappy, sprinkling powder over his little pink buttocks and over that part of him at the front which was different from Lilian. She didn't ask, and Mother didn't tell her, but she knew that it was the thing that distinguished boys from girls. She was intrigued by Tom's maleness, by this secret knowledge that she knew him better than anyone else. Then, as she grew older, she began to realise that she didn't want to share Tom at all, not any part of him, with anyone. It was then, when she was about fifteen, that she had started to be difficult. Her mother, she knew, had found her unmanageable at times, especially as her father had died a few years previously. The adolescent Lilian had had sulking fits and accused her mother of showing favouritism towards her younger brother. It wasn't entirely unjustified – Martha had always had a special love for Tom, her youngest child – but Lilian had exaggerated her feelings of jealousy for fear that someone would realise just how much she cared for him. So, at times, she had pretended to hate him. Poor Tom . . . She remembered the puzzled look that would come into his clear grey eyes as he wondered what he had done to provoke his sister's wrath. He was so even-tempered that it was almost impossible to pick a quarrel with him, but Lilian had tried.

He had always been different from the other lads. Lilian recalled the boys at school in Tom's class; snotty-nosed little urchins, many of them, with their seats hanging out of their trousers, grubby fists clenched in readiness for a fight . . . And Tom, clean and neatly dressed, with his soft sandy hair falling over his forehead, and looking always as though it had been newly washed. The friends he had made were, in the main, quiet, well-mannered boys like himself. They had not minded when Lilian, with few friends of her own, had tagged along with them, joining in their games and accompanying then on their jaunts into the countryside. She had enjoyed their friendship, but not one of them could hold a candle to Tom.

She had been devastated at first when Jenny had come on the scene, although she had known, deep down, that Tom would be certain to marry one day. But she had found it difficult to sustain a dislike for Jenny. Jenny was a dear, sweet girl and Lilian had found that she had grown to love and admire Tom's wife, almost against her will. There were times though – like now – when she felt that she hated her. The last few days had been wonderful, having Tom all to herself, and Jenny had seemed almost glad for them to be alone together. But the nights were hellish; it was then that Lilian's thoughts were tortuous, like black demons chasing round and round in her brain, preventing her from sleeping. Soon it would be dawn . . . As the clear light of a mid-June morning tried to filter through the blackout curtains Lilian fell, at last, into a fitful slumber.

'I've a couple of dresses here that I think would fit you, Lilian.' Jenny came into the girls' bedroom carrying the clothes over her arm. 'I've been sorting out my wardrobe. They keep telling us in the magazines I read to make do and mend, but I think I'm getting a bit too plump to wear these now.' She gave a little laugh as she pulled at the waistband of her skirt. 'Here, let's try them against you.' She held first the blue spotted, then the pink silky rayon dress against Lilian's slender figure, then she nodded. 'I reckon they'd look lovely on you, that is if you don't mind wearing my cast-offs?'

'Of course I don't, Jenny. It's real kind of you.' Lilian smiled, obviously very pleased. 'I don't go in much for posh clothes. They're always covered up with me overall when I'm at work and I don't go out very much apart from that.'

'Well, I'd hardly call these posh,' said Jenny, 'but you're welcome to them. Try 'em on, then if they suit you, you can pop them in your case.'

Lilian was packing to go home and an assortment of clothes, sensible and serviceable, lay on the bed. Her visit had coincided with Tom's leave for five days, but she had to go home today as she was due back at work. Jenny knew that she must be feeling miserable at the prospect and hoped that the dresses might cheer her up. A new dress always worked wanders for her, Jenny, but Lilian was a different kettle of fish altogether.

A few minutes later Lilian shyly entered the kitchen wearing the pink dress, which fitted her as though it had been made for her. 'It's nice, don't you think so?' she asked diffidently.

'Lovely!' said Jenny. 'Look, Tom.'

Tom looked over the top of his newspaper at his sister in her new finery. 'Aye – pink to make the boys wink! You look a real bobby-dazzler in that, our Lilian.'

Lilian smiled with pleasure and a faint pink blush tinged her cheeks. She looked almost pretty.

'I'll walk you to the station when you're ready, love,' said Tom. 'Or we'll get a bus if your case is heavy. It's a shame you've got to go, but it's been real grand to see you – it has that – and such a nice surprise an' all.'

Lilian looked as though she could almost dance with delight as she walked from the room.

'She's a strange 'un all right, is our Lilian,' Tom remarked when he returned from the station. 'I can't make head nor tail of her at times. Did you see how she blushed when I said I liked her dress? You'd have thought I was her young man, not her brother. She's a funny lass. We used to fight like cat and dog when we were youngsters, although – come to think of it – it was usually her as tried to pick a quarrel. She was an awkward little so-and-so. She's a good deal more affable now, but I wish she'd meet somebody she likes and get wed. It doesn't seem natural, somehow . . .'

'I don't suppose she could find anybody like you, Tom,' said Jenny, smiling at him.

'Me? Why the heck should she want somebody like me? No . . . I reckon me mam makes her too comfortable at home. She knows which side her bread's buttered, does our Lilian. Well, I suppose there's nowt so queer as folks . . .' He flopped into the armchair and buried himself again in the depths of his newspaper.

Jenny was pleased to see that Tom was more cheerful and was talking more freely now. She had hardly been able to get two words out of him when he first came home, so tired and dejected had he been. Lilian's visit seemed to have done him good, but Jenny suspected that his return to his unit in two days' time also had something to do with his change in outlook. He was dying to get back to the fray.

He had rallied a little at the stirring words of Winston Churchill: '. . . We shall defend our island, whatever the cost may be. We shall fight on the beaches, we shall fight on the landing grounds, we shall fight in the fields and in the streets, we shall fight in the hills; we shall never surrender.'

'If old Winnie tells us to keep going, then we must,' he remarked to Jenny with a sad smile. He had spoken hardly at all about his experiences during the retreat through France, but the night before his departure it seemed as though he was ready, for the first time, to talk about them.

'Aye, it was a bad do, Jenny love,' he said, sadly shaking his head. 'We were right on the front line, near the Belgian border. We couldn't believe it when we heard that Belgium had surrendered.'

Then had started the long march back towards the Channel ports. They marched by night, Tom explained, there being less danger of attack from the air. They would have stood very little chance if they had been attacked, as during the retreat they saw only one Allied plane. With the coming of each new dawn they dug trenches and took cover, sleeping from sheer exhaustion, but with every nerve keyed up, listening for the whistle of a bullet or the throb of an enemy aircraft.

One night, Tom recalled, they marched about thirty-five miles, from eight o'clock in the evening till ten o'clock the following morning. During the daylight hours they were machine-gunned from the air and by passing troops on motorcycles. Tom didn't mention the losses, but Jenny could imagine the scenes of devastation and carnage that must have surrounded the retreating men.

'Thank God you're safe, Tom,' she breathed.

It was a wonder they had had the strength to march at all. Their only rations throughout the whole of the retreat were what they could loot from discarded lorries – tins of corned beef and Army biscuits.

'I'll never forget the cheer that went up when we finally caught sight of the sea,' said Tom. 'You'd have thought we'd have been too bloomin' fagged out to cheer, but it seemed to give us new life, seeing those little boats bobbing about. I damn near copped it, though, Jenny. I had to duck to dodge a piece of shrapnel that was flying towards me. It knocked me cap off, or else I'd have been a gonner.'

They had waited in the darkness for a boat, the cold water lapping round their ankles, then their knees, then their thighs as they drew closer to the vessels that would ferry them home. Tom had never learned to swim. He was almost out of his depth, but he managed to summon up his last reserves of strength to dive forward and grasp hold of the side of a boat. It was a pleasure-boat that had, in peacetime, carried thousands of happy holiday-makers on jaunts from Brighton pier. The soldiers' soaking clothes dried in the engine room as the boat chugged steadily across the Channel towards Harwich.

'I'll tell you what, Jenny – that tea tasted good.' Tom smiled at the memory of the refreshments they were given on landing, in the dockside canteen. 'And chocolate and cigarettes too. We were treated like bloody heroes . . . and the funny thing is, we weren't heroes at all, were we? We were damn near defeated.'

'Don't say that, Tom,' Jenny said quietly. 'There'll always be an England, you know, like it says in that song. And remember what Winston Churchill said – "We'll never surrender".'

'Aye, you're right, my love.' Tom smiled thoughtfully. 'At least I've lived to fight another day.'

It was hard for Jenny to remember the time, just before the outbreak of hostilities, when she had argued with Tom about enlisting. Of course he had been right to join up. So long as there were men of Tom's calibre in the British Army, Britain would never go under.

Jenny was proud of her husband. She admired him, and she was very, very fond of him. But she knew that there was no excitement or passion in her feelings for him. She wished she could love him more.

Chapter 11

'Atten . . . shun! By the left – quick march! Left, right, left, right . . .'

The diminutive sergeant, red-faced and puffed out with pride like a pouter pigeon, stood on the wall of the boarding house opposite Pleasant View, bellowing out his commands. Jenny and Violet, shaking with laughter, watched him from their vantage point at the dining-room window. He was a continuing source of amusement in the neighbourhood, especially to the children, who found the performance as good as a visit to the cinema.

'He's not as big as six penn'orth of copper,' remarked Violet, 'but what he lacks in size he certainly makes up for with his voice. I bet they can hear him at the other end of North Pier.'

Jenny laughed. 'It's always the same with the little fellows, isn't it? They're so full of their own importance – making a big noise so that you'll forget how small they are.'

'Not always.' Violet shook her head. 'You can't say that about your Tom, can you? He's not so big, but you couldn't say that he was full of himself. Not a bit of it. I don't think I've ever met a more modest chap.'

Jenny glanced affectionately at her sister. 'You'll never hear a wrong word about him, will you, Vi? Tom'll never be short of an ally while you're around, that's for sure. I suppose you're right, though; Tom doesn't make himself heard overmuch. I wish at times he would talk more.' Her husband was a quiet, insignificant sort of chap, thought Jenny; it was amazing how he managed to inspire such devotion. His sister Lilian, and Violet, his sister-in-law . . . Jenny suspected that Violet was halfway to being in love with Tom, and had been ever since she was a little girl, though it was more than likely that she didn't realise it. 'You've got your own young man now, though, haven't you, Vi?' said Jenny. 'How's it going with Tony? You haven't mentioned him lately.'

'He's all right.' Violet's reply was curt. She turned away quickly and started piling the dirty dinner plates on to the trolley. Jenny looked at her concernedly. Her sister's lips were pressed tightly together in a thin straight line and her green eyes were expressionless.

'Violet?' said Jenny. 'What is it? There is something, isn't there?'

Violet didn't look at her sister as she slowly shook her head. There was silence for a few seconds, broken only by the clattering of the crockery which Violet was stacking together far more forcefully than was necessary.

'Violet?' Jenny persisted. 'Come on, love. I know there's something bothering you. Can't you tell me?' She knew Violet well enough to understand that, whatever it was, her sister would feel better if she unburdened herself. Vi had always liked to talk things out with Jenny, often lacking the self-confidence to make decisions on her own.

Violet stood motionless, her knuckles showing white as she gripped the handle of the tea trolley. Then she turned and flopped on to the nearest chair. She put her elbows on the table and leaned forward, her eyes full of anxiety as she looked at her sister. 'Yes . . . there is something worrying me. I've been wanting to talk to you for ages, but it's . . . well . . . it's embarrassing. I don't know how to put it . . .'

'You don't need to be embarrassed with me, love.' Jenny sat down on the opposite chair and grasped hold of Violet's hand across the table. 'Come on – fire away. I'm all ears.'

Violet shook her head in a nervous little gesture. 'Mother might come in. She'll be wondering what we're doing. Perhaps we'd better . . .'

'Be hanged to Mother! It's supposed to be your day off, Vi, but she's got you working. Anyway, she's nipped across the road to see Mrs Barber and you know what it's like when those two get gassing. She'll likely be gone an hour or more.'

'All right then,' said Violet. She paused, then when she started to speak the words came quickly, falling over one another. 'It's . . . it's Tony. I've never had a boyfriend before, you see, and I don't really know . . . Oh heck, Jenny! The trouble is . . . he wants to do more than just kiss me – a lot more – and . . . I don't know whether I should . . .'

Jenny gave an inward sigh. She had guessed it might be something of the sort, and Violet was so innocent, so trusting . . . 'Do you love him, Vi?' she asked quietly, squeezing her sister's hand.

Violet shook her head again as she answered, more slowly. 'I'm
. . . not sure. I like him . . . I liked him a lot at first. I suppose I was
flattered that night at the Tower when he made such a fuss of me. I
couldn't believe he'd want to see me again, but he did. Now he says
that if I really loved him I would want to . . .'

Jenny gave a bitter little laugh. 'That's what they all say, our Vi.
Don't be taken in by talk like that. You've let him do . . . more than
kiss you, then?'

Violet nodded and her cheeks turned a bright pink. 'Yes . . . I
know you'll think I'm awful, but . . . he says he loves me. And if . . .
if I don't, I think I might lose him.'

'And would it matter very much if you did? Lose him, I mean?'

'Of course it would! I've told you – I like him a lot. He's been good
to me, spent a lot of money on me, taking me to the pictures and
dancing, but . . .'

'But you don't think you love him?'

'No . . . I don't think so. We're very different, you know, Tony
and me. He never talks about anything but his bloomin' motorbike
and the garage he worked at in Leeds and all the posh cars he used to
mend. He doesn't read either, only the *Daily Mirror*, so I can't talk
about books to him. I can't have a serious discussion with him about
anything, except the war, and you don't want to be talking about
that all the time.'

'There's more to life than serious discussions,' said Jenny,
smiling. 'You want somebody that can make you laugh as well and
bring you out of yourself. Tony certainly seems to have done that.
You're a lot different since you met him, you know, Vi.'

'Oh, I know. I'm not so shy now. I feel I can talk to people without
tying myself in knots. I used to feel so tongue-tied when I met
strangers, but I'm not so bad now and it's all due to Tony – and Joyce
and Sheila as well – they've helped me a lot. But . . . I suppose I
know really that he's not the one for me.'

'No, I don't think so either,' said Jenny. 'I knew that as soon as I
met him. You want somebody a bit more . . . polished, more . . .
educated.'

'I don't know so much about that,' Violet replied. 'I left school
when I was fourteen, same as Tony did, so there's no point in me
looking down my nose at him because he's not very clever. Anyway,
Mother seems to like him.'

'Leave Mother out of it,' snapped Jenny. 'It's got nothing to do
with Mother. Anyroad, it's just the RAF uniform that she likes. She

131

thinks the sun shines out of 'em all. And I don't suppose she'd be all that keen on Tony if she knew what you've just been telling me.'

'You can say that again!' said Violet with feeling. 'D'you know, Jenny, sometimes when I've been with Tony, when we've been . . . you know . . . I've suddenly thought, Whatever would Mother say? She'd have a fit if she knew.'

'Mmm . . .' Jenny nodded grimly. She found it hard to believe that her mother had ever been young, ever been in love, but she supposed she must have been. She and Violet were living proof of a sexual relationship, within marriage, of course, but that sometimes had very little to do with love . . . 'I know just what you mean, Vi. That should be enough to put you off, if nothing else will. What would Mother say? D'you know, I do believe she thinks that getting pregnant's a worse crime than murder. "Getting into trouble", she calls it. Do you remember when Molly round the corner had to get married? Mother said, "If it was a daughter of mine I'd strangle her, I'd be that ashamed. I'd never be able to lift my head again." I don't suppose she would for one moment, but I wouldn't like to risk it. No – don't do it, Violet. It's not worth it, and if Tony goes off you because you won't, then he's not worth having at all.'

'But . . . isn't there something that I can do, that he can do, I mean, to stop me from having a baby?' Violet's forehead wrinkled in a frown. 'I've heard Sheila say something . . .'

'Then forget it.' Jenny tapped her fingers on the table. 'That Sheila's a flighty little madam, if ever there was one. I don't suppose there's much that she doesn't know, but don't let her lead you astray. And there's more fish in the sea besides Tony, you know.'

'There might not be for me.' Violet sounded regretful. 'Lads don't usually look at me, 'specially when there's somebody like Sheila around.'

'Don't talk so daft, Vi. You look real pretty since you started wearing your hair like that. You could have any amount of fellows. Now, think on what I've told you. Don't do it!'

'All right . . . thanks, Jenny. I've been getting in a right state about everything, but I feel better now I've told you. Come on,' she stood up and took hold of the trolley, 'we'd best get this lot sided away before Mother gets back.'

'You're seeing Tony tonight, are you?' asked Jenny. She was glad to see that Violet was looking much more composed now.

'Yes – we're going dancing, then we usually go for a walk on the prom.'

'Then think on – don't let him take you under the pier!' Jenny wagged her finger at her sister in mock severity. She was pleased to hear Violet laugh.

'All right. I'll remember what big sister has told me.'

It had been passing through Jenny's mind, while she and Violet had been talking, that Robert Cunningham would be ideal for her sister, but she pushed the thought away jealously. Robert liked to talk about books and suchlike, and he had studied at the technical college after he left school to further his education. Yes, he and Violet would probably get along famously, but he didn't know Violet very well at all, except to say good morning to, perhaps, when they met on the stairs. Jenny was glad that Violet didn't know him well, though she couldn't have explained why. She looked forward to the little chats that she and Robert enjoyed each week. Annie's outings to the whist drive were now a regular occurrence and Jenny was only too happy to see to the airmen's suppers on these nights.

She had read *Far from the Madding Crowd*, at Robert's persuasion, and was surprised how easy she found it to understand. Now, interspersed with her usual literary diet of light-hearted romance, she read the occasional classic recommended by Robert. She had read *The Woman in White* the previous month and had found it just as gripping as the Agatha Christie she had borrowed from the library the week before. It gave her something to talk about to Robert. Not that they needed to search for topics of conversation; the two of them always had plenty to say to one another . . .

'I think it's as well to have a good look round before you settle down,' Jenny told her sister as they washed the dinner pots. 'Don't make the same mistake that I did, marrying the first man that asked me.'

'Mistake?' said Violet. She almost dropped the plate she was holding as she looked at her sister in horror. 'Whatever do you mean, our Jenny? I thought you and Tom were happy. You are, aren't you?'

'Yes, we're happy enough,' replied Jenny quickly. Her remark had been a slip of the tongue, following on, no doubt, from her rambling thoughts about the young sergeant. She smiled at her sister and tried to speak confidently and reassuringly. It wouldn't do to let Violet see that her marriage was anything less than perfect. 'But he was almost my first boyfriend, you know, Vi. Like you and Tony. Mother always kept me under her thumb, like she's tried to do with you. Tom and I are lucky it's worked out so well because I certainly didn't have much chance to look around. That's what I meant . . .'

Violet smiled. 'That's all right then. You had me worried for a minute. I thought you were trying to say that you weren't happy. You've got a real good husband there, Jenny. He's one in a million, is your Tom.'

'Yes . . . you're right,' said Jenny slowly. 'I know you're right . . . One in a million.' But her voice lacked conviction and again she was aware of Violet's curious glance.

Violet hoped that all was well between Jenny and Tom. She was thinking about them that evening as she was getting ready to go out with Tony. She'd always liked her brother-in-law and got on well with him. Sometimes she felt that Jenny didn't appreciate him, but perhaps it would do them both good to be apart for a while. Maybe absence would make the heart grow fonder, like in the old saying. Of course, Tom wasn't the most exciting of people – a bit of a stick-in-the-mud, she supposed – but he was sensible and reliable and so very kind. Jenny should think herself lucky.

Violet wished that she felt so sure about Tony. She could feel the chaotic thoughts starting to whirl round and round in her mind, as they did every time she tried to think it through clearly. Conflicting thoughts . . . Did she love him, or did she only imagine that she did? There had been a time when she had envied Jenny her husband and child and her nice little home. It had been lovely to think that now she, Violet, had a young man of her own. That was a start, at least . . . but now she was beginning to have doubts. As she had told Jenny, she wasn't at all sure that Tony was right for her. He was rough-and-ready and – though she hated to admit it, even to herself, because it sounded so snobbish – he was . . . uneducated. But he had aroused feelings in her that she had never experienced before, feelings that she hadn't even known existed.

It had happened the very first time he kissed her, in a secluded tram shelter on the promenade; a churning sensation in the very pit of her stomach – and even lower – and then a . . . moistness. It made Violet blush just to think of it, and she could never, never have told Jenny about that. The next time, she had allowed him to fondle her breasts, just over the top of her dress, but she hadn't minded when his hands had crept inside, opening the buttons and feeling around beneath her underwear till her nipples tensed and tightened. Violet had always been self-conscious about the smallness of her breasts – she hardly needed to wear a brassière at all – but Tony hadn't

134

seemed to mind. It was when his hand caressed her knee, and then started to creep upwards towards that very private part of her that Violet had objected. It was then that the vision of her mother would intrude. She knew that what she was doing was wrong, that it was what Annie would call 'making yourself cheap'. And thoughts of Annie had intervened every time. Violet knew that one thing could lead to another. She had heard the girls at work say so, especially Sheila. It would be easy, so very easy, to let herself go and be hanged to the consequences. It was the thought of what might happen that stopped her every time. If you went 'all the way' you might end up having a baby. And that, according to Mother, was something so shameful that it didn't bear thinking about. But Violet knew that tonight Tony would try and persuade her again. He always did.

Tony was quiet that evening. Violet had learned by now that he was liable to switch from one mood to another, especially if he had something on his mind. He was thinking about his parents back in Leeds, he told her. He still hadn't managed to persuade them to move away from the city. No bombs were being dropped at the moment, but everyone knew that it was only a matter of time before the major cities would 'cop it'. It was July now, and in the skies above the southern counties the Battle of Britain was raging.

'I can't wait to leave here and get a bit nearer to where there's some action,' Tony told her as they strolled hand in hand along the promenade. 'Except that it would mean leaving you, love. I only wish I could have a bash at Jerry meself. You don't know how I envy them fliers . . . and here am I, stuck on the bloody ground. It doesn't seem fair.'

This was a constant cry of Tony's. He said it so often that Violet wondered who he was trying to convince, her . . . or himself?

'You're doing an important job, Tony,' she told him, as she did every time. 'They need good mechanics to keep the aeroplanes shipshape. It isn't everybody that could do it.'

'No . . . you're right there.' Tony was very easily convinced. 'And I'm a good mechanic all right. I am that! I remember back home, one of them toffs with his big Rolls Royce – I forget his name – he says to me, "Any time you want a reference, Tony lad, you just come to me." He tipped me five quid an' all.'

Violet had heard it all before, but she tried to humour him. 'It shouldn't be much longer before you're posted, surely? You must nearly have finished your training.'

'Why? Are you trying to get rid of me?' He turned quickly, grabbing hold of her arm, and his grey eyes glinted dangerously. 'Had enough of me now, have you? I daresay you'd like somebody a bit posher. Somebody as can speak proper. Somebody as reads books.' His tone was mocking.

'Steady on, Tony.' Violet tried to speak calmly, though she felt a little frightened at his sudden change of mood. He had done this before. One minute he would be talking quite normally, and the next he would be flying off the handle or retreating into a stubborn silence. 'Of course I'm not trying to get rid of you. I like going out with you, you know I do. I just wondered . . . how long? You've been in Blackpool quite a while and I know it's only a training centre.'

'Dunno.' Tony shrugged. 'Three weeks, a month, maybe more . . . Come on. Let's go and sit down.' He took her hand and they went down the stone steps to the lower promenade. 'Sorry I got mad. I'm a bit on edge just now, what with one thing and another.'

They sat on a hard wooden seat in a secluded corner. The lower promenade was a favourite haunt of courting couples. They could be seen, any number of them, every night after dusk fell, on the prom or in the tram shelters or under the pier, arms entwined around one another, oblivious to everything except each other. Time was precious. One never knew if this meeting might be the last . . .

The tide was in tonight and the sea looked like black velvet, smooth and unruffled. The supports of the pier were silhouetted against the darkness of the waves, sinister and menacing in the half-light, like some prehistoric monster crouching there with hundreds of stick-like legs. Violet was glad that the incoming tide had prevented them from going down on to the beach, under the pier. Jenny had joked about it – 'don't let him take you under the pier!' she'd said – and Violet had laughed, but she never liked it when Tony suggested that they should go there. It seemed so sordid somehow, leaning against the pier supports and letting Tony's hands roam all over her. Strictly speaking, the beach was out of bounds after dark, but this was a rule that just asked to be broken. It was almost impossible to enforce it, and during the summer months, especially with double British Summer Time, it was light until very late at night.

As soon as they sat down Tony started to kiss her. He pushed her long hair to one side and started to nibble at her neck. She felt the tingling sensation begin again, in her breasts, in the very secret part of her . . . Tony could arouse her now with just the slightest touch. She could hear his rapid breathing and she leaned against him, feeling his hands exploring her body, wanting him to, wanting him so very, very much . . .

Then, 'No, Tony . . . no. We mustn't.' She put her hands against his chest and pushed him away. 'I've told you before. I keep telling you . . . We can't.'

He dropped his hands abruptly and moved away from her, further along the seat. 'You've no idea what you're doing to me, girl,' he mumbled as he reached into his pocket for a packet of cigarettes. He struck a match, a tiny yellow flame in the darkness, and lit his cigarette, then flung the spent match away in a savage gesture. 'Why won't you? You know I love you . . . and I want you so much, Violet.'

Violet didn't answer and for a few moments there was silence as Tony drew deeply on his cigarette, staring sullenly out over the sea.

'I'm sorry,' Violet murmured. 'I'd like to . . . You know I want to really, but . . .'

'Forget it.' Tony's reply was brusque. 'It doesn't matter. It's . . . it's gone off now.'

Violet didn't know what he was talking about. She wished she had more experience of men. Sheila would have understood what he meant, but with Sheila it probably wouldn't have ended like this. Sheila wouldn't have said no . . .

Tony turned back to her and smiled. He put his arm round her in a casual manner and gently stroked her cheek with one finger. 'Sorry, Violet. Forgive me. I hate upsetting you.' His voice was wheedling and she felt the turmoil inside her subsiding a little. He really was a man of many moods; she hadn't realised how much so until tonight. 'I worry, you know, about me mam and dad,' he went on. 'Listen, love, I've got an idea. I've got a forty-eight-hour pass next weekend and I'm going to nip over to Leeds to see 'em. Come with me, Violet. Come and meet me mam and dad. They'd make you right welcome.'

'I can't, Tony.' The words were out almost before Violet realised what she was saying. 'I have to help at home. Mother wouldn't hear of it. You know what she's like and . . .'

'Bloody hell!' Tony viciously stubbed out his cigarette on the stone wall behind them, then threw it down and ground it under-foot. 'Your flamin' mother again! It's always "me mother this and me mother that". How much longer are you going to let her rule your life? You're a grown-up girl now, Violet. It's about time you started pleasing yourself a bit more . . . to say nothing of pleasing me,' he added bitterly.

Violet knew that he was right. She also knew that what she had said about her mother wasn't true. Annie, she was almost sure, would not have stopped her from going to Leeds. She had let Jenny visit Tom in Castleburn long before the two of them were married, and Mother did like Tony. Violet knew that her words had been an automatic reaction, just an excuse. She didn't want to go to Tony's home. She wasn't even sure that she wanted to see him again.

'Come on.' Tony stood up abruptly and pulled her to her feet. 'I'll walk you home . . . or else Mother will be wondering where you are, won't she?' His voice was taunting, malicious almost, and Violet was beginning to think that she didn't know him at all.

They walked back in silence through the dark streets, their footsteps sounding loud in the stillness. Tony didn't even touch her. He walked along with his hands in his pockets, his shoulders hunched as if in despair. Violet had no idea what to say to him.

They paused for a moment by the empty gateway; the gate had been taken away for scrap metal for the war effort. 'See you sometime,' Tony mumbled. His eyes held hers for a brief moment, then he nodded curtly and walked away.

'Hellfire and damnation!' he muttered to himself as he slouched down the street. 'I've made a right muck-up of that and no mistake. But her and her flamin' mother. It's enough to drive a fellow barmy!'

Tony had never met a girl quite like Violet before. When he told her that he loved her they were not just empty words. He was almost sure that he meant it. Her mother was a battle-axe, right enough, but he had soon got on the right side of her. He could be very pleasant when he tried and he'd certainly put on the charm with the old harridan. Violet was a real classy dame, with that gorgeous blonde hair and green eyes. A bit scraggy, not much of a handful, and her nose was too long, but then so was his own. She was real class, though, and he'd felt good going out with her. But a fellow wanted a bit of fun and there wasn't much chance of that with Violet . . . That Sheila that she knocked around with, now she looked a likely lass. She didn't look as though she'd say no . . .

Chapter 12

Annie slammed her shopping basket on to the kitchen table. 'Queues, queues, queues . . . I've never seen such crowds of folk! I don't know about 'em cancelling the Bank Holiday. Blackpool seems busier than ever to me.'

'I suppose it's bound to be, when you think about it, Mother.' Jenny glanced up from the huge pan of potatoes she was mashing in readiness for the speciality on today's menu, shepherd's pie. 'There's not only visitors here, there's the RAF and civil servants and war workers at the factory . . .'

'Humph!' Annie snorted. 'To say nothing of residents – us what lives here.' She tapped her finger on the edge of the table. 'And it's the residents that are getting their noses pushed out, I'll tell you. Would you believe? I stood more than half an hour in a queue for one bloomin' tin of peaches.' She held it up like a trophy won in a race. 'And most of the women in front of me were flippin' visitors. Seems like it's the latest holiday craze, spending their time in food queues instead of walking on the promenade. And then when us what lives here comes along there's nowt left.'

'They didn't cancel the Bank Holiday this time, Mother,' Jenny pointed out. 'Not the August one. It was the one at Whit that the Government cancelled. They thought it might interfere with the war effort. Eileen said she'd heard that there were so many folks in Blackpool last weekend that a lot of them had to sleep outside. On the prom, I suppose, or in the air-raid shelters . . .'

'Serve 'em bloomin' well right!' muttered Annie. 'They should stay at home. Hasn't anybody told 'em there's a war on?'

Jenny didn't answer. She reflected that her mother was glad enough to accommodate visitors in peacetime. After all, it was the visitors who enabled the seaside landladies to earn their living. Annie was preoccupied at the moment, though, with her lovely lads in blue, and refused to see any further than the end of her nose. Jenny didn't blame the holiday-makers for still pouring into Blackpool. If they could manage to get away for a few days to try and forget their worries then jolly good luck to them. Heaven knows, the war news is grim enough, she thought.

There was still very little to signify, on the Fylde coast, that there was a war on, apart from the blackout and the restrictions and, of course, the boys in blue uniforms who seemed to be everywhere. The siren very rarely sounded – when it did it was usually a false alarm – but it was a vastly different picture in the south of England. It must be sheer hell down there, the folk up in the north told one another, at the same time feeling relieved – and a little guilty – that it wasn't happening to them.

Most of the airmen who were billeted at Pleasant View were anxious to finish their basic training and 'have a bash at Hitler'. That was what they said, but Jenny wondered how much of it was bravado. Surely the poor lads must be frightened out of their wits. 'Three times over Germany, then down in flames,' she had heard one young corporal remark to his mate, 'but what a way to go!'

Jenny shuddered and a wave of sickness engulfed her. Please God, let it all end soon, she prayed silently, but she, and millions like her, knew that it was a vain prayer. It was amazing how cheerful and optimistic everyone seemed on the whole, but just occasionally, even at Pleasant View, there were mutterings about the strength of the German forces and the vulnerability of the British Isles. Invasion was a real threat; some feared that it was imminent but Annie, along with hundreds of other landladies, wasn't having talk like that in her house.

'Defeatist talk, that is!' she said, going red in the face. 'Just let me hear 'em talking like that and I'll give 'em a piece of my mind. We'll teach that Hitler a thing or two afore we've done, you mark my words. We're not beaten yet – far from it.'

She put up a notice, as did many of her fellow householders, quoting the words of Queen Victoria at the time of the Boer war which had appeared recently in the national press. Violet painstakingly copied it out in her best italic script: 'Please understand there is no one depressed in this house, and we are not interested in the possibilities of defeat. They do not exist.'

'That'll learn 'em,' declared Annie, gazing approvingly at the framed quotation which she had hung conspicuously over the piano in the lounge.

140

The lads got the message. There was no more defeatist talk. They hadn't meant any harm, they said to one another. They were only weighing up the pros and cons, but it wouldn't do to upset our Annie. She was a grand old lass when all was said and done, and they couldn't wish for a better billet anywhere . . .

Violet shook her head as she looked at her friend's reflection in the cloakroom mirror. 'No . . . I don't think so, Joyce. Not tonight. I've got to wash my hair.'

'That's what you say every time I ask you to go anywhere. It's a wonder you've got any hair left, the number of times you wash it. Aw, come on, Vi.' Joyce put her arm round the other girl's shoulder and gave her a squeeze. 'You'll have to snap out of it, you know. RAF blokes are ten a penny round here, and I never did think that that Tony was much cop, if you want the truth. Nowhere near good enough for you.'

'You shouldn't say that, Joyce. It's not true anyway. There's none of us any better than anyone else, just . . . different.' Violet looked at the reflections of herself and Joyce. They were very different; both were much the same height, but there the resemblance ended. Joyce was brown-haired and she was fair; Joyce had a round face and rosy cheeks whereas Violet was thin-featured and had a pale complexion. In temperament, too, Violet knew they were different. Her friend was easygoing, able to brush things off and face life with an untroubled outlook, while she, Violet, took things so much to heart. Like this business with Tony . . . Joyce was a good friend – she'd been wonderful since the break with Tony – and Violet knew that what she said was right. It wouldn't do any good to go on brooding. She grinned at the other girl in the mirror and Joyce grinned back. 'I might . . .' said Violet hesitantly. 'Yes – I think it might be a good idea to go out for a change. Which pictures are you thinking of going to?'

'George Formby's on at the Odeon,' said Joyce. 'We could go there. It'd be a good laugh.'

Violet nodded. 'All right then.' Until she'd met Joyce and Sheila she hadn't cared much for George Formby, with his gormless smile and his ukulele. After she'd seen a few of his films, however, she had realised that he was just the tonic that ordinary folk needed in war-time, especially folk in Lancashire who seemed to appreciate his humour. 'See you at the bus stop then. What time?'

'About half past six if you can make it. We'd best get there early in case there's a queue.'

'All right. Suits me.' Violet adjusted her hair, shoving most of it back under her turban. 'Is Sheila coming too?'

'No . . . I don't think so. She's got other fish to fry. You know what our Sheila's been like lately. A different bloke nearly every night.' Joyce gave a careless little laugh, but Violet didn't miss the uneasy look in her friend's eyes as she glanced at her.

Violet hadn't seen Tony for about ten days, not since that night on the promenade when she had refused to go with him to Leeds. She was confused. Part of her missed Tony; he had been good fun, most of the time, and had given her confidence in herself. Another part of her felt a reluctant relief; his demands had been getting too much for her and she had a growing suspicion that there was much about Tony that she didn't understand. And part of her had to admit that she was suffering from wounded pride. It had done wonders for her self-esteem to have a boyfriend; she had felt just like the other girls. She could join in their light-hearted prattle and understand many of their innuendoes. But now, she was on her own again . . .

She laughed with Joyce and the rest of the cinema audience as the cheerful king of the ukulele unmasked Nazi spies in Norway and, during a dream sequence, told Hitler to 'put a sock in it'. At the interval they ate ice cream from tubs with little wooden spoons, and Violet felt, at the end of the evening, that she had really enjoyed herself. They stood to listen to 'God save the King', then pushed their way through the red plush seats to the exit.

'Just a minute,' said Joyce, grabbing hold of her arm when they were nearly at the back of the cinema. 'I've dropped my scarf. Help me to look for it, Vi, there's a love. It's me best one.'

Violet stooped to look between the rows of seats, but not before she had seen, emerging from the back row, Tony and . . . Sheila. His arm was round her waist and she was smiling up at him. Her bright-red lipstick was smudged and her baby-fine hair looked as though it hadn't seen a comb for a week. They didn't see Violet and Joyce. They were too engrossed in one another.

'You're too late, Joyce. I've seen them,' said Violet, seeing through her friend's ruse about the scarf. 'Thanks for trying, though . . .'

142

Joyce shamefacedly picked up the scarf, emblazoned with Union Jacks, from where she had surreptitiously dropped it under a seat. 'Aw . . . I'm sorry, luv. I didn't want you to find out like that.'

'You knew . . . ?'

'Yes . . . I knew. But how was I to know they'd be coming here tonight?' She gave her friend's arm an affectionate squeeze. 'Now don't you go worrying your head about 'em. I've told you, he's not worth it. She's not worth it either, that little minx! I tried to warn you about her ages ago, Vi, but you're so kind, aren't you, love? You didn't want to believe me.'

Violet shook her head. No, she hadn't wanted to believe that Sheila would play such a dirty trick, not on one of her best friends. Violet did always try so hard to see the best in people. She had noticed, however, the appraising looks that Tony had given Sheila on occasions, and the 'come hither' glances that little madam had given him in return, simpering and blinking her big baby-blue eyes. But then she did that with all the men . . . Violet was feeling let down, not just by Tony, but by her friend as well, but she mustn't let Joyce see how much she was hurt by them. That was another of the things that her new friends had taught her. To pretend that you didn't care, that there were more fish in the sea . . .

Violet shrugged. 'Why should I care?' she said casually. 'She's welcome to him.' She tried to smile at her friend, but her face felt frozen and her voice lacked conviction. Suddenly all the joy and laughter had gone from the evening and Violet felt . . . empty.

'You should have seen them, Auntie Jenny,' said Rosie excitedly as they sat eating their tea. It was baked beans on toast today, a regular favourite of the children. 'They came running like mad towards this sandbag that was swinging about, and then – pow! – they plunged their knives into it.'

'What were they doing, Mum?' asked Patsy.

'It's bayonet practice, silly,' replied Rosie. 'Isn't it, Auntie Jenny?' She shoved another forkful of the bright-orange beans into her mouth, then paused for a moment, savouring the taste. 'They're pretending that the sandbags are German soldiers, and they're sticking their knives into them and killing them.'

'Ugh!' Patsy shuddered. 'I think that's horrible! I shan't go and watch them again.'

'I hope you two didn't go down to the sands on your own,' said Jenny, trying to change the subject. Bayonet practice on the sand was a regular occurrence, watched avidly by the local children. It was impossible to shield the little girls entirely from the brutalities of war, but Jenny knew she must encourage them not to dwell on it. It was doubtful, though, whether they understood its true significance. To them it was probably just bloodthirsty play-acting.

'No, we weren't on our own,' Patsy assured her. 'We were with Auntie Eileen and the boys – and Ben, of course. Ronnie and Ray wanted to watch the airmen so we all went.'

Eileen and Jenny took it in turns to meet the children from school, although the time was rapidly approaching when they would be able to come and go on their own. They were all growing up so fast. Rosie would be seven later that month. She had been with them a full year now. Jenny grew fonder of the little evacuee with every day that passed, and Patsy and Rosie grew even closer. They were inseparable now.

Daisy White visited Blackpool every couple of months, but there had been no talk of taking Rosie back home. Jenny, though trying to consider Daisy's rights as a mother, as opposed to her own deepening love for the child, never broached the subject. Young Ben Williams was still happily residing at Eileen's. His mother was busy with her war work at a local factory – as was Rosie's mother, though Jenny suspected that Daisy White still had other equally important interests – and there seemed to be no point in moving Ben at the moment. Besides which, the Blitz had started on London, and no doubt the other major cities would soon suffer as well. Ben's mother had decided that he was safer where he was, and with Rosie just up the road to keep a maternal eye on him, things couldn't be better.

'It's Ronnie and Ray's birthday next week,' said Patsy. 'They'll be seven – same as Rosie'll be soon – and they're having a party.' Patsy's eyes lit up at the thought. 'Rosie and me's invited – aren't we, Rosie? – and Auntie Eileen says she's been saving up her rations to make a cake. And guess what she's got hidden away in her cupboard – a red jelly!'

Jenny smiled. You could concoct a party around the simplest of ingredients. As far as children were concerned, a jelly – a red one – was the essential item.

'That's lovely,' she said. 'You seem to be the best of friends now with Ronnie and Ray. They don't tease you any more then, Patsy?'

'No, not now. Rosie sorted 'em out ages ago, didn't you, Rose? She stopped them from bullying little Ben as well.' Patsy beamed at her friend. 'Our teacher said that Rosie did a real nice painting today, Mum. We had to do a poster, you see, called "Dig for Victory", and Miss Bailey said that Rosie's was the best in the whole class. She drew a little man with a big spade, and a garden full of 'normous cabbages and cauliflowers.'

The return to school in September had brought a new teacher and a whole lot of new experiences. It was amazing, though, how many of the lessons were concerned with waging – and winning – the war.

'Your picture was nice an' all, Patsy,' Rosie declared. They always stuck up for one another.

'Not as good as yours, though.' Patsy shook her head. 'The paint kept running and the sky went all smudgy.'

'You're better'n me at writing and spelling, though. Patsy got ten out of ten for a spelling test today, Auntie Jenny.'

'Well done, dear,' said Jenny, in the split-second's pause before Rosie went on.

'Oh, and d'you know what else Miss Bailey said today, Auntie Jenny?' Rosie didn't wait for an answer. 'She said that if a stranger stops us in the street and asks us the way, we have to say "I'm sorry, I can't tell you."'

Jenny shook her head, slightly bemused. 'What do you mean, dear?'

'In case the Germans come,' said Rosie vehemently. 'They might land in parachutes, dressed as British soldiers, or they might pretend to be vicars or nuns, or ladies going shopping or . . . anything. But they'd really be spies, you see, and we couldn't say "I don't know the way", because that would be telling a lie if we really did know, so we have to say "I can't tell you."'

'Oh yes – I understand now,' said Jenny, still feeling bewildered. It was, she thought, a subtle way of getting round the moral issue. On no account should children ever be encouraged to tell a lie, even in wartime. 'Now, come along, you two. If you've finished your tea we'll go and wash up, then we can listen to *Monday Night at Eight* before you go to bed.'

145

'Hurray!'

'Gosh – can we really, Mummy? Just think, Rosie. We'll be up till nine o'clock!'

The wail of the siren broke into Jenny's slumbers. It was a familiar sound – not as familiar to the inhabitants of Blackpool as it was to those of Liverpool say, or Leeds, but familiar enough to rouse her to immediate consciousness. She sat up in bed, every nerve tense, all her senses alert, waiting, fearing what she might hear. It was usually a false alarm, but you never knew.

The first crash was deafening. Jenny heard a scream that could only have come from her own lips, though she was unaware of having uttered it. It was no false alarm this time. It sounded like a direct hit on the house, but thankfully the walls and roof still seemed to be intact. Mercifully for us, thought Jenny, but some other poor blighters must be copping it, and very near, too, from the sound of it.

There followed two more ear-splitting crashes. Jenny sprang out of bed, shoved her feet into her slippers and grabbed her woollen dressing gown from its peg on the door. Hurriedly fastening the cord round her waist, she dashed into Patsy and Rosie's bedroom. They blinked, wide-eyed and startled, as she switched on the light, but they were both already sitting up in bed.

'What's happening, Mummy?'

'That was a terrific crash, Auntie Jenny.'

'It's an air raid,' said Jenny. There was no point in being anything less than truthful. 'Come on, both of you. Quick sharp. Put your dressing gowns on and we'll go downstairs.'

There was an air-raid shelter at the end of the street. They had taken part in the statutory practice, complete with gas masks, instigated by the local ARP warden, but now that it was for real Jenny felt that they would be just as safe under the stairs. It was a triangular space, an open cupboard, just big enough to stand up in, where they kept Wellingtons and an assortment of coats and overalls, plus the ironing board and the vacuum cleaner. Patsy and Rosie huddled under the coats, clinging to one another as several more thunderous crashes followed.

Jenny put her arms round them both, bending herself over them and protecting them with her body, consoling them with words of encouragement.

'It'll soon be over. I think they're going away now.'

'Just think, Auntie Jenny,' said Rosie, in an awed whisper, 'my mum probably has to do this every night. Mustn't it be awful?'

Dreadful, thought Jenny, not answering, but holding the child closer. They had been very lucky so far on the Fylde coast. Please God, don't let it be the start of anything worse, she prayed. Then, after what seemed like an eternity, came the single, unwavering note of the all-clear signal.

'There we are. It's all over. We're all safe and sound.' Jenny smiled at the two little girls. 'Now, let's all have a nice cup of hot milk and a biscuit before we get back into bed.'

At Pleasant View, Annie and Violet were also downstairs, with several of the airmen, who looked unfamiliar in garishly striped pyjamas, their hair standing on end and bluish shadows round their chins.

'I bet that's your factory they're bombing, our Violet,' said Annie. 'There'll be nowt left of it in the morning by the sound of things.'

'We'll have to wait and see, Mother,' said Violet, sounding much more composed than she was feeling. 'There's nothing we can do anyway, more's the pity, except wait.'

'Thank God we're all safe.' Annie breathed a heartfelt sigh of relief at the sound of the all-clear. 'And I hope our Jenny and them bairns are safe an' all.'

'We may be safe, Mother, but some poor folks aren't,' Violet reminded her.

'Aye, I know that, lass.' Annie smiled at her sadly. 'But like you were saying, love, there's nothing we can do about it, worse luck . . . We can have a nice cup of tea, though, before we go back to bed. We can always have a cup of tea, can't we? Come on, some of you lads – we'll go and get the kettle on and have a brew-up.' She caught sight of the sergeant standing quietly to one side, bemusedly stroking the stubble on his chin. It was the first time she had seen him looking anything but immaculate. 'Oh, Sergeant Cunningham . . . Robert. I wonder if you'd mind . . . I don't like asking you really, but I'm a bit worried about me daughter, our Jenny, I mean. D'you think you could pop round and see how she is? I'm sure she'll be all right, but it'd just set me mind at rest. Just round t'corner. Number sixteen Green Street.'

Robert Cunningham smiled in his usual friendly manner. 'Of

course I will, Mrs Carter.' He had never fallen into the habit of calling her Annie, as so many of the lads did. Sergeant Cunningham was a very proper sort of young man, friendly and very polite, but never familiar. 'I'll just put my coat on and go straight round there.'

Annie cast an amused glance at his legs, clad in blue striped pyjamas. 'I reckon you'd best put your trousers on an' all, lad, or else you'll have the bobbies after you.'

Robert laughed then, and his blue eyes twinkled. 'You're right! Don't worry, Mrs Carter. I won't be more than a few minutes.'

Jenny was startled to see Robert Cunningham on the doorstep when she tentatively opened the door and peeped round. She had thought it was the ARP warden. With all the trauma of the past hour it wouldn't have been surprising if she'd left a light showing.

'Robert . . .' Her surprise showed in her voice. 'What are you doing here?' Aware that she sounded unwelcoming, she gave a little laugh. 'Sorry, I didn't mean to be rude, but . . .'

'I'm sorry to disturb you, Jenny,' Robert said softly. 'Your mother asked me to call. She was worried about you.' His voice, though merely a whisper, sounded loud in the quiet darkness of the street. There was not another soul in sight. 'I can see you're all right, though . . . You are, aren't you?' His eyes, glowing like deep inky-blue pools in the absence of light, narrowed with concern as he looked at her.

'Yes . . . Yes, I'm fine, thanks. We were a bit shaken. Very close, wasn't it? But we're all right. I've just got the girls tucked up in bed again.' She glanced down at her feet in their fleecy-edged slippers, suddenly – embarrassingly – aware of her dressing gown and her white nightgown peeping out at the hem. It seemed awful to leave Robert standing on the doorstep, but she couldn't – mustn't – ask him in.

'And that's where you should be too,' he said kindly. 'Tucked up in bed.' He patted her arm. 'I'll tell your mother that you're OK. She was quite concerned about you. Good night then . . . Jenny.'

'Goodnight, Robert. Thank you . . . for coming. It was kind . . .'

His smile was warm and his eyes held hers for several seconds longer than was necessary before he turned and walked away down the pitch-black street.

Jenny watched him go. She gave a deep sigh of regret as she went in and closed the door, but she wasn't sure why . . .

It wasn't the factory that had been bombed. Violet realised when she arrived for work the following morning that it was Seed Street, a row of terraced houses near the bus station, that had borne the brunt of the attack from the air. Violet, with Joyce and Sheila and several more of their colleagues, stared, horrified, at the scene of devastation. A mountainous pile of rubble faced them, bricks and roof tiles and timbers, window frames and doors all heaped together like some colossal bonfire. From the midst of the pile a staircase, carpeted with threadbare Axminster, led to nowhere. An iron bedstead hung crazily at an angle, the mattress sagging beneath it belching out clouds of fluffy white feathers. Here and there in the pile of rubble they could see glimpses of coloured material; a peg rug, a gaily striped cushion, someone's Sunday frock now lying in tatters. A teddy bear lay on his back, stuffing oozing out of his innards, his boot-button eyes gazing sightlessly into the grey sky. ARP workers and Local Defence Volunteers were still searching amongst the ruins. Rumour had it that eleven people had been killed and thirty-three injured. It had been Blackpool's blackest night so far, 12 September 1940.

'Come on,' said Sheila, her big blue eyes clouded with tears. 'Let's get into work and make some more planes to blast Jerry to bits.'

'But why?' bewailed Violet. 'What's the point of it all? Will somebody tell me what it's all about? It'll do no good making more aeroplanes and more bombs to blow one another to bits. Why can't they all just stop fighting?'

Joyce put an arm round her friend. 'Come on, love. You're right, of course. God knows you're right. There's no sense in it at all, but we'd best get on with it and do our bit.'

Jenny walked briskly along the north promenade towards the cliffs. It was her favourite spot, away from the crowds that always milled around the centre of the town. She longed for peace and solitude. She had been depressed by the recent bombing in the town, not that she knew any of the victims personally, but it had brought the grim reality of war so much nearer.

It was a cold, blustery evening, with a touch of rain in the air, but Jenny tied her headscarf more firmly under her chin and strode purposefully forward, battling against the north-west wind that was blowing in from the sea. She had a couple of hours to herself – a very rare occurrence – while Patsy and Rosie were at the twins' party.

She stopped opposite the Boating Pool and leaned against the railings, staring out towards the horizon. The tide was fully in, and the breakers, dark-grey and white-capped with foam, dashed fiercely against the sea wall, scattering spray that reached rioht to the upper promenade where Jenny was standing. The Boating Pool was deserted, shut up for the evening. The wooden animals that made up the automated ride were covered with a sheet of tarpaulin, the gaily coloured paddle boats were crowded together at the side of the lake, and the shutters were closed on the stall that sold ice cream and fizzy pop. It was a favourite haunt of Patsy and Rosie, and Jenny, too, as a child, had loved her visits here.

'Jenny – how nice to see you.'

She turned, startled at the sound of the familiar voice near to her elbow. It was Robert Cunningham.

Chapter 13

'Robert – what are you doing here?'

'The same as you, I suppose. Walking, thinking, getting away from the crowds for a while.' He came and leaned against the railings next to Jenny. 'You're on your own I see. No children with you today? That's unusual.'

'Yes. The girls have gone to a party so I found that I had some time to myself. I like it up here, especially when there are no people around. "Far from the madding crowd", I suppose you might say.'

She gave a little laugh and Robert smiled back at her.

'I think we all need some time to ourselves occasionally,' he remarked. 'To take stock of things and to sort out the muddle in our minds.'

'Mm . . . My mind's certainly been in a muddle this last day or two. I've been terribly depressed since those bombs fell on Blackpool. I know it's nothing compared with what's happening in other parts of the country, but it made it all feel so much nearer, so much more real. What do you think about it, Robert? Do you think it might be the start of something bigger? Full-scale bombing raids on Blackpool, perhaps?'

Robert shook his head. 'I very much doubt it. I think it was just an isolated incident. A lone bomber dropping his load. He may have been trying to hit the factory, or the station. Who knows? But I think that if they'd been going to bomb Blackpool in earnest they would have started before now.'

'Why do you say that?'

'Well, just think about it. There's a huge aircraft factory at Squire's Gate and other smaller ones dotted about. And there are thousands of us airmen training here. I'm quite sure Jerry knows all about it, but for some reason he's decided to leave us alone.'

'I hope you're right. It seems so selfish, though, doesn't it? It's

151

almost as though you're wanting the bombs to drop on someone else.'

'I shouldn't worry about it, Jenny. Self-preservation is the strongest instinct known to man. In battle, of course, it would be called cowardice. You're trained to put your fellow men first, but it doesn't come naturally. We're all basically selfish when it comes to the crunch.'

'So you think we're reasonably safe here?'

'I think so. The Tower's a good landmark for the German planes. It wouldn't make much sense to demolish it. Or maybe Hitler thinks that Blackpool would be a good recreation centre for his troops when he's conquered Britain!'

'That's defeatist talk, Robert.'

'It's all right. Your mother's not here to listen. Anyway, you don't think I mean it, do you?'

'You don't think there's any chance . . . ?

'Not a bit of it. What does it say in that song? "England unconquered yet, o'er land and sea." No, we'll never be conquered, Jenny. You can rest assured. Not that I understand it all – the war, I mean, and nations wanting to fight one another. I suppose I'm a pacifist at heart. I'm certainly not a natural warrior, but I couldn't sit back and see my friends enlisting and not do my bit. I would have joined up even if there hadn't been conscription.'

'My husband, Tom – I suppose he's a natural warrior, as you put it. He couldn't wait to get into the Army. He'd always been interested in military campaigns and strategies. He and his father used to play for hours with their toy soldiers – not that I remember his father, but Tom told me all about him – so I daresay it's an instinct that he's inherited.'

'I expect he's finding that it's much more than a game now, isn't he? I spoke to him once or twice, you know, when he came back from France.'

'Yes. He was very disillusioned when he came home from Dunkirk. All the heart seemed to have gone out of him. He was glad to get back to the fray, though . . . Let's not talk about the war any more, Robert. You must hear enough about it, day after day. Sometimes it seems as though we can't stop talking about it.'

'Yes, you're right. This blasted war worms its way into all our conversations, doesn't it? Let's try to forget it.' Robert placed his hand, well shaped, she noticed, with long tapering fingers, upon Jenny's gloved one as it lay on the railings. He left it there for a few seconds and they looked at one another, their eyes meeting in a steady, unwavering gaze. Then, quickly, they looked away again.

'This is a nice part of Blackpool,' said Robert, gazing out to sea once more. 'Do you often come up here, Jenny?'

'Yes. I love it up here. It's my favourite spot. The children like the Boating Pool, of course, and you seem to get the full benefit of the sea here.'

'We're certainly getting the benefit of it now. You're not too cold, are you?'

'No.' Jenny shook her head. 'You get used to the sea breezes when you live in Blackpool. I don't feel the cold very much.'

The wind had increased in strength while they had been talking and at times their words were almost drowned by the noise of the waves crashing against the sea wall.

'You're lucky living near the coast,' Robert remarked. 'In Coventry we're right in the heart of England. Until I was billeted here I'd never been to Blackpool, believe it or not.'

'Never been to Blackpool?' said Jenny, finding the idea incredible. 'Then you hadn't lived!'

'I know that now.' Robert turned and looked at her steadily, and again their eyes met and held for several seconds.

'You'd been to the seaside, though? You must have been.'

'Oh yes. We used to spend family holidays at Llandudno, my mother and father and my sister Ruth and I. It's a pretty place, but there doesn't seem to be the same vastness about it that there is here. I've been fascinated by the sea here. It has so many moods. Wild, like it is now, and then so gentle that you can scarcely believe the strength that it holds. And so many colours too – blue, green, grey, almost black sometimes – always changing. It's with you all the time in Blackpool, isn't it? Even when you can't see it, you can hear it and smell it in the air.'

The sea was in an angry mood now. A sudden freak wave hurtled against the wall, sending up a shower of spray that drenched Jenny and Robert.

He seized hold of her hand. 'Quick – run. We're getting soaked.'

Shrieking with laughter, they ran for the safety of the nearest shelter, about twenty yards along the promenade. They sat on the wooden bench, not speaking, staring out at the threatening landscape. It was all grey now; grey sea, grey sky, and the rain which had just begun, sweeping across the deserted promenade in a silvery-grey sheet. Here on the cliffs, Jenny felt as though they were marooned on the edge of the world, far away from everything and everyone except the limitless panorama of sea and sky.

Robert turned to look at her, his eyes a deep, intense blue, glowing with unspoken longing. 'Jenny . . . Oh, Jenny,' he whispered as he put his arms round her.

His lips brushed against her hair as he turned her gently towards him. She felt the coldness of his cheek against hers, then she was aware of nothing but Robert's hands on her shoulders and her own ardent response, as though all her life she had been waiting for this moment. His mouth came down on hers, gently at first – she could taste the faint trace of salt on his lips – then more fervently as he felt her responding to his caress. She closed her eyes, dissolving, drowning in the strength of her feeling for him.

'Jenny – oh, Jenny,' he whispered again. 'I've dreamed about this so often.' His mouth was in her hair, whispering the words . . .

> 'Say I'm weary, say I'm sad,
> Say that health and wealth have missed me,
> Say I'm growing old – but add,
> Jenny kissed me.'

'That's nice,' she whispered back. 'Poetry, is it?'

'Yes – it's by a man called Leigh Hunt. I don't know of anything else that he wrote, but I've always liked that piece. I like it even more now. I thought about it the moment I met you. Will Jenny ever kiss me? I wondered. Now it's come true – I can hardly believe it.'

'I've thought about it too,' Jenny said quietly, 'but it shouldn't have happened.'

'I know – dear God, I know . . .' Robert's voice rose, almost breaking with emotion. 'But don't expect me to say that I'm sorry. I can't . . .'

'I'm not sorry either . . .' Jenny's voice was the merest whisper. Robert kissed her again, and as he drew her closer to him she felt the hardness of his body against hers. She experienced a feeling of desperate longing that she had never known before.

'We really ought to be going,' she whispered. 'The girls will be

154

home from the party soon and I must be there. I didn't mean to be out so long. Look at it, though – it's raining cats and dogs.'

'We'll get a tram. Look – there's one coming. Come on – let's run for it.'

He gave her a quick kiss, then hand in hand they ran through the rain to the nearby tram stop. They sat close together on the hard leather seat as the tram clanged its way southwards towards the North Pier tram stop. They didn't speak, but Robert reached for her hand and gently felt inside her glove, caressing her palm. She almost cried out with the depth of the desire that enveloped her.

They walked quickly across the rain-swept promenade towards Pleasant View, keeping a distance between them now, as though they had met casually. Of course they had, but it was as though it were preordained. They stopped briefly on the corner of Green Street.

'Jenny – may I come and see you later this evening?' Robert's voice was soft and deep, and she could sense the urgency in his question.

'Yes . . .' she replied simply, hardly knowing what she was saying. Robert had so completely overwhelmed her senses that her response to him seemed to be beyond her control. 'The girls should be fast asleep by half past eight . . .'

'Thank you, Jenny.' Robert looked at her for a moment, his eyes glowing with tenderness, then he turned and walked purposefully up the road towards the billet.

She hummed softly to herself as she took the guard away from the fire and stirred the glowing coals until they burst into vivid flames of yellow and orange. It was dusk already. The nights were drawing in, heralding the approach of autumn. This was the season that Jenny loved best. Some, she knew, welcomed the spring with its promise of new life and new hope, but to Jenny, the turning of the year had a charm that was unique. There were few of the obvious autumnal signs in Blackpool. She recalled her first visit to Tom's home in Yorkshire; the trees had been glowing with the red, orange and yellow of the fall as though they were bursting into life, but it was really a gradual dying. Here, near the sea, one was aware of a clammy mistiness in the air in the early morning and evening, and the lengthening of the shadows cast on the pavement. In Stanley Park, no doubt, the trees would be resplendent in their autumn glory. Perhaps she could take Patsy and Rosie there at the weekend. It was a long time since they had been. Life was suddenly full of promise.

She smiled happily as she drew the blackout blinds, then the folk-weave patterned curtains across the windows. It wasn't quite dark yet, but she loved the feeling of security that the closed curtains gave her. She enjoyed the autumn evenings; the warmth of the fireside, a good book to read, the companionship of the wireless set. She hadn't missed Tom nearly as much as she had expected to. She found that her own company was quite satisfying; after all, if you couldn't enjoy your own company, there wasn't much chance of anyone else enjoying it either. Tonight, though, she would not be alone. She felt her heart miss a beat at the thought.

She heard running footsteps on the pavement outside the window and a loud knock at the door. The girls were home from the party. They ran in excitedly, cheeks aglow, bright with enthusiasm.

'It was a lovely party, Mummy.'

'And, d'you know, Auntie Jenny,' interrupted Rosie, 'we had loads and loads to eat. I'm nearly bursting. Corned-beef sandwiches, cut all fancy in triangles, and meat-paste sandwiches. And Auntie Eileen made some buns with icing and all little coloured bits stuck on 'em.'

'And we had red jelly and orange squash . . .'

'And a birthday cake an' all. It had seven candles.'

'And then we played games, Mummy. Pin the tail on the donkey, and blind man's buff, and musical bumps. And Auntie Eileen gave us a piece of cake to bring home. Come on, Rosie – show Mummy what we've got.'

The two little girls felt in their pockets and each brought out a serviette which they carefully unwrapped. The cake – obviously an austerity one with a smattering of currants and a rich brown colour that could only have been achieved by gravy browning – was squashed and sticking to the paper, but to the girls, it was the highlight of the party. A souvenir to bring home.

'Well, that sounds like a fantastic party,' said Jenny, beaming at them. 'You can have the cake for your supper with a cup of milk, and then it's off to bed with you.'

The children were tired with all the excitement, and when Jenny peeped into their room at half past eight, they were both asleep.

She switched off the main light in the living room and turned on the lamp. The light from the huge glass beach ball held by the gilded lady cast a comforting orange glow. The fire flickered welcomingly as Jenny waited.

She hurried to the door at Robert's quiet knock, and without speaking he followed her along the hallway and into the living room. Hurriedly he took off his greatcoat and flung it on to the nearest chair. Then he took her once more in his arms.

'Jenny, my darling,' he whispered as he stroked her hair, then his lips closed over hers.

There was no need for them to speak, there was no question that needed to be asked or answered. This was the moment for which they had both been waiting. What had happened in the past was of no consequence. The future with its threat and imminent danger could not touch them. There was only the present and the two of them in all the world.

Their bodies moving as one, fused together in a perfect whole, they sank into the depths of the armchair. The light from the lamp bathed their lovemaking in a radiant glow. The feeling of desire deep inside Jenny swelled and then burst, like the waves crashing against the cliffs. Wave after wave of surging desire swept over her. Nothing could stop the oncoming tide of their love.

All passion spent, she lay in Robert's arms as he covered her face with teasing little kisses. His eyes in the dim glow cast by firelight and lamplight looked almost black, deep and yet sparkling with light. She stared into their depths, seeing a small image of herself mirrored in each of them.

'I can see myself in your eyes,' she said, laughing. 'Very, very small, like looking through the wrong end of a telescope.'

'Mirror'd small in paradise,' Robert murmured.

'Mm?' she said lazily.

'It's a quotation – it's by Keats.'

'You and your quotations!' She pushed at him playfully, planting a kiss on the end of his nose. 'Go on then – tell me about it. Educate me.'

'You don't need much educating, my darling Jenny.' His hand caressed her breast, and she saw the flame of desire once more in his eyes.

The force of their love overwhelmed them again, but this time it was more peaceful and tender, like the gentle waves caressing the sand, as they took their time, finding delight in pleasuring each other.

'Now – tell me about Keats,' said Jenny, running her fingers through his hair.

'It's from "Lamia" – a love story set in ancient Corinth.'

'With a happy ending?'

'I think not, darling. But you will have to read it for yourself. It's full of the most beautiful language. We read it in my last year at school and I was enthralled with it. That was what started my love of poetry, especially the poetry of Keats. But "Lamia" is still my favourite. She was the embodiment of woman. "A virgin," Keats says, "yet in the lore of love deep learned to the red heart's core." A real woman, like you are, Jenny darling.'

'I can't pretend I'm a virgin, though. But it was never like this . . .' Jenny realised with a sudden stab of surprise that she had never before experienced a full and perfect consummation.

'Nor for me,' said Robert softly.

'But . . . you're not married. I wasn't the first then? You mean that you've . . . ?'

'No, you're not the first, but it doesn't matter. They weren't important.'

'What about Marjorie?'

'Marjorie?' A slight frown furrowed Robert's brow.

'Your girlfriend, the one in Coventry. You showed me a picture of her.'

'Yes . . . Marjorie,' said Robert thoughtfully. 'She's not impor-tant either.' He shook his head slowly. 'Marjorie and I didn't . . . We're just close friends, more than anything else. I'm very fond of her. We grew up together and went to school together, and our parents more or less expected us to get married. But you can't always fall in with your parents' wishes. At one time I thought I might marry her, but now . . . Oh, Jenny – what are we going to do? I love you so much.'

'I love you too, Robert, but there's nothing we can do, darling, except take each day as it comes. We can't look too far into the future – we daren't. I should be feeling guilty. I should be thinking about Tom, but I can't. I can only think about you and about how glad I am that we met.'

She ran her fingers through his hair again, blue-black and glossy as a raven's wing, that waved back from his forehead. He was so very handsome, but that wasn't why she loved him. She had to admit to herself now that she was deeply in love with him.

'Tell me,' she said. 'How old are you?'

'Twenty-three. I'll be twenty-four at Christmas. Boxing Day, to be exact.'

'And I will be twenty-eight next month. That means I'm four years older than you.'

'Good gracious! You are an old lady, aren't you? You'll be wearing a night-cap and shawl before long.' Playfully he kissed the end of her nose.

'You don't mind then, about me being older?'

'Why should I mind? What does it matter? What does anything matter, Jenny Wren, except that we've found one another?' Once more he folded her in his arms, overwhelmed by the strength of his feeling for her.

'Your birthday is in October then?' he asked a little while later. 'What date?'

'The seventeenth.'

'You're an October sort of person, Jenny.'

'What do you mean?'

'You have an autumn look about you. "Mellow fruitfulness" – that's Keats again – all ripe and rosy and ready for the picking.'

Jenny laughed. 'Then maybe that's why I like the autumn so much, because it's the time of the year that I was born.'

'What do you like about it?'

'Oh – the long evenings, the warm fire and the cosiness you feel when the curtains are drawn. The feeling that you're safe in your own little world and that nobody can touch you.'

'Nobody can touch us, Jenny. They'll never be able to take this away from us, whatever happens.'

Jenny felt a stab of fear and a shiver of premonition ran through her. Oh God – whatever were they to do? She reached silently for Robert's hand and felt the reassuring touch of his fingers closing round hers. She lay quietly in his arms and they watched the fire burning low until there was nothing left but the glowing embers.

'I must go, darling. Look at the time – I could stay here all night, but I mustn't.' Robert kissed her again, but gently this time, then rose to his feet.

The hands of the square wooden clock on the mantelpiece stood

159

at half past eleven. Jenny gave a start. 'Oh, goodness me! Mother will have locked you out. Whatever will she think?'

'Don't panic, Jenny Wren. I've got my own key – one of the privileges of being sergeant-in-charge, though I've never used it before. Are you frightened of your mother, Jenny?'

'No, not exactly frightened. It's just . . . No, of course I'm not frightened of her. We'll have to be careful, though, Robert.'

'I know. Oh, Jenny darling – I feel like shouting it from the rooftops, but I know we'll have to be discreet. I can come and see you again, can't I?'

'Of course.' She nodded, then looked at him pleadingly, like a small child. 'Soon, darling?'

'Very soon, my love.' He kissed her fleetingly. 'Don't come to the door. I'll let myself out.'

She heard the door close quietly behind him and the sound of his footsteps dying away down the street. She sank to her knees on the hearthrug, closing her eyes and folding her arms tightly round her body, hugging to herself the thought of Robert Cunningham. Dear God, how she loved him.

Chapter 14

Was this then what it was like to be in love, this feeling that was both pleasure and pain? Jenny was aware of a strange aching inside her as she relived every moment of their time together. As she lay in bed at night, alone and wide awake in the quiet darkness, she felt again, in her imagination, Robert's hands caressing her body. She heard his voice, soft and seductive, as warm as a glowing fire on a winter's evening, whispering words of love. She could smell the clean freshness of him – the faint scent of carbolic soap and brilliantine – and feel the roughness of his uniform greatcoat against her cheek as he took her in his arms for a final good-night kiss. And when sleep came at last, Robert filled her dreams, as he now filled most of her waking thoughts.

Never by a word or a glance did they give themselves away when they met day by day at Pleasant View. They spoke and smiled and laughed together as though they were casual acquaintances. But just knowing that he was in the same room sent a shivery tingling up Jenny's spine.

She felt as though she had been reawakened. Suddenly she was more sensitive to everything around her. She saw colours more brightly; the sapphire-blue of the autumn sky, the dark, brooding grey of the sea, the dull gold of the sand. Everything seemed much more vibrant, bursting with life. She began to feel things more deeply. For the first time the words of popular songs she heard on the wireless had a meaning for her. Now she knew what they meant when they sang of their beloved's eyes and lips and hair, of the world being upside down, of the beauty of moonlight and starlight.

'Yours till the stars lose their glory,' Jenny sang to herself as she did the ironing.

They met whenever they could at Jenny's home. Robert would have liked to have come every evening, but they both knew that they must be discreet. Who could tell if inquisitive eyes were watching as the young sergeant took his regular stroll down Green Street, always stopping at number sixteen? The evenings were growing darker now and the blackout curtains were drawn at all the windows. There was little chance of Robert being observed by nosy neighbours peeping through the curtains, but the other airmen were beginning to wonder where their sergeant disappeared to several times a week. He had always seemed such a stick-in-the-mud before, a permanent fixture in the lounge with his head buried in a book. Now he was obviously finding entertainment elsewhere.

One or two of the bolder lads asked him what he was doing with himself.

'Ask no questions and you'll be told no lies,' Robert replied with a laugh, tapping the side of his nose.

After a while they stopped asking. They had their own lives to lead when they were off duty – dancing, picture-going, sampling the ale in the Blackpool pubs, and sampling the local talent too. If Robert Cunningham, dark horse that he was, had found himself a girlfriend, then jolly good luck to him.

Jenny still took charge of the supper arrangements on Annie's whist nights, and on these evenings Robert stayed in the lounge. They spoke to one another only briefly. Jenny made a point of chatting at length to some of the other lads, to their great delight – she was such a pretty young woman and so popular with them all – but she was aware all the time of the vibrant current of attraction flowing between her and Robert. The atmosphere seemed so charged with their mutual empathy that she felt sure that everyone else must be aware of it.

Jenny knew, deep down inside her, that their behaviour was wrong. She had a good husband, selflessly serving his country. She had a child – two children really, for Rosie was almost like her own flesh and blood by now. She knew all this, but when she was with Robert all other considerations were swept aside. Nothing mattered but that they should be together. Their feeling for one another was not just physical, nor was it any passing infatuation. It was a meeting of true minds, each of them finding in the other the perfect soul mate.

Jenny felt that she must confide in someone about the wonderful and yet terrifying thing that had happened to her. She wondered if lovers always felt the need to talk about their beloved, to pour out their feelings and fears and forebodings to a sympathetic ear. To talk was to ease the anguish, to allay the doubts, to find reassurance that what she was doing was not really wrong.

Eileen gazed at her friend in open-mouthed astonishment. 'You mean to say that you and Robert Cunningham . . . ? You've let him make love to you? Oh . . . Jenny!' Eileen's eyes behind the circular lenses looked rounder than ever.

'It wasn't a question of letting him, Eileen. It just . . . happened. It had to happen. Can't you see?'

Eileen shook her head as she stared unbelievingly at her friend. 'Not really. I . . . don't understand.'

'Then that makes two of us,' said Jenny, 'because I don't understand it either. I only know that I love him, and he loves me, and I've never known anything like this before.'

'But what about your Tom? He's always been such a good husband to you. And there's Patsy, and now there's Rosie as well. You wouldn't leave them, would you, Jenny, and go off with . . . him?'

'Of course not. Robert wouldn't want me to. We haven't talked about anything like that. He's a very nice young man, you know, apart from the fact that I love him so much. He wouldn't want to do anything to hurt anyone.'

'But Tom would be very hurt if he found out. And aren't you afraid of him coming home on leave unexpectedly?'

'Not really. There's no leave being granted at the moment, except in very special circumstances. They're keeping all the troops down in the south of England in case of invasion. Of course they don't admit it, and Robert thinks there's not much chance of Hitler invading, but they're keeping the bases fully manned just in case.' Jenny paused, staring at the pattern of leaves on Eileen's carpet, then she went on, speaking slowly, 'Yes – I know that Tom would be hurt if he found out about Robert and me. That's what I find so confusing. You see, I still love Tom. Not in the way I love Robert – I never loved Tom that way – but I'm still fond of him. Oh, why should it be wrong to love two men?' Jenny leaned forward, looking pleadingly at her friend. 'I love both the little girls, don't I, Patsy and Rosie? Before Rosie came I didn't think that I could ever feel about any child the way I felt about my Patsy, but now I love them both. Why can't I love both Robert and Tom? Who makes the rules to say that we can't love more than one man?'

Eileen put her empty teacup on the table beside her. She was silent for a moment. Then, 'God makes them, I suppose,' she said quietly. 'It's in the Bible, and in the prayer book too. It's one of the

Commandments – "Thou shalt not commit adultery".'

'And I'm sure it's the one most often broken,' Jenny retorted. 'How can it be adultery when we love one another so much? It doesn't feel like adultery. I just want to . . . belong to him.'

'It's there in black and white, though, isn't it, whether we want to take notice of it or not. Do you remember, Jenny, all those years ago in Sunday school when we were reading the Ten Commandments and Lily Slater asked the teacher what adultery was?'

'Oh yes – Lily Slater – that fat girl with buck teeth and greasy hair.' Jenny giggled. 'And poor Miss Walters was all covered with confusion. She went all red and dropped her prayer book.'

'Do you remember what she said to Lily?'

'Yes – something about a castle. "Your body is your castle," she said. "Always keep your castle sparkling and bright and you'll never commit adultery." I didn't know what she was talking about, did you?'

'Well, I'd a vague idea it was something to with "that",' said Eileen. Remember, Jenny, how we were always so curious about it?'

'Yes, I remember.' Jenny giggled again. She found that she laughed so much more these days, in spite of her mind being continually in a turmoil. 'I was expecting Lily to say that she didn't live in a castle, just an ordinary house. Poor old Lily – I don't suppose she has ever had the chance to commit adultery.'

Eileen got up abruptly and started to poke at the embers of the fire. 'Very few of us have, Jenny.' Her voice was sharp, and Jenny sensed that she was annoyed.

'You're condemning me, aren't you?' she said, looking sideways at her friend. 'You think I'm dreadful, don't you?'

'No – of course I don't think you're dreadful,' said Eileen, more kindly. She came over to sit next to Jenny, on the arm of the chair, and put an arm companionably round her friend's shoulder. 'I've told you – I don't understand. Nothing like that has ever happened to me. I suppose I'm jealous in a way, to tell you the truth. Making love with Charlie is nothing to write home about. Just a bit of a fumble under the bedclothes on a Saturday night when he comes home from the pub. That's all it amounts to. It must be nice to be swept off your feet by a grand passion.'

'It wasn't all that marvellous with Tom either,' Jenny replied. 'I was quite happy at first, but this last year or two I must admit I've had to grin and bear it.'

'It isn't everything, though, is it? That side of marriage, I mean. Tom loves you, and you've got a nice home and your little girl. I know he's a bit of a stuffed shirt at times, your Tom, but none of 'em are perfect. My Charlie certainly isn't, but we just have to make the best of what we've got.'

Eileen paused for a moment, as if deep in thought, then she got up from her seat on Jenny's chair arm and went to sit on the settee on the opposite side of the fireplace. She leaned forward, her hands clasped between her knees, her big round eyes behind the big round lenses staring earnestly into Jenny's. 'You know, Jenny . . .' she began diffidently, 'I hope you don't mind me saying this, but a marriage has to be worked at. It doesn't just . . . happen. It's not all roses round the door and happy ever after like it is in those books you read. Real life isn't like that. It's . . . well, marriage is hard work at times, if you want it to work, that is.'

'I did work at it. Really I did,' said Jenny indignantly. 'Tom and I were all right together. We still are, I suppose . . . but he's not here, is he? It's hard to work at something when he's hundreds of miles away and . . .'

'And Robert's here . . . I know,' said Eileen quietly. 'Robert's so near, and poor old Tom's so far away. And Robert's so very good-looking. You've been swept off your feet, haven't you, love?'

'Not really,' replied Jenny simply. 'I do love him. I'm not just imagining it. At times I wish I didn't . . .'

'You were very young when you married Tom, weren't you?' said Eileen. 'I know I was, too, when Charlie and I were married, but not quite as young as you were. I daresay you didn't know just what to expect.'

'I don't think Tom did either,' said Jenny with a little laugh. 'We were both inexperienced when it came to . . . that. But you don't need to think that we didn't try, Eileen, because we did,' she added, a trifle hotly. 'And – I've told you – we were all right. It just wasn't very exciting, that's all. And . . .' Jenny paused, fiddling absent-mindedly with a button on her cardigan, 'I've never said this to anyone before, but – d'you know? – I think sometimes that I got married to get away from me mother. That sounds awful, doesn't it?' she added in a shocked voice.

'Not at all,' said Eileen, laughing. 'She can be a bit much, your ma. I reckon I did the same when I come to think of it. I know I was glad of a bit of independence. Mothers round here seem to want you to be tied to their apron strings, don't they? Anyway, this . . . thing between you and Robert, it'll all come to an end, won't it, when Robert gets posted?'

'He'll be around for quite a while yet,' said Jenny. 'He finished his wireless operator's training very quickly. He knew most of it because he'd studied at the tech when he left school, so they've asked him to stay on as an instructor. I don't know for how long – he doesn't know himself – but I'm afraid he won't be conveniently whisked away, much as you would like it, Eileen.'

'Oh, come on, love. I'm not blaming you. Any girl could fall for him. He's quite a dish, your Sergeant Cunningham. But I care about you, Jenny. We've been friends for ages, haven't we, and I don't want you to get hurt or be unhappy.'

'That's something I'll have to risk. I don't suppose we are meant to be happy all the time.' Jenny sighed. 'I had to tell somebody about it, and who better than you? Keep it under your hat, though, won't you, love? I haven't told anybody else.'

'Of course I will! What do you take me for? I won't breathe a word. I say, Jenny, your mother would go mad if she knew, wouldn't she?'

'She'd go stark raving barmy! I'm frightened to death of her finding out. Robert thinks I'm daft, always worrying about what my mother would say, but he doesn't know what she's really like. She can be as nice as pie to those airmen, and they think she's wonderful. If only they knew!'

'Yes, your ma's quite a tyrant, I must admit. How's your Violet, by the way? Is she still seeing that young fellow she met at the Tower?'

'No . . . it all seems to have fizzled out. He wasn't really suitable for our Violet. She was upset at first, but she seems to be all right again now.'

'Does she know about it?' asked Eileen. 'What you've just been telling me, about you and . . . ?'

'About Robert? Good heavens – no! Our Violet's a very virtuous young lady. She'd have a fit. Besides, she thinks the sun shines out of Tom.'

'And what about the children? Aren't you scared of them finding out? I suppose they're all tucked up in bed before Robert comes round?'

'Yes. There's a lock on the living-room door, so I always turn the key. They never wake up once they're asleep, but if they did, they couldn't just walk straight in. It would give us time . . . Oh, it makes it all seem so shameful, and it isn't like that at all. It's . . . wonderful.'

'I've no doubt it is,' said Eileen drily. 'But you know what they say about wives who play around while their husbands are away . . . Oh, I'm sorry, Jenny. I shouldn't have said that. It was unkind – but do be careful, love.'

Jenny looked anxiously at her friend. 'Whatever am I going to do, Eileen? I love him so much.' She sighed, knowing that it was a pointless question. What was there to do except to go on loving him? 'Oh, gosh! What a mess and a muddle it all is. Thanks for listening to me. I don't know what I'd do without you.'

'Be happy, Jenny,' said Eileen simply, leaning forward and kissing her cheek. 'I'll be thinking about you.'

Jenny could feel her friend's eyes watching her thoughtfully as she walked back down the street to number sixteen.

'Come on, you two. Let's listen to *Children's Hour*,' Jenny called to the two little girls. 'Princess Elizabeth's going to broadcast today.'

They sat and stared at the wireless set with the sunray design cut into the woodwork, hearing first the jolly voice of Derek McCulloch – Uncle Mac – then the precise, cultured tones of the young heir to the throne speaking to the children who had been evacuated overseas.

'. . . I can truthfully say to you all that we children at home are full of cheerfulness and courage. We are trying to do all we can to help our gallant sailors, soldiers and airmen, and we are trying too to bear our own share of the danger and sadness of war. We know, every one of us, that in the end all will be well . . . My sister Margaret Rose and I feel so much for you, as we know from experience what it means to be away from those we love most of all . . . My sister is by my side, and we are both going to say good night – come on, Margaret.'

Both sisters joined in the final message – 'Good night and good luck to you all.'

'She's got the same name as me, that little 'un,' said Rosie proudly. 'Princess Margaret Rose. Me mum called me after her, see. I think she's nice, don't you, Auntie Jenny?'

'I think they're both lovely little girls,' said Jenny. 'Princess Elizabeth's not so little now, though, come to think of it. She must be about fourteen.'

'What did they mean, Mummy,' asked Patsy, 'about being away from the people they love? They've not been 'vacuated, have they?

167

Wouldn't it be nice if they'd been sent here?'

Jenny laughed. 'No, dear. They haven't been evacuated. They stayed up in Scotland when the war started, and their parents came back to London, so they were all separated for a while. That's what happens in wartime. I expect they missed their parents, like you miss your mum, Rosie, and like you miss Daddy, Patsy.'

Patsy did miss her dad. Not that he'd ever played with her very much, or read stories to her, or sung to her like Mummy did. He had played with them that Christmas, though, soon after Rosie came. He had been much jollier then, but Rosie always seemed to make people laugh. She even had the teachers at school in stitches laughing at her sometimes, with the funny things she said. Daddy had always been there, though, reading his newspaper, or listening to the wireless, or playing quiet little games with his toy soldiers. Not speaking very much, but just being there, safe and steady and dependable.

Mummy had been tired and cross before he went away. She'd been snappy and she'd shouted at Patsy sometimes, but Rosie had seemed to make her happy again. Rosie made everybody happy . . . There was no doubt that Mummy was happy now. She laughed a lot and was forever dancing round the room and singing to herself. She looked so pretty too. She had always been pretty – Patsy loved her dark curly hair and wished that her own hair was like that – but now she was prettier than ever.

'Come on, you two,' Jenny called now. 'Here's your favourite song. Let's dance, shall we?'

'Tiptoe through the Tulips' was playing on the gramophone, and Jenny seized the hands of both little girls and they all cavorted round the room, singing and dancing and shrieking with laughter.

> 'Tiptoe . . . from your pillow,
> To the shadow . . . of the willow tree,
> Come tiptoe . . . through the tulips . . . with me.'

Patsy hoped that Mummy would stay happy like this for ever.

'I suppose you had the idea that he wasn't good enough for you.' Annie turned round from the sink where she was washing up and glared indignantly at her younger daughter. 'Just because he gets his hands dirty earning an honest bob, you looked down your nose at him.'

'No, Mother. It wasn't like that at all.' Violet spoke through clenched teeth. 'It's just that . . . I didn't think that Tony and I had much in common. He thought so as well.'

'What do you want then? A doctor or lawyer or summat? You could have done a lot worse than settle for Tony Harris, I'll tell you, my girl.'

'I'm a bit young to settle for anyone, surely? I'm only twenty, Mother. I haven't had much chance to look around yet.'

Annie slammed another plate on to the draining board. 'What do you want to look around for? Our Jenny was married when she was nineteen. I'll admit I thought she was a bit young at the time, but it's worked out splendidly. She couldn't have a better husband than Tom, and he was only an ordinary working lad. She's never wanted to look around since she met Tom. She's happy with what she's got. You could learn a lot from our Jenny.'

Jenny felt a guilty flush stain her cheeks. She didn't look at her mother or Violet, but went on steadily drying the pots, keeping her head averted. She felt sorry for her sister. Since Annie had found out that Violet's friendship with Tony had come to an end, she had never let the matter drop. Poor Violet. She had been upset enough as it was, without her mother harping on about it. Mother had taken a fancy to the young man – one that Jenny knew was misplaced – but neither of the sisters could tell their mother the real reason for the break-up.

'And your father too – God rest his soul,' Annie continued. 'He was only an ordinary sort of chap. He worked down the pit when I met him, so he wasn't afraid of hard work, and he was none the worse for that. No good comes of it when you start getting ideas above your station.'

'Let it drop, can't you, Mother!' Violet exclaimed, more sharply than Jenny had ever heard her speak before. 'It's over and that's all there is to it. I'm sick and tired of hearing you go on about it.'

'Huh!' Annie grunted. 'Well, at least I have to admit that you're staying in a bit more now, instead of gadding out every night.' Her tone was a little less cantankerous, Jenny was pleased to notice. It didn't do any harm to stand up to Mother once in a while. 'It's about time you spent a few nights at home.' This was Annie's parting shot as she turned back to the sink.

Behind her mother's back Violet looked at her sister and raised her eyebrows. Jenny grinned back sympathetically. With Mother you just couldn't win.

* * *

'Happy birthday, darling.' Robert reached into the pocket of his overcoat and took out a small package. 'I thought it was better not to send you a card – I know how you worry about people finding out – but this says far more than any card could do. Read it, and think about me.' He drew her into his arms and kissed her. 'Goodnight, my love. I'll see you tomorrow.'

Jenny smiled happily to herself as she knelt on the hearthrug before the glowing embers of the fire. She was still like a child about birthdays and Christmas. She loved the excitement and the anticipation, and especially she loved surprise presents. She should really wait until tomorrow – presents should always be opened on the correct day – but she was too impatient to wait until then. Besides, Patsy and Rosie would be clamouring for attention in the morning.

Eagerly she pulled off the brown paper to reveal a book, beautifully bound in green leather with gold lettering on the spine: *A Selection of Favourite Romantic Poetry*. The inscription on the flyleaf was simple. 'To Jenny with my love. October 17th 1940. Robert.'

She thumbed through the fine pages – Browning, Byron, Keats, Shelley, Wordsworth. She had read some of the poems at school and quite enjoyed them, those that she could understand, but she had never owned such a beautiful book before.

Which was the poem that Robert had quoted from, that first night that he came here, the night when they had declared their love for one another? Something by Keats . . . Yes, there it was – 'Lamia'. She settled down to read the poem, strange but fascinating, about the youth from Corinth who fell in love with a lovely girl, only to discover that she was a serpent in disguise. Their love was based on an illusion.

'Do not all charms fly at the touch of cold philosophy?' Jenny read the chilling words and felt a shudder of premonition run through her. But her love for Robert was no illusion; it was warm and vibrant and real. Like the lovers in the poem they too were 'happy in beauty, life and love and everything'. Nothing could touch a love such as theirs. Maybe in the eyes of the world it was wrong. Eventually there may come a day of reckoning, but for the moment their secret was safe. Their love was inviolate.

'Too short was their bliss . . .' Once again the words of the poem seemed to leap from the page, sounding a warning note in Jenny's brain. They seemed strangely prophetic, and again she shuddered.

170

Chapter 15

Jenny pulled her belt more tightly round her waist as she hurried through the station entrance. She was aware that her tweed coat was shabby – it was two years old – but a new red beret had added a splash of colour to her appearance.

They had arranged to meet at ten o'clock at the station and Robert was already there, waiting at the barrier.

'Jenny, darling – come on. I've got the tickets.'

He took her hand as they pushed their way through the crowds to the waiting train. Jenny breathed a sigh of relief as the train pulled away from the station. That was the worst part – getting away from Blackpool without being seen – but they had done it. She leaned back in her seat and smiled shyly at Robert who was sitting opposite her. 'Is your journey really necessary?' the poster above his head asked accusingly, but Jenny considered that it was.

She had needed some persuading at first to come away for the weekend. It had involved telling lies, which Jenny hated doing. Besides, Mother could always see right through her – she had been able to do so ever since Jenny was a little girl. But, surprisingly, Annie had agreed that she had worked hard and that she deserved a weekend way. She had believed, too, Jenny's tale that she was going to stay with her old school friend Joan, who lived in Preston.

At Preston station they had to change for the train to Lancaster and Morecambe. Here, on the crowded platform, they were jostled by soldiers and airmen, and a few sailors, carrying bulging kitbags. There were very few people in civilian clothes, except for the women, dressed mainly as Jenny was in tweed coats that had seen better days and woollen hats. They had nearly an hour to wait for a connection so they sat in the refreshment room drinking tepid tea from thick white cups.

'Did you get away all right, darling?' Robert asked. 'No problems?'

'No – none at all. The girls are excited at the thought of staying at Ada's tonight. They're having their dinner at my mother's first. She's been marvellous about it really – Mother, I mean – I feel terrible deceiving her like this.'

'Don't, Jenny.' Robert leaned across and squeezed her hand. 'The girls are being taken care of, and your mother's happy about it. Don't spend your time feeling guilty, just enjoy the weekend, mm?'

She smiled back happily. Robert, as always, was able to charm away all her fears. 'Of course I will,' she said. 'It's going to be wonderful.'

In Morecambe they found a boarding house with a Vacancies sign at the end of a long street leading from the promenade. Here, as in Blackpool, there were still several establishments that catered for the occasional weekend visitors.

After they had unpacked their few belongings they dined, in the middle of the afternoon, at a small café near the pier. Jenny thought that she had never tasted such delicious fish and chips; succulent cod, covered with crispy brown batter, and golden chips, gently steaming as her knife cut into them. Or perhaps it was because it was their first meal together, their wedding breakfast, as it were. The red and white checked tablecloth, the blue rims round the plates and cups, the sauce and vinegar bottles on the table – all these homely details imprinted themselves on Jenny's mind. She knew she would remember them for ever.

With their arms round one another they sauntered across the promenade and down the steps to the beach. The sand stretched for miles, with the sea just a glimpse of silver in the distance.

'That's one of the things I remember best about Morecambe,' said Jenny, 'what a long way the tide goes out. It must come in sometimes, I suppose, but there always seems to be more sand here than there is at home.'

Here, as in Blackpool, you could smell the sea in the salt-laden air. It was a golden autumn afternoon. The sun hung low in the sky, a red fiery ball, and above their heads the seagulls wheeled and screeched.

'Come on – I'll race you to the sea.' Robert set off at a run, and Jenny followed him, shouting with laughter.

'Catch me,' Robert yelled. 'There's a prize if you can catch me.'

His voice rang out clearly in the still air – there was hardly any wind today – as Jenny chased after him, following the footprints that his feet made in the wet sand. Nearer the sea the sand was crinkled and the ridges left by the tide hurt her feet.

'Stop – Robert, stop!' she yelled. 'I've got a stitch in my side and my feet are hurting. I give up. You win.'

Robert turned and ran back towards her. Laughing, he swept her up in his arms and whirled her round and round until she was dizzy.

'Help!' she shrieked. 'Put me down!'

'Gladly,' said Robert, panting in an exaggerated manner. 'I couldn't say that you're as light as a feather.' His hands wandered over her body. 'Mm,' he murmured. 'Soft and round, like a ripe apple, just the way I like them.'

'Can I have my prize?' asked Jenny teasingly. 'I didn't win, but I'm sure you've got something for me, haven't you?'

Robert grinned at her, his eyes twinkling with amusement. As his lips closed over hers Jenny felt that she had never been so happy in her life, and never had she loved Robert so much.

They leaned on the railing and watched the sun gradually disappearing below the horizon, painting the clouds in softly glowing colours of pink, orange and crimson. The sea glittered with millions of golden coins scattered by the sun's dying rays, and in the distance the hills of the Lake District stood out stark and black against the darkening sky.

'God's in His heaven, All's right with the world,' Robert whispered, laying his cold cheek against Jenny's.

'Do you believe in God, Robert?'

'Yes – I do. When I look at all this around us – the sea and the sky and so much beauty – I can't help but believe in Him. But there's part of me that can't believe in a God that allows wars to happen. Wars that cause so much misery and suffering.'

'I don't suppose God's very happy about it either. I'm sure He doesn't want it all to happen. It's people that cause it all, isn't it, not God? People getting greedy and wanting more than their fair share of everything. That's what causes wars, when you think about it.'

'God's very real to you, isn't He, Jenny – more like a person?'

'I suppose so. I've not thought about it much. I haven't been to church for ages, but I still remember what we were taught in Sunday school, about God caring for us. I have to believe that He's there somewhere, in charge of it all, or else none of it would make sense. Not that I understand it. Sometimes it seems like a great big muddle. I only hope that God can sort it all out.'

Robert smiled at her. 'You're lovely, Jenny. Very lovely.' He gently stroked her eyelids and nose with the tip of his finger. 'Sometimes I can't believe that you're real, that all this is happening to me. Oh, darling, I'm so happy that you agreed to come away with me.'

'I'm happy too, love.' Jenny leaned her head contentedly against his shoulder. 'So very happy. I know that it's wrong, though, to be here with you like this. If anyone were to find out, they would think we were dreadful. But when I'm with you, nothing else seems to matter.'

'Don't let's waste time thinking about the rights or wrongs of it, my love. We have these two days – whether we should have them or not is beside the point. Let's just make the most of our time together. This is our honeymoon, darling.'

'Only two days,' said Jenny wistfully. 'Such a very short time. And tomorrow we will have to be home again.'

'If every minute were an hour, then we would have several weeks together. Let's make the most of every second, Jenny. Let's make it a weekend that we will remember for ever.'

For ever . . . For ever was eternity, and Jenny didn't dare to think about the future. There was only the present, the here and now.

'Oh, Robert,' she cried, burying her head against his shoulder. 'I don't want to think of a time when we're not together. It frightens me. I want to think that we'll always be together like this, loving one another.'

'We will be, Jenny,' said Robert softly, 'so long as we have our memories. I read somewhere once – I can't remember where – that everything we do, everything we say, exists for ever and ever so long as there is someone to remember it. So we'll always be together, darling, together in our minds, every time we think of one another.'

He kissed her gently and, as always, Jenny forgot everything but the strength of Robert's arms around her, the softness of his lips upon hers.

The evening meal, cooked by the homely landlady Mrs Bates, was, to their surprise, delicious. Shepherd's pie, with the potatoes fluffy and nicely browned, the meat tender and well cooked with not a trace of gristle. Ginger pudding and creamy custard completed a most satisfying meal.

'That was grand,' said Jenny. 'I couldn't eat another thing. Even my mother couldn't have cooked it any better.'

'And that's praise indeed,' added Robert, laughing. 'I must admit your mother's a fine cook, and her daughter's not so bad either. Remember the Woolton pie, Jenny? That was the first time I really spoke to you.'

Jenny nodded. That was the day when she had first realised that she was attracted to Robert. 'I think I began to fall in love with you then,' she said, 'when you came with your plate asking for a second helping.'

'I started to love you long before that,' said Robert. 'From the first moment I saw you, serving in the dining room in your frilly apron, blushing so prettily at the lads' remarks. I daresay they all fancy you, if the truth were told, Jenny. I knew that you were married, but it didn't make any difference. I couldn't forget you, and I don't think I even tried. It was enough, at the beginning, just to see you each day. Knowing that you were there was all that mattered. Then, when we met that day on the cliffs and I kissed you, I just couldn't believe it. Oh, my darling, it was all I'd ever dreamed about.'

They reached out and held hands across the starched white tablecloth. Jenny felt as though they were floating in a time bubble, just the two of them, oblivious to everything and everyone else in the world. She didn't dare to admit to herself that bubbles could burst, and their happiness might be transitory. It didn't seem possible that it could ever end.

Robert squeezed her fingers. 'Come on, love. Get your glad rags on and we'll go out for the evening.'

In the bedroom, chilly in the early November evening, Jenny slipped off her woollen skirt and red jumper and reached into the wardrobe for her dress. It was her only good one; emerald green, which highlighted the colour of her eyes, in silky rayon with a sweetheart neckline and a skirt of flaring pleats. Like her coat it was two years old, but Jenny had rejuvenated it by adding a touch of lace to the neckline and a wide black belt which accentuated the smallness of her waist. She was faintly embarrassed, feeling Robert's eyes upon her as she stood there in her plain blue rayon slip. She didn't know why she should feel like this – Robert's

lovemaking had taught her to be unashamed of her nakedness –
but tonight it was different. The room was an unfamiliar one and
for a moment Jenny felt afraid. What was she doing here, miles
away from home, with a man who wasn't her husband? Tentatively
she undid her suspenders, changing her everyday stockings for a
pair of new, pure silk ones. She looked up and smiled shyly at
Robert and when he smiled back at her – his glance not
provocative, just loving and tender – she knew that it was foolish to
be frightened. He didn't speak, nor did he reach out for her. It was
just as well, or they would never have got out that evening.

The Palais de Danse was a small, intimate room up a steep flight
of stairs in a side street, as unlike the Tower or the Winter Gardens
as you could imagine. But the clientele was similar – mainly
soldiers, sailors and airmen with their wives or sweethearts –
probably more of the latter – plus the local lads of eighteen and
under who hadn't yet been called up.

It was heavenly to float round the ballroom floor, feeling
Robert's strong arm around her and his lips brushing against her
hair. Violet had told her about the Tower and the Wurlitzer organ,
and the thrill of dancing there, but Jenny was more than content to
be here, listening to the wailing saxophone and the tinny voice of
the young girl vocalist crooning into the microphone:

'It's a lovely day tomorrow,
Tomorrow is a lovely day.
Come and feast your tear-dimmed eyes
On tomorrow's clear blue skies.'

A song for lovers who were parted, who looked forward to the
tomorrow when they would be together again. But for Robert and
Jenny, today was of the essence. There might never be a
tomorrow.

The band stopped playing on a sudden discordant cadence. They
clapped like the other couples around them. Then, as the lights
came on again, they walked hand in hand off the ballroom floor to
the small red-plush chairs arranged round the walls.

'You're a good dancer,' said Jenny. Where did you learn?'

'In my last year at school. We had dancing lessons with the local
girls' school. I used to dance with . . . some girls I knew.'

Jenny was aware that he had been about to mention Marjorie,

176

but she wasn't jealous. She knew him too well to be envious of anything that had happened before. She and Robert were inseparable, two matching halves of a perfect whole.

'I'm not much of a dancer,' she admitted. 'I used to go now and again when I was younger – when Mother would let me off the leash – but I've not been lately. Listen – they're playing a waltz. I can do that best. Come on.'

She seized his hand, and they drifted round to the strains of 'One Day when we were Young'.

'You told me you loved me,
When we were young one day,'

trilled the reedy voice of the singer.

'Shall we go soon, darling?' Robert murmured.

Jenny smiled up at him, seeing the warm glow of desire shining from his eyes. 'Yes.' Her voice was the merest whisper. 'Let's go now, love.'

The streets were dark and the few buses that trundled past were lit with a dim blue light, painting the passengers' faces an eerie purple hue. There were few stars and the merest sliver of a crescent moon, but Robert's pocket torch lit the way for them up the steep slope to the boarding house.

Jenny shivered as she slipped her pink celanese nightdress over her head. It was a chilly night – warm winceyette pyjamas would have been more appropriate – but she knew that very soon Robert would provide all the warmth that she needed.

When she returned from the bathroom he was sitting up in bed. His blue and white striped pyjamas were hanging from the brass bed rail – he'd brought them along for modesty's sake, no doubt, in case the landlady should enter the room in their absence.

He threw back the blankets and the quilted eiderdown, and Jenny thrilled at the lean lines of his naked body as he strode to the doorway and quickly put out the light. Then he walked across to the window and pulled back the curtains and the blackout blinds.

There was very little light from the moon and stars, but their eyes gradually grew accustomed to the darkness. Jenny opened her arms to him and they sank into the soft depths of the feather bed.

'Oh, my darling,' he whispered, as he had done so many times before.

And it was as though it was for the first time ever. They came together rapturously and without restraint. They knew one another so intimately by now, their minds as well as their bodies, that the act of love was 'a thing of beauty . . . a joy for ever', its loveliness increasing with each consummation.

Jenny woke to find Robert raised on one elbow, gazing down at her. She had slept peacefully, cradled in his arms, knowing that for tonight at least nothing and nobody could touch them and their love.

'Lazybones,' he teased, touching the tip of her nose with his finger. 'I've been watching you for ages. Shall we get up now . . . or . . . ?'

'Or, I think,' she said mischievously, holding out her arms to him.

'You're a wicked, wanton woman,' he mumbled into her hair as she joyously opened herself to him.

She felt almost detached in her happiness, as though she were viewing a scene from far away. She reflected that Robert's lovemaking, like everything else about him, was beautiful. If ever that adjective could be used to describe a man, then it described Robert. Jenny loved not only his looks, but everything about him. His air of quiet, well-bred modesty was one of the first things that she had noticed. As she grew to love him more, she realised that he was not shy and withdrawn as she had first thought; he was reserved, unwilling to commit himself until he was sure. Now they were unashamedly committed to one another. There could be no going back, but the way forward was unknown.

The rest of the day passed all too quickly, despite their pretence of counting every minute as an hour. They wandered into a little park just off the promenade where the trees were shedding their last remaining leaves, a harbinger of the approaching winter. Some of the trees, victims of the northerly gales, were already bare, their branches forming a tapestry of lacework against the grey sky. Jenny was gripped by an unaccountable feeling of sadness, as though the dying of the year was symbolising the end of everything for them.

The day was cold, with low-hanging clouds, and the light was already beginning to fade as, in the early afternoon, they boarded the train for Preston.

'Cheer up, darling,' said Robert, looking at her glum face. 'We're not saying goodbye, you know. I'll see you tomorrow at home, and the day after, and the day after that.'

Jenny smiled at him. 'I know – but it's been so perfect, I don't want it to end.'

'Our love will never end, darling,' said Robert quietly, 'but this weekend must, I'm afraid. Listen, love – I'm going to get off the train at South Station. I don't want to, but it wouldn't do for us to be seen together. You'll be all right, won't you? You go on to Central Station and get out there, just as though you've been away on your own.'

The journey ended all too soon and sadness enveloped Jenny as she watched Robert's tall figure stride briskly away into the gathering darkness, turning once to wave and blow a kiss. At least she had two days to remember, two golden days which she could pluck from the storehouse of memories in her mind and think about when the future looked dark. There was a song that they used to sing at school – 'Fond memory brings the light of other days around us.' God, in His infinite wisdom, must have known that mere mortals could never exist without memory.

She had a feeling that, very soon, memories would be all that she and Robert had to keep them going. The future was uncertain, not just for them, but for everyone, but their memories would keep the flame of their love glowing even when they had to part. 'For how long?' whispered a niggling little voice, deep within her. Would the flame of their love burn as brightly when they were parted, when it could no longer be rekindled by voice and touch and presence, or would it be extinguished by the passing days, months, years . . . ? Jenny felt a cold fear grip her as she stared through the carriage window into the gloom of the November evening. 'We'll always be together,' Robert had said earlier that weekend, 'so long as we have our memories.' Jenny's heart warmed again as she thought of him, and she tried to push away the depressing doubts. Their love would live for ever . . .

Chapter 16

'We had a lovely time at Auntie Ada's,' Patsy said happily. 'Did you have a nice time, Mummy?'

'Er . . . yes, thank you, dear. Very nice,' Jenny replied, feeling somewhat disorientated.

She had been in the house only about ten minutes when Violet arrived with the girls. It was hard to adjust to her normal surroundings after a weekend which was already beginning to take on the semblance of a dream.

'You're looking tired, Jenny,' said Violet, eyeing her sister with concern. 'I expect you've been up half the night chatting about old times, haven't you? Or were you and Joan out painting the town red?'

'Joan?' Jenny gave a puzzled frown. 'Oh yes – Joan. Yes . . . like you said, Vi,' she added quickly, 'we were chatting till all hours.' She was aware that her sister was looking at her searchingly. Oh, crikey! She'd nearly given herself away. She must pull herself together and try to act normally. 'I'm sorry. I was miles away. I am feeling tired. The train was crowded and I had to stand most of the way home. It's not really worth going away at all. They try to put us off by saying "Is your journey really necessary?" and I suppose they're right. We ought to leave the trains free for the servicemen. It isn't fair to go gadding about for pleasure when there's a war on.'

Jenny was aware that she was chattering inanely. 'I was just going to make a cup of tea. You'll have one, won't you, Vi?'

She was glad to escape to the kitchen to put the kettle on. She put her hands to her burning cheeks and took several deep breaths to still the trembling inside her. Automatically she took four cups and saucers from the cupboard and set them on a tray. The normality of the actions helped to steady her shaking hands and to focus her attention on the present. The weekend away had now, of necessity, become the past. A secret shared by her and Robert, to

181

be plucked from her memory and relived in every minute detail when she was alone.

When she returned to Violet and the girls she was more composed and the hand that poured out the tea was steady and unwavering.

'You had a good time then, did you?' she asked brightly. 'I'm sure I don't need to ask if you were good girls for Auntie Ada.'

'Yes, 'course we were, Mummy, and we helped her ever such a lot, didn't we, Rosie? Miss Alice is poorly in bed and we carried up cups of tea and magazines for her to read.'

Jenny looked anxiously at Violet. 'Miss Alice is ill, is she? Oh dear – I hope it wasn't too much for our Ada having the children. It's not anything serious, is it?'

'No – I don't think so,' Violet assured her. 'Just a bad cold that's settled on her chest. She gets a lot of bronchitis in the winter and the doctor said she'd better stay in bed for a few days. Ada didn't tell you because she was looking forward to having the girls, and she thought you should have your weekend away, like you'd planned.'

Jenny felt a stab of guilt. 'Cousin Ada's a real gem, isn't she? She seems to have spent most of her life running about after other folk – mainly Miss Alice and Miss Maud. I must call and see the old lady tomorrow, then I can say thank you to Ada for having the girls.'

'Auntie Jenny?' Rosie's blue eyes were looking puzzled and her forehead was creased in a frown.

'Yes, dear?'

'Well, I was wondering. Why do you always call those two old ladies Miss Alice and Miss Maud? They don't call Auntie Ada Miss Ada, do they? Why doesn't she call them Alice and Maud, same as they call her Ada?'

'Well, I suppose it's because she's a servant, dear.' Jenny realised that she had never given it much thought before. 'Miss Alice and Miss Maud employ her – they pay her to do their work for them.'

'Why? Can't they do it themselves?'

'I suppose they could, but they've never been used to doing housework.'

'Why?'

Oh dear! It would be far easier to tell Rosie not to ask so many

182

questions, but Jenny didn't believe in telling children to be quiet when they wanted to know things. But how did one begin to explain the complicated business of class structure to a child such as Rosie?'

'Their father was a doctor,' Jenny explained. 'They had a lot of money, so they've always paid somebody to do their work for them. That's what it's all about, I suppose.' Jenny smiled at the little girl. 'Some people have a lot of money, and others have very little. It doesn't seem fair, but that's the way it is. If you have money you can afford all sorts of things – like servants, for instance.'

'You've hit the nail on the head there, Jenny,' said Violet. 'It all boils down to the haves and have nots. Them as has got a bit of brass, as Mother would say, and them as hasn't. There's far too much inequality in this country of ours, but when this lot's over there'll be a sort out, you mark my words. The Labour Party'll come into their own – you see if they don't. They've had one or two goes at it, but they haven't amounted to much yet. But their day will come, you can be sure.'

'Steady on, Violet.' Jenny wagged a finger at her sister. 'Don't let Mother hear you talking like that. She'd disown you. You know she never has a good word to say for Labour folks. "Always wanting summat for nowt" – that's what she says about them. You know what people say about the Conservatives – stick a blue ribbon on a pig and they'll vote for it. That's Mother to a T. She's voted Tory all her life and she's not going to change her ideas now. She'd have a fit if she heard what you've been saying.'

Violet laughed. 'Yes, I know. You remember that hymn we used to sing in Sunday school, Jenny? "The rich man in his castle, The poor man at his gate. God made them high or lowly, And ordered their estate." Well, that's what Mother believes. A place for everyone, and everyone in his place. Oh, I got so mad with her when she was going on about Tony, do you remember? Telling me that I thought he wasn't good enough for me. Of course I didn't think that . . .'

'Do you hear anything of Tony now?' asked Jenny. 'I didn't like to mention him at first, you seemed so upset about it all . . .'

'Oh, I've got over it now,' said Violet. 'It was a shock seeing him with Sheila that night, but I don't think he lasted very long with her. No . . . I haven't heard anything of him since he was posted down south. And thank goodness Mother has stopped talking about him!'

'And you and Sheila are still the best of friends?'

'Yes, of course we are. There's no point in falling out over fellows. They're not worth it, are they?' Violet laughed. 'I must admit, though, that I like Joyce better than Sheila. Sheila's a flighty piece . . . Oh gosh!' Violet put her hand over her mouth. 'I sound like Mother, don't I? But they've both been very good friends to me. Do you remember what I was like before I went to work at the factory? I wouldn't say boo to a goose!'

'You've certainly changed a lot, our Vi,' Jenny remarked. 'I didn't know you were a budding Socialist, though.'

'Oh, I've had leanings that way for some time. Your Tom agrees with me too. We both think the country's ready for a change. But you must know all about his political views, Jenny. You're married to him.'

Jenny didn't answer. She thought again how very little she knew about Tom and how he seemed to be able to communicate with Violet so much more easily than with herself.

'You get on very well with the Misses Frobisher, though, don't you?' said Jenny, getting away from the subject of Tom. 'And you couldn't find two more dyed-in-the-wool Tories than they are.'

'It's the way they've been brought up. They're the remnants of an archaic society,' said Violet. 'Of course I like them – they're dear old souls and they're so kind in their own way – but I don't think they've ever realised that Ada's a person in her own right. They just see her as an extension of themselves. Poor Ada – she's never had a place of her own, being in service all her life.'

'I shouldn't worry too much about Ada,' said Jenny. 'She seems contented enough. That little parlour is like a palace to her.'

'But it doesn't even belong to her, does it?' said Violet. She shook her head impatiently. 'She makes me so cross at times with her servile attitude. "Yes, Miss Alice" and "No, Miss Maud" all the time. There were big changes after the last war, you know, and not before time either. A lot of women found employment elsewhere instead of going into service, and there'll be even more changes when this war comes to an end. I'm thinking of doing something more worthwhile with my life when this lot's over.'

'What do you mean, Vi?' Jenny looked at her sister in surprise. 'I thought you wanted to get married. Eventually, I mean, when Mr Right comes along. Not that that isn't worthwhile,' she added hastily, 'but you didn't mean that, did you?'

'No – I don't see why marriage has to be the be all and end all for women. It's all right when you meet the right man, like you did, but lots of girls don't.' Violet paused, idly stirring her spoon round and round in her cup, then she looked up at her sister and smiled. 'I'm thinking of studying to be a teacher. I always wanted to, but Mother wouldn't hear of it.'

'Fancy that – a teacher in the family! Mother'll be right proud of you, in spite of all she says.'

'Oh, it's early days yet, but I've started reading again since I stopped seeing Tony. I'd been neglecting my books, gadding about with Joyce and Sheila, and then meeting Tony.'

'Don't work too hard, though.' Jenny smiled at her sister. 'You know what they say: All work and no play . . . and you've seemed much happier since you started going out more.'

'Yes, I know. I'll go out once or twice a week, and the rest of the time I'm going to catch up with my reading. I'll do the airmen's supper on Thursdays, by the way, while Mother's at her whist drive, so you won't need to come round.'

Jenny made a mental note to tell Robert that she would be free those evenings.

Ada appeared flustered when she answered the door to Jenny's knock the following day.

'Oh, it's you,' she said, a faint flush tingeing her cheeks. 'Well, you'd best come in.' She continued to stand in the doorway, barring Jenny's entrance.

Jenny laughed. 'I will, if you'll shift and let me get past.'

Whatever was up with Ada? she wondered. It wasn't like her to be so unwelcoming. Her cousin grunted and led the way up the hall to her own private domain. She paused at the door.

'I've got company,' she said over her shoulder to Jenny, giving a curt nod.

There was a man sitting in one of the armchairs, his feet outstretched to the glowing fire. So that's it, thought Jenny. Ada was a dark horse and no mistake!

He sprang to his feet as they entered and looked enquiringly at the cousins. His shrewd brown eyes gave the impression that he didn't miss much. He wasn't very tall – about five foot five, the same height as Ada. He had sleek black hair and a little moustache – like Hitler – but there the resemblance ended. This man's eyes were kind and his lips curved in a humorous smile. He was smartly dressed in a dark suit – his courting suit, Jenny smiled to herself.

'This is Fred,' said Ada abruptly. 'He used to be our milkman. This is me cousin Jenny that you've head me speak about.'

'Pleased to meet you,' Fred said in a precise voice as he shook Jenny's hand. 'Come and sit down by the fire and get warm. Ada was just going to make a cup of tea.'

'First I've heard of it,' that lady retorted, folding her arms across her starched white apron. 'You certainly know how to make yourself at home, Fred Bottomley, I'll say that for you. I've only just finished washing up my ladies' dinner pots. I can't sit here for hours on end talking to you and making cups of tea. There's work to be done. I reckon I'd best put the kettle on, though, or I'll get no peace. I daresay Jenny'd like a cuppa.'

'Don't bother for me,' replied Jenny. 'I've only called to say thank you for looking after the girls, and I'll pop up and see Miss Alice if I may?' She nodded at Fred. 'Nice to meet you. I expect I'll see you again sometime.'

'I'm sure you will,' he said seriously, but his eyelid flickered in the faintest trace of a wink.

He was obviously undeterred by Ada's good-natured grousing. He'd probably heard it all before, realising, as Jenny did, that there was no malice in it, and from his easy manner at Ada's fireside it seemed as though he was only too willing to hear it all again.

'I'll tell you about it another time,' Ada mouthed silently to her cousin as they went down the hall. Then, in a louder voice, 'We loved having the girls. Good as gold they were and my ladies were thrilled to bits with them. Go right up, Jenny. Miss Alice will be pleased to see you.'

'Seems as though you've clicked, our Ada,' said Jenny, giving a sly wink.

'Go on with you, you cheeky monkey,' Ada retorted, but the corners of her mouth twitched in a rare smile and her sharp eyes were unusually bright.

Miss Alice's eyes were bright too, but they had a feverish look and her face was unnaturally flushed. She was sitting up in bed with a pink woolly bed jacket round her shoulders, and Jenny was shocked to see her gaunt cheeks and skeletal-looking hands and arms. Miss Alice was delighted to see her, and enthused over the simple offerings she had brought – a get well card painstakingly made by the girls before they went to bed last night, and a feather-light sponge cake baked by Jenny that morning.

They exchanged pleasantries about the weather and 'the dear children and dear Tom and Violet', then Miss Alice leaned forward and asked in a hoarse whisper, 'Is that Fred here again?'

Jenny told her that she had just been introduced to him.

'He's never been off the doorstep since he came round about the blackout,' said Miss Alice peevishly.

'I thought he was a milkman,' said Jenny, mystified.

'Blackout,' replied Miss Alice frostily. 'At least that's what he says, but I think it's just an excuse to get our Ada into his clutches.'

Jenny excused herself as soon as she could. The heat from the fire in the small grate and the cloying sickroom smell of camphor and stale sweat were combining to make her feel nauseous.

The atmosphere in the living room where Miss Maud was sitting in solitary state was none too pleasant either. Jenny could never understand why they had the fire built halfway up the chimney, or where they managed to get the coal. They'd probably hoarded tons of the stuff before the war started.

Miss Maud was in high spirits today, very much the mistress of the house with her elder sister safely tucked away in bed. Now she could, for once, express some opinions of her own.

'You've met Fred, have you, dear?' she twittered excitedly. 'Such a nice man and he's so fond of our dear Ada. We don't mind her having gentlemen callers,' she added primly, 'provided they don't interfere with her work.' Just as if Ada was sixteen and employed as the scullery maid, thought Jenny, instead of running the house single-handed as she did.

Miss Maud went on to explain, far more succinctly than her sister had done, what had brought Fred Bottomley to the house again.

'He used to be our milkman, dear, but he was moved to another round. Well, would you believe it? – a fortnight ago he knocked at the door to tell Ada there was a light showing. Frightened us out of our wits, he did – it was ten o'clock at night. He's the ARP warden for our area. Ada got on her high horse, I can tell you. Very particular about the blackout, she is. But Fred's been round to see her a few times since then.' She leaned forward and whispered conspiratorially, 'Do you think we might hear wedding bells, dear? Wouldn't that be lovely?' She clasped her plump hands together in delight.

'I think we'll have to wait and see, Miss Maud,' said Jenny tolerantly. Poor old soul. She had so little in her life in spite of all her money.

'My sister was cross with me for saying that.' Miss Maud put her hand up to her mouth and gave a little giggle, like a small girl who was being naughty. 'She's frightened Ada might go and leave us, you see. But I know she wouldn't let us down – she's a good lass.'

'I wouldn't say too much to Ada, if I were you,' said Jenny kindly. 'She'll have to make up her own mind, won't she?'

Knowing Ada, she'd more than likely jump in the other direction if she thought someone was pushing her. And Jenny was sure that Miss Maud hadn't even considered that if Ada did get married she would have to go and live with Fred.

Jenny and her mother heard a little more of the story – as much as Ada wanted them to know – the next day when she came to Pleasant View.

'So I says to him, "If there's a chink showing then I'm a Chinaman." Would you credit it? Knocking on the door, as bold as brass, at ten o'clock at night! Anyroad, he had me out in the street, pointing up at the bedroom window.'

'And was there a chink showing?' asked Jenny, hardly able to suppress her laughter.

'Was there heck as like! None as I could see at any rate, but that Fred has got eyes like a hawk. No – I reckon it was just an excuse to get his feet under the table.'

'What's he doing, Ada? Trying to warm up the old porridge?' asked Annie, casting an amused glance at her niece.

'He may try, Aunt Annie, but whether he succeeds or not is a different story. It'll take more than Fred Bottomley, with all his cheek, to make me leave my cosy little home. Besides, there's my ladies to consider.'

Annie put down her rolling pin and leaned across the kitchen table. For once, she looked kindly at her niece. 'Ada – don't you think it's about time you started considering yourself? Never mind them old biddies. You've spent a lifetime fetching and carrying for them. Don't leave it too late.'

Ada was silent for a moment, obviously taken aback by the unaccustomed warmth in her aunt's voice. Then a half-smile played round the corners of her mouth. 'Well, I suppose he's all right. He's better than a wet weekend in Wigan, at any rate. And he says he'll take me to see *Gone with the Wind* when it comes round again, so that can't be bad. Fellows are all alike, though, cluttering up the place with their muddy boots and wanting you to wait on 'em hand and foot. I wouldn't give any of 'em house room and that's a fact.'

Jenny noticed, though, in spite of her vehement denials, that there had been a subtle change in Ada's appearance lately. Her hair was now arranged in a roll round her head, instead of being tightly pinned back. Her pointed nose and her ruddy cheeks were toned down with a light dusting of face powder. And could it be possible that she was wearing just the faintest trace of pink lipstick?

Jenny lay contentedly in Robert's arms, idly playing with the brass buttons on his tunic.

'Would you like me to make a cup of tea, darling?' she asked lazily.

'I can think of something else I'd much rather have,' said Robert, a suggestive gleam in his eyes as he ran his hand up and down her silk-clad leg, 'But I mustn't be greedy. Yes, darling – tea would be lovely. And one of your special cakes. Off you go, wench.' He speeded her on her way with a playful slap on her bottom.

Jenny skipped joyfully across the room, pausing in the kitchen doorway to put out her tongue at him. How happy he made her. When they were together in the evening like this, it was hard to imagine a time when she hadn't known him. Her previous life with Tom seemed to belong to a different life. Another existence, completely removed from what she was experiencing now. She smiled contentedly as she put the cups and saucers on a tray, with a plate of homemade cakes, and waited for the kettle to boil.

'No repercussions abut the weekend, love?' Robert asked as he sipped his tea. 'Nobody's asked any awkward questions, have they?'

'No – none at all. Mind you, I've kept pretty quiet. I didn't want to tell too many lies, so I've said very little. It was wonderful, wasn't it, darling?'

'Indeed it was, my love. You were so depressed when I was leaving you, as though it was all coming to an end, and it wasn't, you see. We're together again, just you and me and . . .' His words were interrupted by a knock at the door. 'Good gracious! Who can that be?'

'That's what I'm wondering. I don't often have callers at night, apart from you, of course. I'd better go and see. I'll close the door, love, because of the blackout.'

'That's probably who it is, Jenny. The ARP warden. You haven't got a light showing, have you?'

'Not that I know of.' The knock sounded again, not loud, but persistent. 'Hold your horses, whoever you are. I'm coming.'

Jenny hurried down the hallway and tentatively opened the door. Then she gave a gasp of horror. 'Mother! Whatever are you doing here?'

Chapter 17

'Well, that's a fine greeting, I must say.'

Annie stood on the doorstep, breathing heavily. From what Jenny could see at her first panic-stricken glance, her mother was holding a cardboard box in her arms, hugging it tightly to her chest.

'I've just come from the whist drive and – would you believe it – I won first prize. I had to come and tell you – I was that thrilled.'

'Very nice, Mother.' Jenny looked more closely at the box, noting that it contained a chicken, surrounded by potatoes and carrots and a large cooking apple, and, at the end, reposing between the bird's legs, a box of sage and onion stuffing.

'Our Sunday dinner – all ready and waiting. All it needs is cooking.' Annie hadn't sounded so excited for a long while. 'Well, aren't you going to ask me in? What's up with you? You look as though you've seen a ghost or summat.'

'Yes . . . of course . . . Come in, Mother. I was just . . .'

'It was like waking the dead. I thought you were never coming to the door.'

Jenny preceded her mother up the hallway, a sick feeling in the pit of her stomach. Annie was still going on about that damned bird . . .

'There'll not be enough for the lads, but it'll do nicely for me and our Violet, and perhaps you and the girls might like to come round. I'll put it in the larder where it's cool. D'you reckon it'll keep till Sunday, Jenny?'

Jenny paused with her hand on the living-room door. 'Sergeant Cunningham's here, Mother,' she said brightly, trying to force her voice into tones of normality. 'We were just having a cup of tea.'

Annie followed her daughter into the room, her face set in grim lines. 'So I see . . . Good evening . . . Sergeant Cunningham.' Her voice was ominous and her eyes darted quickly round the room, taking in the scene at a glance: Robert's greatcoat slung casually over a chair; the young man himself seated in an armchair, his long legs outstretched to the glowing fire, his jacket unbuttoned, a cup of tea in his hands; the tray on a little table set with teapot, sugar basin, milk jug, a plate of buns; the intimate light shed by the lamp in the corner – that disgraceful naked lady, holding a beach ball; and the guilty flush beginning to stain Jenny's cheeks.

'Good evening, Mrs Carter.' Robert, ever the gentleman, leapt to his feet. 'Won't you sit down?'

'Yes . . . sit down, Mother. I'll pour you a cup of tea.' Jenny bustled over to the little table, her agitation showing in her every movement.

'Indeed I won't! This is a fine carry-on, I must say. I'm surprised at you, our Jenny, and you with a husband serving his King and Country. A finer young man never drew breath than Tom Bradshaw, I'll tell you, Sergeant Cunningham!' The last two words were delivered with no uncertain emphasis.

'Calm down, Mother. We're not doing any harm. I told you, we're just having a cup of tea.' Jenny smiled weakly in her mother's direction, but her face felt frozen.

'Huh! That's a likely story. Pull the other leg – it's got bells on it. I'll have something to say to you in the morning, young woman.' Annie's face, under her black velour hat, was growing redder and redder as she stood there, feet set firmly apart, still clinging tightly to her box of goodies. 'I'm going now. I'll not stay a minute longer. And as for you, young man, if you're not down that street after me in less than five minutes, I'll report you to your superiors, you see if I don't!'

'Mrs Carter,' said Robert placatingly, 'you've got it all wrong, you know. Jenny's been very kind to me. We lads get lonely when we're away from home – and where's the harm in us having a cup of tea together?'

'Huh!' Annie grunted again. 'That's as may be. I daresay you do get lonely,' she added, a trifle less aggressively, 'but I reckon Tom's lonely too and I can't see him carrying on like that. Anyroad, I've had my say. Just think on – don't be long.' She nodded curtly in Robert's direction, then turned and marched off down the hallway. 'You needn't bother to come to the door. I can let myself out.'

As the front door closed behind her they looked at one another, Jenny in dismay, Robert, in spite of everything, with a twinkle in his eyes.

'Oh, Robert! How awful.' Jenny's voice was scarcely audible and her eyes were beginning to fill up with tears. 'I've been dreading something like this happening. Whatever are we going to do?'

'There's nothing we can do, darling, except bluff our way through it. Look – she can't prove anything. We were only having a cup of tea, like we told her.'

'And do you really think she believed that? Not on your life! Mother doesn't miss a trick. Ever since I was a little girl she's been able to see straight through me.'

'And she still treats you like a little girl, as I've told you many times before. Anyway, my love, we won't go into all that now.' Robert reached for his greatcoat. 'One thing I won't do is incur her wrath any further. She'll probably be waiting behind the door with a rolling pin at the ready. What did she come round for anyway, at this time of night?'

'Didn't you hear what she said? She won first prize at the whist drive – a chicken – and she'd come to tell me.'

Robert burst out laughing. 'So that's what she was clutching to her bosom! Oh dear! We really took the wind out of her sails, didn't we? Poor old Annie!'

'It isn't funny,' Jenny snapped. 'I don't know what you're laughing at. I wanted the ground to open up and swallow me, I was that embarrassed.'

'Don't take it all so seriously, darling.' Robert put his arms round her, holding her close. 'I've told you – she can't prove a thing. You don't want me to stop coming to see you, do you?'

Silently Jenny shook her head.

'Well then, she can't stop me. And you're a big girl now. She can't tell you what to do.' Gently Robert put a finger under her chin and lifted her face so that her eyes looked up into his. 'Now promise me you won't worry any more, darling.'

'All right – I'll try not to.'

Very gently he kissed her. 'Just stand up to her. Don't let her browbeat you, Jenny Wren. Look – I really must go, or she may very well carry out her threat. I'll see you tomorrow, darling.'

When he had gone, Jenny collapsed wearily into an armchair, burying her head in her hands. Don't worry, Robert had said. That was easier said than done. With the thought of tomorrow's meeting with her mother hanging over her like the threat of doom, Jenny envisaged a sleepless night.

'You want a good hiding, Jenny Bradshaw, and you're lucky I don't give you one an' all.' Annie's voice quivered with indignation and her ample bosom rose and fell heavily beneath her flowered crossover pinny. 'Carrying on with one of them la-di-da RAF chaps, and you with a husband who's a soldier.'

Annie seemed to have forgotten momentarily that she had previously thought that the sun rose and set with the Royal Air Force.

'We're not carrying on, Mother,' Jenny protested, though she knew she was fighting a losing battle.

'Just you look me straight in the eye, young woman, and tell me that he hasn't been in your bed – and you with two bairns asleep in the next room. Disgusting, I call it!'

Jenny looked steadily at her mother. 'Robert hasn't been in my bed, Mother,' she said, slowly enunciating each word. 'I don't know how you could suggest such a thing.'

That, at least, was true. She and Robert had never made love in the bed that had belonged to her and Tom. It would have seemed wrong, and Robert had never suggested it.

Annie appeared somewhat mollified. 'All right then. I know you've never lied to me, Jenny. You can't, because I can read you like a book. But you were up to summat, that's for sure. Kissing and cuddling, no doubt. It was written all over you as soon as you came to the door. You needn't worry, though – I shan't follow Sergeant la-di-da Cunningham every time he goes out. I've too much pride to go snooping round corners. I'll just leave it to your conscience to think what you're doing to Tom.'

'It's got nothing to do with Tom.' Jenny could have bitten off her tongue as soon as she had spoken the words. That wasn't what she had meant to say at all. She meant that her love for Robert was something distinct from her feelings for Tom; a part of her life that was completely separate from anything that had gone before. She might have known that her mother would misunderstand.

'Oh, hasn't it? I'd say it has everything to do with Tom when his wife's playing games behind his back. But I shan't tell him. I think too much of him to go breaking his heart, and that's what it would do to him if he found out. I just hope you come to your senses before it's too late. And I'm surprised at that sergeant an' all. I thought he was a right decent young man. But you live and learn. I don't wonder Tom doesn't think much of the RAF if Robert

Cunningham's an example of what they're turning out. Glamour boys, Tom calls 'em. Well, handsome is as handsome does, that's what I say, and I don't reckon much to a fellow that'll pinch another man's wife when his back's turned.'

Oh, for God's sake, Mother, let it drop, Jenny said to herself. On and on and on she went, like a damned gramophone record. There were times when she positively disliked her mother. She loved her, she supposed – you did love your parents when they'd brought you up and looked after you – but liking was something different. Liking was to do with friendship and compatibility, and never in a thousand years could Jenny have made a friend of her mother.

'Anyroad, I can't stand here all morning, Sergeant Cunningham or no Sergeant Cunningham.' Annie wrung out the dishcloth, squeezing it between her hands until her knuckles grew white with the effort. An expression almost akin to hatred gleamed in her eyes as though she was imagining herself squeezing someone's throat. Robert's, more than likely, thought Jenny. 'You'd best get off to the butcher's before they've sold out. See if he's got any lamb's liver for tomorrow's dinner. Then you can go to the cobbler's and see if my black shoes are ready yet. He's had 'em a fortnight. And get a move on. The morning's half over already and we've done nowt yet. And we know whose fault that is!' Annie cast a baleful look in Jenny's direction before she disappeared through the door, dustpan and brush in hand, to vent her displeasure on the already decidedly worn staircarpet.

Fetch me this, carry me that. Come here, go there. And never once did Annie think of thanking her. That was how it had been ever since Jenny started work in the boarding house when she was fourteen, and things hadn't altered much since she got married. She found herself thinking, not for the first time, that Tom should have insisted on them moving to Yorkshire, or at least buying a house a long way from her mother's. Irritably she grabbed her coat from the peg behind the door. She'd better hurry. If the butcher had sold out of lamb's liver her mother would have something else to blame her for.

'Whatever's up between you and Mother?' Violet whispered as she and Jenny cleared the tables. 'You haven't spoken two words to one another for the last couple of days and there's an atmosphere you could cut with a knife. Have you had a row or something?'

'She hasn't told you then?'

'Told me what? I wouldn't be asking if I knew what it was all about, would I?'

Jenny sighed. 'I suppose you might as well know, Vi. You'll be sure to find out sooner or later. I'm only amazed that Mother hasn't blurted it out already. She came round the other night – you know, when she won the whist prize – and Robert Cunningham happened to be there . . . and she was mad with us . . . That's what it's about.'

'Why should she be mad about that?' Violet stared at her sister, a guileless expression in her green eyes. 'What's wrong with Robert being there? He lends you books sometimes, doesn't he?'

'Oh, don't be so naïve, our Vi! Robert and I have got rather . . . friendly. Mother could tell when she saw us together. I know I went as red as a beetroot.'

There was a split second's silence. Then, 'What do you mean by friendly?' asked Violet, a note of suspicion creeping into her voice.

'Oh, use your imagination!' Jenny snapped, losing control. She was sick of all the cross-examining. First her mother, now her sister. 'What do you think I mean?'

'I see.' Violet pressed her lips together primly and two red spots of colour burned on her cheeks. The expression in her eyes changed in a flash. Now they were cold and hard, like green pebbles, as she stared at her sister. 'Yes – I certainly do see. You and . . . him. I've noticed you chatting in corners when you thought nobody was watching. I didn't think anything about it at the time, but I can see now . . . Well, I think it's disgusting. Mother's quite right to be mad at you. And what about Tom? Haven't you spared a thought for your husband? You've got the best husband in the world, Jenny Bradshaw. You should be ashamed of yourself.'

Jenny realised, too late, that she shouldn't have told her sister. She should have guessed what Violet's reaction would be, particularly with regard to Tom, but the words had been out almost before she realised what she was saying.

'And when I think about all that you said to me,' Violet went on. 'Don't do this and don't do that. "If Tony goes off you because you won't, then he's not worth having at all."' Violet's tone was mocking. 'That's what you said to me. You're nothing but a damned hypocrite, Jenny Bradshaw And it's all your fault that I lost Tony. I'll never forgive you for that. Never!'

'I'm sorry, Violet,' Jenny said quietly. She knew that her sister didn't mean what she had just said about Tony – only last week she had said that she was better off without him – but it certainly must seem now as though she, Jenny, was being two-faced. 'What else can I say? I know I should be ashamed – but I'm not. It's the sort of thing that happens in wartime. You meet someone you care about . . . and all the while you feel that time's running out. I can't expect you to understand, but try not to think too badly of me. We've always been such good friends, Vi.'

'Not any more,' said Violet hotly. 'I shan't ever feel the same way about you. Not ever! And I'll never forgive you!'

As her sister turned and flounced out of the room Jenny felt hot tears spring to her eyes and course slowly down her cheeks.

'So you were caught with your pants down, the pair of you?'

'Don't be so crude, Eileen!' Jenny snapped. 'No, as a matter of fact, we weren't. It was later. We'd had time to . . . I don't know what you're grinning at. It wasn't funny, I can tell you.'

'I was just imagining your mother's face when she came in and saw Robert sitting there. It's a good job she didn't come barging in half an hour earlier or the fat would have been in the fire.'

'She couldn't walk straight in. She hasn't got a key. Oh, she'd have liked one all right, but I've never given her one . . . Yes – I suppose it was funny really.' Jenny felt her mouth begin to twitch at the corners for the first time for two days. 'She was standing there going redder and redder, her eyes nearly popping out of her head, and all the time she was clutching that damned bird to her bosom. Oh, Eileen – it was hilarious really!' Jenny suddenly burst into hysterical laughter and the tears which had been very near the surface since her mother's discovery brimmed over and rolled down her cheeks. 'Oh dear! I don't know whether to laugh or cry.'

'Well, have a good laugh then, Jen. It'll do you a world of good. You looked as miserable as a wet week's washing when you came in. I'm glad you've seen the funny side of it at last. Eeh – I bet it was a scream!' Eileen took off her glasses and wiped the tears of merriment from her eyes. 'Anyroad, there's nowt you can do about it, except stop seeing him, and I don't suppose you'll do that, will you?'

197

Jenny shook her head. 'We've played it cool for the last day or two, but I think he'll be round tonight . . . You're a great friend, Eileen. I can always rely on you.'

'I should hope so, love. But . . . must you take it all so seriously? Robert may well be gone soon – posted, I mean. Can't you just look upon it as a little fling? It's daft to eat your heart out about somebody who's here today and gone tomorrow.'

Jenny gave a sad smile as she silently shook her head. How could she possibly explain to Eileen that in the two months that they had been lovers, Robert had become her main reason for existence.

'Thanks for listening, love,' was all she said. 'I feel tons better now.'

'Always glad to oblige,' said Eileen cheerily, 'but it would be better, you know, if you could think of you and him as ships that pass in the night.'

Eileen was a wonderful friend, but she didn't understand.

'I'm sorry you've been so miserable, darling,' said Robert later that evening. 'Come on – cheer up. She didn't kill you, did she? If looks could kill I'd be dead all right, with the glances Annie's been casting at me through the serving hatch. But she'll soon forget about it, you'll see.'

'That she won't! You don't know her like I do. I'm not sure how I'm going to stick it, Robert. There's a terrible atmosphere, and now our Violet won't speak to me.'

'You worry too much about your family, Jenny. You're far too wrapped up with your mother and your sister. It's about time you broke free from them. The trouble is, you've never left home.'

'I have. Of course I have.' Jenny sounded indignant. 'When I got married we moved into our own home straight away.'

'Yes – and where is it? Just round the corner from your mother's. You're still tied to her hand and foot. I suppose you can't help it. I've noticed that it happens a lot in this part of the country – mothers hanging on to their daughters like grim death.'

'In the north, you mean?' Jenny's eyes flashed angrily.

'I didn't say that.'

'No, but you meant it, didn't you? You southerners are all alike. You think there's something peculiar about all of us up here.'

'I'm not a southerner – I'm from the Midlands.' Robert's voice was still calm. 'And of course I don't think there's anything peculiar about northern folk – they're great – but I can't imagine it happening where I come from. My sister Ruth isn't married yet, but when she does get married I can't see my mother wanting to hang on to her like your mother does.'

'Maybe they care more up here,' Jenny snapped. 'If it's so flippin' marvellous where you come from, why don't you go back there?'

'I can't. There's a war on. Hadn't you realised?'

For the first time in their relationship Robert raised his voice and, at the shock of it, Jenny burst into tears.

'Oh, darling – I'm sorry. I didn't mean to shout.' Robert immediately sprang from his chair and took Jenny in his arms. 'We're quarrelling – oh, darling, we mustn't ever quarrel. Forgive me? I wasn't criticising your family. Really I wasn't.'

Jenny sniffed and wiped her eyes. 'You're right, though. She does cling to me, and if our Violet doesn't watch out the same thing will happen to her. We should have gone to live in Yorkshire when we got married. Tom had a good job there, but Mother insisted on us living here. I was under twenty-one, you see, so I suppose she did have some claim over me. We should have moved, though, as soon as I was old enough. I know that now . . . Oh, darling – whatever am I saying?' Jenny looked up at him, smiling through her tears. 'If we'd moved, I'd never have met you, would I?'

'We would have met, my love,' said Robert quietly. 'Somewhere, somehow, we would have met. Can you imagine us going through life not knowing one another? We mustn't argue again, though, darling. Other people don't matter – they're not worth arguing about. They didn't guess about our weekend away, did they?'

'No – funnily enough I don't think they've cottoned on to that. No, darling. That's our secret. They can't take that away from us, whatever happens.'

Robert held her close to him. 'Let old Hitler do his worst. We've still got that to remember, my love.'

Jenny recalled Robert's words a few days later as she listened to the sombre voice of the BBC announcer telling of the previous night's heavy raid on Coventry. Hitler had indeed done his worst. The devastation was phenomenal. Poor Robert . . . Please let his family be safe, Jenny whispered under her breath.

She caught a glimpse of him as she and Annie dished out the breakfast of scrambled egg – made from the now familiar yellow powder – and toast. He was laughing unconcernedly with some of the other lads, obviously having not yet heard the grim news. She hadn't the heart to tell him. Bad news always travelled fast and he would hear the sad tidings sooner or later, but she prayed that it hadn't touched him personally.

A telegram arrived the next morning, addressed to Sergeant Robert Cunningham. Annie handed it to him silently as he came in through the front door at lunch time. His expression was grim, as it had been since the previous day when he first heard of the destruction of his home town.

'Thanks,' he murmured. 'I think I've been expecting it.' His face was ashen and his fingers trembled as he took the dreaded yellow envelope.

'You know where I am if you want me, lad,' Annie said gruffly, but not unkindly. 'You'd best go and open it in your room.'

'The sergeant's had some bad news. There's a telegram come for him,' she said curtly to Jenny, avoiding her daughter's eye by turning her back and busying herself with dishing out the potatoes.

Jenny gave an involuntary gasp. 'Oh no – who is it?'

'I've no idea, but it must be somebody close. I'll send one of the lads up in a minute or two to see if he's all right. Happen he'll want a bit of dinner on a tray. I don't suppose he'll feel like facing that lot in there.'

Mother could be quite human at times, Jenny thought, but she couldn't trust herself to speak. She was longing to go to him, to put her arms round him and comfort him, for it must be bad news that the telegram contained, but propriety – and her mother – insisted that she stay here straining the cabbage, pouring the gravy, dishing out the mince – as if any of it mattered when Robert needed her so badly.

He was still wearing his greatcoat when he came up to them at the serving hatch. His mouth was unsmiling, and his eyes, more grey than blue now, were dark with pain.

'It's my father,' he said, his voice almost inaudible. 'He's . . . dead. The telegram was from my mother. I suppose I must be thankful that it's not all of them.'

'Eeh . . . I'm right sorry, lad,' said Annie shaking her head. 'It's a bad do.'

'Yes . . . it is. Very bad. For all the people of Coventry, not just for us. I won't have any dinner, thanks. I'm going for a walk now, on the promenade. I expect I'll be granted compassionate leave. I'll let you know, Mrs Carter . . . Jenny.' His eyes softened momentarily as he glanced at her, then quickly, his head averted, he hurried from the dining room.

'Poor lad,' sighed Annie. 'I know I've said some harsh things about him lately, and I've meant them too. I don't take any of it back, but I wouldn't wish this on anyone. Eeh – that so-and-so Hitler's got a lot to answer for and no mistake . . . Come on, lass. There's no point in standing there like cheese at fourpence. Start dishing out that rice pudding before it goes cold. We've got to feed the inner man whatever happens.'

'I've never seen anything like it, Jenny. Whole streets of houses gone. The cathedral's in ruins, and the school that I used to go to. My father's shop's gone too . . . Not that it matters now, I suppose, now that he's . . . not there. I just thank God that Mum's alive, and Ruth, and that they've still got the house. Poor Marjorie, though. I find that harder to bear than anything. Can you understand that, darling? You know how much I love you, but Marjorie and I . . . we were children together. She was too young, Jenny. Oh, God – what a waste!'

'I know, darling. I understand,' said Jenny soothingly, as though to a child, as she put her arms round him again. He laid his head against her breast and she gently stroked his hair, hoping that he could draw some small comfort from her nearness.

He had been in Coventry for almost a week, making the arrangements for his father's funeral. Mr Cunningham had, ironically, not been killed in the bombing raid, but had met his death a few hours later when a pile of rubble had collapsed on him as he was carrying out rescue work with the Civil Defence. The street in which they lived had, miraculously, escaped untouched apart from a few broken windows. But what Robert had found most difficult to cope with was the death of his childhood friend Marjorie. The hospital where she worked as a nurse had received a direct hit, resulting in the deaths of many patients and staff.

Jenny realised, to her dismay, that she could hardly find the words of consolation. These people – Marjorie, Mr and Mrs Cunningham, Ruth – they were just names to her. She had known

201

Robert for such a short time, whereas they had known him all his life. She felt so inadequate, and yet she knew that the very fact of her being there was a solace to him.

They sat silently for a while, holding one another, staring at the flickering flames of the fire. There was something very comforting about firelight. Jenny was sad for Robert, yet strangely contented too. She had felt that their relationship might be spoilt by the setbacks they had encountered recently. Firstly there had been her mother's discovery, seeming to leave a black stain upon the pristine whiteness of their love for one another. Then their first quarrel, then the overwhelming sorrow of Robert's bereavement. She had wondered if things would ever be the same again, but how wrong she had been to doubt. Robert's arms were around her, holding her so closely that she could feel the beating of his heart. With love such as theirs they could face whatever might be in store for them. His next words came as a chilling shock, shattering her complacency, scattering wide her hopes and dreams.

'There's something else that I haven't told you yet, darling. I found out about it the same day that I heard about my father – that was certainly a black day, my love . . . I'm being posted.'

Jenny gave a gasp of dismay. 'Oh, no . . .' The words were the merest whisper on a drawn-out breath.

'They want me to carry on as an instructor, but I'm being sent to a training camp in the south of England . . . I'm going next week, darling.'

Chapter 18

Christmas 1940 was by no means a merry one. The Blitz on London was still continuing, and other major cities and towns – Southampton, Bristol, Hull, Liverpool, Birmingham – had their own tales to tell of death and destruction. The recent massacre of Coventry was fresh in everyone's minds and there seemed to be little cause for celebration. It was not to be wondered at that the phrase 'Merry Christmas' did not spring readily to the lips this year.

Annie managed to scrape together the necessary ingredients for a Christmas dinner. A chicken was the essential item, and this she had managed to procure as a regular customer of the local butcher. It was pathetically small, barely enough for one decent meal for the six of them, but at least it was a bird of sorts and Christmas wouldn't be Christmas without a bird. With tasty sage and onion stuffing, generous helpings of vegetables and three or four roast potatoes apiece, all covered in lashings of gravy, they would never notice the meagre amount of white breast meat on their plates.

Most of the airmen had gone home on leave for the Christmas period. The half-dozen or so who were still around – because it was too far for them to travel, or because, poor lads, some of them had no homes to go to, having lost them in the bombing raids – were enjoying the same Christmas meal, the only difference being that they were having roast mutton instead of chicken. Mr Jenks the butcher was very sorry, but rules were rules, and it was only one bird per family, no matter the size or circumstances.

Jenny had heard with mixed feelings the news that Tom would be home for Christmas, although she had assumed that he would be granted leave. The thought had hovered continually at the back of her mind, but she hadn't allowed herself to dwell on the reality, on what it would mean to her when she actually saw him again. In one sense she dreaded his return, but she would have found it hard to explain why. Could her feelings be tinged with fear? she wondered. A dread that Tom would be able to see right through to her innermost soul, laying bare the precious secret of her love for another man. She found herself, inexplicably, thinking of the marriage service, of the vows that she and Tom had made. Forsaking all others . . . one flesh . . . to love, honour and to obey. The promises had been made in good faith, with Jenny believing that she would keep every word of them, but that was so long ago, before she had met Robert.

She had hardly given her marriage vows a thought until recently. She had been able to keep her two loves – Tom and Robert – in separate compartments, as it were, in her mind, like two parallel lines that would never meet. But as the time fast approached when she would see Tom again after a separation of more than six months, she found that the lines were beginning to converge. Her affair with Robert would be bound to affect her meeting with her husband. The marriage bond, even in the unhappiest of relationships, was a close one, and she and Tom had been as happy together as many married couples were. Surely he would be able to tell, just by being with her, that she had been . . . unfaithful. She used the word, even in her innermost thoughts, guardedly. Her love for Robert had been so overwhelming that she hadn't stopped to think that she was betraying Tom.

Jenny had also feared, at first, that her mother might give her away, perhaps without even meaning to, with indiscreet references about her friendship with the young sergeant. But since Robert Cunningham had left, almost a month ago, for the south of England, it was, for Annie, as though he had ceased to exist. Never once had she referred to him and though she remained somewhat cool still in her dealings with her elder daughter, Jenny felt, to her intense relief, that her mother now regarded the incident as a closed book.

Violet had tentatively extended an olive branch to her sister, and by Christmas Jenny was happy to feel that they were good friends again.

'Jenny,' she had said falteringly, when the two of them were alone in the kitchen the week before Christmas, 'I'm sorry . . . for what I said about you and . . . him. I didn't mean to upset you.'

Jenny looked up, startled. It was the first kind word that Violet had spoken to her for several weeks. The only words, in fact, that she had spoken when the two of them were alone together. The rift had been a deep one, all the more alarming considering their previous closeness, and Jenny had wondered if it could ever be mended. She felt tears of thankfulness spring to her eyes as she smiled warmly at her sister.

'That's all right, Vi,' she said quietly. 'I can understand how you must have felt, especially with all that business about Tony as well. I'm really sorry about that.'

Violet shook her head. 'Tony doesn't matter. I don't think he ever did . . . But I think I know now how you must have felt.' She put a protective arm round her sister. 'You must have felt lonely with Tom being away, and that sergeant was such a handsome man. I can't blame you for flirting with him. I might have done the same if I'd had the chance, but he never looked at me, did he? They don't look at me when you're around.' She gave a self-conscious laugh. 'And you needn't worry that I shall say anything to Tom. I shan't breathe a word.'

'Thanks, Vi – I know you won't,' said Jenny warmly. 'I'm glad we're friends again.'

'So am I. I hated seeing you so unhappy, and I know it was all my fault for being so horrid to you. Tom'll be home next week, won't he? That'll be lovely for you. You'll forget all about . . . him, when Tom comes home.'

Jenny nodded, the cheerful smile that she put on for Violet's benefit masking her turbulent thoughts and the dull ache that she had felt inside for the last month. Neither her sister nor her mother could know how bereft she felt, as though some vital part of herself were missing. It was perhaps as well that Violet had dismissed it as a harmless flirtation, and that, to her mother, it was a question of out of sight, out of mind. They knew nothing of the enormity of her feelings, nor did they know of the letters which were arriving every day or two. Letters in which Robert spoke of his undying love, of the desolation he was feeling without his beloved Jenny. He didn't speak of the future – how could he? Nor did he speak of the time when they would meet again. Who could tell when that might be? Their separation had only served to strengthen the bond that there was between them.

Jenny's letters to Robert were more matter-of-fact – she found it difficult to express her feelings on paper – chatty news about the lads whom he remembered from the billet, or funny things that the children had said. Her letters to him were, in fact, very much like her letters to Tom, except that the ones to Robert always ended with simple phrases telling of her love for him. It was a long time since she had declared her love to her husband, either by the spoken or the written word.

Tom arrived at dusk on Christmas Eve. Jenny was in the bedroom, drawing the blackout curtains, when she glanced out of the window and saw him turn the corner. He strode purposefully through the grey twilight of the cold December evening, his kitbag on his back, his sandy hair flopping over his brow beneath his forage cap. Jenny recalled another such occasion when she had seen him striding towards her; the time when he had come to meet her from the train at Castleburn station on her first visit to his home. Now his step was a little less jaunty, his shoulders slightly bowed beneath the weight of his heavy bag, but he was still her Tom, dear and familiar, and she felt her heart warm to him in an unexpected rush of tenderness. When she opened the door to him she saw his grey eyes shining with joy at seeing her again after so long, as they had done on that day long ago in Castleburn.

'Jenny, my love. It's been so long.' He closed the door behind him, took off his kitbag and flung it on to the hall floor with a heavy thud, and enveloped her in a bear hug.

'Too long, love,' she replied, her voice muffled against the prickly serge of his army greatcoat.

She found, to her surprise, that she meant it. Six months was too long to be apart. Why ever had she been afraid of seeing him again? She knew, suddenly, that it would be all right. She would be able to behave naturally with him. The children would be a help, and already, at the sound of Tom's voice, they had come rushing into the hall.

'Daddy! Daddy!' Patsy flung herself against his legs and put her arms round his waist.

'Whoever's this big girl?' Tom stared at his daughter in mock surprise. 'Well, I do believe it's Patsy! Goodness me! You must have grown at least three inches. Come here and give your dad a kiss.' He lifted her high in the air till she almost reached the ceiling, and she squealed with delight. 'And you too, Rosie. My! You're bonnier than ever.'

Rosie, a little overawed by the exuberance of Tom's homecoming, was hanging back self-consciously, her thumb in her mouth. She was unused to such demonstrations of affection. Her own mother was always afraid of smudging her lipstick or spoiling her hair, and her customary greeting to Rosie was a perfunctory peck on the cheek. Auntie Jenny, to be sure, was a great one for hugs and kisses, and Rosie, during her stay in the Bradshaw household, had changed her former opinion that such behaviour was soppy. But it was a long time since she had seen Patsy's daddy, and now she felt shy of him.

On his last leave, she remembered, he had looked unhappy. He had hardly spoken to her and Patsy, just smiled at them sadly now and again, his eyes grey and misty, like the rain clouds that you saw so often in this part of the country. But now he was like a different person, all jolly and noisy and laughing. Rosie was glad to see that Auntie Jenny was laughing too. She had looked so sad just lately.

Rosie took her thumb out of her mouth and put her hand into the one that Patsy's daddy was holding out to her. Then, as he stooped down to her, she stood on tiptoe and planted a kiss on his smooth, cold cheek. The children followed him into the living room, watching him intently as he divested himself of his overcoat and cap and woolly scarf. He flopped into an easy chair, laying his head against the padded cushion. His eyes travelled round the room, resting on each object – the wireless, the lamp, the mirror, the pottery jug on the sideboard – as though he were seeing them all for the first time. Then he gave a contented sigh, and the smile that he gave, first to Jenny, then to the two little girls, lit up his face with a happiness that had been missing the last time he was at home.

'My! It's good to be home again,' he said with feeling. 'It is that! I could do with a cup of tea, Jenny love.'

Patsy sat on his knee, snuggling up against his chest, not speaking, just familiarising herself once more with the scent and feel of her dear daddy who had been away for so long. Rosie stood by the arm of the chair and he put his arm round her, drawing her closer to him and Patsy.

'D'you remember?' Rosie said thoughtfully, 'I used to call you Pop when you were here before, didn't I? D'you think . . . would you mind if I called you Daddy, like what Patsy does? It seems daft to have two names – and it means the same thing, doesn't it?'

'Of course you can, lovey,' said Tom happily, and Rosie beamed at him.

She would have loved to call Auntie Jenny 'Mummy', like Patsy did. She had done so once or twice, by mistake, and Auntie Jenny had laughed, that merry, melodious chuckle that she had, and smiled fondly at her. To Rosie's disappointment she hadn't said 'It's all right, dear. You can call me Mummy.' Anyway Rosie knew, though she couldn't have put it into words, that to do so would be disloyal to her own mother. Daisy White in Liverpool was her mum, and Rosie loved her – of course she did – but, oh, how she loved Auntie Jenny as well. With every day that passed she became more and more a part of this close-knit little family group, and the image of her own mother grew more and more hazy until Rosie found it difficult to recall her features or the sound of her voice.

The little girl didn't know that every time, by a slip of her tongue, she uttered the name 'Mummy', Jenny felt a pang of joy and yet anguish at the same time. How she longed to tell Rosie that it was all right to call her that. But Jenny knew that this chid, much as she loved her, belonged to another woman, and the day would surely come when she, Jenny, would have to part with her.

Jenny hummed contentedly to herself now as she put the kettle on and took the cups and saucers from the cupboard. What a panacea for all ills was a pot of tea. A convenient way of bridging the gap caused by strangeness or embarrassment or sadness. Any strangeness that she felt at Tom's homecoming would be overcome too by the cheerful presence of the children, especially at the Christmas season when they would be more high-spirited than ever. Wartime restrictions and the gloom and doom spread abroad by scaremongers could do little to quell their enthusiasm. Yes, the children would help . . .

They both came running to her in the back kitchen as she washed up the tea things.

'Mummy, me and Rosie's been thinking . . .' Patsy pulled at her mother's apron. 'Listen, Mummy . . .' She turned to her friend. 'Go on. Tell her, Rosie, what we were talking about.'

'No . . .' Rosie, to Jenny's amazement, was looking down at her feet, as if overcome by shyness. It wasn't like Rosie to be at a loss for words. 'No . . . I don't like. You tell her.'

'All right then.' Patsy sighed. 'But it was your idea, Rosie.'

'It never was! Not just mine. It was yours an' all.'

'Well, come on then. What is it?' said Jenny, laughing. 'I'm dying to know.'

'We was wondering, Rosie and me,' said Patsy seriously, 'if she could call you Mummy, like I do. She's going to call me dad Daddy instead of Pop, an' it seems a bit daft, doesn't it, to go on calling you Auntie Jenny? I've heard you say to people that you've got two little girls now, an' Rosie's like me sister, isn't she, so we just wondered . . .'

'It's . . . not quite as easy as all that, Patsy,' said Jenny slowly, trying to find the words to explain this complex problem to the two little girls to whom it was obviously no problem at all. 'Here . . . make yourselves useful while we're talking.' She thrust teatowels into both their hands. 'You can help me to dry these pots . . . Like I was saying, Patsy, it's not as easy as all that.'

'Why not?' asked Patsy. Her little chin stuck out aggressively and her brown eyes held a touch of defiance. 'She can call you Mummy if she wants to, can't she?'

'But she's already got a mum, in Liverpool,' said Jenny quietly. She turned to Rosie. 'Haven't you, dear?' Rosie nodded, her blue eyes serious. 'You can't have more than one mum,' Jenny went on. 'I think it's all right for her to call your dad Daddy, because Rosie hasn't got another dad, but she's got a mum who loves her very much.'

'She doesn't see her, though. Not much,' Patsy persisted.

'No . . . but you both know why that is,' said Jenny. 'Rosie's mum wants her to be safe, that's why she's decided to let her stay in Blackpool.'

'But most of the kids have gone back,' argued Patsy. 'There were ever so many of them at first at our school, and now there's hardly any. Why hasn't Rosie gone back then, like the others?'

Oh dear, why, why, why? thought Jenny, and how was she to answer when she didn't really know the answers herself? 'I think Rosie's mum is being very sensible,' she said firmly, 'and little Ben's mum as well. He's still here, isn't he, with Auntie Eileen? You remember what it was like when those bombs dropped on Blackpool a few months ago. We were all scared, weren't we? Well, it's quite often like that in Liverpool, so Rosie's mum thinks she'd be better here until . . . until the war ends.' She turned to smile at Rosie, who still hadn't said a word. 'So I think you'd better go on calling me Auntie Jenny, dear, don't you? It doesn't make any difference. I'm still the same person. I'm Mummy to Patsy, and Auntie Jenny to you, and my mother and my sister call me Jenny, and people I meet in the street call me Mrs Bradshaw. But I'm still me, aren't I?'

'Mmm . . .' Rosie was thoughtful. 'Auntie Jenny . . . you just said that I'd be here till the war ends. How long will that be?'

'Oh dear, Rosie. I don't know.' Jenny shook her head. 'That's something that none of us knows, isn't it, love? We just have to go on hoping and praying that it won't be too long.'

'And . . . when the war's over, will I have to go back to Liverpool then?'

'Well, of course, dear. Back to your mum and all the friends you've got there. And Ben will be going back as well.'

'But I like being here, Auntie Jenny, with you and Patsy and Auntie Violet and Patsy's grandma. I think it's lovely here. I don't ever want to go back.'

And I don't want you ever to go back, my dear little Rosie, said a voice inside Jenny. How she would bear to part with the child when this wretched war came to an end, God alone knew. 'Don't let's worry about that at the moment, dear,' she said kindly. 'It's Christmas and we're all going to have a happy time together. Come on now. Have you finished drying those pots? You'd best hurry up, the pair of you. It's Christmas Eve and you'll have to find some stockings to hang up.'

'Yes, come on, Rosie.' Patsy pulled at her friend's hand. 'Let's go and get those grey socks we wear for school. Those'll be nice long ones for Father Christmas to fill.'

Rosie gave a sideways glance at Jenny, a sly little grin on her face and one eye half closed in a semblance of a wink. Jenny had to suppress a laugh. She had thought for some time, from odd remarks that the child had made, that Rosie was no longer fooled by stories of the magic midnight visitor. But Patsy still believed in him implicitly and Jenny wanted to keep it that way. Behind Patsy's back, she raised a warning finger at Rosie and pursed her lips to say 'Shhh.'

Rosie nodded gravely, then her face lit up in a delighted grin. 'I'm going to try an' stay awake, then I'll see him,' she said. 'Bet I can stay awake longer'n you, Patsy.'

'Bet you can't . . .'

Jenny watched them, her heart overflowing with love for both of them, as they darted off upstairs. It was almost impossible to believe that Rosie wouldn't be here for always, but, as she had told the child, they mustn't think about that. Not now . . .

She had tried to make it a happy Christmas for the children, though money and luxuries were scarce. She had been busy with her knitting needles and they each had a bright woollen pixie hood – Patsy's blue and Rosie's red – with gloves and scarves to match. Their beloved black dolls, too, each had a new outfit and the little girls were thrilled to find them at the bottom of their beds on Christmas morning in their fine regalia. There were books by their favourite author, Enid Blyton, and jigsaw puzzles and games and, in spite of rationing, even a few sweets and chocolates.

Jenny was so busy throughout the Christmas period that her all-pervading thoughts of Robert had begun to recede, not into the background, but into that special compartment of her mind that she had reserved for him. Jenny was thankful, in one sense, that he was far away in the south of England – or at home in Coventry, as he probably was at this moment. If he had been here, goodness knows how she would have coped with the problem.

However, it was one thing to be at ease with Tom when surrounded by the bolstering companionship of her family, but quite another to be alone with him in the evenings when their support was withdrawn. Especially to be alone with him in bed . . .

Jenny had dreaded the nights, the thought of the claustrophobic darkness, of Tom's body close to hers, his breath heavy with desire, his arms closing around her possessively. How would she be able to respond to him after the tender yet rapturous loving that she had known with Robert?

At first she had used the age-old excuse. It was the 'time of the month', she said. it wasn't true and Jenny hated telling lies, but she felt that she couldn't face Tom's ardour . . . not yet. However, she knew that she couldn't continue with this pretext for longer than five days at the most. She had been happy enough to snuggle up to Tom the first night, safe in the knowledge that he would kiss her good night and, aware of her condition, go no further. It was then that he had told her that his leave was an extended one – ten days' embarkation leave. They hadn't been told where they were going, but, if rumours were to be believed, it was the African desert, and the issue of tropical kit seemed to substantiate this.

'Are you worried, love?' she asked him, feeling a stab of fear at the thought of him going into more immediate danger.

'Not really. I'll be glad to be seeing some proper action again after six months of doing what amounts to sweet Fanny Adams.' He put his arm round her and pulled her closer to him in the comfortable warmth of the feather bed. 'It's you I'm worried about. Leaving you on your own – I know you're not really on your own – you've got the girls and your mother and Violet – but you must feel lonely at times.'

'Yes, but you get used to it,' said Jenny evasively, her conscience pricking more than a little. 'I keep myself busy. I'm always knitting or reading. It's amazing how quickly the evenings fly past, and of course during the day I've hardly time to turn round. Mother sees to that. The last think I want you to do is to worry about me. Just

211

concentrate on beating that old Hitler and getting the war over as quickly as possible . . . It's lovely to have you home again, though, Tom.' Once more, to her surprise, she found that she meant it.

But the acid test was still to come. How would she react when he finally tried to make love to her? On the fifth night of Tom's leave, Jenny knew that there was no point in postponing the moment any further. It would only alert his suspicions if she were reticent or tried to invent any more excuses. She had a bath, dusted herself liberally with Yardley's lavender talc, dabbed some Californian Poppy – a Christmas present from Patsy and Rosie – behind her ears, and lay in bed waiting for Tom to finish reading his newspaper and come and join her. She was prepared to lie back and think of England, and to simulate, if necessary, a token response. Tom had never been a particularly skilful lover, but tonight she found his lovemaking unusually tender and she was able to respond with reciprocal embraces of her own. Though she didn't reach the heights of bliss that she had known with Robert, she nevertheless found the act of love soothing and felt her pent-up tension gradually drifting away.

When the ten days' leave was over, it was with genuine regret that she said goodbye to him at Central Station.

'Take care, love,' she whispered, as he held her close to him, although she knew it was a forlorn plea. How could he take care when he might have to face God knew what dangers?

'Don't worry – I'll do that,' he answered cheerily. 'Keep your pecker up, Jenny love, and I'll be home before you know where you are. And look after those little lasses. It cheers me up no end just thinking of you and those two little girls. It makes it all worth while. Ta-ra, love. Don't come to the train with me. It only drags it out. I'll say goodbye here.'

He kissed her fondly, and she watched his slight figure stride away through the barrier to the waiting train.

It was when she arrived home that the doubts began to assail her again. There was a letter awaiting her from Robert which had come by the second post. He loved her, he missed her, his next leave – whenever it might be – would be spent in Blackpool. He must see her again . . .

Jenny sighed, and her hands trembled as she returned the letter to its envelope and pushed it to the back of the dressing-table drawer with his other missives, hidden behind piles of underwear and stockings. Her face was wet with tears, but whether she was weeping for her husband or her young lover, Jenny herself had no idea.

Chapter 19

'Well, it's to be hoped you've said yes.' Annie paused with a pot towel in one hand and a frying pan in the other and looked questioningly at her niece. 'You could do a lot worse, our Ada, from all accounts.'

'Aye – I've said I'll marry him,' Ada answered in her usual gruff tones, but she couldn't disguise the note of elation that crept into her voice. 'Though goodness knows why! I reckon I must want me head seeing to. I'm getting a bit long in the tooth for getting wed.'

'Indeed you're not!' Jenny smiled encouragingly at her cousin. 'I think it's wonderful news, and from what I've seen of Fred Bottomley, he'll make you a real good husband. What does Miss Maud say about it?'

'Oh, she's tickled pink,' Ada replied. 'She took a fancy to him the first time he called round about the blackout. It's more than her sister did – God rest her soul. I'm afraid Miss Alice never liked him much.'

'I think she was jealous – frightened that you'd go and leave them,' said Jenny. 'How's Miss Maud coping without her sister? Does she miss her?'

Ada shook her head. 'Not so as you'd notice. She was upset at first. She was bound to be, of course. They'd been together all their lives. But there's a big change in her now, right enough. I've never heard her chatter so much.'

'Miss Maud hardly spoke two words of her own when Miss Alice was alive, did she? Too much under her sister's thumb, if you ask me.' Annie returned the frying pan to the top of the stove with a forceful bang. 'Repeating everything Miss Alice said like Little Sir Echo.'

'She's making up for it all right now,' said Ada, laughing. 'Oh – by the way – she says she wants to be called Miss Frobisher now, not Miss Maud, seeing that there's only one of 'em left. It takes some getting used to, but she reminds me if ever I forget. She's getting to be a proper bossy-boots, I can tell you.'

The elder Miss Frobisher had died in January following a severe attack of bronchitis, and Ada certainly hadn't wasted much time before giving an affirmative answer when Fred popped the question.

'You'll find it hard, won't you, when you're living at Fred's?' asked Jenny. 'I suppose Miss Maud – I mean, Miss Frobisher – will still want you to see to her meals and everything. Not much good at looking after herself, is she? Or are you going to leave when you get married?'

'Am I heck as like!' retorted Ada. 'I know when I'm well off, and I told Fred before that I'd no intention of going to live in his poky little place. No – I was just going to tell you – she's asked us if we'd both like to live there – me and Fred – so he's selling his house and moving in with Miss Frobisher. When we're wed, of course.'

'Whatever are you thinking about, Ada? Have you taken leave of your senses?' Annie scowled at her niece. 'Making Fred give up his home like that. A man always likes his own place and his own fireside. Of course you wouldn't know much about that – you've not had much to do with fellows – but you don't want him to go blaming you if it doesn't work out and he's left with no roof over his head.'

'It wasn't a question of making him,' countered Ada, glaring back at her aunt. 'It was Fred's own choice. He can be quite determined when his mind's made up – he's not an ARP warden for nothing – and he thinks it's the best thing to do. It'll give us a bit of money in the bank, and if anything happens to Miss Frobisher – God forbid – then we'll have enough to make a fresh start. And I've always been careful with me wages. I'm not without a bit of brass stacked away.'

'We'll all have to get our glad rags out,' said Jenny cheerfully. 'Are you having a white dress, Ada?'

'Don't talk so bloomin' daft! Can you see me all dressed up like a dog's dinner with a bunch of flowers stuck in me hand? No, my grey costume'll have to do. It was new just before the war started. I might run to a new hat, but you can't go spending money on fancy togs these days. It's not patriotic.'

'And when's the big day?' asked Annie. 'I hope you'll give us

214

time to save up a bob or two for a wedding present.'

'June or July, we think – when it gets warmer – but we haven't fixed a definite date yet. Anyroad, you'll know in good time . . . Well, I can't stand here all day gassing to you two. I've all them bedrooms to do. This won't buy the baby a new bonnet.'

'Ada! Fancy!' Jenny's eyes opened wide in mock astonishment. 'And you never let on. So that's the reason for the hurry, is it?'

'Go on with your bother, you cheeky monkey!' Ada's normally grim features broke into a broad smile at her cousin's words.

Ada smiled a lot more nowadays, Jenny had noticed, and what a difference it made to her appearance when she did. She looked years younger and Jenny suspected that beneath the forbidding exterior there lurked an amiable side to her personality which Fred, to his credit, was bringing to the fore.

But Annie was not amused. 'That's enough of that mucky talk, our Jenny,' she retorted, resolutely polishing the inside of a saucepan until you could see your face in it. 'You never used to talk like that before these RAF lads came. You're getting too saucy by far, young woman.'

'That'd be a turn-up for the book, wouldn't it?' Ada whispered to Jenny as she went off to do the bedrooms. 'I can't see myself pushing a pram along the promenade, but you never know your luck.' She gave an impudent wink as she disappeared through the door.

Jenny was still smiling to herself as she walked back to her own home later that afternoon. She was feeling happy today. Maybe the springlike weather was partially responsible for her mood. It was still only early March but the weather was surprisingly mild. It was lovely to see the sunshine again, however fleeting, after the darkness of winter. But there was another reason too; there had been a letter from Robert that morning, saying that he was due for a forty-eight-hour pass next weekend and that this time he would be spending it in Blackpool. She was overjoyed at the prospect of seeing him again. Not that he would be able to stay at the house or at Pleasant View, but they would be able to spend a few precious hours together.

She hadn't heard from Tom for a few weeks, but the last time he had written he'd seemed cheerful. Mail was sure to be delayed from somewhere as far away as Africa, so she wasn't unduly worried. That was why it was such a shock, as she approached the house, to see the telegram boy standing on the doorstep.

Silently she took the envelope from him, aware that as he handed it to her he didn't look into her face. The boy didn't wait for an answer; what answer could there be? She closed the door behind her and, feeling as though she were at the beginning of a nightmare, stumbled along the passage and into the living room.

She held the dreaded yellow envelope in her hands, feeling the colour drain from her face and her fingers turn to stone, as clumsily she tore it open. The black printed words jumped from the page, forcing themselves upon her unbelieving brain.

'Regret to inform you . . . Corporal Thomas Bradshaw . . . missing in action . . .'

'Oh no. He can't be. Please, God – let it not be true,' Jenny moaned as she sank to her knees in front of the dull embers of the fire. She didn't know how long she knelt there in dry-eyed misery. She could cry so easily over little, unimportant matters. Now, with the grief seeping through her, a dull ache suffusing every part of her body, the tears would not come. After what seemed hours she became aware of the monotonous tick, tick of the clock, abnormally loud in the oppressive silence of the room. She glanced at the dial. Half past three. The girls would be home soon from school. She must get some coal in and mend the fire. She rose to her feet, noting with surprise that she was still wearing her coat.

It was amazing how the simple actions – filling the coal scuttle, putting the kettle on, cutting the bread – had a calming effect on her. She wouldn't say anything to Patsy, she decided. There would be no point. To the little girl, her daddy was already missing by the very fact that he wasn't here, so it was no use alarming her unduly. And through the numbness that seemed to have paralysed her brain, one faint ray of hope emerged, the merest flicker of a candle flame in the darkness. The all too familiar words 'presumed killed' were missing from the telegram.

'But, Jenny, I don't understand you. You're saying that you don't want to see me again? It doesn't make sense.' Robert shook his head in bewilderment and his eyes were dark with pain.

'It isn't that I don't want to see you again. I mustn't . . . I can't. Surely you must see that?'

'I can't see anything except that I love you,' replied Robert wearily. 'You're not being reasonable, darling. You were willing to see me – to make love with me – when Tom was alive. Now that there's a chance that he may be . . .'

'Don't say that!' Jenny spoke loudly in protest. 'Don't ever say that. Tom isn't dead. I know he isn't. They would have told me if he were. The telegram said that he was missing . . . that's all.'

'I know that, darling. But you may have to face up to it sooner or later. He may be alive, or he may . . . not be. And if that were to happen, then we could be together, love, for always.'

Jenny shook her head sadly. 'No, Robert. I'm sorry – we can't. I mustn't see you again. I've got to wait now for Tom to come back.'

'Then you don't love me any more. Perhaps you've never loved me.' The desolation in Robert's voice and the sadness misting the clear blue of his eyes made Jenny cry out as if in pain.

'Of course I love you! God knows how much I love you. Don't ask me to explain it, darling. I can't even explain it to myself. But I know – now – that we can't go on. I'm not saying that it was wrong. It was too wonderful to be wrong. But . . . it's over, darling.'

Jenny had known, with a terrifying certainty, ever since the dreaded telegram had arrived, that this marked the end of her love affair with Robert. The thought that she might now be free had entered her mind only fleetingly. She knew, for better or worse, that her future lay with Tom, her husband, the father of her child. To leave Robert would be to lose part of herself – had they not said so many times that they were twin souls, two matching halves of a perfect whole? – but nevertheless, she knew, inexplicably, that it had to be done.

The words of the marriage service had sprung, unbidden, into Jenny's mind as she lay in bed that first night after the dreadful news had come to her. She could see again, as clearly as if he were standing near to her, the clergyman, tall and forbidding-looking, who had married them, and she could hear in her memory his sonorous tones echoing round the church: '. . . to have and to hold . . . for better, for worse . . . in sickness and in health . . . to love, honour and obey . . . till death us do part . . .'

'No, he can't be!' She almost cried out loud in her anguish. He can't be dead . . .' Then, as the scalding tears burned her eyelids and trickled down her cheeks she prayed. Please God, let him be alive. Please God, I'll love him and obey him, like I promised . . .

She didn't promise in her fervent prayer to give Robert up, but she knew, nevertheless, that that was what she had to do.

But when Robert came on leave the next weekend he didn't understand. He closed the door behind him and strode purposefully across the room. The next instant she was in his arms, feeling the eager hardness of his body against hers, smelling the so familiar, dearly loved scent of his skin, his hair. For a split second her resolution began to waver, then she put her hands against his shoulders and struggled to push him away from her.

'No! Darling – don't. You'll only make it worse.'

'Please, Jenny. Let me make love to you. Just once more. Please, darling.'

'No, no.' Jenny shook her head. 'We mustn't.'

'Then you can't stop me kissing you,' said Robert harshly.

His arms encircled her again in a vicelike grip. His mouth came down fiercely on hers, bruising her lips with the intensity of his frustrated desire. As he felt her responding to him, he held her more gently, stroking her hair, her breasts, the curves of her body. Their last kiss encompassed all the tenderness, the sweetness and the joy that they had known together over the last few months. As a drowning person, it is said, sees his life flash before him, so Jenny relived again in those few seconds the precious moments that she had known with Robert. The clifftop at the height of a gale; the waves crashing against the sea wall; the scent of the spray; the crunch of autumn leaves beneath their feet; the warmth of the flames upon their bodies as they made love by the glowing fire. These moments she would cherish and remember for ever.

'That's it then, darling?' Robert's voice was sad as he gradually released her from his arms, gently stroking her cheeks, her nose, her eyelids with the tip of his finger.

'I'm afraid so, my love. Just go – now. Don't say goodbye. Just go quickly, before . . .

'I've no intention of saying goodbye, darling. Just *au revoir*, like the French do. Till we meet again. And we will meet again, my love, somewhere, somehow . . .'

'Just go, Robert,' repeated Jenny sadly. 'But remember that I love you. I'll always love you.'

As she heard the door close behind him Jenny sank to her knees in front of the fire, as she had done the day that the telegram arrived, a week ago. The longest week of her life.

'Please, God, keep him safe,' she whispered fervently. 'I do love him. I love him so much.' It was no longer possible to keep them in separate compartments; her love for Tom and her love for Robert had become hopelessly intermingled. 'And please, please show me what to do . . .' she whispered. 'Dear God, it's such a muddle . . . please help me . . .' Never had Jenny prayed more fervently, for now she was praying, not only for the safety of her husband and her young lover, but for something that she hadn't revealed to Robert, something that Tom might never know. The anguished prayer that issued from Jenny's mind was just a plea that God, somehow, would make it all come right . . .

At first she had ignored the subtle changes in her body, the telltale signs that would make most women jump to the obvious conclusion. Jenny's periods had always been irregular; it had been nothing unusual for her to go for eight or nine weeks without any loss, especially since Patsy's birth. Her waistline had thickened slightly and her breasts had become fuller, but these signs, too, she had disregarded. She knew that her figure, like her mother's, tended towards plumpness, and she had refused to give credence to the thought that was trying to push itself to the forefront of her mind.

The doctor had told her, when Patsy was born, that it was extremely unlikely that there would be any more children. She and Tom had made love without taking the precautions that she knew so many women favoured nowadays. Jenny was still naïve about such matters. She knew that large families were becoming a thing of the past, that there were ways and means now of preventing conception, but these measures had seemed irrelevant to Jenny. She and Tom had wanted another child so very much, but none had come along. Now, Jenny knew without a shadow of a doubt what these bodily changes meant. She was pregnant, but it was only now, after she had forced herself to say goodbye to Robert, that her mind would allow the thought to be admitted.

She stood in front of the wardrobe mirror, turning sideways and smoothing her skirt over the slight bulge of her stomach. It was not noticeable yet, especially as when she was working she always wore an apron, but very soon it would become apparent. Dear God, whatever was she to do? Before long her mother would notice – her astute glance missed very little – and Violet, too . . . She had become a shrewd young woman lately, and though the sisters were now friendly again on the surface, Jenny knew that her affair with Robert still rankled in Violet's mind.

It never entered Jenny's head for one moment that she could get rid of the child. It was there, for better or worse, the result of her indiscretion, and she would have to face up to it. For Jenny presumed that the child she was carrying was Robert's. It was very unlikely that it could be Tom's; six years had passed without her conceiving his child, and Robert was younger and stronger, much more virile . . .

Jenny knew that she would have to dissemble. The best thing to do would be to tell them quickly, her mother and Violet, before it became too apparent. Tom had been home on leave at Christmas and they had made love more than once. Nothing could be proved; her family might have their suspicions, but there could be no proof . . . could there? Even after the child was born there would be no way of telling . . . Robert's hair was dark, but then so was Jenny's own, and babies' eyes were always blue at birth . . . weren't they?

Jenny sighed; the questions she was asking herself were futile. She nodded at her reflection in the mirror. You'd best get it over with, my girl, she told the apprehensive face that gazed back at her. You know there's no turning back. 'What's done can't be undone' was a favourite expression of her mother's, and Jenny knew that she must tell them quickly – now – before her courage failed her.

A visit to the doctor only confirmed what she had known all along.

'It's good news, Mrs Bradshaw.' The doctor beamed at her across the consulting-room table, after he had examined her. 'There's no doubt that there's a baby on the way.'

'Yes, it's . . . good news,' Jenny repeated. 'But I thought I'd better make certain, before I told my . . . family.'

'Indeed . . . yes.' Dr Norris looked grave for a moment. 'I was so sorry to hear about your husband, Jenny.' He had been the family doctor for many years and often used her Christian name. 'One hardly knows what to say . . . but the gift of a child can compensate such a lot. I really did think, after the birth of your little girl, that it wouldn't be possible. This seem like a miracle after so long.'

'Yes . . . a miracle,' said Jenny, aware that she was foolishly repeating the doctor's words. 'And it will be wonderful news for Tom, if . . . when I hear from him,' she went on quickly. 'I haven't given up hope, Dr Norris.'

'And you mustn't give up. Now, off you go home, and take good care of yourself. I'll see you regularly, and there's no reason at all why you shouldn't have a fine, healthy child. You can spread the glad tidings now . . .'

'Well, I'm blowed!" said Annie, sitting down suddenly in the easy chair. 'A baby . . . after all this time? I can hardly credit it . . .' Her eyes narrowed speculatively behind the thick lenses as she glanced at her daughter's waistline. 'You don't seem to be showing much yet, our Jenny. When did you say it was due?'

'I didn't,' Jenny replied quickly. 'You know how irregular I've always been, Mother . . .' Now, speak calmly, she said to herself. There's no need to panic . . . She can't prove anything. 'But Tom was home at Christmas, so I should imagine it will be the end of September . . . or thereabouts,' she added casually.

Just what she would do when the child arrived in August, as she was sure it would, Jenny didn't know, but there would be time enough to think about that when it happened. The biggest hurdle – telling her mother – had been overcome, and if Annie suspected anything, she had the good sense, at the moment, to keep it to herself.

'I believe congratulations are due,' said Violet the next day. 'Well, it's certainly time we had some good news for a change.' She raised her eyebrows questioningly and Jenny could see that her sister's face was unsmiling. Violet hadn't smiled much lately, though. She had seemed to be getting over her break-up with Tony and hadn't mentioned him for months, but the news that Tom was missing had saddened her, as it had all of them. 'It is good news, is it, Jenny?' she asked, and Jenny was aware of a note of scepticism creeping into Violet's voice.

'Of course it is.' Jenny gave a little laugh. 'A baby coming is always good news . . . and you know that Tom and I had given up hope.'

'Yes . . . We'll have to start knitting then, won't we?' said Violet.

Jenny knew that no matter how much knitting any of them did, she wouldn't be able to pull the wool over Violet's eyes. The war and the experiences it had brought had changed her sister into a most perspicacious young woman.

Daisy White leaned back in the corner seat of the compartment and watched the drab little houses of central Blackpool flash past the window. One town was pretty much the same as another, especially near the railway station and she supposed that Rosie was as well off here as she would be at home in Liverpool. The child certainly seemed contented enough. Very happy, in fact . . . Too happy? A tiny niggle of doubt creased Daisy's smooth white forehead, and her big blue eyes, so like her daughter's, clouded over as she stared unseeingly at the vista of sand dunes and wheeling seagulls as the train approached St Annes.

She didn't now whether Rosie had been glad to see her or not. She had seemed pleased, and had chatted readily enough, as usual, but it was 'Auntie Jenny this' and 'Auntie Jenny that' all the time, until Daisy was sick and tired of hearing the woman's name. It wasn't that she didn't feel grateful to Mrs Bradshaw for making Rosie so welcome, but when all was said and done she wasn't a relation, not a proper auntie at all. Daisy was thoughtful . . . The bombing raids on Liverpool had slackened off lately. Maybe it was time to be thinking of having Rosie back home again. Mrs Willams across the road was talking about having Ben back. He was living just up the street from Rosie. Maybe they could travel home together? She would pop across and see his mother later tonight.

Daisy wasn't sure, though. It needed careful thought. It was much easier, with Rosie out of the way, to work longer hours at the factory. Then there was her other . . . job. She supposed it was a job to her now, although it hadn't started off as one. Daisy had always enjoyed the company of men and when they started buying her gifts – flowers and chocolates at first, then stockings, dresses, even furs – how could she refuse? The next stage had been accepting money as payment . . . It had provided a few luxuries, and her Rosie was the best-turned-out little kid in the street. Nobody could deny that. Having her daughter home again would certainly curtail her activities, but Rosie was getting far too fond of that Jenny Bradshaw.

The next train, which she boarded at Preston station, was crowded, but Daisy just managed to find a seat – the last one in the compartment – between a soldier and a red-faced sailor.

'There's room for a little one,' she prattled cheerfully as she squeezed her shapely bottom into the few inches of space.

She peered into the flyblown mirror opposite as the train drew out of the station, and adjusted the angle of her saucy red hat and her fox fur – a gift from an admirer – which she always wore over her best black costume. Damn! There was a smut on her nose. She pulled a lace-edged hanky from her pocket and licked the corner of it.

'Allow me,' said the sailor, who had been watching her with interest.

'Ta very much.' Daisy grinned at him as he took her handkerchief and wiped away the offending black smear.

He continued to watch her as she idly examined her scarlet-painted nails and then stretched out one silk-stockinged leg, then the other, to make sure there were no ladders.

'Whooo!' he whistled appreciatively, and Daisy grinned at him again, this time closing one eye in a suggestive wink.

'Joining your ship, are you, lovey?' she asked cheerily.

'That's right, lady. Liverpool docks, tomorrow morning.'

'Well – fancy that! What a coincidence,' Daisy chirruped. 'That's where I live. Right near to the docks. Got anywhere to stay tonight, ducky?'

'I was going to stay with a mate, but I don't suppose he'll worry if I don't turn up. What do you say, darling?'

'I'll make sure you don't miss the boat, lovey!' Daisy giggled. She looked hurriedly round the compartment at her travelling companions. The soldier was asleep and the other occupants were either dozing or reading their newspapers.

The train rattled on, gathering speed as it left Preston. No one paid any attention to the couple cuddling in the corner . . .

Dusk was falling rapidly and by the time the train, which had stopped and started every few minutes, drew nearer to Liverpool, the view outside the window was nothing but inky blackness. If you didn't know the area there was no telling where you were at all, because the signs had long since been taken away from the stations. Suddenly, the wail of the siren sounded above the rhythmic clatter of the train wheels, and all the lights went out. Now there was total blackness both inside and out.

'Shall we get out at the next station, or take our chance?' whispered Daisy's companion.

During an air raid, passengers were given the choice of leaving the train at the next stop and taking shelter, or continuing the journey at a snail's pace.

'Let's risk it,' Daisy whispered back. 'We can't be more than fifteen miles from Lime Street station.'

'OK, darling. Suits me.' The sailor put his hand on Daisy's thigh and pulled up her skirt. He fondled the bare flesh at her stocking top. 'Let's make the most of this blackout . . .'

An ear-splitting crash drowned the last of his words, and as they threw themselves to the floor, burying their heads in their arms, the roof and walls of the carriage shattered around them.

Jenny stared in disbelief at the second yellow envelope which she held in her hands. Oh, dear God, no! This time it must be the news she had dreaded to hear. Tom must be . . . Her fingers trembled as she drew out the thin white paper and forced herself to read the words. But she couldn't comprehend for a moment what she was reading.

'Daisy White killed in air raid . . . Letter following . . . Jean Williams.'

Who on earth was Jean Williams? She shook her head bemusedly. Of course – Ben – Eileen's evacuee – he was called Williams. It must be from his mother. But how dreadful for poor little Rosie. However would Jenny be able to find the words to tell her? Then a feeling of relief which almost amounted to joy gripped her, to be followed immediately by one of guilt that she should inwardly rejoice at such devastating news. From the recesses of her mind came the memory of a text heard long ago at Sunday school: 'The Lord giveth and the Lord taketh away. Blessed be the name of the Lord.'

Rosie's blue eyes clouded over for a moment, but Jenny, who was watching her intently, thought that it was more with puzzlement than grief.

'Then . . . where is she, my mum?' the child asked, and, almost to her relief, Jenny caught a glimpse of tears welling up in the corners of her lovely blue eyes.

'I've just told you, darling. Didn't you understand?' She put her arm round Rosie where they sat on the settee and drew the little girl closer to her. 'There was an air raid, and Mummy was . . .'

'Yes . . . I know that.' Rosie shook her head impatiently. 'I

know she's dead . . . but,' her forehead creased in a frown, 'but
. . . at the Sunday school I go to with Patsy they told us that when
people die they go to heaven to live with God. Them that love
Him, that is. Me mum didn't go to church an' all that, an' I never
heard her talk about God. I don't think she knew much about Him.
I just wondered . . .'

Jenny could hardly speak for the lump in her throat, but she tried
to answer calmly. 'Don't worry, love. Your mum will be in heaven.
I don't think it depends on how much we love God . . . It's how
much He loves us.' And, in her heart, that was what Jenny
believed. She could have no faith in a God who was so unforgiving
as to allow into His kingdom only those who were continually
falling at His feet in adoration. Jenny believed in an all-powerful,
all-embracing God who would find room for everyone. She wasn't
sure whether her simple view of theology was an accurate one –
who could really know with any certainty? she asked herself – but it
was a comforting one at this moment for a little girl who was sad
and perplexed. 'Don't worry, Rosie,' she said again. 'God will take
care of your mum.'

'Then – can I stay here, Auntie Jenny?'

'Of course you can, darling. Where else would you stay?'

'I mean – for always?'

'Yes – for always.' Jenny put her arms round the child and Rosie
leaned her head against Jenny's breast.

'And – Auntie Jenny – can I call you Mummy?'

'Of course you can, darling,' said Jenny again, her eyes wet with
tears of both thankfulness and sorrow.

It was at that moment that she made up her mind that she would
take steps to legally adopt the little girl. Rosie was hers now, and
no one was going to take her away.

Chapter 20

'Why don't you go and stay with Tom's mother for a while? You're looking a bit peaky, our Jenny. That's not to be wondered at, of course, with all the shocks you've had lately and then this baby coming an' all. A week or two in Yorkshire'd do you a world of good, and the two little girls.'

'Mm . . . yes, I might,' said Jenny thoughtfully. Annie had been much more sympathetic recently in spite of – or could it possibly be because of? – the expected child, and Jenny responded with a smile to the unusual warmth in her mother's voice. 'It would be a nice change for Rosie, wouldn't it, to see a bit of real countryside? I don't think she'd seen much outside Liverpool before she came here. Do you know, Mother, she never mentions Daisy White? I don't know whether to be glad or sorry.'

'I expect she thinks about her, though, for all she doesn't let on about it. Poor little mite – it was her ma when all's said and done – but you'll make up for it, I'm sure, Jenny lass. Have you got any nearer with the adoption?'

'Mr Davenport's sorting it all out for me,' replied Jenny. 'These things take time, especially when there's a war on, but he doesn't think there'll be any problem. There don't seem to be any close relatives. Nobody's come to lay any claim to her at any rate, poor little lamb.'

Mr Davenport, a local solicitor, was the husband of the billeting officer who had been in charge at the church hall the day that Rosie had arrived in Blackpool. A meek, mild-mannered little man, in sharp contrast to his overbearing wife, he had willingly agreed to take care of the legal formalities for Jenny at a nominal cost. Jenny was happy, for her part, that the proceedings had been set in motion. Before long, all being well, she would have her second little girl. She knew that in this venture she would have Tom's full support, and what a lovely surprise it would be for him when he found out about it.

There would be two surprises for him, for surely the news of the coming child would be the biggest wonder of all.

Jenny was remarkably well, and the paleness that her mother had remarked upon was just a result of the sunless winter months. At times she could hardly believe that a new life was growing within her. She had felt poorly for a lot of the time when she was carrying Patsy, but this time the only sign of her pregnancy was her expanding waistline. She knew that some explaining – prevaricating, more like – would have to be done when the child arrived prematurely, but, by and large, she was able to push the disturbing thoughts about this to the back of her mind.

Her main concern was for Tom. For most of the time she still firmly believed that he was alive. Sometimes, in the small hours of the morning, when the world, and her thoughts, too, was at its blackest, the powers of darkness would take hold of her. She felt certain, as she lay wide wake in the suffocating blackness, that tomorrow another dreaded telegram would come telling her the worst. But, with the arrival of the new dawn, came renewed hope and the certainty that her night-time fears were unfounded. Now it was April, the sun was shining, and she knew that her mother's suggestion – that she should visit Tom's mother in Castleburn – was a wise one.

She was determined to put on a brave face for Martha Bradshaw; Tom's mother would be badly in need of reassurance and comfort. It was with some trepidation that Jenny, together with the two girls, got out of the battered taxi at the end of the slow journey to Castleburn, and walked up the garden path between the rows of daffodils.

Martha, who had been watching from the window, opened the door before Jenny had a chance to knock. She seemed smaller than ever – not much taller than Rosie – and more wrinkled, if that were possible, but her beady brown eyes were as bright as ever. At the sight of her the tears, which Jenny was usually able to hold in check, threatened to brim over again. She blinked rapidly – Martha mustn't see her crying – and put her arms round the little old lady, feeling the papery dryness of her skin, smelling again the faint, familiar scent of eau-de-Cologne.

What a joy it was, after their long journey, to sit by the kitchen fire, drinking tea from Martha's old willow-pattern cups. Rosie stared in wide-eyed delight around the old-fashioned kitchen. Jenny remembered how she, too, had been fascinated by it on her first visit. This was the heart of the house, virtually unchanged – apart from the introduction of electric lighting instead of the original gas mantles – since the end of the last century, when Martha had come to live here as a young bride. Here she had brought up her five children, and it was here that Martha and Lilian still ate most of their meals.

Jenny gazed round contentedly at the familiar scene. The cooking was done on a black cast-iron range. The fire burned, winter and summer through, in the centre of the range, and on the hob a copper kettle continually simmered, providing endless cups of tea. On either side of the grate were brick-lined ovens used for baking and roasting meat. Martha baked all her own bread and cakes and Jenny knew that her mother-in-law's cooking could not be surpassed by any of the more modern housewives with all their up-to-date equipment.

On the wooden mantelpiece was an assortment of family treasures that had been there since Jenny's first visit, over ten years before. A Toby jug portraying General Kitchener; two curly brass candlesticks; a tea caddy with a portrait of King Edward VII and Queen Alexandra; a china shell with the inscription 'A Present from Bridlington'; a square wooden clock; a carved wooden holder containing coloured spills; and a host of family photographs. On a dresser at the back of the kitchen Martha's willow-pattern pottery was displayed, together with more mundane articles – baking dishes, basins and bowls made from heavy, partly-glazed clay. In the centre of the room was the large scrubbed pine table with the wooden Windsor armchair at the head. Jenny wondered if it was still left unoccupied as a tribute to the memory of Albert Bradshaw. and would there now be another chair left vacant, the place that was once occupied by the youngest son? Jenny gave a shudder and pushed the thought away.

The fireside chairs were comfortable, in spite of the sagging cushions and the threadbare moquette. Jenny leaned back and smiled at her mother-in-law.

'Would the girls like to go and play in the garden?' Martha asked. 'I reckon they'll be getting a bit bored sitting here.'

'Yes, I daresay they would,' Jenny replied, 'so long as they don't go trampling all over your plants. Be careful now, you two. Granny Bradshaw's very proud of her flower garden.'

The old lady laughed. 'Not so many flowers now, Jenny dear. Our Lilian's turned nearly all the flowerbeds over. Digging for Victory, she calls it. We've got carrots and onions and Brussels sprouts and goodness knows what else out there. We've always grown our own potatoes, of course, but now we don't need to go to the market for any of our veg. She's always liked gardening, has our Lilian. I thought we'd have a nice little chat, just you and me, dear.' Martha nodded at Jenny as the two little girls skipped happily out into the garden. 'It doesn't do to say too much in front of the bairns.'

'I haven't told them anything,' Jenny replied. 'It must have been a shock to Rosie, losing her mother, though she doesn't say much. She thinks the world of Tom. I wouldn't want to upset her even further. Or Patsy either – she's got used to her daddy being away. Time enough to tell them when we know definitely whether . . .'

'My Tom isn't dead.' Martha leaned forward, her bright eyes looking intently into Jenny's. 'I know that as sure as I know I'm sitting here. Don't you think I would feel it, right here' – she tucked her hand under her left breast – 'if he were dead? A mother would know, my dear, and we were always so close, Tom and me. I know you're his wife, and he couldn't have a better one anywhere in the world.' Jenny looked at her feet feeling embarrassed, and rather guilty too. 'But when you've borne a child,' Martha went on, 'they're part of you for always . . . and that little lad was God's precious gift to me, coming along so late in my life. I know I've told you before that he was my favourite. Oh, I know a mother shouldn't have favourites, but that's the way I feel and there's nowt I can do about it. And how wonderful that you're having another bairn, Jenny lass. I was that pleased when you wrote and told me, and our Tom'll be delighted when he finds out.'

Jenny smiled and nodded in agreement, feeling even more guilty. 'Yes, he will be pleased,' she said quietly, 'and I'm so glad that you feel he's still alive, Mam. That's what I think too – most of the time.'

Jenny had been ready to give comfort and moral support to the older woman, to offer a shoulder to cry on if the need should arise. Now she found, not entirely to her surprise, that it was Martha who was better able to offer consolation. She had always been a strong character. Though tiny in stature she was, and always had been, a

230

veritable matriarch to her family. It had always come easy to Jenny to call her 'Mam' as Tom did, and she had a genuine affection for the old lady which was sadly lacking, alas, in her relationship with Annie.

'Aye, he's a grand lad, is my Tom,' Martha continued, 'and I'm right proud of him, serving his King and Country. I know his father would have been proud of him an' all. He's the only one of my lads in the Army, though to be fair to them, it's not their fault. Joe's working down the pit – Bevin boys they call 'em now, don't they, Jenny? – and our Jack's not been called up. Of course he's turned fifty now, and I reckon he did his bit at the end of the Great War. He was in Palestine then. Have I told you, Jenny?'

Jenny smiled and nodded. Martha had told her – many times.

'I should think one war's enough in any man's lifetime, don't you think so, dear?'

Jenny nodded again in agreement, but she didn't need to speak because when Martha started talking there was no stopping her. She went on like a river in full spate.

'The war to end all wars they called it, didn't they, dear, but a fat lot of good it did I must say. Oh, there are some wicked people in the world, dear. Really wicked – wanting to cause wars like this. But what can young fellows do? They've got to go and do their bit if they've got owt about 'em. I wouldn't have had my Tom any other way.'

'How's Lilian?' asked Jenny, to change the subject. 'She's still working at Woolworth's, I suppose?'

'Aye, she's still at Woolie's. Our Lilian isn't much of a one for change.' Martha paused for a moment, then her bright eyes clouded over with anxiety. 'I'm worried about her, Jenny, and that's a fact. She's always been a strange girl, but I reckon she's worse than ever now. She's so close I can hardly get two words out of her. She always used to chat about her job when she came in of a night. To tell you the truth, I sometimes got a bit fed up of hearing about it.' Martha gave a dry little laugh. 'But I reckon she's not got much else to talk about. She's never been one for getting out and about much. But she doesn't even talk about Woolie's now.'

'I daresay she's worrying about Tom,' said Jenny. 'He's her brother when all's said and done, and she's bound to be upset. She may not have the same faith as you, Mam, that he's still alive.'

231

'Happen you're right. I know I couldn't get through if I didn't believe that the good Lord was in charge of it all. And He is, you know, Jenny. He'll be looking after our Tom, you mark my words. He'll not let him come to any harm.'

Jenny nodded slowly, but she didn't speak. What a childlike faith Martha had; it was obviously a great comfort to her, but, to Jenny's mind, it was too simple. What about the thousands of deaths that there had been already during the first two years of the war? Was God not looking after those people as well? And if the mothers and wives of the victims had prayed for their loved ones' safety, as Martha did, surely they must feel now that God had let them down, that He did not care . . . It was a problem of such magnitude that Jenny's uncomplicated mind could not cope with it. She, too, would love to think that God was in control, but at times she had her doubts. Why did He permit such misery and mayhem if He was all-powerful . . .?

'Yes, I daresay she's concerned about Tom,' Martha continued. 'She never mentions him, though. When I first told her she went as white as a sheet, then when I said as how I knew he were still alive she gave me such a strange look, Jenny. It fair put the wind up me, I'll tell you. Sometimes I can't weigh her up at all.'

Poor Lilian, thought Jenny. It wasn't the first time since hearing the news about Tom that she had spared a thought for her sister-in-law. She knew that Lilian was fond – very fond – of her brother and that at times in the past she had been jealous of his wife.

'They got on well when they were bairns, our Tom and Lilian,' Martha continued, 'though she were always a bit jealous. Then when they were growing up, she seemed to turn right against him. It were uncanny. Maybe she's sorry now that she weren't nicer to him . . . Aye, she's a funny lass.'

When Lilian came in at tea time Jenny could see that Martha had cause indeed to be worried about her. Lilian had always been of a slight build, but now her clothes hung on her like a scarecrow's garb. The young woman's expression was blank and apathetic, as though all hope had gone. She smiled briefly when she spoke to the children, but the smile didn't reach her eyes, and her enquiry after Jenny's health was merely perfunctory.

It was intuition, rather than the noise, that woke Jenny around midnight. She could hear the regular breathing of the two little girls in the opposite bed, but there wa another sound, coming from downstairs. She strained her ears, listening, her common sense telling her that it was nothing to worry about. No doubt it would be Martha, unable to sleep, making herself a cup of tea. Jenny frowned . . . There was someone talking down there; the words were indistinguishable, but she could hear the low murmur of a voice. A presentiment of something sadly amiss made her spring out of bed. She grabbed her dressing gown from behind the door and hurried downstairs.

The kitchen was in darkness, but the sound of quiet sobbing was coming from there and she realised at once that it was not Martha, but Lilian. When she pushed open the door Jenny could see the huddled figure slumped over the kitchen table, and she noticed, in spite of her anxiety, that Lilian was sitting in the large Windsor chair, the one normally left vacant to the memory of Albert Bradshaw. Lilian looked round, startled, as Jenny switched on the light. Her face was red and blotchy with weeping and her eyes held the look of despair that had so worried Jenny earlier in the day.

'Lilian . . . love, whatever's the matter?' Jenny went across and put her arm round the young woman's thin shoulders.

'The light . . . put it out. I want it to be . . . dark,' Lilian stammered. 'Leave me, Jenny. Just . . . leave me.'

It was then that Jenny noticed that the blackout blinds had been opened. It was indeed necessary to put out the light before an ARP warden came snooping round, and this Jenny did quickly before returning to Lilian's' side. 'Indeed I won't leave you, Lilian,' she said quietly. The light from an almost full moon shone through the window, illuminating Lilian's white nightgown and her pale, thin arms. Surely she must be cold, sitting there without a dressing gown? Then Jenny saw, to her slowly mounting horror, the glass in front of Lilian, the bottle a quarter empty, and a smaller bottle the contents of which – small, round white pills – were strewn across the table top.

'Oh, dear God, no!' Jenny gave an involuntary gasp of fright and, though her instinct was to shake Lilian and shout at her, she knew that she must try to act calmly. Harsh words and anger might only serve to drive Lilian even further over the brink of despair. And she must already be very far gone in her misery to attempt to . . . What she was attempting to do didn't bear thinking about. 'Lilian, listen to me.' Jenny took her sister-in-law by the shoulders, speaking to her gently but firmly. 'How many have you taken? Come on . . . you must tell me.'

Lilian shook her head. 'Two, three . . . I don't know.' Her voice was almost inaudible. 'I was just counting them. I didn't know how many . . .'

'You're quite sure?' Jenny took a quick glance at the tablets. Aspirin – probably not very powerful unless taken in large quantities, and there didn't seem to be many missing. But combined with the alcohol . . . Jenny saw, to her relief, that the glass was almost full. 'Lilian,' she said urgently, 'you're sure, aren't you? You've only taken two or three?'

Lilian nodded. 'I don't like whisky,' she said in a tiny voice, the complaining voice of a child. Jenny had to suppress an overwhelming desire to laugh out loud. Martha Bradshaw never allowed alcohol in the house. Tom had never dared to let on to his mother that he enjoyed the odd drink, now and again, and as for Lilian, the idea was preposterous. Jenny wondered how she had come by the bottle, but that was irrelevant. The evidence must be got rid of, immediately. Martha must never know what Lilian had attempted to do, or by what means.

She picked up the glass and bottle and quickly poured the contents down the sink, then she washed the glass and popped the empty bottle into a cupboard. She would hide it in her bedroom later until she was able to dispose of it. Jenny was only surprised that Martha hadn't come down already, disturbed by the commotion. Luckily, the older woman slept well, unusually for someone of her age, the untroubled sleep that issued from a tranquil mind. Jenny wished that she, too, could cast all her care upon an invisible deity, as Martha did on retiring, instead of lying awake with chaotic thoughts chasing round and round in her brain.

Her concern at the moment, though, was for Lilian. She was sitting motionless, as though in a trance. Jenny knew that her sister-in-law needed to talk, to unburden herself of the great weight of worry that must be clouding her reason. She sat down in one of the kitchen chairs, then leaned across and took hold of Lilian's hand. 'It's all right, love,' she said gently. 'I understand. It's Tom, isn't it? You're worried about Tom. We all are . . . but we have to go on hoping – trusting – that he's still alive. Your mother thinks that he is . . .'

'Tom . . .' Lilian repeated dazedly. 'Yes . . . Tom.' Her eyes drifted out of focus as she stared across the room, and the emptiness, both in her look and in her voice, frightened Jenny. But thank God she had come down in time. Another few minutes and it could have been too late. Suddenly Lilian gave a strangled cry and, burying her head in her hands, gave way to a paroxysm of weeping. 'I love him . . . as well . . . just as much as you. I don't know what I'll do if . . . he doesn't come back.'

'Shhh . . .' Jenny stroked her hair. It felt greasy, in need of a wash. 'He'll come back, Lilian. I know . . . how much you care for him.'

The look that Lilian gave Jenny was one of such torment that she feared, not for the first time, for her sister-in-law's sanity. 'You can't know how much . . .' Lilian almost screamed. 'Nobody knows. I know it's wrong . . . it's wicked . . . but I can't help it. Oh, God . . . I can't help it . . . and now he's gone.'

'Hush . . . Lilian, hush!' Jenny was afraid that Martha would hear the noise. She cast a worried glance towards the ceiling, but there was no sound, only that of Lilian's muffled sobs. 'Listen to me, love. I do know how you feel . . . about Tom.'

And suddenly, intuitively, Jenny did know. This was more than a normal affection that Lilian had for her brother. It amounted to an . . . obsession. Now Jenny understood just why she had seemed so strange at times. Lilian loved Tom deeply – perhaps in a way that she shouldn't love him – and the thought that it was wrong was tormenting her. Poor Lilian . . . Jenny drew the young woman closer to her. 'I do know how you feel,' she said again, realising that for the very first time she was beginning to understand the complex emotions of her sister-in-law.

'You . . . you know?' A faint glimmer of reason, of normality, returned to Lilian's eyes as she stared at Jenny.

'Yes . . . I've known for a long time. A very long time.' Jenny gave a sad smile. 'It's not wicked. Don't ever think that. It's just . . . well, you've never found anyone to match up to him, have you?'

She was relieved that Lilian's fit of weeping seemed to be at an end and she was looking slightly more composed. If she could be persuaded to talk about it all, it might do her a power of good. That was probably what the trouble was, the bottling up of her emotions – and also the feeling that they were wrong – for so many years.

'It's wrong to love your brother . . . the way I do,' said Lilian, in a monotone. 'I've never told anyone. All these years, I've never told

. . . and now he's not here any more. And I've been jealous of you, Jenny. That was wicked too . . .'

Once the words started to tumble out there was no stopping them. Jenny just nodded from time to time and made encouraging sounds of reassurance, letting Lilian talk it all out of her system: the gradual dawning upon Lilian that she loved her brother, possibly too much; her envy of Jenny, not only of her husband, but of her home and her little girl, and now the new baby that was on the way. Jenny sensed the bitterness that Lilian must have felt. She realised, with a pang of guilt, particularly with regard to the coming child, that she had so much and Lilian so little. But she knew also that the young woman was indulging in self-pity as, Jenny guessed, she had done all her life.

'I'll make us a pot of tea,' said Jenny briskly, when Lilian had stopped speaking. She took her coat from the back of the door and slipped it round Lilian's shoulders. 'There – you must be feeling a bit chilly. And we'd best get back to bed soon or we'll both be like a piece of chewed string in the morning.' She spoke composedly in an endeavour to restore normality to the highly emotional atmosphere.

Lilian, thank God, seemed calmer now. She sipped at the hot, strong tea that Jenny had made, both hands clasped round the mug as though she was trying to draw comfort from its warmth, and watched furtively as Jenny popped the tablets, one by one, back in the bottle. 'You won't be needing these again, will you?' Jenny's voice was stern. She must make Lilian understand what a dreadful think it was she had tried to do. 'It was very wrong, Lilian. You said it was wicked to love Tom like you do, but it isn't. Love can't be wicked . . . but what you were doing was wicked. Just imagine how upset your mother would have been. And all of us . . . We all love you, you know, Lilian,' she added quietly. Jenny wondered, though, if her sister-in-law's action had been more of a cry for help than a serious attempt to take her own life.

'Nothing to live for. No point,' Lilian mumbled, staring down at the mug of tea. 'Now Tom's gone . . .'

'No, Lilian. Don't ever say that. Tom isn't dead. I know he isn't.' Jenny remembered how she had used the same words to Robert. It seemed so long ago now, and she wasn't at all sure whether she really believed them herself. But it was vital that Lilian should not give up hope.

Lilian, she thought, had always seemed to be one of life's losers, a

236

victim of her own introspective personality. Some people were born optimists, always ready to take a sanguine view of life. Jenny knew that she herself was of that temperament, although she'd had her share of troubles lately and it was difficult sometimes to go on hoping. But Lilian's was a totally different disposition, one that was naturally melancholy, finding it easier to descend to the depths of despair than to seek for joy on the mountaintops.

Lilian needed something to live for . . . From the depths of her mind Jenny tried to recall something that she had heard long ago – probably a half-remembered sermon from her church-going days – about the essentials for happiness . . . Something to do, someone to love, and something to look forward to . . . Jenny knew that her own life, though beset with problems, was rich indeed. She had always had so much to do that there were seldom enough hours in the day. She had her children to love and care for, and she looked forward to a brighter tomorrow. Lilian's life, in contrast, seemed so empty . . . Jenny knew that her sister-in-law's job at Woolworth's was not one that would widen her horizons, especially now, in wartime, when young women were finding employment in all sorts of different spheres. Like Violet, for instance . . .

'You know, Lilian,' she said now. 'My sister – our Violet – used to be just like you. She never did anything but work in the boarding house for Mother, until, soon after the war started, she went to work in the aircraft factory. It's made a world of difference to her.'

'She's brainier than me, your Violet,' said Lilian gruffly, her self-pity coming to the fore again. 'She's a right clever girl. Don't see as how she can be much like me.'

'She was quiet, like you,' Jenny persisted. 'She didn't find it easy to make friends, and she'd never had a boyfriend.' She smiled confidingly at Lilian. 'And I'll tell you something . . . I used to think she fancied my Tom, so you're not the only one, you see.' She was gratified to see Lilian's mouth lift slightly in the ghost of a smile. 'Our Violet loves it at the factory. Have you never thought of doing something like that, Lilian?'

Lilian shrugged. 'Don't know. There's no munitions factory near here. Joan across the road, she's joined the Land Army. She's working down in Shropshire . . . but I'd never be able to leave me mam . . .'

Jenny heard a wistful note creep into Lilian's voice. She quickly acted upon it. 'But you'd like that, would you? I think it would suit you down to the ground. Mam was saying how you loved gardening. All those lovely vegetables you've grown . . . you must have green fingers.'

'I like gardening,' Lilian replied. Her voice was still lifeless, but at least Jenny had managed to discover something that she was interested in, and that must be a breakthrough. 'But I can't leave Mam . . .' She shook her head.

'You may not have to. Heaven knows, there's enough farms round here.' Jenny leaned forward and grasped hold of Lilian's hand. 'Think about it. Now, promise me you will. You need a change, something different . . .'

'I know.' Lilian nodded. 'I might . . . You won't tell Mam, will you?' A confused look came into her eyes again. 'About . . . you know.'

'Of course I won't.'

'Or about . . . Tom?' Lilian's voice was the merest whisper.

'I won't breathe a word,' Jenny whispered back.

'Whatever's going on here?' Martha, clad in a red woollen dressing gown, pushed open the kitchen door. 'Lilian, whatever are you doing, child? You'll catch your death of cold down here. You're in Father's chair an' all . . . And you too, Jenny . . .'

'It's all right, Mam.' Jenny smiled reassuringly. 'Lilian was feeling poorly and I heard her come down. Something she's eaten, more than likely . . .'

'Aye – happen that Spam we had at tea time. I've felt a bit churned up meself.' Martha looked concernedly at her daughter. 'You do look a bit peaky, lass. Not that I can see right well with you sitting in t'dark . . . Stop off work tomorrow if you feel no better. I reckon Woolie's can manage without you for one day.'

Lilian smiled weakly at Jenny as her mother departed. 'I'm sorry . . . but don't tell Mam. Promise you won't.'

'I've already told you. It's our secret. Now, come on, let's be having you. Back to bed.' Jenny put her arm round Lilian as they walked up the stairs, and at the bedroom door she kissed her stone-cold cheek. 'Now . . . get some sleep.'

There was silence for the rest of the night. Whether Lilian slept Jenny did not know, but she herself was wide awake for several hours. She heard the dawn chorus, welcoming the start of another day, and then, at last, she fell asleep.

Chapter 21

Lilian returned to work after a day at home, supposedly recuperating from her 'sickness'. She was still subdued, but Jenny was relieved to see that a look of normality had returned to her eyes. Jenny hoped that Lilian's unburdening of her guilt and anxiety would help her in some way. In quite which way, Jenny was not sure. It was difficult to help someone who wouldn't help herself, and Lilian seemed to be her own worst enemy. Jenny kept a cautionary eye on her for the next few days, although she didn't think it was likely that there would be a repetition of the first night's dramatic happening; she was beginning to see it more as a plea for help.

Though she continued to be anxious about Lilian, Jenny was determined that Patsy and Rosie should have a memorable holiday. Children as well as adults needed a respite now and again from the cares of war. The girls were delighted with everything about their visit to Castleburn – more so because they were missing a week's schooling – and Patsy, who had been several times before, joyously showed Rosie the newcomer all her favourite haunts. Woolworth's, to be sure, was a poky little place compared with the huge store at home. Ironmongery, stationery, groceries and toys were all huddled together in a riotous confusion, but it was an exciting place nonetheless, even more so because they actually had an auntie who worked there.

The open-air market was another thrill, especially to the town-bred Rosie, who exclaimed delightedly at the real live hens and chicks. Jenny recalled how she had done just the same on her first visit to Castleburn, the week that Tom had asked her to marry him.

Memories of Tom crowded in on her as she visited the places that he had so proudly showed her when she was a stranger to the town. The countryside around Castleburn was at its loveliest in the spring. Wild daffodils – sometimes called Easter lilies by the countryfolk – bloomed in the woods and lanes and along the banks of the river, with clumps of pale-yellow primroses, celandine and delicate harebells. The hedges were just beginning to whiten with hawthorn blossom, baby lambs frolicked in the fields behind the dry-stone walls, and all round, pale-green shoots were appearing and buds were popping open on the trees. Signs of new life, new birth, renewed hope . . . It was hard to believe, in this oasis of green loveliness, that there was a war on, that from the night skies not fifty miles away bombs were still being dropped, and that in countries across the sea men were fighting to the death to preserve their precious homeland.

On the last afternoon of her stay Jenny found herself, for the first time, completely on her own. Martha had expressed a desire to have the children to herself for an hour or two; the old and the young often got on well together and Martha and her granddaughters were no exception. Rosie had taken an immediate liking to the elderly woman and was now calling her 'Gran', just as Patsy did. Martha had taken the girls on a bus ride to a neighbouring village, and from there they were going to walk to the waterfall, a favourite beauty spot.

Jenny was happy to part with them for an afternoon. Enjoying her freedom, she wandered down to the river, round the ruined Cistercian abbey, then back to the village street. At one end was the parish church of All Saints with its square Norman tower. Jenny had never been inside, Martha Bradshaw and all her family being staunch Methodists, but now she felt that she would like to take a look at the interior.

The heavy wooden door creaked as she pushed it open and tiptoed inside. She was met by the musty, damp smell common to all old churches, but this one showed signs of loving care from the hands of faithful parishioners. Silver salvers, shining with recent polishing, gleamed on the stone altar, which was covered with a blue cloth, exquisitely embroidered with gold thread in a design of arum lilies. Easter was not long past, and tall vases held displays of spring flowers – daffodils, tulips and narcissi, interspersed with branches of pussy willow.

Jenny sat in one of the hard-backed pews. It couldn't be called comfortable – churches in the Middle Ages were not built for ease – but it wasn't bodily comfort that Jenny was seeking. She felt troubled, her mind a turmoil of jumbled thoughts, doubts and fears that she couldn't voice in the company of her mother-in-law. Here in Castleburn, in the bosom of his family, she felt Tom's presence as though he were with her in the flesh; but he was missing. Missing . . . regret to inform you . . . missing in action . . . The words of that dreadful telegram still echoed in her mind like a death knell, and she knew that however much she might try to convince herself that he was alive, his whereabouts were still unknown.

Robert was gone from her too, of her own volition, and though she had told him that he mustn't communicate with her, the fact that he hadn't written had saddened and confused her even now. And there was this new life, growing inside her. Jenny still found it hard to believe, after all these years, that it could be possible, but her increase in weight and the fullness of her face and breasts confirmed that it was so. The child in her womb had still not quickened, though. Jenny had counted back to the end of November, the time before Robert had been posted to the camp in the south of England. That was more than four and a half months ago; she was halfway through her pregnancy, but there was still no movement from the child inside her. There had been difficulties when Patsy was born; Jenny hoped and prayed that all was well this time. Though she knew she may well have to practise some deception when the child arrived, Jenny desperately wanted this baby.

She longed at times to pour it all out, this tangled knot of grief and pain and perplexity that was at the heart of her, but there was no one here whom she could talk to, and at home there was only Eileen who, good friend that she was, had heard it all so many times before. Eileen, she suspected, was getting a little tired of being her confidante. There was so much that her friend did not approve of. Lilian had unburdened herself the other night and seemed better for so doing. Jenny wished that she could ease the load in her own mind in a similar way.

She turned round, startled, as footsteps sounded behind her, echoing hollowly back from the stone walls. From his dark suit and characteristic collar she could tell at once that this was the vicar, and she jumped to her feet, embarrassed, though she couldn't have said why. Churches, she knew, were habitually left open as a sanctuary for passers-by like herself, and she was committing no offence by being there.

'Sit down, my dear,' the newcomer said kindly. 'Don't dash away on my account. I'll come and join you . . . if I may?'

She nodded diffidently in agreement, noting at once the kindness in his grey eyes. He was a tall man with a slight stoop, craggy-featured, with fair hair greying at the temples. He looked quite young, but Jenny guessed that he must be fifty or more or he would be serving in the Forces as padre.

'I'm Brian Martindale, vicar of All Saints,' he said, holding out his hand.

'Jenny Bradshaw,' mumbled Jenny, as she felt his firm grasp round her fingers. 'I'm just visiting.'

'I thought I hadn't seen you before. Are you staying in Castleburn?'

'Yes – with Mrs Bradshaw. She's my mother-in-law. Perhaps you know her – Martha Bradshaw. Of course you might not . . . She goes to the Methodist church round the corner.'

The vicar smiled. 'I'm sure I know her by sight. It's quite a small town, but, sadly, we tend to know by name only those of our own persuasion. I'm always trying to tell my flock that the denomination doesn't matter, it's faith that counts, but it's surprising how much prejudice there is in a small community . . . Still, you don't want to hear all about that. I'm sure Mrs Bradshaw must be very pleased to have you staying with her.' He looked at her questioningly.

'Yes – she is. You see, my husband . . . her son . . . he's missing,' Jenny stammered. 'In Africa. He's in the Army.'

'Oh, my dear – I'm so sorry. I'll call and see her if I may? It must have been very hard for you, trying to comfort her.'

'Not really.' Jenny smiled. 'She seems to be bearing up better than I am. You see, I can't help feeling . . .' She stopped, unwilling to give voice to the troublesome thoughts that had been plaguing her for the past few weeks.

'What is it, my dear? Go on.'

'I feel it might be because of something I've done that Tom's missing. As though I'm being punished.' Jenny blurted the words out quickly, finding it hard to believe that she had said them. This feeling had been tormenting her for ages and now that the words were out she felt a sense of relief.

'No . . . I'm sure that's not true.' The vicar shook his head emphatically. 'I don't know what it is that you've done, my dear, but God doesn't punish us in that way. You can rest assured on that score.' He laid his hand comfortingly over Jenny's. 'Would you like to tell me about it? You don't have to, of course, but sometimes it helps to talk.'

Jenny knew with a sudden blinding certainty that she would have to tell this man. 'Like a confession, you mean?' she said a little warily. 'Like the Catholics?'

'No, my dear.' The Reverend Martindale smiled, then gave a little laugh. 'I'm not a priest. Well – I suppose I am really, but in the Church of England we don't always call ourselves priests. We're very Low Church here, although I do so dislike putting labels on people. The Catholics find that it helps to confess to the priest, but it's my view that you don't really need a mediator. God hears us if we tell Him about it, quietly, in our minds. But it sometimes helps to talk to another person. You can rest assured that it won't go any further.'

Jenny knew that it wasn't likely that she would ever see him again, and he had such a kindly, sympathetic face. She felt sure he would understand. And yet he was an ordained minister, a man of God. He might think that what she had done was terrible.

'How can I tell you? she began. 'You will think I'm dreadful.'

'I'm quite sure I've heard it all before . . . whatever it is.' He looked at her steadily. 'Could it be something to do with your . . . condition, my dear? I can see that you are expecting a child.'

Jenny nodded. 'Yes . . . that's part of it.' Falteringly she began to tell him about Robert, their meeting, the blossoming of their love. '. . . And then all these dreadful things started to happen to us. Robert's father was killed, and now Tom's missing, and then there's the baby . . . Not that I think that's dreadful. I'm pleased about it, but I still know that it was wrong . . . I can't help feeling that it's all my fault that these things have happened . . .'

'It's wartime, my dear. All kinds of terrible things happen in wartime. God hasn't picked you out for special punishment. Yes – what you did was wrong, but it's what you choose to do about it now that's important. Tell me . . . this child that you're carrying, you think that it's Robert's child?'

Jenny nodded again. 'Yes . . . I'm sure it is.'

'What about Tom? Could it be his?'

Jenny paused. 'It's possible . . . but not likely. The doctor didn't think that we could have any more children after Patsy was born. That's why I think it's Robert's. But I've told him – Robert, I mean – that I won't see him again. He doesn't know about the baby.'

'And you mean it? You won't see him again?'

'Yes – I mean it. It hurts like mad, and I still love him – but I mean it. The awful part is that I don't really feel guilty about loving him. I can't truthfully say that I'm sorry it happened, because it was so . . . wonderful.'

'Yes . . . There can be a powerful chemistry at work between a man and a woman, God-given, I believe, if it's between the right people, at the right time.'

'That's what I don't understand. If I hadn't been married when I met Robert, it would have been right, but – because of Tom – you're telling me it's wrong?'

'You made your choice when you married Tom. I know it's hard, but those are the rules and we have to obey them. One man, one woman . . . at one time. We wouldn't be human, of course, if we weren't tempted. We can all be influenced by a pretty face or a winning smile.' The Reverend Martindale smiled now, rather wryly. 'You can't help the first glance, but you can help the second and the subsequent ones. You have to know where to draw the line.'

'It's hard . . .'

'Yes, indeed. Almost impossible, Jenny. I may call you Jenny? But what you must do now is to look to the future. You have a family, my dear? You mentioned a daughter.'

'Yes – I have a little girl. She's six. Well, I have two little girls now . . .' She went on to explain about Rosie.

'Well, there you are then. They are the future generation, your Patsy and Rosie. That's what our lads are fighting for. That's something for you to build on – and Tom too, when he comes home.'

'You say "when", but supposing . . . ?'

'You will still have to carry on and look to the future, for the sake of your little girls and the child that you're expecting. But I pray that he's safe, Jenny.'

Jenny was silent for a moment, deep in thought. Then, 'He trusts me,' she said. 'Tom's always trusted me. I know he'd be terribly hurt, but I sometimes feel that I must tell him about Robert . . . and about the baby.'

'Why must you tell him?'

'Because he's my husband. Because we shouldn't have any secrets from one another.'

'And would you want him to forfeit his peace of mind, just so that you could unburden yourself?'

Jenny didn't answer.

'Just think about it,' said the vicar quietly. 'That's your

punishment, Jenny, if you feel you need one. Keeping quiet about it all.'

'But . . . surely it would be wrong to deceive him,' Jenny persisted, 'to pretend that the child was his.'

'You've already done wrong,' the vicar told her quietly. 'Why should Tom be made to suffer as well? I'm sure he's suffered enough already, Jenny, in this dreadful war. Yes . . . maybe it will be harder to keep quiet than to confess everything, but that's what you must do. You'll manage it, my dear. It's amazing how much courage human beings have when they're put to the test. Now – do you feel any better?'

'Much better,' said Jenny truthfully. 'Thank you.' She felt as though some of her burden had been lifted, as though in sharing it with this man she had now given him a portion of the weight to carry. 'I must be going soon,' she said. 'My mother-in-law will be expecting me in for tea. I'll tell her I've been talking to you.' She smiled. 'Not what it was about though . . . But do call and see her. I know she would be pleased.' Jenny paused. While talking about her own troubles she had, momentarily, forgotten about Lilian, but her sister-in-law, too, needed help. 'To tell you the truth,' she said now, 'it's Tom's sister Lilian who is more in need of comfort than her mother. Mrs Bradshaw's a very strong woman, strong in faith, I mean. But Lilian . . . she's really gone to pieces since Tom was missing. I think she's felt it more than any of us. She . . . cares very much for him.'

Brian Martindale looked understandingly at Jenny. 'Ah . . . a case of brother fixation, maybe?'

'Yes,' said Jenny, looking at him in some surprise. 'That's it exactly. But . . . how did you know?'

'I didn't. I guessed, rightly as it happened. Something in the tone of your voice when you spoke of her. And, as I told you, I've heard it all before. There are very few human problems that a parish priest hasn't encountered, and infatuation with a brother is not uncommon. Would you like to tell me a little about Lilian? I can see that you're worried about her.'

Jenny told him about her concern, how she felt that her sister-in-law needed to widen her horizons. She forbore to mention the incident of a few nights ago, feeling certain now that Lilian had been crying out for help. Besides, she had promised that she wouldn't say a word, and to do so would be a betrayal of Lilian's trust. Jenny felt that she might have said too much already, but it was only out of concern for Tom's sister, and the vicar was such an understanding sort of person.

He nodded thoughtfully. 'Mmm . . . You mention the Land Army. Do you know, I might be able to help there. One of my parishioners is a farmer – well, several of them are, of course – it's a farming community – but I'm thinking of one in particular, Bert Adams. He had a couple of Land Army girls working for him, but one of them had to go home. She was taken seriously ill, and I know he hasn't been given a replacement yet. If your sister-in-law – Lilian, isn't it? – was interested, I daresay we could cut out all the red tape . . .'

'It sounds wonderful.' Jenny was enthusiastic, but also aware that it was Lilian's life that they were organising, without her knowledge. 'But it all depends on Lilian, of course. And I know she feels that she can't leave Mam . . . Mrs Bradshaw.'

'I see no reason why the young lady couldn't live at home,' said the vicar. 'I know the Land Army girls usually live in, but in this case . . . the farm's only a hop, skip and a jump away. Anyway, leave it with me, Jenny, and I'll make some enquiries. As you so rightly say, though, it all depends on how Lilian feels. Perhaps you could broach the subject first with Lilian and her mother? And I'll call and see Mrs Bradshaw before long. She sounds a great lady. I know her minister won't mind – we get on very well. It might be a way of bringing our churches closer together, who knows?'

Jenny was comforted by the strength of his handshake as he said goodbye to her, and by the wealth of compassion she could see in his grey eyes. 'I'm glad I met you, Jenny,' he said. 'I shall be thinking about you, my dear . . . and Tom, and your children.'

It was during the second week in May, the week of the last major air raid on London, that the official letter arrived from the War Office. Tom was alive, but he was a prisoner of war in the hands of the Germans.

Jenny sank to her knees in gratitude. 'Thank you. Oh, thank you, God . . .' she whispered, tears of relief flowing down her cheeks. 'Thank you . . .' That was all that she could think of to say, two simple words, but they came from a heart that was overflowing with gladness.

It was the evening of the same day that Jenny felt the child

246

quicken. She put her hand over the bulge just below her waistline. There it was again, a definite movement, a stirring of the life inside her. And Jenny knew, at that moment, that the child she was carrying was her husband's, stirring miraculously into life, it seemed, by the news of his safety. She knew that this was a fanciful thought, but she had no doubt whatsoever now that the child was Tom's. She was halfway through her pregnancy now, she realised; she must have conceived at the end of December. She had been mistaken all along in her belief that she was carrying Robert's child, but she knew, nevertheless, that her love for the young airman had opened her up, both physically and emotionally. Her inhibitions had been cast aside and so she had conceived. The impossible had happened. She was to have Tom's child . . .

Jenny was relieved that Tom was out of danger for the duration of the war, but she knew that it wasn't what he would have wished. To be a prisoner of war would be, to him, a waste of time, when all he had ever wanted to do was to fight and defeat the enemy. How eagerly he had gone off to war on that September day which now seemed so long ago, his eyes shining with his desire to serve his country. Now, less than two years later, the war, for Tom and for thousands like him, was virtually over. And Jenny was glad.

She had adapted to her life without Tom – and without Robert – because she had no choice. Her parting from Robert still hurt, a dull ache inside her that couldn't be assuaged, but as the weeks and the months passed, so the pain grew less. She was able to think of him without the relentless surging of desire which, at first, had accompanied every thought of him. Now she remembered him fondly, recalling his laughter and the sound of his voice, visiting again in memory the places they had known during that unforgettable weekend, as though she were reading a well-loved book.

She busied herself in an orgy of spring-cleaning. When she wasn't working at her mother's, she occupied her time in her own little home, cleaning it from top to bottom, polishing every stick of furniture, washing all the curtains and covers, making it into a home that Tom would be proud to come back to. The work was therapeutic, occupying both her body and her mind, so that at the end of the day she would roll into bed exhausted, too tired to lie awake thinking.

The children, too, were a great blessing. Jenny loved to hear of their day-to-day happenings at school and she gave them her undivided attention, helping them with their problems and all the time marvelling at the development of their different personalities. With Rosie it was 'Why, why, why?' all the time, a mind continually grasping for knowledge. Patsy was more introspective – like her father – preferring to think things out quietly for herself rather than bombarding adults with questions. They were still inseparable. Bosom friends soon, to Patsy's great joy, to become real sisters. Jenny was ever grateful for the unexpected quirk of fate that had bestowed on her the gift of this second little girl. They were the future generation, as the vicar in Castleburn had reminded her, the cornerstone on which to build her plans and hopes for the future.

A pleasant diversion from the monotony of war was the wedding in June 1941 of Ada Wainwright and Fred Bottomley. It took place at the Methodist church which Ada attended regularly. Clothes rationing had just been introduced, but that made very little difference to the bride as she had insisted all along that her best grey costume would suffice. With it she wore a jaunty red Robin Hood hat, with a feather in the side, and a red rose to match in her buttonhole. Jenny had never seen her cousin look so contented, or so proud, as she stood on the chapel steps arm in arm with her new husband.

'Get a move on, can't you?' Ada hissed, as both Jenny and Violet snapped away with their Brownie box cameras. 'We don't want all the neighbourhood gawping at us . . . You must take a photo of them two little lasses, though. Come on, Patsy and Rosie. Stand here in front of your Uncle Fred and me. Your dad'll be thrilled to bits to get a picture of his two bonny little girls.'

Ada had maintained that she didn't want 'proper bridesmaids and all that nonsense', but Patsy and Rosie could walk behind her and Fred in church if they liked. It would be a good excuse for them to dress up a bit. Jenny had made them each a plain blue cotton dress with a sailor collar, which they wore with straw boaters with blue ribbons hanging down the back.

The wedding reception was at Miss Frobisher's home, and as it was only a stone's throw from the church the couple had decided, patriotically, to dispense with wedding cars. They had agreed wholeheartedly with Miss Frobisher's idea about the venue. It was to be their home as well, she had assured them delightedly as she raided the store cupboard to provide the wherewithal for a fitting wedding breakfast. Ada had prepared most of it herself, helped by Miss Frobisher, before departing for church, and the guests exclaimed with surprise at the red salmon in the sandwiches, and the huge bowls of tinned peaches and pears. The cream was only mock, to be sure, but it was a banquet, Ada avowed, at which even the King wouldn't turn up his nose.

Between them they had scraped together the necessary ingredients for a tiny wedding cake, all that was needed for such a small gathering, fourteen guests in all. The dried fruit had been in Miss Frobisher's store cupboard, awaiting such an occasion, since before the war, and Annie had unearthed some ground almonds and icing sugar. It was Annie who made the cake, and she decorated it with the silver bells and horseshoes that had been carefully stored away since Jenny's wedding.

'There you are,' she said with justifiable pride as she watched Ada and Fred cut into it. 'That's better than them whited sepulchres as some brides have to put up with these days.'

A feature of many wartime weddings was a huge cardboard structure, resembling a wedding cake, with a tiny cake lurking inside, made, as likely as not, with dried egg, and gravy browning to add colour instead of dried fruit. Ada had her aunt and Miss Frobisher to thank that she hadn't to resort to such measures, and she whispered a word of gratitude before she and Fred set off to Southport for their honeymoon.

'Thanks, Aunt Annie – for the present and the cake an' all. Fred and me have had a right good day.'

'It's not over yet, lass,' whispered Annie, with a sly glance at her niece. 'Off you go, the pair of you, and enjoy yourselves. Eeh, I only wish I was young again!'

Jenny, overhearing the remark and her mother's heartfelt sigh, reflected ruefully that in reality her cousin was well past the first flush of youth. She stole a surreptitious glance at Ada, but that lady, unaware of anyone around her, was gazing at her new husband, her eyes shining with what Jenny recognised, to her astonishment – and with a pang of envy – as unmistakable desire.

Chapter 22

Tony Harris dodged round the back of the newspaper kiosk at Central Station. Those military police seemed to be everywhere, usually in twos, their gimlet-sharp eyes darting about all over the place in the hope of catching some poor bastard who was AWOL. Tony knew that he was well and truly AWOL now; his forty-eight-hour pass had come to an end, but he had no intention of going back to the camp without seeing Violet. If things worked out for him, if he could think of a foolproof plan, he wouldn't go back at all.

The year since he left Blackpool for the camp in Sussex had been hell on earth. The Battle of Britain had been raging when Tony arrived in the south of England. '. . . Never in the field of human conflict was so much owed by so many to so few,' Winston Churchill had said of the brave young fighter pilots who fought in the battlefields of the skies. Tony had been one of the spectators, near the end of the struggle, watching the savage dogfights between the British and German planes. He would never forget the throb and whine of the aircraft engines in the bright-blue sky crisscrossed with vapour trails. Many civilians had seemed complacent about it all; newspaper placards often bore scores – 160 for 32 – as though the battle were some sort of game, but maybe treating it light-heartedly had taken away some of the horror. Many of the pilots themselves were nonchalant about their achievements and disliked references to glory and heroism. Their RAF slang thrived on understatement; pilots referred to the dropping of bombs as 'leaving visiting cards' or 'laying eggs', and the planes that they flew were 'kites'.

Tony used the slang along with the rest of them, adopting a couldn't-care-less attitude, while at the same time thanking his lucky stars that he was one of the ground crew. What he had said to Violet that night at the Tower and many times afterwards, and

251

what he had said to many girls since – that he would like to have a bash at Jerry himself – was just bravado. When he watched the battles, in terror and admiration, from the comparative safety of the ground, he had to admit, though only to himself, that it was mainly in terror. Tony was scared out of his mind at the mere thought of going up in one of those planes.

The Battle of Britain had started off as an unequal struggle. The enemy should have won . . . but they didn't. The Germans were more experienced, more numerous, better armed. Admittedly, the British had great advantages – proximity to their own airfields, and the technical excellence of the Spitfire planes – but everyone knew the odds weighed heavily against them. And yet, they won.

After the Battle of Britain had come the Blitz on the major cities, followed by retaliatory raids over Germany, which, twelve months later, were still going on. Tony watched more and more of his comrades departing on bombing raids, departing . . . and often not returning. Tony often wondered, in retrospect, whatever had possessed him to join the RAF in the first place. He had had to join one of the forces, though; he would have been called up, sooner rather than later, because of his age, and when his mates started enlisting right, left and centre, Tony had no intention of being the odd one out. He supposed the glamour attached to the newest of the armed forces had attracted him. He had heard the gruesome tales from his father and other senior relatives about the appalling bloodshed of the last war, the unspeakable horror of a war fought by soldiers in the trenches. No, Tony certainly had no desire to join the Army. There would be no trenches this time, they had said, but surely there would be other equally horrific ordeals to be faced.

Likewise, the Navy was out. Tony had been seasick once on a pleasure boat trip from Llandudno pier, and anyway he couldn't swim. So only the RAF had remained, but, if he played his cards right, Tony saw no reason why he shouldn't keep out of danger. They trained you for what you were best at, and Tony was a garage mechanic, one of the best though he said it himself. That was how he had started out, training as an engineer, but now several of his colleagues had retrained, as navigators or wireless operators, to replace the poor buggers who hadn't returned. Some of them were volunteers . . . others were not. Tony had no intention of volunteering, of giving up his cushy number on the ground, and he was damned if he was going to let himself be coerced into something that was abhorrent to him. It wasn't very likely – they still needed good ground mechanics – but Tony was terrified. He had known from the start that he was lacking in courage – he possessed little of the stuff that heroes were made of – but what shred of tenacity he might have been endowed with had gradually dwindled away.

Last week had been the final straw. He couldn't erase from his mind the sight of Arthur, one of his best mates, as he had been dragged from a blazing aircraft, his face blackened, his hair singed to a frazzle, a red pulpy mass where his hands should have been. And all around, the flames issuing from the plane that had crash-landed on its return with only one engine remaining. Arthur had died later that evening . . .

Yes, it was the fire that had been the final undoing of Tony. He had had an inbred fear of flames since he was four years old, when a live coal had fallen on to the kitchen hearthrug. There had been no one in the room at the time except his baby sister Marion, asleep in her pram. He recalled the frantic screams of his mother and her flailing arms as she beat against the flames that were creeping towards the pram, then a sizzle and hiss as a bucket of water doused the inferno. Marion had been saved; she hadn't even woken up, but his mother's blistered hands and the charred bodywork of the pram were evidence of a tragedy averted. Now, twenty years later, too many of Tony's comrades had died in the consuming flames of war. His mate Arthur was the latest victim. Tony was determined that he himself would not be next. He had to get out.

A forty-eight-hour pass had been due to him, and he had spent a pleasant weekend with his parents in Leeds. He was relieved to think that at last he might have persuaded his mam and dad to move away from the city to stay with his uncle and aunt on their farm in Ilkley. His sister Marion was in the Land Army now, working on a farm very near to his uncle's, and it was this that had convinced his parents that a move might be expedient. The idea of not returning to camp had been, at the beginning of the weekend, just a germ of a notion floating around in his mind. But as Sunday evening drew nearer, and with it the imminent curtailing of his freedom, Tony knew that he couldn't face up to the idea of going back. He could no more do it than fly to the moon.

He dissuaded his parents from coming to the station with him, then he boarded a train going not south, but west to Preston. From there he would catch a connection to Blackpool. He must see Violet again . . . The memory of Violet – her lovely green eyes and flaxen hair, and her long limbs – had haunted him lately. It had been a comfort to think of her as he lay in his bed at night, instead of letting his mind dwell on hideous memories of burning flesh and agonised screams. He had been a fool ever to let her go. That little tart Sheila and the other girls he'd taken out since had not been a patch on Violet. She'd been a bit of a prude, he had to admit. There had been no way he'd been able to persuade her to take her knickers off, but funnily enough, that didn't seem to matter so much now. When he thought of Violet what he experienced was a soothing of his mind rather than the anticipation of carnal delights. Violet had been kind, and clever – far cleverer than he was, but that, too, didn't seem to matter any more – a calming influence upon him . . . most of the time. That last time they had met, though, he had felt far from calm. He regretted now his angry words and his shabby treatment of her. He would make it up to her . . . if only he could see her again.

It was ten o'clock when the train arrived at Blackpool Central Station, a dark, drizzly September night. The train had been crowded, as always, but Tony had managed to get a corner seat and had spent the journey engrossed in his *Sunday Mirror*, endeavouring to play the part of a young airman returning to camp. No prying military police had questioned him; more than likely they would not do so now, but Tony was taking no chances. He hid until they were out of the way. He wouldn't have been missed, yet, from the camp in Sussex – he was due back there about now – but by morning the news that he was AWOL would have been circulated up and down the country. They would be looking out for him then . . .

It was too late to attempt to see Violet tonight. She would be curled up by the fireside, no doubt, with one of her dry-as-dust books, whereas he would have to spend a night in the open air. No . . . that might be too risky, to be seen in his RAF uniform sleeping out on the prom, but there were lots of convenient air-raid shelters, used by courting couples and sometimes by vagrants or the temporarily homeless. Then, in the morning, he would look out for Violet on her way to work. Violet would know what he should do. She was a clever girl; she would be able to think of a

254

plan to help him to get away. She might even go with him . . .

Violet heard the sound of a whistle as she passed the end of Green Street on her way to the bus stop. She took no notice. Some fellow, no doubt, but fellows didn't whistle at her. She crossed the road, then she heard it again, this time followed by a low, but urgent shout. 'Violet . . . wait.'

She turned round and saw him, just where the back alley to the Green Street houses began. 'Tony . . .' She gaped at him in astonishment. 'Whatever . . . ?'

'Shhh . . .' He beckoned her and she recrossed the road and followed him into the back alley. There seemed to be no one else around. She was a little earlier this morning and Joyce was not yet at the bus stop further along the street.

'Whatever are you doing here?' Violet gasped, looking at Tony in concern. His hair beneath his cap was dishevelled, and his jaw was unshaven. But it was his eyes that Violet noticed more than anything else. They held a frenzied look, and shifted restlessly back and forth, glancing first at Violet's face, then up the street, then back to Violet again. 'You haven't been posted back to Blackpool, have you, Tony?' she asked glancing at the kitbag at his feet.

'No . . . I'm due back in Sussex, but I've . . . I've come here to see you, Violet.' His voice was wheedling, and Violet found herself remembering his former treatment of her.

She looked at him coolly. 'Shouldn't you be seeing Sheila, not me?'

'Sheila!' Tony's lip curled contemptuously. 'She wasn't a patch on you, Violet. Listen . . . I want you to help me. I'm what they call AWOL.' He gave a hysterical laugh. 'I've . . . absconded, I suppose.'

'But . . . Tony, this is dreadful! You can't . . . how can you hope to get away with it? What do you intend to do? You can't hide in Blackpool. It's swarming with RAF lads here.'

'Then there's no better place to hide, surely? I'll be just one among many.' His tone was defiant, revealing a touch of the old, cocksure Tony. 'They'll never notice me here . . .' His voice petered out. 'Help me, Violet. Please help me . . . I can't go back.'

Violet looked at him in dismay. This was terrible. She had no idea what to do, how to help him, but she couldn't walk away and

255

leave him, that was certain. Whatever was she to do? She suddenly thought of Jenny. Of course . . . When she was in a dilemma her thoughts immediately flew to her sister. Jenny might not be able to help this time, but she would listen, and it would be somewhere to take Tony while they decided what to do. 'My sister lives just up the street,' she told Tony. 'Come on . . . pick up your kitbag and we'll see if the back gate's open.'

The high wooden gate was closed. There was a catch that Jenny put down at night, but Violet rattled at the latch and in a few seconds she heard her sister's footsteps across the paved yard.

Jenny's eyes widened in surprise. 'Violet . . . what on earth? And . . . Tony.' She shook her head bemusedly. 'Well, you'd best come in. I'm just getting the girls ready for school.'

'Don't let them see me.' Violet could hear the agitation in Tony's voice, and panic flickered in his eyes like a ripple in a stream. She looked at her sister and gave an imperceptible shake of her head. 'We'll go in the front room till the girls have gone,' she whispered.

Jenny's front room smelt musty and damp from lack of use. Tony dropped his kitbag on the floor and collapsed into one of the big armchairs, burying his head in his hands. Violet watched in silence. He hadn't moved when Jenny came in a few minutes later.

'Now, what's all this about?' Jenny's tone was matter-of-fact, tinged with irritation. Violet knew that her sister had had a poor opinion of Tony Harris since the time she had confided in her about his demands to make love to her. And then, of course, Tony had dropped Violet in favour of Sheila, which had intensified Jenny's antipathy towards him.

Tony looked up. To her horror, Violet could see a trace of tears glinting in his grey eyes, and his mouth quivered slightly. She wondered how she could ever have imagined that she was in love with him, as she had when she first met him. His wide mouth, which she had so often seen curling in a smile, now looked weak and irresolute. All that Violet could feel for him now was pity.

'I'm AWOL,' Tony said in a flat voice as he looked at Jenny. 'I'm due back at camp now . . . but I can't go back.'

'I see,' said Jenny quietly. Her eyes softened as she looked at Tony. 'You look worn out, lad. You didn't have much sleep last night, I suppose?' Tony shook his head. 'Well, I'm sure I don't know what's to be done with you,' Jenny went on, 'but the first thing you need is a good rest. We can talk later. Go on . . . upstairs with you and have a kip in the front bedroom. Nobody'll disturb you. Off you go, lad.'

Tony smiled his thanks and stumbled from the room. He looked dead on his feet.

'I'll come up in a minute or two and see if you're comfy,' called Jenny. 'Well . . . this is a pretty kettle of fish, I must say,' She flopped into an armchair and looked at her sister. 'He'll have to go back,' she mouthed, waiting till Tony was out of earshot. 'There's nothing else for it,' she went on in a low voice. 'If he gets caught he'll be for the high jump . . . What's he doing here, anyway? I thought it was all over between you and him.'

'It is.' Violet shook her head. 'I know no more than you do. He just shouted at me as I was going along the street. You could have knocked me down with a feather. Look, Jen . . . I'll have to go or I'll be late for work. Thanks for . . . for looking after him. I'll call on the way home tonight, then we'll have to persuade him to go back.' Violet paused. Then, 'What about the girls?' she asked. 'Won't they wonder what's going on?'

'It's all right,' Jenny replied. 'They go to Mother's for dinner, don't they? And, as luck would have it, they're going to a party at tea time. I'll see to the wandering boy today . . .' She glanced towards the ceiling, 'but, like you say, Vi, he'll have to go back. I tell you what – you're well rid of that one.'

'Don't I know it,' breathed Violet. 'But I can't help feeling sorry for him. He's got himself in a fair pickle. I wonder what's at the bottom of it?'

'Sheer bloody fright, I shouldn't wonder,' said Jenny. 'Excuse my language . . . Can't say I blame him. It's the fellows as gets the raw deal in wartime. It must be awful trying to be brave when you're really scared to death. All we women have to do is wait . . . See you later, Vi. And . . . don't worry.'

Violet smiled sadly at her sister. 'OK.' I'll try not to. And . . . thanks, Jen. I don't know what I'd do without you.'

Violet hurried along the street to the bus stop. She could see that a long queue had formed – she usually caught an earlier bus to avoid the rush – and she'd be lucky if she made it in time this morning. Still, it couldn't be helped. She couldn't leave Tony in the lurch, though heaven knew what they were going to do with him if they couldn't persuade him to go back. Jenny was wonderful, turning up trumps like that, but Violet had known that she would. She was a sister in a million and Violet was so glad that they were friends again. She'd been mad with her at the time, though. Fancy carrying on with another fellow when she had a good husband like Tom. But it was all over now, thank goodness. Violet had had her suspicions when Jenny announced that she was pregnant, and her manner towards her sister had cooled again. She had counted on her fingers – November, December, January . . . and so on, up to nine – but when August had passed she realised that she must have misjudged her sister. It was nearing the end of September now. The child must be Tom's after all. Violet was sorry for her mistrustful thoughts.

'Tony, there's no way round it. You'll have to go back. Give yourself up, then they may let you off lightly.' Jenny looked across at the tall figure slumped in the armchair. She had never seen such a picture of misery. Her heart had ached with sympathy for him as, earlier in the day, after he had rested, he had admitted that he was scared stiff. The death of his friend had tipped the balance and Jenny felt that his mind was temporarily deranged. She had sensed the incipient madness in him when he had spoken of Violet.

'But what do you intend to do?' Jenny had asked him. 'Why have you come here?'

'Violet . . .' he said, his voice husky with emotion. 'I love her . . . I want her to go away with me. I've got civvy clothes in there.' He pointed to his kitbag. 'We could get right away, where nobody knows us . . .'

Jenny had been frightened then, at her wits' end wondering what to do. Should she make an excuse and run to the phone box on the corner? Ring the police . . . ? But no, she couldn't betray him like that.

After a hot meal and a long talk, when he seemed to get it all out of his system, he appeared calmer. Now Violet was here to add her weight to the persuasion.

'You musn't let the military police catch you,' she told him. 'You'd be branded a deserter and court-martialled or . . .' Violet stopped. She had no idea what happened to deserters now. She knew that in the last war they had been shot, but that was too horrific to think of. 'Go back to camp. Tell them how you feel, that you're sick . . . I'm sure they'll understand,' she finished lamely.

She wasn't sure at all, knowing that cowardice was considered the most shameful crime in wartime, but it would be even worse for Tony – that much she knew – if he were to be arrested.

He was more composed now. The wildness had gone from his eyes, and Jenny was relieved that he hadn't repeated to Violet his nonsensical ideas about them going away together. The poor lass would be terrified.

'Aye . . . Happen you're right.' Tony's gravelly voice sounded more normal. 'Don't know what got into me. Reckon I'd best be off and face the music.' He glanced at the wooden clock. 'Half past six. It'll be dropping dark in an hour or so. I'll get off to Central Station and see if there's a train going south.' He smiled weakly at Jenny, then at Violet, but made no move to embrace her. 'So long . . . Be seeing you.'

Violet gave a whimper, like an animal in pain, as the door closed behind him. 'Oh . . . poor Tony. What will they do with him, Jenny?'

'I don't know. Probably not very much . . . It's the best thing, Vi, for him to admit what he's done. Thank God we were able to persuade him. You'd best be off home now, love. Mother'll be wondering where you are.'

'Don't tell her,' said Violet, with a terse look at her sister. 'It's best she doesn't know.'

'No, not a word to Mother,' said Jenny. 'And don't worry, Vi. He'll be all right.'

Tony walked to the end of the street and turned right, towards the promenade. He had no intention of going to Central Station, at least not yet. He'd have a walk along the prom and try to sort out the mess and muddle in his mind. He walked northwards, heading towards the cliffs at Bispham. He felt conspicuous with a kitbag, but there were few people around and there would be even fewer further north. Tony walked and walked until dusk fell.

He leaned on the iron railings, staring out towards the horizon. The tide was far out tonight, gently lapping against the sand in tiny wavelets, like an edging of frothy lace on black satin. He'd like to see Violet dressed in black satin, in one of those posh nightdress things, négligés they called them. He could imagine running his hands up and down her long silk-covered limbs . . . But Violet wasn't for him, not yet, not till this lot was over. The vast expanse

259

of sand, shimmering grey in the moonlight, looked inviting. Tony recalled seaside holidays as a child with Mam and Dad and Marion . . .

He walked down the stone steps and threw his kitbag on to the sand. He suddenly realised how bitterly weary he was. He had had a few hours' kip at Jenny's, but he hadn't slept at all last night in that dank, smelly air-raid shelter. Now his overburdened mind was desperately crying out for oblivion, for a blacking-out of all the frenzied thoughts that were chasing round and round like demons in his brain. He stretched out on the sand, glad to rest his tired limbs which seemed to have been walking for ever. His kitbag was a lumpy, uncomfortable pillow but, nevertheless, he slept . . .

When he woke, an hour or so later, the darkness was complete: black sky, for the moon had vanished momentarily behind a bank of cloud, dark-grey sand, and black sea with tiny silver wavelets edging nearer. And total blackness in Tony's mind. 'No, no . . . Stop them! Don't let them come near me . . .' He was aware of a voice, very near to him, shouting out as if in agony. 'Keep away. Get away from me, you bastards . . .' He put his hands over his head, protecting himself from the unseen menace coming at him from out of the blackness and from the screeching voice yelling in his ears. Then he realised that it was his own voice . . .

The nightmare had been horrific: Arthur, and Tony's mother and his sister Marion, all consumed in the devouring flames, and all around the bombs falling, exploding, bursting open. He almost laughed with relief that it was only a dream . . . except for Arthur. Arthur was a goner. He glanced around. The grey sand and black sea stretched for miles with not another soul, and Tony felt afraid, very alone in the midst of a vast expanse of nothingness. He started to walk towards the sea. His head was clearer now, but it was at times like this, when he thought he was safe, that the torment would start. Images of flames, of burning flesh and anguished screams, of Arthur with his hands and his face burned away . . . They were beginning now, those terrifying pictures in his mind. He must get rid of them. He'd have a paddle in the sea, like he used to when he was a little lad . . .

He took off his shoes and socks and rolled up his trousers, like Dad used to do. The icy-cold water would cool his brain, rid him of these horrific fears. The waves lapped round his ankles and his knees and Tony stood motionless, gazing out across the limitless ocean. His fear had gone. He was beyond fear now. He had been terribly afraid for so long, but now something had snapped inside him. He no longer felt fear, or hope, or pain . . . or anything. He strode further out into the sea, letting it envelop his thighs, his arms, every part of him . . .

His body was washed up by the tide in the Wyre estuary at Fleetwood, three days later. The first that Violet knew of the tragedy was when she read it in the evening paper.

'Whatever's the matter?' said Annie, as her daughter gave a strangled cry, then burst into tears. Violet couldn't answer. She just pointed numbly at the paragraph of newsprint.

Annie read it through, her lips silently mouthing the unbelievable words: '". . . body of a young airman . . . A/C 1, Anthony Harris, from Leeds . . . next of kin have been informed . . ." Eeh, that poor young lad,' she sighed. 'Such a lovely lad he were an' all. Eeh, that bloody Hitler's got a lot to answer for, he has that . . . Whatever was he doing in Blackpool, I wonder . . . ?'

It was the first time that Violet had ever heard her mother use such a violent swear word. She made no comment, neither did she answer Annie's question. She knew that it didn't require an answer and the less her mother knew about it, the better. Let her keep her illusions about Tony. It could do no harm . . .

Jenny's baby – a boy – was born on the first day of October 1941. Surprisingly, the birth was much easier than Patsy's had been, but the tiny red-faced bundle that the midwife placed in Jenny's arms was the image of his sister. So much so that Jenny cried out in wonder; he had the same nose and mouth, the same sandy red hair, though a shade less bright than Patsy's had been. And not only was the baby the spitting image of his sister, but also his father.

She looked at the child in her arms, so very small and helpless, at the fingernails like miniature seashells, the delicate, almost translucent eyelids, now closed in sleep, the tiny blue veins throbbing beneath the mottled skin, and she wondered again at the miracle of birth. Every newborn baby was a miracle – didn't every mother feel the same? – but this child, surely, more so than most, arriving when Jenny had believed she could have no more children and rekindling her love for her husband. For Jenny felt now, as she looked at her baby, a resurgence of the love which, deep down, she had always had for Tom but which had been overshadowed by her feelings for Robert. Dear Tom . . . Her heart warmed now at the thought of him, and this child, so like his father, would be a constant reminder of him. Jenny had never doubted, since she had felt the child quicken, that Tom was the father, but now there could be no doubt in anyone's mind.

Annie said as much when she bent over the cot a few minutes later. 'Hmm . . . It's easy to see who this little lad belongs to . . . And a good job too, our Jenny,' she added with a meaningful nod at her daughter. She kept her voice quiet so that the midwife, busy at the other end of the room, could not overhear, but there was no doubt as to what she was referring to. 'You're a lucky lass. You are that . . .' Her tone was as brusque as ever, but Jenny noticed, to her surprise and great joy, a tiny tear glinting in the corner of her mother's eye. A very tiny tear, almost hidden behind the thick lens of her glasses, but proof that Annie was not as hard-boiled as she liked to pretend.

She bent over the cot again. 'Aye, he's a grand little lad and a chip off the old block all right. Have you thought of a name for him yet?'

'Yes,' said Jenny, without hesitation. 'Victor. That's what we'll call him. Victor . . . Thomas.' Until that moment she had had no idea what name to give the child, but this one had sprung to her mind in a flash of inspiration. Victory might be a long way off, but it would come eventually, she felt sure of that. Little Victor would be one of a new generation to reap the benefit of a lasting peace, God willing, grimly fought and won. Jenny prayed that it would not be too far in the future before Tom would see his son for the first time.

Chapter 23

On 7 December 1941, Japanese planes attacked Pearl Harbor and the next day America entered the war. In spring 1942, American troops descended on Britain, and Warton airfield, near Blackpool, became a training camp for the US Army 8th Airforce. And in June 1942, Violet met Charles Clifford . . .

She was browsing in Sweeten's bookshop, a regular haunt on her half-day of freedom from the factory. Her head was buried in the pages of Charlotte Brontë's *Shirley* when she collided in the narrow aisle with a tall figure in uniform.

Her first reaction – apart from the awareness of a sharp pain in her left foot where the stranger had stood on her toe – was that she seemed to be making a habit of this. First there had been Tony at the Tower – she had literally fallen at his feet . . . Poor Tony . . . Violet still felt a pang of remorse whenever she thought of him, though she doubted that she and Jenny could have done any more to help him. He was just one of the many thousands of wartime casualties, not always killed in action.

She pulled her wandering thoughts back to the present and looked up into a pair of kind brown eyes filled with concern. He appeared to be all brown; greeny-brown uniform, brown suntanned face, and chestnut-brown hair cut very short, from what she could see of it under his cap.

'Gosh! I'm sorry,' he said. 'I guess I wasn't looking where I was going. I hope I haven't hurt you?'

'No. It's all right.' Violet smiled weakly. 'It was my fault. I'm always the same when I get my head stuck in a book. I never notice anything.'

'Same goes for me. I'd better introduce myself now that I've nearly knocked you into the middle of next week. Charles Clifford – my friends call me Chuck – corporal – US Army 8th Airforce. I'm stationed at Warton.'

Violet noticed that the hand he held out to her was brown too, as though he had spent much of his time out of doors. The most comforting things in life were brown, she mused. The polished sheen of her mother's old oak table, the coarse brown coats of the donkeys on the sands, a mug of hot chocolate with the steam gently rising from it . . .

She smiled at him and shook his hand. 'I'm Violet Carter. I'm pleased to meet you.'

The smile that he gave her in return, and the tone of his voice, held all the warmth of a glowing fire on a cold winter's evening. To her amazement and delight, Violet felt as though she were coming home.

'And you live in Blackpool, do you, Violet?' Charles Clifford asked.

'Yes. At the north end of the town. My mother has a boarding house there. We've got the RAF billeted with us now, of course.'

'I'm just getting acquainted with the place. Blackpool sure is a fine city. I guess I've never seen so much sea and sand. And the hotels – gosh! – there must be thousands of them.'

Violet didn't tell him that, strictly speaking, Blackpool wasn't a city. In Britain a town had to have either a cathedral or a university to be worthy of that name, but she guessed that to Americans any town of a fair size was classed as a city.

'Have you time for a cup of coffee, Violet? Do say yes.' He looked at her eagerly, his brown eyes shining with enthusiasm. 'I must make amends for trampling all over you with my big feet.'

'Yes – thank you. I'd like that.' Goodness knows what her mother would think of her, being picked up by an American GI of all things, but Violet didn't care. This meeting seemed so natural, as though it were fate that planned it, although she hadn't until this moment believed that things like this ever happened outside the books she read.

'Great. We'll be on our way then. Just a minute – I guess I'd better pay for this book. I'd almost forgotten.' Charles Clifford held up a volume bound in maroon leatherette with gold lettering on the spine, similar to the one that Violet was holding.

'Oh, gosh! Yes – so had I.'

She held up her own book and Charles looked at it with interest. 'What have you chosen? *Shirley* by Charlotte Brontë. Well, great minds think alike, I guess, except mine's by her sister. I already have a copy of *Wuthering Heights* back home, but it's falling apart I've read it so much. I just had to buy a replacement copy, seeing that I'm so near to where they lived.'

They sat companionably in Lockhart's café, drinking anaemic-looking coffee.

'I daresay you think we don't know how to make coffee over here,' Violet remarked. 'We're more for tea in this part of the world.'

'No. It's fine,' said Charles, but it obviously wasn't the coffee that interested him. He leaned forward over the blue checked table-cloth. 'I can't get over meeting someone who shares my love for the Brontës. You've read all their books, have you?'

'Most of them,' Violet replied. 'I started reading them at school – because I had to – then I went on reading them because I enjoyed them. I'm collecting these bound volumes now, when I can afford them.'

'And you'll have been to see the place where they lived, of course – Haworth? I really must get over there while I'm so near.'

'No.' Violet shook her head. 'I've never been to Haworth.'

'You've never been . . . ?' Charles stared at her in astonishment. 'Why ever not? It's only just over the mountains. The next state, isn't it?'

Violet laughed. 'Yes – Yorkshire's the next county. It's just across the hills – the Pennines. But it isn't all that easy to get to when you've no car. And what seems not very far away to you may well be a long journey to us.'

'Yes. I guess so,' said Charles thoughtfully. 'It only looks a stone's throw away on the map. But the States is such a vast country that we think nothing of travelling a couple of hundred miles.'

'And you have a car, I suppose?'

'My father has an old jalopy – a Buick – nothing elaborate, but it sure can go. I was saving up for my own vehicle when this lot happened.'

'Where are you from, Charles?' Violet asked. 'I hope you don't mind if I call you Charles and not Chuck,' she added. 'I think it's a much nicer name.'

Charles laughed. 'Sure – anything you like, honey. I'm from Burlington in Vermont. It's one of the smaller states, up near the Canadian border. I say small, though it would probably seem quite enormous to you. It is small, though, compared with the vast states like Kansas and Colorado. Vermont's one of the prettiest states in the whole of the USA. I admit that I'm prejudiced, but I'm sure there can be no finer sight anywhere than Vermont in the fall . . . You call it autumn, don't you?'

Violet nodded, listening entranced to Charles's eager way of talking and the soft American drawl which was so easy on her ears. 'I guess so,' she said, grinning at him. 'And what's your job, Charles? What do you do in Civvy Street?'

'Civvy Street.' Charles laughed. 'I sure do like that expression everyone's using over here – Civvy Street . . . I'm a bank clerk.' He pronounced it to rhyme with 'work'.

'Good gracious! I felt sure you must have a job working out of doors. You're so suntanned.'

'I guess we see rather more of the sun than you do here. And I make the most of it during the summer – cycling and swimming and playing tennis.'

'Hot summers and cold winters, I suppose?'

'Gosh, yes! The sort of snow that you folks only see on Christmas cards. It sure is pretty, though.'

Violet could see in her mind's eye the sparkling snow nestling on pine trees and wooden houses, against a backdrop of mountain peaks. A far cry from the slushy grey mess left behind in the gutters after a snowfall in Blackpool. 'It sounds like another world,' she said thoughtfully.

'Oh, I don't know. The scenery may be different, but folks are pretty much the same the world over. I heard such tales before I came here about how reserved the British are, but I sure have met some kind folks. The people round here are swell. I just adore those jolly bus conductresses who call everybody "luv", and the shop assistants are so happy and friendly. No one would guess that you've ben fighting a war for damn near three years.'

'I daresay they're making a special effort to please our overseas visitors,' Violet told him. 'But there's no point grumbling about it. We've just had to tighten our belts and get on with the job.'

'And what's your job, Violet?'

'Making aeroplanes!' She laughed. 'Fastening the rivets together, at any rate. I've been there two years now. It's boring work, but we have a good laugh together and I keep telling myself that I'm helping to win the war . . .'

When Violet glanced at her watch she saw, to her surprise, that it was four o'clock. They had been talking for over an hour.

'Gosh!' she cried in alarm. 'Look at the time. Mother'll be

wondering where on earth I am. I promised to get back to help with the airmen's teas. Oh heck!' She hurriedly sprang to her feet. 'Thanks for the coffee, Charles – and everything. I'll have to dash now and catch the bus.'

'I'll walk you to the bus stop,' said Charles, glancing at her in amusement. 'What's the big hurry? I thought you said it was your half-day?'

'Oh, Mother doesn't recognise half-days. "Hard work never killed anyone", that's her motto. No – I'm not being fair. I usually have my half-day to myself, but my sister Jenny has gone to the dentist this afternoon, so I said I'd give Mother a hand.'

'I hope you'll be free tonight,' said Charles, tucking his hand beneath her elbow as they walked along the street. 'I thought we might go to the cinema.'

Violet grinned up at him, her green eyes dancing with pleasure. 'Thanks, I'd love to,' she said eagerly, not feeling that she was being the least bit forward in agreeing so readily. She felt as though she had known Charles for ages and she had known instinctively that he would ask her for a date.

'A Yank? One of them GIs?' said Annie with undisguised horror when Violet told her where she was going later that evening. She put down her knitting – a grey woolen sock for the war effort – and glared angrily at Violet. 'Have you taken leave of your senses, girl? I thought you were up to summat when you came in this afternoon all hot and bothered, but I never thought I'd live to see the day when my daughter took up with one of them foreigners.'

'How can you say that, Mother?' said Violet indignantly. 'After they've come over to help us to win the war.'

'Huh! They only came in because they were forced to. Like they did in the last one. They came over here throwing their weight about, then they had the cheek to say that they'd won it for us . . .' Annie's steel knitting needles clicked together so furiously that they almost caught fire. 'And you want to watch 'em too. They're all alike when they get hold of a nice young lass, especially one as hasn't been around much.'

'I can look after myself, Mother,' said Violet calmly. She knew there was no point in losing her temper. That would only make Annie worse. 'Charles is very nice. It isn't fair of you to lump all the Americans together like that. Anyway, it doesn't make the slightest difference what you say, I'm going out with him tonight.

I'm well turned twenty-one now, and you can't tell me what to do any more.'

She walked from the room without a further glance at her mother, leaving Annie gaping in open-mouthed astonishment.

The summer of 1942 was a memorable one for Violet and Charles. They visited the cinema several times. They saw *In Which We Serve* starring Noël Coward, and Violet was able to identify with Patricia Roc as a factory girl in *Millions Like Us*. They danced at the Winter Gardens and the Tower to the strains of 'In the Mood' and 'Deep in the Heart of Texas'. The dance halls were packed to capacity that summer, the girls standing three or four deep on the edge of the ballroom floor waiting to be asked to dance by the flying corps of various nationalities – the RAF, the Polish airmen, or the bright and breezy newcomers to the scene, the American GIs.

Charles and Violet watched with amusement as some of the more exuberant Yanks swept the local girls literally off their feet in a frenzied rendering of the jitterbug. This dance was frowned upon by the authorities; it had been officially banned because it required a great deal of space and would have been dangerous for the other dancers on the floor, but there were ways of getting round this. There were plenty of places off the ballroom floor, isolated alcoves where the music could be easily heard, and here the GIs and their willing partners indulged in their rhythmic acrobatic cavorting.

Charles and Violet were content dancing the more conventional waltz or quickstep, but they were at their happiest when they were away from the crowds. They walked hand in hand along the seven-mile stretch of golden sand. They rode on a tram the length of the promenade from Squire's Gate to Fleetwood. Some Sunday afternoons they went on bicycle rides, Charles riding Tom's old machine, to secluded spots – the sand dunes near St Annes, or the old-world village of St Michael's on the River Wyre. And Violet soon knew that she was truly in love, for the first time in her life.

She leaned back contentedly against the prickly grass of the sand dunes, one warm Sunday afternoon in mid-July, feeling the hot sand caressing her bare arms and legs. Idly she scooped up a handful of the soft golden grains and let them trickle through her fingers. Violet couldn't remember a time when she had ever felt so happy, so much at peace.

'A penny for them?' Charles plucked a blade of the tough grass and tickled her cheeks and chin, then he bent forward and kissed her gently, first on the forehead then, more lingeringly, on the lips.

'I was just thinking how happy I am,' said Violet. 'Here . . . with you.' She reached up a finger and tenderly traced the firm line of his jaw. 'The war seems a million miles away. But . . . if it hadn't been for the war, we wouldn't have met.'

'We did meet, honey. We had to meet . . . you know that, don't you?' Charles smiled at her – that glowing smile that released all the warmth in his brown eyes and awakened an answering warmth in Violet's breast – then he bent and kissed her again.

Violet felt the hardness of his body against hers and her own reciprocal response; a yearning sensation in that very secret place, an opening up . . . She knew that now, with Charles, she no longer wanted to keep that private part of herself inviolate. She wanted to share all of herself – every last little bit – with him. She remembered with a pang of guilt how, with Tony, it had seemed sordid. Now, with Charles, because she loved him so much, it seemed so right . . .

She felt his hands, firm yet gentle, unbuttoning her blouse and fondling her breasts, then stroking her thighs, her buttocks . . . Violet sighed and pressed herself closer to him. Now she understood . . . Thoughts of 'What would Mother say?' intruded no more. Nothing else mattered now, save her consuming love for Charles. She even understood now how her sister must have felt about Robert. She had never realised before that love between a man and a woman could be such a glorious thing . . .

But Charles stopped, as he always did. 'No, honey . . . no,' he said, kissing the tip of her nose. 'I can't take advantage of you. It wouldn't be right . . .'

'I want you to,' said Violet softly. 'It's all . . . right. It's what I want, as well.'

'No, darling. Don't let's spoil it. I love you too much to spoil it all. Some day . . . we will. Very soon, I hope . . .'

And Violet knew that very soon Charles would ask her to marry him.

The only stumbling block preventing Violet's happiness from being complete was Annie's attitude. For the first few weeks she refused, to Violet's embarrassment, to invite Charles to the house.

'Don't worry, honey,' he said. 'She'll come round, you'll see. I guess it must be a shock to her: her daughter going with a Yank. I know some folks regard us as creatures from another planet.'

'If only she would meet you,' said Violet, her green eyes clouding with anxiety, 'she would see how wrong she is to make such sweeping statements about Americans.'

And that was more or less what Jenny, knowing how worried her sister was about the situation, said to Annie. 'You're wrong, Mother,' she told her. 'Charles is a right decent young man. You've only to look at him and our Violet together to know how happy they are. And he's real kind and considerate too. The only thing spoiling it for Vi is that you won't meet him.'

'I reckon I can choose who I invite to my own house, can't I?' said Annie aggressively. 'Don't you start telling me what to do, our Jenny.' She sighed, and her next words were uttered with a great deal less vehemence. 'To tell you the truth, I'm worried about her. I can't bear to think of her marrying one of them Yanks.'

'She's not said anything about marrying Charles Clifford,' said Jenny. 'You're jumping the gun there, Mother. They've only been going together for a few weeks.'

Nevertheless, Jenny knew that marriage would be the inevitable step. She had known that as soon as she had seen her sister and her American boyfriend together, but she didn't say so to Annie. It would be up to Violet to tell her mother herself when she was good and ready.

'What about your plans to become a teacher?' Jenny had asked her sister with a teasing gleam in her eye.

Violet had laughed. 'Do you remember . . . I also said it would be different if the right man came along? Well – he has.'

Jenny was relieved to hear her mother's next words, though they were spoken grudgingly. 'All right. You can give over mithering, our Jenny. I'll tell our Violet that he can come for tea on Sunday.'

Annie, to Violet's relief, was polite enough to Charles. She didn't welcome him as wholeheartedly as she had welcomed Tony Harris, but she couldn't help but be impressed by his polite manners, his free and easy friendliness and, above all, the tender respect with which he treated her younger daughter.

'Do you think your mother would be offended if I brought something to help with the rations?' Charles asked as they strolled along the promenade after his first visit.

'I'm sure she wouldn't,' Violet replied, 'but you don't need to. Whatever faults Mother has, she always believes in making visitors welcome. She's generous to a fault at times.'

Charles nodded. 'She sure is. She's a swell old lady.'

Violet smiled to herself, wondering how her mother would react to that description.

'But I'd kinda like to help,' he went on. 'I know your rations don't go far and your ma must have used a hell of a lot of her points on that tin of red salmon.

'She's had it in the cupboard for ages,' Violet told him, 'awaiting an important visitor – like Winston Churchill, for instance. You're honoured, I can tell you.'

'I was on my best behaviour this afternoon,' said Charles, laughing. 'We've ben told to mind our Ps and Qs when we visit your homes. In fact they issued us all with a booklet, so that we wouldn't offend our hosts.'

'Really?' Violet raised her eyebrows. 'What does it say?'

'Well, the main thing is never, never, never to say "We came over here and won the last one". And to go easy on the food if you're told "Eat up – there's plenty", like your mother said. It may well be the family's ration for a week.'

'Oh, I shouldn't worry about that. If Mother tells you to eat up you can be sure that she means it. I'm relieved that we've got over the first hurdle. I knew she would like you once she met you.'

Charles tightened his grip on Violet's slim shoulders and leaned over and kissed her cheek. 'It can only get better, honey.'

Annie smiled and muttered a gruff acceptance when Charles came on his next visit bearing gifts of a large tin of pineapple, a tinned fruit cake and an enormous block of Hershey's milk chocolate.

'You needn't have bothered, lad. All Violet's friends are welcome here.' She significantly emphasised the 'all'. 'I don't expect 'em to provide their own tea. But thanks all the same.'

Violet was thrilled to receive a gift of French perfume and her first pair of nylons on her twenty-second birthday in August. And when, later that evening, Charles asked her to marry him, she agreed without hesitation.

Annie received the news unenthusiastically.

'There's a lot as could happen between now and the end of the war,' she remarked churlishly to Jenny a few days later. 'She may well be flashing a diamond ring now, but time will tell. He might change his mind – foreigners are good at that – or he might be . . . Well, anything could happen. If that wedding comes off I'll eat my hat.'

Then you'd better have your knife and fork ready, Mother, said Jenny to herself, but she made no comment. She knew only too well that the balloon would go up really and truly when Annie heard – as Jenny had already done – of the young couple's plns.

Violet broke the news to her mother late that same evening.

'You're getting married in October?' Annie's voice went up an octave in a shrill crescendo. 'What's the flamin' hurry? You've only known him five minutes. Whatever will folks think? Dashing up the aisle with a fellow that you hardly know, and to crown it all he's not even one of us.'

'We're getting married in October,' Violet repeated calmly, 'and that's all there is to it, Mother. Charles thinks that he'll be posted soon, and we want some time together first. We hope you'll be happy for us, but if you're not then I'm sorry, there's nothing we can do about it.'

'And what the heck am I going to do if she goes gallivanting across the other side of the Atlantic?' Annie moaned to her elder daughter as they prepared the midday meal the next day.

Jenny recalled, with wry amusement, that her mother had used exactly the same words when she, Jenny, was getting married, but then it had been 'to the other side of the Pennines'. Now, ten years later, her argument was just the same.

'How can I be expected to run a boarding house with nobody to help me? Our Ada's got her head stuck in the clouds ever since she married that Fred. I did think Violet'd come back and help me when this bloomin' war comes to an end.' She paused, then added thoughtfully, 'He works in a bank, doesn't he, that Charles of hers? Well, I reckon bank clerks are ten a penny. Happen he could get a job over here.'

Jenny could hear despair in her mother's voice and when she glanced at her she saw, to her alarm, that her eyes behind the thick lenses were moist with tears.

'I shouldn't pin your hopes on that, Mother,' she said kindly. 'You'd better make up your mind to it that Violet will be joining him in Vermont. But it won't be for a while yet. She'll be with you till the end of the war.'

'She's my little girl,' said Annie wistfully, in gentle tones far removed from her normal manner of speaking. 'Oh, I know I'm not one for fancy words and all that lovey-dovey nonsense, but I can't bear to think of her going so far away.'

272

'Then give her your blessing now – while she's still here,' said Jenny. 'You'll feel a lot happier, and our Violet will too. Then you can start saving up, Mother, for a trip to America.'

'What – me? Don't talk so bloomin' daft! How do you think I'm going to get to America?'

'On a ship, the same as other people do. And I daresay before long, folk will be flying to America and think nothing about it.'

'And I reckon I'll be pushing daisies up long before that happens,' said Annie, with a return to her customary dryness.

'Don't you believe it.' Jenny walked across the kitchen and put her arm round her mother's shoulders. 'Start saving up, Mother, like I said. It'll be something to look forward to when this lot's over. It's time you had a good holiday. And try to be happy about it – for Violet's sake.'

'Aye, happen you're right, lass,' said Annie with a sniff. 'But it came as a real shock. It's a wonder I didn't have a heart attack right on the spot when she told me. Eeh! We've certainly had some knocks one way and another with this flamin' war. And it's not over yet. Anyway, whatever happens, you'll still be here, won't you, lass?'

Jenny smiled, but she didn't answer. She knew that this was not an opportune moment to tell her mother that after the war she and Tom and the girls – and little Victor, the son that Tom had not yet seen – intended to return to Yorkshire. Tom's letters from the prisoner of war camp were full of it.

On her wedding day Violet looked radiant in a white satin dress with a high neck and long sleeves tapering to a point over the wrist. It was perfectly plain – frills and flounces wouldn't have suited Violet – the flowing lines enhancing her slim figure. Jenny, feeling a lump come into her throat, thought that she had never seen her sister look so beautiful.

'You're having a white wedding, Vi,' Jenny had told her emphatically. 'Be hanged to the expense and to the coupons. It's going to be a day to remember. I'll make your dress, and the bridesmaids' too.'

Joyce, dressed in pale-blue silky rayon, and Patsy and Rosie, in dresses of the same colour, complemented the bride's elegant loveliness. Joyce was engaged now, to a 'buddy' of Charles's from Kentucky. Sheila was not at the wedding. She had married one of the many RAF lads whom she had welcomed so wholeheartedly to the town, and she was now nursing at home her month-old son. A few eyebrows had been raised, but no one had been very surprised, when the child had arrived only five months after the wedding.

Charles had insisted that their few days' honeymoon would be spent in Yorkshire. Where else would they go when, as he reminded Violet, it was the Brontës who had brought them together?

They stayed at a small boarding house on the outskirts of York, near to the city walls. There, in the massive mahogany bed, their marriage was consummated, and Violet was glad – so very glad – that they had waited. Their love, like vintage wine, had improved with the keeping, and now overflowed, surprising them both with undiscovered delights and the rapture that they felt for one another.

Charles was entranced by all that he saw that week. 'Gee, that sure is something!' he gasped in quiet amazement as he gazed at the medieval gates to the city of York and the ancient walls. 'I can almost see the Roman legions marching along those walls.'

They wandered hand in hand through the narrow streets where the old timber-framed houses leaned together as though they were whispering secrets, and in the afternoon they took the bus to the ruined Fountains Abbey.

The highlight of the week was the visit to Haworth. They climbed the steep cobbled street to the old parsonage, which stood foursquare and dour, overlooking the churchyard. They had a lunch-time drink in the Black Bull Inn where, reputedly, Branwell had drunk himself to death, then climbed to the bleak ruins of Top Withens, high up on the moors which surrounded the town.

'Gee, this sure is something,' Charles whispered again as the wind, fresh with the tang of the moors, whistled round the rocks, whipping at their clothes and their hair. 'Can't you just see Cathy and Heathcliff racing across these slopes and flinging themselves down on the bracken? I've never ever seen such vastness of sky and land.'

'Not even in America?' said Violet, laughing.

'Not even there, honey,' said Charles. 'I guess Yorkshire's like no other place on earth. Of course, it could be because you're here.'

He drew her close to him and kissed her as they stood there alone beneath the brooding grey sky. There was no one in the world but the two of them, the silence broken only by the distant bleating of a sheep, and the haunting cry of a curlew far above them.

Chapter 24

By 1943 Jenny, together with most people in Britain, felt as though the war had been going on for ever. What was more, she thought it seemed likely to continue for ever. Now and again there were cheering items of news to boost morale and lift sinking spirits – the capture of Tripoli by the 8th Army; the surrender of the last German troops in North Africa; the raid of the RAF Dambusters on the Ruhr dams – but, on the whole, the worst aspect of the war, to ordinary folk, was the boredom.

Day followed day, a continuous road of restrictions, rules and regulations. How Jenny longed to fling apart the blackout curtains, to let the moonlight shine in and the lamplight shine out; to be able to buy herself and the girls new dresses without feeling guilty; to fill her shopping basket to overflowing with oranges and bananas and pears, and to see the shop windows adorned with gaily coloured clothes and unnecessary frivolities.

All you could do was live a day at a time, coping somehow with the queueing and the rationing, the shortages and the blackout. Victory would come one day. That was what everyone prayed for and everyone believed. Morale was still surprisingly high and everyone looked forward to the day when Europe would be free once more, when the servicemen and prisoners of war would return home and loved ones would be reunited. It was just taking such a long time to come . . .

Patsy and Rosie seemed happy and contented. They found it difficult to remember a time when there had not been a war going on. Little Victor was now nearly two years old, a merry-faced child with a sunny disposition, a great favourite with all the RAF lads who were still billeted at Pleasant View. His grandmother often avowed that he was a 'right little scallywag' and 'into everything', but she thought the world of him, as they all did. Jenny often spoke to him of his daddy and it was a word that Victor, just beginning to

275

talk, found easy to repeat. But, as yet, it was a word in his vocabulary that held no meaning for him.

The war infiltrated the children's education, the popular campaigns providing many an art lesson or a composition topic. Jenny was very proud when Rosie won first prize in a school competition for a 'Wings for Victory' poster. Her picture showed brightly coloured aircraft, such as were never seen in the night skies, raining bombs on to red-painted houses, and airmen in bluer than blue uniforms marching two by two round the border. The large sheets that were provided for the children were cut from the back of a roll of wallpaper, as there was a shortage of paper in school, as well as a scarcity of pencils and text books.

The next week Patsy, too, won a prize, for her composition about the 'Squander Bug' campaign.

'We can help the war effort,' she wrote, 'by buying National Savings stamps. Every Monday morning we take our sixpence to school and the little blue stamps are stuck into a special book. The money goes to the Government and they use it to make aeroplanes and ships and tanks and all the things that are needed for us to win the war.

'It is patriotic to save and not to spend and to "Make do and Mend". My mum is a very good sewer and she has put a piece of blue material round the bottom of my yellow dress that was too short for me, then she made a blue belt and sewed on some blue buttons. Now it is just like a new dress.

'I am trying to go without sweets and to save my money instead, but that is very hard because I like sweets.

'When we have won the war my dad will come home. He is a prisoner of war. That is why I must save up and do all I can to help him.'

Jenny smiled sadly to herself when she read Patsy's composition. She was sure that Patsy must find it difficult to remember her father. Jenny herself found it hard at times to recall the sound of his voice or even his features. She had photographs to help her; without them the memories would have been hazy. It was now two and a half years since she had seen Tom. She was relieved, of course, that he was safe for the duration of the war, that there would be no more fighting for him, but she worried about his well-being, about trivial things mostly. Did he get enough to eat? Was he warm enough, especially in winter time? And how did he occupy his time? If anyone had told her, or millions like her, at the beginning of the war that it would drag on for so long, she wouldn't have believed it possible. And there was still no end in view. It was like being in a long, dark tunnel, the freedom of the past far behind and the longed-for peace still not visible.

Letters from Tom provided a glimmer of cheer and hope to brighten up the monotony of the days. He hadn't written much for the first year; he had been injured in his right shoulder and arm, and writing had proved impossible. He had spent several weeks in hospital before being shipped to the camp near Munich where he would now remain for the duration of the war.

He assured Jenny that they were not badly treated. Many of the camp officials, though brusque and humourless, were kind enough in their own way.

'They are just lads, like we are,' Tom wrote, 'a long way from home and wanting this blasted war to come to an end.'

Reading between the lines Jenny could see that Tom's attitude towards the war was gradually changing. Now, like Jenny had done from the beginning, he was realising the futility of it all. The worst aspect of camp life was the boredom – as it was for the wives waiting at home – as day followed endless day. What was there to do but to look forward to the future and to a brighter tomorrow?

'My very dear Jenny,' he had written in his last letter, '. . . The scenery round here is lovely. It reminds me so much of the hills in Yorkshire around Castleburn. Not that they'll let us go out for walks – I wonder why? We don't get much of a change of scene, but we are surrounded by mountains. This part is called Bavaria and it's very near to Austria which I hear is a very beautiful country.

'I'm sure it's not as nice as Yorkshire, though. Do you remember, Jenny, the great times we had walking by the river and up into the hills? When this lot's over I would like to buy a little house in Castleburn, for you and me and the two girls, and little Victor, of course. I can't tell you how much I'm looking forward to seeing our son. Blackpool is great and we've been very happy there, haven't we, love, but you know how I've always wanted to go back home. I'm sure there will be plenty of building jobs going there after the war, and we can easily find a school for the girls. It's something for me to look forward to. I wouldn't survive, Jenny, if I couldn't look forward to happier times ahead for all of us.

'Give the children a big kiss from me and ask Patsy and Rosie to drop me a line. Keep your pecker up, Jenny love, and remember that I love you. Yours for ever and ever, Tom.'

His letters were always in the same vein and Jenny had made up her mind that he should have his wish. They would go back to Yorkshire. Annie would have to be mollified, especially with Violet departing for foreign shores, but there would be time enough to deal with the problem of her mother when the war came to an end. Tom deserved a fresh start – Jenny knew that she owed him that – and she felt that her marriage would stand a better chance of renewal and survival if they were to move away from Blackpool.

It was also more than two years since Jenny had seen Robert, on that early April evening in 1941 when they had said their last anguished goodbye. He had written once during the summer, after a silence of a couple of months. He had been unable, he said, to control his feelings any longer. He must know how his Jenny was going on. Did she still love him? Was there any news, was there any hope for the two of them . . . ? She had replied with the news that Tom was alive and, as far as she knew, in good health. She assured Robert that she loved him and would never forget him, but then she had gone on stoically – remembering her conversation with the vicar in Castleburn – to tell him that she musn't see him again. He hadn't written since then. Neither had Jenny told him about the child she was expecting, not even when, mistakenly, she had believed that it was Robert's.

She had no photographs of Robert, as she had of Tom, to enable her to call his features to mind. When she thought of him, as she still did, it was the presence of him that she recalled – the evocative scent of his skin and his Brylcreemed hair; the feeling of his strong arms around her; the recollection of the places they had visited on their stolen weekend together – rather than his individual features and the sound of his voice. The memories were not fading; they could be brought to mind immediately by a casual word or glance – the mention of Morecambe, perhaps, or the sight of a tall, dark figure in RAF uniform striding along the beach – but they no longer hurt with the same agonising intensity.

A happy and welcome event at the beginning of August 1943 was the birth of a baby son to Violet and Charles. Gary Charles

Clifford weighed in at 8lb. 8oz., a red-faced youngster with chestnut-brown hair, a strident voice and tiny clenched fists flailing the air. The birth took place at home in Violet's first-floor bedroom, and Annie and Jenny and the two girls – plus a procession of delighted airmen – tiptoed into the room when the midwife had gone and peeped adoringly into the cot at the side of the bed. His ecstatic father, now stationed in Lincolnshire and taking part in bombing raids over Germany, was home the next weekend.

'He sure is wonderful,' he exclaimed in delight as he picked up the minute bundle cocooned in a blue blanket. 'You're a clever girl, honey. I guess I've never seen such an intelligent-looking baby. Like his mother, of course, but I do believe he's got my hair . . . I can't wait to show him to the folks back home. All we have to do now is win the war. It won't be long now, honey . . .'

Jenny was glad that her sister was finding fulfilment in her marriage, culminating in the birth of her son. She prayed for all their sakes that Charles's hopeful prediction would be true, that it wouldn't be long before it was all over.

Jenny's thoughts, one sunny afternoon in August, were all of her sister. The girls had gone to the beach with Eileen's three boys and Ben, the evacuee who, after all, had not returned to Liverpool. Patsy and Rosie were now nine years old – Rosie would be ten next month – old enough to be trusted to go on little excursions on their own, so long as they remembered to watch out for trams as they crossed the promenade and to come home as soon as the tide started to come in. Victor was having his afternoon nap, so Jenny set to work to clean the front windows. It was not a task that she enjoyed, but a necessary one with the summer sunshine showing up all the rain streaks and the dirt left behind by the smoky chimneys.

As she glanced down the road, preoccupied with her happy thoughts of Violet, she saw someone turn the corner into Green Street. A tall man, in RAF uniform, his cap set at a rakish angle on top of his dark, wavy hair . . . She felt her heart turn somersaults, jumping up to beat wildly in her breast, then plummeting to the pit of her stomach. When she looked again, more closely, she saw that it wasn't Robert, just someone very much like him in stature and colouring. This man was an officer – she could tell by the superior quality of his uniform – but it proved to her how very near to the surface of her mind, still, were her thoughts of Robert.

The man was walking uncertainly up Green Street, glancing at the numbers. He paused at number sixteen, then, to her surprise, he knocked at the door.

'Good afternoon,' he said, politely touching his cap as Jenny opened the door. 'Mrs Bradshaw? May I come in?'

He followed her along the short hallway into the living room. 'May I sit down? I think you'd better sit down too – it's Jenny, isn't it? I'd like to call you Jenny, if I may. And I'm Martin. Martin Willoughby. I'm afraid I have some . . . disturbing news for you.'

His voice was quiet and refined, like Robert's. Jenny sat down hurriedly in an armchair, knowing instinctively what this man had come to tell her.

'It's Robert, isn't it?' she said bluntly. 'You've come to tell me . . . about Robert.'

'Yes, my dear. I'm afraid so.'

'He's . . . dead, isn't he?'

'Yes, my dear. I'm afraid so,' he said again.

Jenny waited for the anguish, for the agonising pain to take hold of her, but she could feel nothing. She only thought, detachedly, what a mess she must look, wearing an apron, with her hair bundled up in a turban and a yellow duster still clutched in her hand. She stared at him stupidly. 'How . . . ? When . . . ?' she muttered.

'It was last week. A bombing raid over Berlin.'

'But Robert didn't . . . he was an instructor. He didn't fly.'

'He was a flier, Jenny,' said Martin Willoughby quietly. 'Soon after you last saw him, he applied for operational duties. He was given a commission – he was a flying officer, and a damned fine navigator. You'd have been proud of him.'

Jenny opened her mouth to speak, but the words wouldn't come.

'He asked me, if anything happened, to let you know,' Martin went on gently. 'He asked me to write, but I felt that it would be kinder to come and see you. And I wanted to meet you. I'd heard such a lot about you. Robert talked to me. I think I was the only person he talked to in that way. He was a very private sort of person, as you know. He didn't tell me everything, of course, but he felt he had to talk to someone.'

'About me. About how badly I treated him.' Jenny found her

voice at last, but it sounded strange and far away from her ears, not like her own voice at all. 'I sent him away.' A sudden thought struck her and she looked at Martin Willoughby in horror. 'Is that why he did it, why he volunteered to fly, because I told him . . . ?'

'No, Jenny.' Martin shook his head. 'He felt that he had to do his bit. He didn't think that it was fair that married men – like myself – should take all the risks while he had what he was beginning to think was a cushy number. It wasn't, of course. We'll always need first-class instructors like Robert . . . was, but he was determined.'

Martin Willoughby looked with compassion at Jenny, this pretty, vivacious – yet so ordinary – young woman, with her hair tied up in a turban and a smudge of dirt on her cheek. Robert had loved her; Martin knew that, though his friend hadn't, he was sure, told him the whole story. He had loved her so much that without her he had felt that life had lost its meaning. The war had claimed his father and his childhood friend and then – though in a different way – Jenny, the young woman he had truly loved. She had chosen to remain faithful to her husband. So Robert had decided that there was very little worth living for. Yes, there was his mother and his sister, as Martin had pointed out to him, but the mainspring in his life – his love for Jenny – was a fruitless passion. She could never be his. And so Robert Cunningham had volunteered for active service. What Martin had told Jenny was true; Robert had regarded his job as an instructor as a 'soft option', but it was only half the truth. Martin knew that he couldn't burden this lovely young woman with the knowledge that her rejection of Robert had been the impetus for him volunteering.

'And there couldn't be any mistake? There's no chance that he might still be . . . ?'

'I'm afraid not.' Martin shook his head regretfully. 'I was in the plane just in front. I saw . . . what happened. I'm sorry, Jenny.'

Jenny closed her eyes, visualising, against her will, the horror of it all. The smoke and the flames, the explosion, the falling aircraft . . . and Robert. Oh, dear God . . . not Robert. She couldn't bear it. She shook her head bemusedly. 'He never wanted to fight at all. He hated the war.'

'Don't we all?' Martin smiled sadly. 'Some of the lads may have joined up with ideas of death and glory and all that, but it's beginning to pall now. I thought at first that Robert may have volunteered because of the raid on Coventry – tit for tat, so to speak – but he wasn't interested in reprisals.'

'No, he wouldn't be . . .'

'He knew the dangers – we all do – and he knew that if anything went wrong, you would never be informed. His mother was his next of kin, but I know that he still thought of you as his closest . . . friend.'

'I treated him badly,' said Jenny again. 'I told him we musn't meet again, and now it's . . . too late.'

'He understood, Jenny. He had come to accept it, though he still loved you, you know. And he was glad when you heard that your husband was safe. That's ironic, I know, but Robert was such a decent lad that he wouldn't have wished anyone ill. I was proud to have him as a friend.'

'It's good of you to come and tell me,' said Jenny shortly. 'Let me make you some tea.'

'No – thank you. I must be going. I'm on my way home – to Kendal. I have a few days' leave, so I decided to break my journey here as it's practically *en route*.' Martin stood up and held out his hand. 'Goodbye, Jenny. Take care of yourself, and the children. You have two children, I believe? Your own little girl and an evacuee. Is she still with you?'

'Yes.' Jenny nodded. 'And I have a little boy now. He's . . . nearly two.'

She sensed, rather than saw, Martin's slightly raised eyebrows and his unspoken question. 'No . . .' she said quietly. 'He's . . . Tom's child. Robert didn't know about it. I thought it best that way.'

'Of course.' Martin smiled understandingly. 'And let's hope it won't be long before your husband is home again.'

She was still sitting there, motionless, when the girls came in from the beach. They dashed through the back door, then stopped dead at the sight of Jenny crouched in a pathetic huddle in the armchair, instead of bustling brightly around the kitchen as she usually was. She glanced up, staring at them unseeingly as though she couldn't remember who they were.

'Mum, what's the matter?'

'Are you all right, Mum? You look . . . funny, somehow.'

'Yes . . . I'm all right.' Jenny blinked rapidly. 'I've just had a shock.'

'It's not Dad, is it? asked Patsy in alarm.

'No, dear,' said Jenny gently. 'It's not your father. But I've had some bad news. Do you remember Sergeant Cunningham? He was billeted at your gran's about . . . oh, three years ago.'

'I think so.' Patsy gave a puzzled frown.

'Yes, I do,' said Rosie, nodding emphatically. 'You know, Patsy. That very good-looking one.'

'Oh, yes,' Patsy replied, and the two girls grinned at one another. 'Just like a film star, wasn't he?'

Jenny smiled to herself in spite of her sadness. The girls were growing up, beginning, as she had noticed before, to take an interest in the opposite sex, even if it was only to recognise male comeliness.

'What about him?' asked Rosie.

'I'm afraid he's been killed. In a bombing raid.'

'Gosh, that's terrible!'

'I'm afraid it happens in wartime,' said Jenny wearily. 'It's happening all the time . . .' She glanced towards the ceiling, listening. Victor had woken up. She could hear him rattling the bars of the cot and singing tunelessly to himself. He would be hungry and wanting his tea. So would the girls, after a few hours in the fresh air. Life had to go on . . .

'What's up, our Jenny? You look as white as a sheet.' Annie looked
at her daughter with concern as they prepared breakfast the following morning. 'You've had some bad news, have you? It's not . . . Tom?'

'No, it's not Tom, Mother. I'll have to tell you about it, though I know you were annoyed with me at the time. It's Robert Cunningham . . . He's been . . . killed.'

Jenny heard her mother's gasp of horror. It wasn't the first time that news had filtered back to them of the death of one of the young men who had stayed at the billet. It was happening again and again.

'Eeh lass, that's terrible! That poor young man,' said Annie in a voice choked with emotion. Jenny found her distress hard to understand; her mother had once castigated her so severely about Robert.

'I know how you must be feeling, lovey,' her mother went on. 'I know only too well. It was seeing you and him together – you remember, at your house that night – that brought it all back to me.'

'Brought what back, Mother?' asked Jenny, staring in surprise at Annie.

The older woman's eyes were misty. 'It was at the beginning of the war – I mean the last one, of course. Your father was away at the Front. He'd joined up early on. I got friendly with a young soldier who was home on leave. I'd always known him – he lived in the next street – but we got talking and, well, you know how it is, lass. I was lonely with Frank being away, and one thing led to another. Nothing much, mind you. We never did anything wrong. Well, not much, anyroad. But when I saw you and that young chap it reminded me. That's why I went for you both . . . but I understood, lass. Oh yes, I understood.'

'What happened to him, Mother?' Jenny's voice was scarcely audible.

'He was killed – at Ypres, in 1917. Your dad came through it all. He never knew owt about it, and I just picked up the pieces and carried on.' She sighed. 'You have to, lovey.'

'I loved him, Mother,' said Jenny softly.

'Aye. I know you did, lass.' Annie walked across the kitchen and put her arms round her daughter.

Jenny buried her head in her mother's comfortable breast, the first time she had done so since she was a little girl. Annie stroked her hair. 'You've still got your Tom – praise the Lord – and he's a good lad. And your family – the little lasses and young Victor. You've got to think about them. And it'll soon be over, lovey. It'll soon be over. Go on – have a good cry if you want to.'

Jenny felt closer to her mother than she had ever felt before. There was such a tightness in her chest that she felt as though she would burst open with it, but the tears which had been stinging her eyelids since yesterday still would not flow freely. She was suddenly aware of her mother's sharp indrawn breath and she looked up to see Annie's face contorted in pain and her hand clasped to her breast.

'Mother – what's the matter?' Jenny's own anguish was momentarily set aside. 'You're not ill, are you?'

Annie tried to smile. 'No, I don't think so, lass. Just a little spasm. Happen something I've eaten. I've had it once or twice lately. Just get us a drop of brandy, there's a good girl . . .'

Jenny went to the sideboard for the bottle, remembering another occasion, just after the outbreak of war, when Annie had been similarly affected. It had been stress that had brought it on then and no doubt it was the same now. Hearing the news about Robert, and then talking about her own unhappy little affair.

Annie was soon back to normal. She insisted that she was as right as rain – she dismissed it as 'summat and nowt' – but Jenny was worried. Her mother wasn't getting any younger and Jenny suspected that her system wouldn't always withstand the shocks that this war was continually bringing in its wake.

Jenny lit a small fire, for the evening was chilly although it was August, then she curled up in an armchair, with the volume of poetry on her lap. She thumbed through the pages. Keats – Robert's favourite poet. 'Ode on a Grecian Urn' – what strange titles some of these poems had, and what an odd thing to choose to write a poem about. She read on. About the lovers, the maidens and men, captured and held in one brief moment of time. Like herself and Robert.

'For ever wilt thou love and she be fair.' Their love – hers and Robert's – would never fade, would never have the chance to grow dull and tarnished with overfamiliarity. Robert would always be young, as she had seen him on that April day two years ago, his hair black and glossy, never streaked with silver as hers was beginning to be; his clear blue eyes shining with love for her; fresh-faced and firm-limbed, with the warmth and joy of springtime about him, as it would be for ever.

'For ever warm and still to be enjoyed,
For ever panting and for ever young.'

What was it that Robert had said to her that weekend? Their love would never die so long as they had their memories . . .

'We'll always be together, darling,' he had said, 'together in our minds, every time we think of one another.'

Memories, memories . . . Jenny closed her eyes now, remembering . . . She saw the vast stretch of beach, and herself and Robert running, laughing, shouting with delight as they raced towards the sea, that day in Morecambe, so long ago. So long ago, and yet it seemed as if it were only yesterday. She felt the hard ridges of sand hurting her feet, she smelt the freshness of the salt-laden air and she experienced again the wonder of that moment when Robert's lips, so firm and yet so tender, had closed upon her own, his cheek cold against hers in the deepening November dusk.

But now Robert was gone from her, gone for ever. Robert was dead . . . and Jenny felt so very alone.

But still the memories flooded back. She recalled his laughter, the joyous brilliance of his smile illuminating his serious face, the flicker of merriment that would light up his clear blue eyes whenever she said something that amused him . . . as she often did. And the feeling of his strong arms around her, the warmth of his body next to hers, the soft whisper of his voice, '. . . You're so lovely, Jenny. My lovely Jenny Wren . . .'

'Oh, Robert . . . I loved you so much. I still love you,' Jenny murmured.

And then her tears came at last, falling like rain on the pages of the open book.

Chapter 25

'Here is a special bulletin read by John Snagge. D-Day has come. Early this morning the Allies began the assault on the north-western face of Hitler's European fortress . . .'

These were the words that Jenny, along with millions of other Britons, heard on the wireless on the morning of the sixth of June 1944. It was the beginning of the end. In August, Paris was liberated, followed by Brussels in September.

But not before the Germans countered with a last, desperate attack. A week after D-Day, on the twelfth of June, the first V1 pilotless plane crossed the English coast, and during the following month about 8,000 of these deadly missiles were launched. On the eighth of September, the longer-range V2s began to fall. It was too late for Germany to win the war, but the effect was demoralising on the war-weary civilians of Britain.

The north of England escaped the attack but, as in 1939, the evacuation of schoolchildren took place. Patsy and Rosie found their classroom bursting with this latest influx of wartime visitors, this time from London and the surrounding area. Many of them stayed until the end of the war and when, in February 1945, the local children sat for their scholarship examination, their new friends did the same.

Everyone now began to be more concerned with what would happen after the war ended than about winning the war itself. Victory was by now a foregone conclusion. There were still battles to be fought and dead to be mourned, but the worst of the pressure had gone. The blackout restrictions were relaxed, the Home Guard was demobilised, and now it was just a question of waiting for the final news of victory.

'It's a lovely day tomorrow,' sang Vera Lynn when Jenny switched on the wireless on the morning of the seventh of May 1945.

> 'Tomorrow is a lovely day.
> Come and feast your tear-dimmed eyes
> On tomorrow's clear blue skies.'

They had been playing that song when she and Robert had danced together that memorable weekend in Morecambe. She recalled the flashing lights, the crush of bodies on the dance floor, and the tinny voice of the young girl vocalist.

> 'If today your heart is weary,
> And every little thing looks grey,
> Just forget your troubles and learn to say
> Tomorrow is a lovely day.'

There had never been any hope of tomorrow for her and Robert. Right from the beginning, deep down, she had known that there would be no future for them together, but she had refused to let the thought take root in her mind. They had had to live for the moment, to cram a whole lifetime of loving and giving and sharing into a few short months. Jenny had no regrets. All her memories of Robert were happy ones and she had come to terms, as much as she ever would do, with her loss. She saw their love affair as a joyful thing, encapsulated in one brief moment of time. Nothing and nobody would ever be able to take it from her. She was glad that she had known him, however briefly. But now . . . now there would be a tomorrow, a bright and hopeful one, for her and Tom and the children, and for the millions of Britons awaiting the end of this wearisome struggle.

The news came the next day, the eighth of May. The Germans had surrendered and the war was over. A mood of exultation swept through the whole country. Patsy and Rosie were delighted when schools were closed for the day, and even more pleased when Pablo's ice-cream parlour, in the centre of Blackpool, handed out free ice-cream to all comers.

There was a party the following week in Green Street, as there was in streets, avenues and terraces in every town and village in Britain. Jenny was one of a small committee of women who went from door to door collecting gifts of money, or the promise of food, to give the children the best party they had ever known.

The long trestle tables, borrowed from the nearby church hall, were set out in the middle of the road and covered with cloths of different shapes and sizes contributed by the various households. Every child brought his or her own cup, plate and dish, and of course his own chair, and then the food and drink flowed fast and furiously. Meat-paste and fish-paste sandwiches – eked out with the ever popular jam sandwiches – sausage rolls, blancmanges, jellies, and buns and cakes of every description, many iced with red, white and blue icing. There were gallons of orange juice, and large enamel pots of tea – strong and black for once – for the grown-ups, who didn't sit down, but waited on the happy and excited children. Their turn, for those so inclined, would come later, when the children were in bed, in the pubs and dance halls around Blackpool, where the ale flowed freely and the light spilled out once more from the open doors and curtainless windows.

Red, white and blue bunting fluttered gaily from the tops of windows and lampposts, forming a zig-zag pattern the length of the street. Union Jacks waved wildly in jubilant hands and nearly every little girl wore red, white and blue ribbons in her hair.

After the food came the races at the far end of the street. Jenny watched as they ran the three-legged race. Rosie was stepping out boldly with Ronnie, one of Eileen's twins, who had once, Jenny recalled, been the new evacuee's deadly enemy. Now they were the best of friends, and well matched both in height and confidence. They won the race easily, yards ahead of the others. Patsy and Ben, smaller and less sure of themselves, were partners, and Jenny watched with amusement as they giggled together, struggling to get their legs synchronised, and then collapsed in a laughing, tangled heap.

Ben would be going home the next morning, back to Liverpool. He had stayed a few extra days as a special concession from his mum, so that he didn't miss the party. He was upset and confused, Eileen had told Jenny, at the thought of leaving what was virtually his second home, but he had tried manfully to hide his tears in front of the boys. Of course he was looking forward to being with his own parents again, but he felt 'all muddled up', he had tried to explain to Eileen. She comforted him by telling him that he could come for a holiday, perhaps later in the year, knowing as she said it that if she were his mum she wouldn't be able to bear the thought of parting with him again.

It must be so for all who were returning home, Jenny reflected, this feeling of unreality. It might well prove difficult to exchange a way of life that had, over the war period, become routine, for one which, though once familiar and loved, was now strange and alien. She hoped that Tom would be able to readjust to his home and family again, and she determined to do all in her power to help him, even to the extent of moving away from her friends and relations here.

And she said a silent prayer of thanks, as she did so often, that she had been spared the anguish of one parting. Rosie, who had come to her as a stranger more than five years ago, was now, legally, her own daughter, as she had been in Jenny's own mind ever since Daisy White was killed.

'Mummy, Mummy . . .' Jenny looked down, diverted from her thoughts of Tom and her two daughters by a small hand pulling her apron. Little Victor, now nearly four years old, was demanding her attention. 'Mummy . . . it's the egg and spoon race. Come on . . .'

Jenny took his hand and ran with him to the starting point, further down the street where the younger children – three-and four-year-olds, like Victor – were assembling. They each clutched a dessert spoon tightly in their fists, topped by a counterfeit egg. The eggs were golf balls, collected hastily from sideboard drawers or from the depths of golfing bags where they had lain dormant for the duration of the war. It would be too risky to use the real thing with the young children; besides, this precious commodity was still in short supply.

The onlookers cheered as the youngsters set off, tiny brows furrowed in concentration as they kept their eyes glued to the all-important egg in front of them. Victor was way ahead, and Jenny felt a glow of maternal pride at her son's achievement – be it only in an egg and spoon race. Then, two yards from the finishing line, his egg rolled off the spoon and bounced to the side of the road. He was pipped at the post by young Johnny, an exuberant lad from the end of the street, who beamed with delight at the cheering crowd.

Oh dear, thought Jenny. I hope there won't be tears. She could see the puckered lips of a few of the three-year-olds who didn't understand that there could be only one winner, and hear murmurs of 'It's not fair . . .' But Victor just looked at her and shrugged his shoulders, then grinned widely and ran off to join his adoring sisters.

'Jolly good, our kid,' said Rosie, ruffling his sandy hair. 'You nearly won.' She seized him under the armpits and whirled him round and round, then each girl took a hand and they ran off with him to the far end of the street where a game of 'The Big Ship Sails through the Alley-alley-o' was just beginning.

Jenny smiled to herself. She might have known that there would be no tears from Victor. He was a tough little customer, and easy-going too, unlike Patsy who had been timid at his age and easily upset. He was more like Rosie in temperament although, biologically, there was no kinship between the two of them; maybe environment played a larger part in the make-up of a child than hereditary traits. Jenny had never ceased to be thankful for the small miracle – which was how she thought of it – that had given her little Victor.

He was always called by his full name. Annie had remarked, in her usual blunt manner, on hearing Rosie refer to him as 'Vic', 'It sounds like summat as you rub on yer chest! Call him by his proper name, if you don't mind, young lady!' Rosie had grinned at Jenny and given her a sly wink, but from then on the little boy had always been Victor.

Jenny looked at the three heads, one dark, one undeniably ginger, and one sandy, going through the archway of the Alley-alley-o and knew that she was blessed indeed. She retired to her own little kitchen to tackle her share of the washing-up, and was joined by Violet and her little son, Gary, who, at not quite two years old, was too young to join in the party games. From the end of the street, drifting towards them on the still evening air, she could hear the strains of children's voices . . . 'The Big Ship Sails through the Alley-alley-o, on the last day of December . . .' Jenny smiled. It had been a happy day.

The celebrations continued the next week with a Victory concert at the local school.

'You'll come, won't you, Mum?' Patsy had said excitedly. 'We're both in it. Well, all the class are in it, but me and Rosie – Rosie and I, I mean – have got important parts. Rosie's is more important than mine, though, She's . . .'

'Don't tell her!' Rosie interrupted. 'I want it to be a surprise.' Her vivid blue eyes gleamed with delighted anticipation as she smiled at Jenny. 'You'll be ever so pleased, Mum. I know you will. And with Patsy, an' all.'

The last two words had slipped out unconsciously, Jenny knew, because the girl was excited. Jenny had tried to steer Rosie away from some of the more blatant colloquialisms that she was apt to use and to encourage her to speak more correctly. To say 'as well' instead of 'an' all' was but one example, and Rosie usually remembered. Jenny was well aware that her own speech often tended towards the vernacular of her native Lancashire; so did her mother's, but she wouldn't have wanted Annie to be any different. The Lancashire idiom was as much a part of Annie as her buxom figure and her flowered crossover pinny. Jenny was surprised to find that her thoughts of her mother were now often tinged with affection. But as far as the next generation was concerned – the girls and young Victor – Jenny wanted the best possible start in life for all of them. A good education; extra music and dancing lessons, maybe – opportunities that she and Violet had lacked – and to speak nicely, according to Jenny's lights, was to have one foot on the first rung of the ladder to success. Now that the war was over, there was no telling what possibilities would be open to them . . .

Jenny smiled at Patsy and Rosie. 'I know I'll be very proud of you – both of you – whatever you're doing in the concert.' The girls still championed each other's achievements and, as yet, there had been no suggestion of jealousy in their relationship. 'Do you think I could invite Grandma to come as well? I'm sure she'd love to see you both.'

''Course you can, Mum,' said Rosie. 'And Victor an' all . . . I mean, as well.'

'I think we're only allowed two guests, Mum,' said Patsy, her brown eyes clouded with concentration. 'But if Victor sits on your knee, I 'spect it'll be all right.' She nodded precisely. 'I'll ask our teacher tomorrow and make sure . . .'

As it happened, Patsy need not have worried. The more the merrier, was the attitude of all the teachers. It wasn't every day that Victory was celebrated, and when the great day arrived, the school hall was packed to overflowing, with several guests – mainly mums and grans – standing at the back. Jenny and Annie had arrived early and had seats in the middle of the second row.

Jenny wondered what the important part was that Rosie had been chosen to play. The girl had asked for the loan of a white sheet – 'Just an old one will do, Mum' – but she was still determined on absolute secrecy. When the makeshift curtains were drawn back to reveal the opening tableau, Jenny saw her standing, tall and regal, in the centre of the impromptu stage. She was Britannia, her long toga-like dress, fashioned from the white sheet, draped with a Union Jack, and a helmet moulded from silver paper and cardboard on her head. She had grown into a most attractive girl with her bright blue eyes and black hair, but Jenny felt that she had been chosen not only for this reason, or because she was the tallest girl in the top class, but because she radiated self-confidence. Around her were scores of children dressed as soldiers, sailors and airmen, with some of the girls as nurses, all singing,

'Rule, Britannia, Britannia rule the waves,
Britons never, never, never shall be slaves.'

Jenny swallowed to try to free the lump in her throat, but it was still there as they continued with a selection of patriotic songs. But her tears fell unashamedly as she heard Patsy, chosen for the clarity of her voice, recite with a chorus of several other girls and boys, Lawrence Binyon's poem, 'For the Fallen'.

'They went with songs to the battle, they were young,
Straight of limb, true of eye, steady and aglow,
They were staunch to the end against odds uncounted,
They fell with their faces to the foe.'

Jenny stole a glance at their mother. Annie's eyes, too, were moist with unshed tears. Jenny smiled understandingly, then quickly reached out and squeezed her hand. All around, people were reaching for their handkerchiefs and trying to blow their noses with as little noise as possible. Jenny didn't know how much the children would really understand of the beautiful words they were reciting – very little, she imagined – but the effect on the audience was cataclysmic. There was silence for a few seconds after they finished speaking, then thunderous applause.

The concert continued for about an hour with a display of Physical Training, further songs and recitations from the younger children, then the final tableau, concluding, fittingly, with 'There'll Always be an England'. 'Three cheers for Victory!' shouted the head-master, then the walls rang and the roof nearly lifted off with the deafening cry of exultant voices.

Tom stepped off the train, his eyes gazing over the heads of the other homecoming soldiers towards the barrier. Jenny had said she would be there to meet him, and Tom was longing to see her again. His heart and his mind and his body cried out for her and yet, in a way, he was afraid. It had been so long . . . Tom had always been a solitary, introspective person, not very quick to make friends, although the friends he had made recently in the camp he knew he would never forget. The circumstances in which he had found himself, as a prisoner of war, had forced him to retreat into himself, into a world of his own secret thoughts and imaginings. He feared that Jenny might have changed too, that they might be unable to adjust to one another. His letters to her had been full of yearning to be with her again, but now that moment was here Tom was filled with trepidation. And would he recognise her? Don't be ridiculous, he told himself. Not recognise his own dear Jenny? And yet it had been so long . . .

There was a crowd milling round the barrier, women and children and toddlers. Tom narrowed his eyes, searching for a familiar face. There was a little sandy-haired lad jumping up and down excitedly – a grand little lad he looked too, Tom thought – aged about three or four. A dark-haired young woman was laughingly trying to restrain him; at the same time her eyes were searching the faces of the approaching crowd. Tom's heart almost stopped. It was Jenny! His own beloved Jenny. And the little lad . . . it must be . . . well, just fancy that! It must be Victor! At that moment she caught sight of him and a delighted smile lit up her face. She waved frantically and lifted up the little boy, who waved too, but hesitantly, not quite sure where he was supposed to be looking.

Tom hurried through the barrier and put down his kitbag, then he folded Jenny in his arms. 'Oh, Jenny. Jenny, love . . .' he murmured, completely at a loss for words. And there was Patsy, unmistakably his Patsy with her bright ginger hair, but now several inches taller. And Rosie, who had changed more than any of them, smiling shyly at him. How attractive she was, and so tall for her age, nearly as tall as Jenny. But all of them, even Rosie, seemed to have temporarily lost the power of speech. Little Victor just stood there and stared.

'This is your daddy,' said Jenny, quietly. 'Say hello to Daddy, Victor.'

'Hello . . .' The child was unsure. His little forehead creased in a frown and his grey eyes looked perplexedly into Tom's grey eyes, so like his own. Tom's heart nearly burst with wonder and pride as he looked at this little boy, his son, and so much like him that it was almost uncanny. But he was aware of the child's bewilderment. Who was this stranger that he must call Daddy? Tom could read the thought taking shape in the little boy's mind.

He bent down and ruffled his son's hair. 'You're a grand lad. You are that,' he said shyly, and Victor smiled, but still uncertainly. Tom knew that it would take time for both of them, but that was something they had plenty of now. All the time in the world.

It was the end of June when Tom arrived home to a Britain buzzing with election fever, but he showed little interest in this or in anything else going on around him. After his first emotional, but somewhat silent meeting with his family, he retreated back into his own private world. Jenny regarded him anxiously as he sat motionless, staring into space, or with a book he was supposed to be reading open at the same page for an hour or more.

'Are you all right, dear?' she asked concernedly, and his reply was always more or less the same, given with a distracted, far-away smile. 'I'm fine. Don't worry about me, Jenny love. I'm . . . thinking.'

She had, the night before he was due home, taken out Tom's beloved toy soldiers and arranged a selection of them, marching two by two along the top of his chest of drawers, as they had been before he went away. The day after his arrival, she found them scattered on the carpet, obviously flung aside by an impatient hand. Sadly she picked them up and returned them to the drawer, realising, too late, that Tom, having experienced the horror of the reality, now had no time or inclination for infantile war games. She had acted with the best of intentions, thinking that by surrounding him with his own familiar possessions she would enable him to settle down more quickly. Now she realised that her gesture had been a foolish one.

Tom didn't speak much about the war itself, though he often mentioned his fellow prisoners, wondering how they were faring. Occasionally, when his feelings became too much for him, he would rage about the futility of war. Not only was it futile, he stormed, it was monstrous, an obscenity beyond all belief. If God was a God of love, as Tom had always been told, why then did He allow it? He refused to go to church, saying that he didn't see the point in it any more, although he had been a regular attender before the war. And Jenny, sensibly, left him alone.

Neither did Tom mention their proposed return to Castleburn, though his letters whilst he was in captivity had spoken of little else. His mother wrote, urging them to go for a visit and Tom said that they would go before long, but their long-term future plans were never mentioned. He took himself off for long walks on the promenade, at first not even wanting the company of the children. He ate very little, to Jenny's consternation, picking at his food in an absent-minded manner. It was Annie who explained to Jenny that it was most likely due to the natural shrinking of his stomach.

'I remember how your dad was when he came back from the last lot,' she told her daughter. 'Messing about with his food and pushing it round his plate. He'd an appetite like a sparrow. He wasn't used to big meals, you see, and your Tom won't be either. I reckon he's been damn near starved for four years. It'll take time, Jenny lass. It'll take time, but he'll come round, don't fret yourself.'

And so he did, gradually. When school closed for the summer holidays Tom began to spend more time with the girls. Jenny was overjoyed to see, also, the steady consolidation of the bond between Tom and his son as they became less apprehensive of one another. The family links were being forged once more and Tom, heartened by the love of his children, began, slowly, to return to normality. Jenny hoped that her love for her husband was strengthening him too, but they had not yet come together, fully, as man and wife.

Towards the middle of August Tom felt ready for a visit to Castleburn, and this proved to be a turning point in their relationship. There, in the bosom of his own family, who loved him so well but had seen so little of him for many years, Tom began to talk more freely again. Not about the war very much, but about family matters, reliving his childhood with his mother and brothers and sisters.

Jenny was delighted to see Lilian again. There was such a change in her that Jenny could hardly believe she was the same person who had, a few years earlier, felt driven to the brink of despair. Her cheeks glowed with health, her eyes with happiness, and on the third finger of her left hand there gleamed a solitaire diamond ring. Martha had written of Lilian's deepening friendship with Bert Adams, a widower, at whose farm she had worked as a Land Girl, and now that the war was over they had decided to name the day.

Jenny had to suppress a laugh when she met him. With his ruddy cheeks and corpulent figure he was the archetype of the farmer portrayed in Patsy and Rosie's reading books. 'All he needs is a straw in his mouth,' she said afterwards, laughingly, to Tom. But she knew that he and Lilian would be happy together.

'Do you like him?' Lilian had asked her shyly, one afternoon when she had brought her young man home for tea. Not that he was so very young; approaching fifty, Jenny guessed, some ten years older than Lilian. 'I do want you to like him, Jenny.'

'Of course I do,' Jenny assured her. 'I think he's a fine man. But the point is . . . do you?'

Lilian nodded happily. 'I love him,' she replied simply. 'And . . . it was all thanks to you. The Reverend Martindale introduced us, after you'd met him in the church that day. And – before that – you helped me, Jenny, that night . . .' She glanced across the room to where her brother was engaged in an animated conversation with her fiancé. Jenny followed the direction of her eyes and the two women looked at one another in perfect understanding. 'I'm all right now. Honestly I am,' said Lilian. 'Thanks, Jenny . . .'

'More than all right, I would say,' replied Jenny. She reached out and squeezed her sister-in-law's hand. 'I'm so glad you're happy, love.'

It was on the first night of their holiday, in the big double bed that he had once slept in with two of his brothers, that Tom took Jenny in his arms and, for the first time since his return home, made love to her. They came together quietly and gently, without a great display of passion, but Jenny felt comforted by Tom's nearness and his murmured words of endearment. She knew from his heartfelt sigh and the stillness of his body as he lay silently beside her, that from now on he would be all right again. Much of the strain and stress of the last few years had drained away from him. It would take time – there would still be occasions, she knew, when bad memories would return to haunt him – but with the help that she was determined to give him they would both win through.

'Thanks, Jenny love,' said Tom, resting his head against her shoulder. 'I didn't know if I would be able to . . . you know. That's why I haven't tried before. But it was all right, love, wasn't it? It's still the same, isn't it? We still love one another.'

She sensed the anxiety in his voice and she answered reassuringly. 'Yes, love. It was . . . wonderful. It's still the same.'

But Jenny knew in her heart that it was not the same. It was much better than before. Her love for Robert had taught her so much, how to give as well as to receive, and now she welcomed Tom's embraces knowing that she was able to respond fully and meet his ardour with her own.

He put his arm round her and snuggled his head against the softness of her breast. 'And you're still the same, Jenny love. You haven't changed at all. I could hardly believe it when I saw you again after all that time. You look younger than ever.'

297

Jenny knew that this wasn't true. She was only too conscious of the tiny grey streaks in her hair and the lines of tiredness on her face that hadn't been there the last time Tom was home. She knew that it was useless to try to disguise them, to pretend that time had stood still. A lot had happened to bring about the subtle change in her appearance. The war had left its mark upon her, as it had upon millions of others, but a better time was coming . . .

Jenny decided to broach the subject that she believed was very dear to Tom's heart. 'What about your idea of moving back here, love?' she asked now. 'Don't you think it's time we were making plans? Looking for a house and . . . everything?'

'Jenny!' Tom sat bolt upright in bed. 'Do you mean it? You'd really come and live here?' His excited voice betrayed his surprise – and a slight disbelief. 'I hadn't mentioned it because – well – it was just a dream to keep me going. I thought that when it came to the crunch you might not want to move.'

'Of course I want to, Tom. Anything you want is all right with me, my love.' Jenny knew now that wherever Tom was, there she would be too. The words of the thought passing through her mind were familiar. Wherever had she heard them before? Of course . . . *Far from the Madding Crowd*, the book that Robert had lent her so long ago. She tried to recall the words. What was it that Gabriel Oak had said when he came courting Bathsheba?

'And at home by the fire, whenever you look up, there shall I be – and whenever I look up, there will be you.'

That's how it would be with her and Tom. Not the most exciting of existences, but Jenny didn't crave excitement. All she cared about now was security for herself and the children, and the freedom to live their lives in the new-found peace that had been so grimly fought for and won. There would be love as well, for she knew now, without a shadow of doubt, that she loved Tom with a deep and abiding affection that would stand the test of time.

And he loved her too in the same way. Tom was like Gabriel Oak, in the story that Robert had loved so much, though he was of another generation and from a different part of the country. Tom was as dependable and unchanging as the grey limestone hills of his native Yorkshire. He would always be secure and reliable, and Jenny knew that she and the children would provide the warmth and gaiety, and together they would be a happy, well-balanced family.

They started looking for a house the next day, and by the end of the holiday they had not only found the house they wanted, but also

a job for Tom with a local firm of building contractors, and places for
the two girls at the Castleburn Girls' Grammar School. Patsy and
Rosie had both passed their scholarship examination, to Jenny and
Tom's pride and delight, and they had been looking forward to
attending the grammar school in Blackpool with all their friends.
But what did it matter where the school was so long as the two of
them were together? And to be coming to live in Castleburn – well –
it was like a dream coming true.

The house was about a minute's walk from Tom's mother's, a
small terraced grey-stone house, not much bigger than the one in
Blackpool, but there was a small garden at the front and a larger
one at the back with an apple tree and a view of the surrounding
hills.

'Now, all we have to do is to tell your mother,' said Tom as they
finished unpacking their suitcases back home in Green Street.

Jenny sighed. 'Yes . . . I think we'd best go and get it over with as
soon as possible. I can't say I'm looking forward to it, but there's no
turning back now.'

'I can't help feeling guilty,' said Tom, 'planning a new life and
leaving your ma here in Blackpool, especially when I think of your
Violet going as well. She'll be sailing for the States before long,
won't she?'

'I'm not sure. It could take a few months. She'll have to wait until
they can arrange a sailing, and Charles has only just gone back
home.' Jenny picked up the empty suitcase and humped it to the top
of the wardrobe, then she turned and smiled pensively at Tom. 'Yes
. . . I feel guilty too, love, but there's no reason why we should.
Mother's had more than her money's worth out of me all these years,
and we've got to think of ourselves now. I know you've always
wanted to go back to Yorkshire and I'm determined that you're
going to have what you want. We'd best go and tell her. Like I say,
our Violet'll be at home for a while yet, so Mother may not feel too
bad about us going . . .'

Annie opened the door to them and they followed her along the
passage and into the kitchen. 'Aye, I thought as how you'd be
coming,' she mumbled, but there was no warmth in her greeting.
She slumped into the sagging easy chair and stared gloomily into the
grey ashes in the fire grate. Jenny thought it was strange that her
mother had let the fire go out.

'What's up, Ma?' said Tom. 'You look as though you've lost a
pound and found a tanner.'

'It's our Violet,' said Annie, still staring at the dead fire. 'She's off to America. Week after next.'

'What . . . but . . . whatever do you mean, Mother?' stuttered Jenny. 'I thought she'd be here for ages yet.'

'Aye . . . so did I, lass. But she got word as there's been a cancellation. She'll be off in a fortnight.' Annie looked at her elder daughter and tried to smile, but her short-sighted grey eyes looked as lifeless as the ashes in the fire grate. 'I reckon we'll have to make the best of it, you and me. At least I know as you'll be here, don't I, lass?'

Jenny and Tom exchanged glances and she knew intuitively what her husband was thinking. 'Yes, Mother,' she answered calmly. 'I'll be here . . .'

'But what about . . . ?' began Rosie. She was quelled by a nudge from Patsy, who shook her head at her sister. 'Not now . . . Grandma's upset,' she whispered, and Rosie put her hand to her mouth and glanced apologetically at Jenny.

Annie, uncharacteristically, hadn't noticed the exchange. She was too distracted by her own despondent thoughts.

'Never mind,' said Tom, later that night when the children were in bed. He perched on the arm of Jenny's chair and put his arm round her. 'We'll wait a while, until your ma's got used to the idea of Violet going. There's no rush. If we lose the house, there'll always be another. And another job for me an' all. And the girls can start at the grammar school here, like you'd planned. Don't worry, love. We'll get to Yorkshire, you'll see . . .'

But Jenny could see their plans slipping further and further from their grasp.

Violet, of course, was over the moon about her imminent departure for the States. Jenny went round to help her with the packing of her suitcases and trunk, doing her best to be cheerful and enthusiastic. It was difficult, though; not only was she losing her beloved sister, but her own plans had been thwarted, and she was also worried about her mother. Annie was still depressed about Violet going and she seemed to have lost much of her vitality and zest for living. Jenny stared absent-mindedly through the bedroom window of Pleasant View at the familiar vista of boarding houses – the street seemed strangely empty, though, without the swarms of RAF recruits – idly nursing a pile of Violet's cardigans in her arms.

'Penny for them, our Jenny . . .'

She turned to see her sister eyeing her curiously.

'You were miles away, Jen. Come on, cheer up, love. Like I told Mother, it's not as if I were going a million miles. You and Tom'll have to save up and come and see us . . . You've been out of sorts ever since you came back from Yorkshire. There's something else wrong, is there, Jenny?'

'No, not really.' Jenny sighed. 'I don't like you going, of course, Vi. Not that I'm not pleased for you – but I'll miss you, love.'

'There is something else wrong, though, isn't there, Jen? Come on . . . I know there is.'

Jenny knew that she could confide in her sister. They had always been close and had shared all their secrets – well, nearly all of them – and Jenny knew that Violet would only go on pestering until she told her. She dropped the piles of cardigans on to the floor and sat down on Violet's bed with its heavy quilted eiderdown, a present from Charles. 'I'm worried about Mother. Not that I think you shouldn't go, Vi. You've got to go, but Mother has taken it so badly. And . . . well, I've got to admit that there's a selfish reason for being worried about her. You see, Tom and I had been planning to go and live in Yorkshire . . .'

She told Violet about the plans they had made, the house and the school and Tom's job, and how it had all come to nothing. 'But we can't go and leave her now, you see, not while she's so upset.'

Violet listened in silence, staring at the carpet, then she looked up at Jenny, her green eyes clouded with concern. 'Oh, Jenny. I'm so sorry. It's all my fault. If it wasn't for me . . . Oh dear. I'm getting things all my own way, and you . . .' Her eyes filled up with tears.

'Look, it doesn't matter. It's just the way things have worked out, and it can't be helped. We'll get to Yorkshire eventually, but we'll just have to wait a month or two to see how Mother settles down.' Jenny smiled at her sister. 'Oh dear, now it's you that looks all down in the dumps. We are a couple of weary Willies, aren't we? Oh, by the way, Mother doesn't know about this – Yorkshire, I mean – so you won't let on, will you?'

'No, I won't say a word. And I hope you get what you want as well, Jen. You deserve it, you and Tom.' Violet put an arm round her sister and gave her a squeeze. 'Shhh . . . I think I can hear Mother coming now.' She sprang to her feet, hastily brushing a tear from the corner of her eye. 'Come on, we'd best look as though we're busy.'

'Have you two not finished yet?' Annie eased herself slowly on to the bed and looked round at the chaos and clutter surrounding them: a trunk and two large suitcases with their lids flung back, one already filled with little Gary's clothes; heaps of underwear, skirts and jumpers on the bed; Violet's precious books – she couldn't bear to leave those behind, whatever the weight – in piles on the floor; shoes neatly arranged in pairs, ready for packing; the dressing table littered with make-up, scent bottles, tins of talcum powder . . . 'My goodness! It looks as though you intend staying for a week or two, our Violet.' Annie's tired face twisted in a travesty of a smile and her eyes softened as she looked at her younger daughter. She nodded. 'I've decided I'm going to try to make the best of it, lass. You've got to join your husband, I know that, an' I'm going to do what our Jenny says. I'm going to start saving up me pennies to come and see you.'

'We'll be pleased to see you, Mother,' said Violet quietly, and Jenny knew that her sister's voice was choked with tears. Her mother in a gentle mood, as she was so much more often nowadays, was in some ways much harder to understand and to come to terms with than the old, belligerent Annie. But Jenny was glad that, at long last, her mother seemed to be coming to terms with Violet's departure and giving the girl her blessing. Maybe it wouldn't be too long before she and Tom would be able to go ahead with their own plans to fly the nest at last.

Chapter 26

'I'll be all right, our Jenny. You don't need to come in with me.'
Annie paused at the gateway to Pleasant View and smiled at her
daughter. 'Off you go home, lass, and wait for the kiddies. Ada'll
be bringing them back soon, won't she?'

'If you're sure Mother,' Jenny glanced concernedly at the older
woman. 'I'll pop round tonight and make sure you're OK.'

'I will be, lass. I've told you . . . I'm all right.' Annie's voice was
tinged with annoyance. 'Stop mithering, can't you?' Then, more
gently, 'Thanks for coming with me,' she said. 'We had to give the
girl a good send-off, didn't we?'

Annie closed the front door behind her and breathed a sigh of
relief. Jenny was a good lass, but right now Annie wanted to be on
her own. Alone with her thoughts . . . with her grief. She hobbled
into the living room and eased her feet out of the shiny black lace-
up shoes and into her carpet slippers – her bunions weren't half
playing her up today – then took off her tweed coat and velour hat
and slung them over the back of the chair. Then she took off her
spectacles, and the tears that had been threatening all afternoon
began to flow unrestrainedly. She pulled a hanky from the pocket
of her skirt and mopped her eyes and her hot face. Whatever was
the matter with her, for heaven's sake? It wasn't as if the girl was
dead. She was only going to America, to start a new life. And as
Jenny was constantly reminding her, it wasn't a million miles away.
She could easily save up and go over for a visit.

She would miss Violet, though. God knows, how she would miss
her. Violet was a good lass. And so was Jenny . . . Annie knew that
she'd been lucky with her two girls, though she hadn't told them so.
It didn't do to spoil 'em; that was when they started taking
advantage. She'd been closer to them both, though, thank God,
these last few months . . . But why on earth did the silly lass have
to go and marry one of those Yanks?

Annie recalled now the scene at the Liverpool docks. The hundreds of women, many with young children, leaning against the ship's railing, waving, blowing kisses; the families and friends on the wharf shouting their last farewells; the streamers and flags – the red, white and blue of the Union Jack and the Stars and Stripes; the band blaring out patriotic tunes, and the deafening sound of the horns signalling the departure of the ship. And Violet, her blonde hair streaming in the wind, holding up little Gary to wave goodbye to Gran and Auntie Jenny. Dear God in heaven . . . would she ever see her again?

Annie felt the tears pricking at her eyelids again and she shook her head impatiently. This wouldn't do at all. She was getting soft in her old age. Old age? Whatever was she talking about? She wasn't old yet – far from it. There was a lot of life in the old dog yet and, by heck, she was going to prove it. She had a boarding house to run. The visitors would come flocking back now the blasted war was over and they'd be sure of a welcome at Annie Carter's. Oh aye . . . It was a big house to manage on her own. Her neighbours kept telling her as much, and Ada too – interfering young madam that she was – but she'd show 'em all right.

She riddled the lifeless ashes through the bottom of the fire grate and shovelled them into a bucket, then she went into the back yard to get some coal. The scuttle felt heavy, heavier than usual today, and Annie found that it took all her strength to carry it through the back kitchen and into the living room. She was tired, that was all it was. She was feeling tired after the traumatic day that she had had. She had felt a bit peculiar on the dockside, and again in the train coming home – her head swimming and her eyes going out of focus – but she hadn't mentioned it to Jenny.

She dropped the coal scuttle on the hearth with a clatter as a sudden pain stabbed at her ribs. She cried out and put her hand to her head. She felt dizzy again; everything was going black . . . she staggered towards the easy chair, reaching out for it – if she could sit down she'd be all right – then the pain came again. Annie gave a cry of alarm and fell heavily to the floor.

'Hello there. Anyone at home?' Ada poked her head round the back door. 'Hello, Aunt Annie. It's only me.' There was no answer, so she stepped inside. She wasn't surprised to find the back door unlocked – it usually was when Annie was at home – but she was surprised at the silence that greeted her. She had expected to hear the wireless going – Annie had become a great believer in music while she worked since the war days – and the kettle bubbling on the stove, but maybe her aunt wanted to be quiet. Poor soul; she would miss Violet, though she pretended to be as hard as nails.

Ada pushed open the living-room door that opened off the back kitchen, then she gave a cry of horror. Annie was lying on the hearthrug, her arms stretched in front of her, her glasses askew, her face deathly pale and her eyes closed, the eyelids not even flickering.

'Aunt Annie . . . Aunt Annie . . .' Ada knelt beside her and put her hand on Annie's brow. It was beaded with perspiration and felt cold and clammy. 'Oh dear . . . Oh dear . . .' Ada heard herself making little whimpering noises, like an animal in pain. She seized one of her aunt's hands and felt desperately for a pulse beneath the blue, knotted veins in her wrist. 'Please God, don't let her be . . .' She waited, praying fervently that she would feel the faint throb of life. Yes, there it was, very feeble, but it was definitely a pulse. Thank God! She put her arm under the older woman's head, holding her close. 'Aunt Annie. It's me, Ada. Come on, love . . . Oh, Auntie . . . speak to me . . .'

But Annie remained motionless. Ada began to panic. Whatever could she do? If she ran to fetch Jenny it would mean leaving her aunt on her own, and she didn't want to do that. But she knew that she would have to get a doctor, and quickly too. Ada didn't like the look of her aunt at all. Gently she eased her arm away from Annie's body, but still the old lady didn't stir. Ada ran to the front door and opened it, frantically looking up and down the street for any sign of life, anyone that she could get to help her. Oh, thank God. There was Mrs Barber, Annie's friend from across the road, just returning from a shopping trip.

In a few minutes Jenny had been fetched, and Dr Norris too. He knelt down and felt Annie's pulse and gently pushed back her eyelids. He looked grave. 'I think she's suffering from concussion,' he said. 'She probably knocked her head when she fell.' He pointed to the brass fender by Annie's head. 'Apart from that . . . I can't tell. We must get her into hospital.'

'Hospital?' said Jenny, her voice tinged with alarm. She knew her mother's abhorrence of hospitals, and Jenny herself had to admit to an aversion to such places, though she knew that her fears were unjustified. But she couldn't rid herself of the notion that once you went into hospital you might never come out again . . .

'Yes, it's the best place for her,' said Dr Norris. 'We've no choice, Jenny. I won't be answerable for the consequences if we don't get her there right away.'

Jenny and Ada sat one on each side of the hospital bed, watching the elderly woman who meant so much to each of them, though they hadn't always realised it. Neither of them knew what they would do if they were to lose her, difficult though she could be at times. They looked at one another and smiled sadly, both realising just what the other was thinking, though they had said very little since they began their vigil. It was nearly the end of visiting hour at Victoria Hospital and soon they would have to go home, but Annie still hadn't regained consciousness. Jenny looked at her mother lying there, so still and pale, seeming different, younger somehow without her glasses and garbed in the winceyette nightdress they had hurriedly found in one of her drawers. Jenny realised that it was almost the first time that she had seen her mother in bed. 'You die in bed . . .' That was what Annie had so often said. Oh, Mother . . . Mother, please don't go, Jenny cried silently, gazing at her, willing her to open her eyes.

And then Annie did . . . She stared round, blinking unfocusedly. Her sight was dim without her glasses, but she could make out Jenny, and Ada . . . 'Where on earth am I?' she murmured. 'What's happened?'

'You're in hospital, Mother,' said Jenny, hardly able to speak for relief. 'You had a little fall and bumped your head.'

'Hospital! I want no truck with any hospital. You'd no business bringing me here, our Jenny. You die in bed . . .' Annie tried to glare at her daughter, but her tone lacked conviction. 'And I don't want no doctor neither . . .' Her voice trailed away, and she bit her lip as the tears welled up behind her eyelids. Her head dropped to one side and she closed her eyes again. 'All right . . . I know when I'm beat . . .' Annie sighed. 'I must admit I do feel a bit queer. I reckon I'll have to do as I'm told for once in me life.'

Ada grinned. 'It'll be the first time, Auntie.' She patted the older

306

woman's cheek. 'Now, you just have a good rest and don't worry about anything. An' Jenny and I'll go and tell that nice young doctor that you've come round . . .'

'I'm afraid your mother won't be able to look after that big house on her own, Jenny.' Dr Norris leaned on the consulting-room desk and looked over the top of his horn-rimmed spectacles, his face grave. 'She's reasonably fit for a woman of her age – it wasn't a heart attack, thank goodness; her heart seems pretty strong – but she's had a hard time for the last few years.' He sighed. 'Haven't we all . . . ? But your mother has worked harder than most women I know, and now it's taking its toll. Violet going to live in America . . . that seemed to be the final straw.'

'And what is the problem, Doctor? What's wrong with Mother?'

'Stress . . . nervous tension. A touch of high blood pressure, but mainly stress. Her body couldn't take any more and rebelled against all the pressures. And of course the concussion didn't help. That's why I say she will need someone to help her, if she intends to keep on running the boarding house. And, from what she says, that's her intention.'

Jenny smiled. 'Mother's a fighter, all right. You know what she's always said – hard work never killed anyone.'

'And she's right . . . to a point. I think it would be wrong for her to give up work entirely, but she'll need help. And she shouldn't really live alone. I know boarding houses are filled up with visitors during the summer, but that's not the same as having someone of your own living with you. Anyhow . . . you're only round the corner, aren't you, my dear?' The doctor smiled at Jenny. 'I'm sure you'll be able to come to some arrangement.'

'Yes . . . We'll think of something,' Jenny replied flatly, her eyes staring unfocusedly across the room. Then, aware that she must sound ungracious, 'Yes, of course we will, Doctor. There's no question of us letting Mother live alone . . .'

'I'm sorry, love,' she said to Tom, later that evening. 'I know how you'd set your heart on going back to Yorkshire. And so had I, I must admit, once I'd got used to the idea of leaving Blackpool. And there's the lovely little house we'd found, and your job . . . and the girls'll be disappointed . . .'

'Never mind about the lasses. They'll get over it. Kids always do.

307

And I reckon I don't mind all that much . . . not really. So long as I'm with you, love, that's all that matters to me.' Jenny was sitting on the hearthrug leaning against Tom's knees, and he gently stroked her hair. 'I've got my job here, and the kids, and you, Jenny lass. There'll be other chances – we're young enough yet, love – and we've got to look after your mother.'

'All right, Tom,' said Jenny resignedly. She sighed. 'We'll move in with Mother – just for the moment, mind you – till we see how the land lies.' She smiled up at her husband and put her hand against his cheek. 'Like you say, love – being together is what matters most.'

'And how are you feeling today, Aunt Annie?' Ada perched on the edge of the bed and looked anxiously at her aunt. 'My goodness! You didn't half give us a fright, I can tell you.' Annie had been discharged from hospital after a few days and was now in bed at home.

'I'm not so bad, lass. Me knees still feel a bit wonky, but I reckon I'll live.' She laughed sardonically. 'Our Jenny's making sure I do as I'm told. It's not like me to be poorly in bed with a shawl on, but she says as how I've got to stay put for a day or two. They insisted on moving in with me, her and Tom and the kiddies. She's a good lass, is our Jenny. It worries me, though, Ada . . .' Annie leaned forward and grasped hold of her niece's hand. 'I know as how they'd been planning to go back to Yorkshire, and it seems as though I'm putting the tin hat on their plans, good and proper.'

'Going to Yorkshire?' Ada stared in amazement at her aunt. 'It's the first I've heard of it. I'm sure you're mistaken, Aunt Annie. They've not said owt to me.'

'Nor to me, lass.' Annie shook her head. 'But they don't need to. Jenny's me daughter, isn't she, and I can read her like a book. I know what's been in their minds, and I'll not stand in their way. She's been good to me, has our Jenny, and I'll see she gets what she deserves. I'll be up and doing afore long, I will that . . .' Annie settled herself more comfortably against the feather pillow and folded her arms in a decisive manner. 'And how about you, Ada? I reckon you and Fred'll be swaggering around like Lord and Lady Muck in that big house, won't you?'

Ada glanced covertly at her aunt, noting that there was a glint of kindness and humour in Annie's eyes in spite of her sarcastic tone.

Acerbic comments flew to Annie's lips as naturally as breathing and it was doubtful if she would ever be any different. 'Yes,' Ada replied evenly. 'It takes a bit of getting used to, living on our own, now that Miss Frobisher's gone . . . God rest her soul. It was real generous of her to leave us the house, and what a surprise it were an' all. You could have knocked me down with a feather when the solicitor told me.'

Miss Maud Frobisher had died a few weeks previously, from the same chest complaint that had claimed her sister. Her money had all been left to charity, but the house and all its contents had been bequeathed to Ada, 'in grateful recognition of a lifetime of devoted service'.

'It's no more than you deserve, Ada lass.' Annie smiled cordially at her niece. 'She had you at her beck and call for donkey's years, and her sister before her. I tell you what, though . . . I had a shock when I found out she was eighty. She didn't look a day over seventy, but I reckon that's what comes of taking it easy. It certainly wasn't hard work as killed that one. You want to ease up a bit now, Ada. Get out and enjoy yourself. Be a lady of leisure for a change.'

'Me? Take it easy?' Ada threw back her head and laughed. 'Not on your life! I reckon you and me are two of a kind, Auntie. Hard work comes as easy to us as breathing . . .' She leaned forward, looking seriously at her aunt, for a plan had been taking root in Ada's mind while she had been listening to Annie. She would have to be careful how she broached the subject, though, or Annie would fly off the handle. 'Listen, Aunt Annie. I've been thinking. How would it be if . . .' She paused, wondering how to phrase it.

'Go on. Spit it out. I can tell you've got summat on your mind,' said Annie abruptly. Then, more kindly, 'Go on, lass. I'm listening . . . and I think I've got an idea what you're going to say . . .'

Annie leaned back in the easy chair with her arms folded, a sly grin tugging at the corners of her mouth. 'I'm as fit as a fiddle again now, as you can see. So you can go right ahead, the pair of you, with your plans for moving to Yorkshire.'

'What!' Jenny's shout could have been heard at the other end of the street, and she stared at her mother in disbelief. 'How did you know? We didn't know ourselves till we went over to Castleburn, and nobody else knew anything about it. Well, I did mention it to

309

our Violet, but I'm sure she didn't tell you. Anyhow, we've changed our minds. We're staying here, with you.'

'Well, you can think again, lass, because I've been making plans of me own, and they don't include you!' Annie grinned at Tom and Jenny, then she paused, obviously dying for them to ask her what she had in mind. They didn't disappoint her.

'Well then, come on, Ma,' said Tom. 'Spill the beans, What are you planning? Are you going to America to join our Violet, or are you thinking of retiring?'

'Retiring? Me? Don't talk so daft. I'd sooner wear away than rust away, and the holiday business'll be booming again before long, you mark my words. I've already had dozens of enquiries from folk that used to come before the war. I couldn't do owt this year, worse luck, with me being ill an' all, but next year it'll be different. Mind you, I must admit I'm not as young as I used to be, and I can't run this place single-handed. No . . .' Annie paused dramatically. 'I'm going into partnership – sounds posh, doesn't it – with our Ada!'

'What!' said Jenny again, her voice shrill with astonishment. 'Ada? But . . . Mother, you know very well that you and Ada don't get on. She's all right in small doses, like you've said yourself. But to work with her all the time – it just wouldn't do.' Jenny shook her head. 'Besides, she's no need to work since Miss Frobisher died and left her the house.'

'Being a lady of leisure doesn't suit Ada,' said Annie. 'She's straining at the leash already. She's like me . . .' She gave a chuckle. 'She's like me in a lot of ways. I reckon we'll get along well enough. She's mellowed since she got wed. Anyhow, her and Fred are coming to live with me. They can have a couple of rooms on the first floor, and we'll turn it into a flat, like. But they're keeping the house on as well, till we see how things go. Maybe I could get a young lass to live in and help with the work. We don't know properly yet . . . But you needn't worry about me any more, Jenny lass. I'll be all right. You and Tom can go right ahead with your plans.'

Jenny went on staring at her mother, hardly able to speak for surprise. 'It beats me how you knew, Mother. We never said a word . . .'

'Oh, I must be psychic, I suppose.' Annie shrugged. 'I could tell as there was something in the wind. It's not so much what you said, as what you didn't say. I knew your mind wasn't on planning a future in Blackpool. It stands to reason that Tom would want to go back home eventually, him being a Yorkshireman born and bred. Anyroad, like I say, me and our Ada's going into partnership. And we'll split all the takings fifty-fifty.'

'You're becoming quite a businesswoman, Ma,' said Tom in admiration. 'Don't overdo it, though. Don't work too hard. You want to enjoy yourself as well.'

'Aye . . . I shall be saving up,' said Annie. 'Jenny was trying to persuade me to take a trip to America, and I reckon I shall do when I've saved up enough brass. Not just yet mind. It's only fair to give 'em a while to settle down. And I shall be nipping across the Pennines to see you lot, when you've settled. Don't think you can get rid of me so easily. That's if you'll have me?'

'Of course we will, Ma,' said Tom, grinning at her.

'You'll always be welcome, Mother,' added Jenny quietly. 'You know that.'

Jenny knew that she meant it. The war had wrought changes in them all, not least in her mother. Jenny could see the beginnings of a new and closer relationship, a friendship which at one time she would have thought impossible. Ada wasn't the only one who had mellowed. Annie, too, was now a much more amiable and sympathetic person. Or it could be that she, Jenny, having experienced great sadness, was now able to view the world and its problems – in particular her mother – with more tolerance and understanding.

Jenny's heart missed a beat as she saw Tom idly pick up the green leather volume of poetry. She hadn't wanted to hide it away – the inscription inside it was innocent enough – although she had destroyed all Robert's letters after hearing of his death. The book had remained on top of the sideboard with a few other volumes, on a carved cedar-book rest that Tom's brother Jack had brought back from Palestine after the last war. Tom and Jenny didn't own many books – just the *Pear's Encyclopaedia*, a dictionary, a medical book, a Bible, and a few childhood classics. Tom, no doubt, had noticed a stranger in their midst.

'I didn't know you were interested in poetry, Jenny,' he commented, opening the book at the flyleaf. 'To Jenny with my love. October 17th 1940. Robert,' he read out aloud, glancing at her curiously.

'Robert Cunningham,' Jenny answered, trying to keep the tone of her voice casual. 'You remember him, Tom. The young sergeant who was billeted at Mother's. He used to call round sometimes and have a cup of tea. I suppose that – the book – was his way of saying thank you. He said I made him feel welcome.'

Tom nodded. 'Yes, I remember him. Nice young chap. I spoke to him now and again when I was home after Dunkirk. Good-looking lad, wasn't he?'

'Yes. Very . . .'

'What happened to him, Jenny?'

'He was killed, over Berlin – a couple of years ago.'

'Oh no . . . That's a bad do. What a waste.' Tom shook his head sadly. 'What a wicked waste of a young life . . .' He looked at her and smiled. I'm glad you made him welcome, love. I reckon he fancied you, you know.'

'Why do you say that, Tom?' Jenny's voice was nonchalant, betraying nothing of the turmoil inside her.

'Oh, I noticed the way he looked at you when you were serving the dinner. Mind you, he wasn't the only one. I reckon quite a few of those lads fancied you. I can't say I blame them . . . They've all gone now, though, haven't they, Jenny? There's just you and me . . . and the lasses and little Victor, of course.'

Jenny sat down on the arm of Tom's chair and rested her cheek gently against the top of his head. 'That's right, Tom,' she said fondly. 'Just you and me . . .'

Robert Cunningham was never mentioned again.

The afternoon sunlight filtered through the stained-glass window, casting pools of coloured light upon the chancel steps, as the choir and congregation rose to sing the final rousing hymn. It was the Thanksgiving Service at the local church, and Jenny had managed to persuade Tom to come along. They had so much to be thankful for, not just the end of the war which the service was celebrating, but their children, their new home to which they would soon be moving, and their new-found happiness in one another.

The little grey-stone house in Castleburn had still been vacant after the trauma of Annie's illness, and the Bradshaw family was moving there at the end of October. Patsy and Rosie had started at the grammar school in Blackpool, but a transfer had been arranged, and now, as Annie put it, 'Everything in the garden's lovely'.

Jenny could tell that Tom had been moved by the simplicity and reverence of this special service, and she knew that in coming he had taken the final step along the road to the healing of his mind and his complete recovery. He had turned to smile at her several times, as though in agreement with the quiet words of praise and thanksgiving.

'. . . We pray that thou wilt keep thy children from the cruelties of war, and lead the nations into the way of peace. Teach us to put away all bitterness and misunderstanding . . .' intoned the vicar, and Jenny heard Tom's fervent whisper, 'Amen to that.'

Her heart was so full of joy at hearing Tom's enthusiastic singing of the final hymn that she was hardly aware of the words that were being sung until they reached the sixth verse.

'The golden evening brightens in the west,
Soon, soon to faithful warriors comes their rest . . .'

Warrior . . . That was the word that Robert had used, that day that they had met on the cliffs, the day when it had all begun . . .

'I'm certainly not a natural warrior . . .' he had said.

Robert hadn't wanted to fight at all. He had been a reluctant warrior, but a faithful one all the same.

Tom had been faithful too, and he, thank God, had been spared.

'But lo, there breaks a yet more glorious day . . .' sang the chorus of triumphant voices.

Jenny turned to smile at her husband, knowing the future was full of promise.

313